Crosscurrents / *Modern Critiques*
Third Series

Edited by Jerome Klinkowitz

In Form: Digressions on the Act of Fiction
By Ronald Sukenick

*Literary Subversions: New American Fiction
and the Practice of Criticism*
By Jerome Klinkowitz

*Critical Angles: European Views
of Contemporary American Literature*
By Marc Chénetier

American Theater of the 1960s
By Zoltán Szilassy

*The Fiction of William Gass: The Consolation
of Language*
By Arthur M. Saltzman

*The Novel as Performance: The Fiction of
Ronald Sukenick and Raymond Federman*
By Jerzy Kutnik

The Dramaturgy of Style: Voice in Short Fiction
By Michael Stephens

*Out of Egypt: Scenes and Arguments
of an Autobiography*
By Ihab Hassan

*Pynchon's Mythography: An Approach
to* Gravity's Rainbow
By Kathryn Hume

*The Spontaneous Poetics of Jack Kerouac:
A Study of the Fiction*
By Regina Weinreich

*Who Says This? The Authority of the
Author, the Discourse, and the Reader*
By Welch D. Everman

David Cowart

History and the Contemporary Novel

Southern Illinois University Press
CARBONDALE AND EDWARDSVILLE

Printed in the United States of America
Edited by William Jerman
Designed by Design for Publishing, Inc.
Production supervised by Linda Jorgensen-Buhman

91 90 89   4 3 2 1

Library of Congress Cataloging-in-Publication Data

Cowart, David, 1947–
  History and the contemporary novel.

    (Crosscurrents/modern critiques/third series)
    Bibliography: p.
    Includes index.
    1. History and literature. 2. Fiction—20th
century—History and criticism. 3. Historical
fiction—History and criticism. I. Title.
II. Series: Crosscurrents/modern critiques. Third
series.
PN3343.C68   1989   809.3′9358   88–18230
ISBN 0–8093–1479–7

Part of chapter 4 originally appeared under the title "Being and Seeming:
The White Hotel." *NOVEL: A Forum on Fiction,* vol. 19, no. 3. Spring 1986.
Copyright NOVEL Corp., 1987. Reprinted with permission.

"The Persian Version" from *Collected Poems, 1975,* by Robert Graves.
Copyright © 1975 by Robert Graves. Reprinted by permission of Oxford
University Press, Inc., and A.P. Watt, Ltd., on behalf of the executors of
the Estate of Robert Graves.

The paper used in this publication meets the minimum requirements
of American National Standard for Information Sciences—Permanence of
Paper for Printed Library Materials, ANSI Z39.48–1984. ⊚

For Rachel

Contents

Crosscurrents/Modern Critiques/Third Series
Jerome Klinkowitz   ix
Acknowledgments   xi

1 Time Present and Time Past: History and the
   Contemporary Novel   1
2 The Way It Was   31
      The Secret of the Springs: *Memoirs of Hadrian*
      Clio Swived: *The Sot-Weed Factor*
3 The Way It Will Be   76
      The Terror of History: *Riddley Walker*
      Puritanism and Patriarchy: *The Handmaid's Tale*
4 The Turning Point   120
      Entropic Stasis: *The Leopard*
      Abreaction of the West: *The White Hotel*
5 The Distant Mirror   165
      Through a Glass Darkly: *Go Down, Moses*
      Face to Face: *The Name of the Rose*

   Notes   217
   Works Cited   227
   Index   234

Crosscurrents/ Modern Critiques/ Third Series

IN THE EARLY 1960s, when the Crosscurrents/Modern Critiques series was developed by Harry T. Moore, the contemporary period was still a controversial one for scholarship. Even today the elusive sense of the present dares critics to rise above mere impressionism and approach their subject with the same rigors of discipline expected in more traditional areas of study. As the first two series of Crosscurrents books demonstrated, critiquing contemporary culture often means that the writer must be historian, philosopher, sociologist, and bibliographer as well as literary critic, for in many cases these essential preliminary tasks are yet undone.

To the challenges that faced the initial Crosscurrents project have been added those unique to the past two decades: the disruption of conventional techniques by the great surge in innovative writing in the American 1960s just when social and political conditions were being radically transformed, the new worldwide interest in the Magic Realism of South American novelists, the startling experiments of textual and aural poetry from Europe, the emergence of Third World authors, the rising cause of feminism in life and literature, and, most dramatically, the introduction of Continental theory into the previously staid world of Anglo-American literary scholarship.

These transformations demand that many traditional treatments be rethought, and part of the new responsibility for Crosscurrents will be to provide such studies.

Contributions to Crosscurrents/Modern Critiques/Third Series will be distinguished by their fresh approaches to established topics and by their opening up of new territories for discourse. When a single author is studied, we hope to present the first book on his or her work or to explore a previously untreated aspect based on new research. Writers who have been critiqued well elsewhere will be studied in comparison with lesser-known figures, sometimes from other cultures, in an effort to broaden our base of understanding. Critical and theoretical works by leading novelists, poets, and dramatists will have a home in Crosscurrents/Modern Critiques/Third Series, as will sampler-introductions to the best in new Americanist criticism written abroad.

The excitement of contemporary studies is that all of its critical practitioners and most of their subjects are alive and working at the same time. One work influences another, bringing to the field a spirit of competition and cooperation that reaches an intensity rarely found in other disciplines. Above all, this third series of Crosscurrents/Modern Critiques will be collegial—a mutual interest in the present moment that can be shared by writer, subject, and reader alike.

Jerome Klinkowitz

Acknowledgments

I HAVE MANY friends and colleagues to thank for their maieutic assistance with this book. Kathryn Hume at the Pennsylvania State University, Michael Beard at the University of North Dakota, and Eva Mills at Winthrop College all helped in numerous ways. Professor Beard sent an interview with Umberto Eco I might have missed, and Professor Mills shared a tremendously helpful bibliography on historical fiction. Professor Hume read the manuscript and suggested books to discuss. I especially appreciated her comments on my discussion of *Riddley Walker*. I have had wonderfully stimulating conversations about the books under consideration here with my good friends William and Jerry McAninch, who also read part of the manuscript. I am indebted, too, to Dianne Luce, who shared her considerable expertise on Faulkner with me and provided other help in the final stages of my work.

I am fortunate to be surrounded by supportive colleagues at the University of South Carolina. Many have sent books and other materials my way; all have provided active encouragement. I would especially like to thank John Kimmey, Ina Rae Hark, Patrick Scott, Joel Myerson, Jeffrey Helterman, John Ower, Gregory Jay, Benjamin Franklin V, Eve Bannet, Buford Norman, Nathalie Racklin, Richard D. Mandell, and Antonio di Giacomantonio.

My graduate assistant, Dean Shackleford, typed several chapters onto floppy disks. My good friend and esteemed colleague Donald J. Greiner took the trouble to read several chapters in manuscript. He provided much sage counsel and needed encouragement.

I would also like to thank George Geckle, formerly my department chair, and two successive deans, Chester Bain and Carol Kay, for the release-time necessary to complete this project. A grant from the Office of Sponsored Programs and Research at the University of South Carolina helped me get to some hard-to-find secondary materials.

History and the
Contemporary Novel

1

Time Present and Time Past: History and the Contemporary Novel

THE HISTORICAL NOVEL, like the genus *Chrysanthemum*, exists in a wide variety of forms, from the weedlike *Sweet Savage Love* (1974) to the highly cultivated *War and Peace* (1863–1869). Prismlike as well, it generates the entire spectrum of critical hues, from the contempt of Henry James to the qualified admiration of Georg Lukács. Indeed, as the critics wax more or less respectful, the historical novel itself proves subject to history. But the increasing prominence of historical themes in current fiction suggests that the novel's perennial valence for history has acquired new strength in recent years. Produced by writers sensitive to the lateness of the historical hour and capable of exploiting technical innovations in the novel, this new historical fiction seems to differ from that of calmer times. A sense of urgency—sometimes even an air of desperation—pervades the historical novel since mid-century, for its author probes the past to account for a present that grows increasingly chaotic. To gauge the significance of this development, one must consider the claims of both art and history to insight into the past. In doing so, one finds the past often less accessible to history than to historical fiction.

1

The origins of modern historical consciousness extend back into the nineteenth century, and perhaps back to the Enlightenment or the Renaissance. But only in the twentieth century (and especially since World War II) has change become truly vertiginous. History seems to have accelerated; indeed, it unfolds at present with the queer jumpiness of those early newsreels in which, at the beginning of the century, viewers began to witness what Pound called "the march of events." On the screen now these events seem to speed toward secular apocalypse as the nuclear age takes its course, and those watching the newsreels are faced with the likelihood of an empty projection booth, a projector out of control.

But the arts, especially the novel, have kept pace. The contemporary novelist has embraced the task of historical analysis, the task of gauging the historical forces responsible for the present. In a pivotal book, *The Naked and the Dead* (1948), the youthful Norman Mailer examines these historical forces at work among a diverse group of Americans under wartime stress. Mailer's characters embody every American social identity—all the vitality, coarseness, lunacy, inversion, and heroism that figured in the hour when the nation moved toward the apogee of its strength, energy, and will. In the high relief afforded by the tensions and horrors of war in the Pacific, these characters represent the permutations of class, psychology, and sexuality that define America as a historical phenomenon.

Mailer treats World War II with a historical acuity comparable to that with which an earlier generation of novelists responded to World War I. Thus *The Naked and the Dead* bears some resemblance to books like Dos Passos's *Three Soldiers* (1921) and Thomas Boyd's *Through the Wheat* (1923). It also invites comparison with Hemingway's *A Farewell to Arms* (1929), another novel in which a botched campaign figures as the ironic emblem of war. Hemingway's narrator, Frederic Henry, is the tragic survivor of violence at once human and elemental, for Hemingway, like Mailer, emphasizes the helplessness of decent individuals at the mercy of enormous forces. Mailer, however, presents an even darker, more Jacobean tragedy, and he conceives of the forces arrayed against his characters in more explicitly historical terms. His Lieutenant Hearn represents a set of values endangered by the forces unleashed at mid-century; like Hemingway's Catherine Barkley, he does not stand a chance. He leaves the postwar stage to the brutish Sergeant Croft and to sexually inverted reactionaries like General Cummings. These characters project a rottenness at the heart of the national character that Mailer refuses to ignore or rationalize. He probes politics and sex, and unlike Hemingway, for whom sex is what refreshes the warrior and politics merely a remote obscenity, he seeks to capture the strange chemistry of sexual repression and political power in American life. Thus he gauges what he would later call the "lines of force" among his characters, in their actions, and, more broadly, in the American ethos itself. Unlike Hemingway, Mailer makes clear the prominence of history among these lines of force.

Another, more recent example of this sensitivity to the way the past molds the present is George Steiner's brilliant and underrated *The Portage to San Cristobal of A. H.* (1982). Readers of Steiner's nonfiction know that he has spent a lifetime seeking to come to terms with the Holocaust, the implications of which would seem to render illusory the most cherished ideals of Western civilization. Repeatedly he asks: How could Buchenwald spring up in the very shadow of Goethe's oak? What are the prospects of a civilization capable of Auschwitz? Steiner's novel concerns the capture, deep in a Brazilian jungle, of the aged but still malevolent Adolf Hitler by a group of Israeli commandos. The climax comes when the hitherto mute prisoner finally breaks his silence to deliver a long monologue on history and racial identity. The German attitude toward the Jews, Hitler admits, had its inception in racial jealousy and took the form of bizarre imitation. All the features of the Nazi myth—Aryan supremacy, the chiliastic Reich, *ein Volk, ein Führer,* and so forth—parallel prominent features of the Hebraic ethos: the chosen people, millennial expectations, the Mosaic leader and lawgiver. Hitler declares that the Nazis, if they were to impose their own vision of historical and cultural election on the world, had to obliterate a people that made a rival claim to historical uniqueness.

Ostensibly neither Steiner's novel nor Mailer's is "historical," yet each breathes a historical consciousness typical of the novel in the age of Hiroshima. Indeed, however determined to record the manners of their own age, novelists ignore the past at their peril. In *The Historical Novel,* written before the war, the Marxist critic Georg Lukács goes so far as to attack the distinction between novel and historical novel. The novel, he argues, is intrinsically historical in that it concerns social currents and forces that are the products of historical antecedents. "A writer's relationship to history is not something special and isolated," says Lukács; it amounts to "an important component of his relation to the whole of reality and especially society."[1]

For formal reasons too, Lukács argues against viewing the historical novel as a separate genre. The author of a historical novel, he maintains, must observe the same artistic conventions with regard to characterization and narrative technique as any other novelist. Yet what looks like an inclusive esthetic proves otherwise, for at the same time that he admits the historical novel's stature as serious fiction, he denies such stature to all fiction that fails to demonstrate adequate sensitivity to a particular conception of history. In effect, all fiction that fails to pass the test of Marxist ideology by unfolding the historical dialectic gets dismissed as "bourgeois decadence."

Other critics allow the novel, including the historical novel, more latitude, and a brief consideration of their work will provide a background for further analysis of the relationship between history and the novel, as well an introduction to some new critical proposals regarding the primacy of historical fiction as a means of knowing the past. The work of these critics does not lack for quantity or variety. Ina Schabert, in the bibliography of her 1981 book *Der historische Roman in England und Amerika,*[2] includes well over a hundred entries under nine headings. She cites book-length studies and bibliographies, special issues of periodicals (notably *Clio,* the journal devoted to the relationships between history and literature), and numerous articles in various sources. The critics address theoretical questions, weigh individual writers like Scott, Stevenson, and Kipling, or attempt broad surveys, most often of historical fiction in nineteenth-century England. Yet they have not exhausted the subject, especially if one considers the historical novel since 1945. No book, thus far, focuses exclusively on contemporary historical fiction. The books that touch on the subject, like Schabert's, which comes up into the 1970s, or Harry B. Henderson's *Versions of the Past,*[3] which comes up into the 1960s in America, do so only as part of a much broader survey.

The authors of such surveys define historical fiction in various ways, and their need to circumscribe the subject can dictate some curious grounds for inclusion and exclusion. Thus Avrom Fleishman, in his fine book *The English Historical Novel,* excludes novels set less than "two generations" back in time, novels without "a number of 'historical' events, particularly those in the public sphere (war, politics, economic change, etc.)," and novels that do not involve "at least one . . . . real person among the fictitious ones."[4] Schabert, by contrast, includes perhaps too much; she risks attenuation in the name of comprehensiveness. Unlike the monistic Lukács or the cautiously pluralistic Fleishman, she divides and subdivides types of the historical novel until discrimination, pushed to the limit, begins to short-circuit. Her overwhelming typology includes such headings and subheadings as "Fictionalization of Historical Gaps" ("The Fictional Biography"); "Fictive Action in

Historical Space" ("The Novel as Illustration of History," "The Story as Interpretation of History"); "Fiction as Historical Experience" ("Historical Revision," "History as Phenomenon of Consciousness"); and "Parasitical Forms" ("Alternative History," "Parody and Burlesque"). With examples and elaboration, these rubrics make more sense, but such an extensive typology leaves little room for substantive analysis of individual works.

As a vehicle for criticism, this kind of exhaustive taxonomy proves unsatisfying. One requires a definition of the form that avoids the ideologically tendentious inclusiveness of Lukács, the arbitrary exclusions of Fleishman, and the categorical plenitude of Schabert. I myself prefer to define historical fiction simply and broadly as fiction in which the past figures with some prominence. Such fiction does not require historical personages or events (the reader finds none, for example, in John Fuller's 1984 novel *Flying to Nowhere*), nor does it have to be set at some specified remove in time. Thus I count as historical fiction any novel in which a historical consciousness manifests itself strongly in either the characters or the action. Many a novel set in the present satisfies the proposed criterion because of its author's attention to the historical background of current reality. Historical fiction of this type would include *V.* (1963), by Thomas Pynchon, or *Sophie's Choice* (1979), by William Styron, as well as the previously cited works by Mailer and Steiner.

To evaluate historical fiction adequately, one must devise an analytical approach that will allow the critic at once to generalize and to discriminate. One must divide the various manifestations of the historical novel into a manageable set of categories that will illuminate each other. My own approach occupies a kind of middle ground equidistant from the positions of Lukács, Fleishman, and Schabert. For profitable discussion of historical fiction, one requires latitude for exe-

gesis and for noninvidious comparison; consequently one rejects outright the ideologically straitjacketed approach of
Lukács, and one steers between methodologies like those of
Schabert and Fleishman, avoiding at once excessive pigeon-
holing and unnecessary principles of exclusion. The present
book, at any rate, is intended not as a survey but as an essay
in the theory of the historical novel and as a vehicle for close
readings of some recent and especially distinguished examples
of the form.

These recent works have raised the reputation of a form
all too often sneered at, patronized, or dismissed—a form, as
Zoé Oldenbourg ruefully notes, "that so-called serious readers
do not take seriously, that the 'average' reader considers above
all as an instructive diversion."[5] Serious writers, too, sometimes
disparage historical fiction. Henry James, for example, wrote
to Sarah Orne Jewett: "The 'historical' novel is, for me, condemned . . . to a fatal *cheapness.*" However carefully worked
up the historical background, says James, "it's all humbug."[6]
Yet James's own favorite subject was the effect of an old culture
on a person from a young culture, and in a sense one Jamesian
protagonist after another, from Christopher Newman to Mag-
gie Verver, stumbles over history itself. At his death, in fact,
James left an unfinished novel in which he makes explicit the
historical dimension of his characteristic theme. Instead of
simply crossing the Atlantic, like the characters in James's
earlier novels, the American hero of *The Sense of the Past* (1917)
actually exchanges bodies with an eighteenth-century English
ancestor. As Edmund Wilson has observed, James's posthumous novel bears a remarkable resemblance to *A Connecticut
Yankee in King Arthur's Court.*[7]

But James's interest in history per se remains marginal, even
in *The Sense of the Past.* By contrast, the more self-consciously
historical novelist sets out to deal directly with the Ur-historical
question: What in the past made the present? In his *Auto-*

biography, R. G. Collingwood remarks that "the chief business of twentieth-century philosophy is to reckon with twentieth-century history,"[8] and one might say the same of modern historical fiction. Indeed, the German historian, novelist, and playwright Lion Feuchtwanger has argued that historical fictions, from Homer on, always have as their object an oblique commentary on contemporaneous issues and problems.[9] But such a formulation, though supported by the number of reviewers who see in every important new historical novel a rendering of the past as "distant mirror" of the present, recalls the critical monism of Lukács. It belies the richness and multiplicity of historical fiction.

The reflection of the present—though always, ideally or theoretically, something that enriches historical fiction—may not in fact be the primary or even a secondary goal of the historical novelist. One agrees with Feuchtwanger's assertion only in the broad sense noted previously: the past depicted in historical fictions must, by flowing toward the future, eventually create the present. But the historical novel, which exists for more than the single purpose asseverated by Lukács, exists also in more than the single mode posited by Feuchtwanger. Thus with an eye to the mythic quaternities of Blake, Jung, and Northrop Frye, one can at once improve on Feuchtwanger's distant mirror thesis and avoid the multiple categories of a pluralist esthetic by organizing a discussion of historical fiction under four rubrics:

(1) The Way It Was—fictions whose authors aspire purely or largely to historical verisimilitude.

(2) The Way It Will Be—fictions whose authors reverse history to contemplate the future.

(3) The Turning Point—fictions whose authors seek to pinpoint the precise historical moment when the modern age or some prominent feature of it came into existence.

(4) The Distant Mirror—fictions whose authors project the present into the past.

In the first of these categories the novelist attempts to re-create the past as vividly as possible, dramatizing a world whose values may diverge radically from those of the present age. In works like Yourcenar's *Memoirs of Hadrian* (1951), Mailer's *Ancient Evenings* (1983), and the novels of the late Mary Re-nault, the reader learns to understand the past by entering into its mental life, thereby avoiding those cheap assumptions of superiority that constitute the most insidious failure of historical thinking. This category also subsumes revisionist historical fiction, whose authors aspire to "the way it was" with special iconoclastic fervor, usually seeking to subvert chau-vinist pieties, to present a more credible version of the past. Examples include Styron's *The Confessions of Nat Turner* (1967), Barth's *The Sot-Weed Factor* (1960), and several of Robert Graves's novels, notably *Sergeant Lamb's America* (1940) and *King Jesus* (1946).

In the second category, fictions of the future reverse the conventions of fictions of the past to show the way it will be rather than the way it was. Though vulgarized by science fiction, visions of the future have a long and distinguished pedigree, from Mary Shelley's *The Last Man* (1827) to Orwell's *1984* (1949). An exercise in reverse historical thinking, these commonly extrapolate the future from the present. But the most sophisticated of these fictions, like Walter M. Miller's *A Canticle for Leibowitz* (1959) or Russell Hoban's *Riddley Walker* (1980), depict a future at once growing out of the present and ironically reflecting the past, for authors who meditate on "things to come" often rely on extensive historical knowledge. H. G. Wells, who hypostatized the future in *The Time Machine* (1895), also knew the past well enough to write *The Outline of History*. He contrived, too, to view his own age historically;

thus in the effete future landscape of *The Time Machine* the reader discovers the remains of the Crystal Palace, that monument to Victorian assumptions about progress.

The third category, the turning point, ranks as perhaps the most important in this schema, at least in terms of the quantity and quality of books that fall into it. Turning point fictions address directly the question: When and how did the present become the present? Shaw's *Saint Joan* (1923), though not a novel, provides a good example. Here the playwright shows his audience the moment in the fifteenth century when the modern world crystallized with the advent of nationalism, the rise of secular power, the development of total war, and the emergence of *Realpolitik*. Similarly, *Freddy's Book* (1980), by John Gardner, locates in sixteenth-century Sweden the origins of such modern political realities as print propaganda, the subjection of private conscience to public expedience, and the unscrupulous exploitation of charisma. Less ambitious but more deftly executed, Giuseppe di Lampedusa's *The Leopard* (1958) concerns the currents that transformed feudal Sicily into a new bourgeois reality in the nineteenth century. Other contemporary novelists have attempted to trace the emergence of the twentieth-century *Zeitgeist*. Some of these—Mailer, Steiner, Pynchon—have already been noted. Though set in the present, Steiner's *The Portage to San Cristobal of A. H.* contains, in Hitler's peroration, much reflection on the modern turning point, as does Pynchon's *V.* or *Gravity's Rainbow* (1973). Other examples include D. M. Thomas's *The White Hotel* (1981) and Timothy Findley's *Famous Last Words* (1982), both of which probe the mind of the twentieth century and the historical origins of its neuroses.

The fourth and last category, that of the distant mirror, contains fictions that make special demands on the ingenuity of the novelist; consequently the distant mirror proves somewhat less common than one might expect. The possibilities for subtlety, complexity, and thematic range, however, are extensive. Novelists who depict their own age in the distant mirror of the past may thereby (a) offer a fresh perspective on the present, (b) suggest that historical change might be largely illusion, (c) discover rich possibilities for allegory, or (d) demonstrate a cyclical theory of history. A number of reviewers saw a reflection of the present in Mailer's *Ancient Evenings*, but the author's projection of a trilogy from antiquity into the modern era would seem to call such readings into question. As suggested previously, this novel is primarily a vivid re-creation, the reflections of the present age being secondary, perhaps even adventitious. Stronger candidates for inclusion here are Umberto Eco's *The Name of the Rose* (1983), a novel set in the fourteenth century yet reflecting events on the contemporary political scene in Europe, or John Gardner's *Grendel* (1971), a retelling of the *Beowulf* story from the monster's point of view. Gardner's monstrous narrator, who debunks the glorious annals of Anglo-Scandinavian origins by rubbing the reader's nose in the decidedly inglorious reality, attempts a revisionist exercise in "the way it was." The author, however, undermines Grendel's iconoclasm. Readers discover in ancient Scandinavia a distant echo if not a distant image of their own time, for Grendel, modeled on Jean-Paul Sartre, speaks with the dreary voice of twentieth-century existentialism. Thus Gardner cleverly intimates the difference between an age of heroism and an age of futility. The ancient Scyldings knew Grendel for an enemy and measured their sense of heroic purpose against his nihilism. The modern descendants of the Scyldings, by contrast, embrace their Grendel and miserably concede the logic of his world view.

The four categories proposed here contain few pure examples. Many of the titles illustrating individual categories would prove at least partly congenial to other categories as well. The more multifaceted the novel, the more likely it will manifest features from more than one category. In Jungian psychology, which provides one version of the quaternal model, individuals seldom represent only one of the four personality types, and the fictional norm, like the psychological, generally involves emphasis on one primary and one secondary mode. Following the model of Jungian psychology, one might expect that the ideal would be an equal blending of all four modes— a "centered" historical novel like, say, Alasdair Gray's *Lanark* (1981), that interesting hybrid of past, present, and hereafter in a surreal Glasgow. But one risks getting carried away with a helpful analogy. A novel that blends the four modes equally is not necessarily superior to one that focuses primarily on one or two—nor is it, for that matter, as common. The centered personality, after all, is seldom encountered in Jungian psychology—just as, in Blake's myth, unity or integration is either prelapsarian or apocalyptic.

I invoke Blake and Jung with a certain irony, for the four-fold schema offered here does not require mythic sanction. The four categories will serve their purpose if they prove sufficiently inclusive and if they compose some kind of unity. Each, in fact, functions as part of a continuum with the present, which, knowing itself in the distant mirror and shaped by the way it was and the turning point, is in turn shaper of the way it will be. This unity, this mutualistic relevance to the present, also makes for the desiderated inclusiveness, so that one can resolve the problems of classification posed by even the more heteroclite or encyclopedic historical novels. Broch's *The Death of Virgil* (1945), for example, seems to need its own history-as-rhapsody classification, and novels like *Finnegans Wake* (1939), *One Hundred Years of Solitude* (1967), and *Terra Nostra* (1975) seem to require a history-as-myth rubric. Perhaps a similar problem exercises Polonius, who divides dramatic forms into "tragedy, comedy, history, pastoral, pastoral-comical, historical-pastoral, tragical-historical, tragical-comical-historical-pastoral" (*Hamlet*, II.ii.415–18), and so forth. If one is to avoid this kind of absurdity, the temptation to create a new category for every variation must meet with firm resistance.

To dispense with such hermeneutically pointless rubrication, one must examine prospective anomalies and describe them in terms of the proposed categories—graph them, if necessary, on a grid provided by all four. *The Death of Virgil,* to take just one problem novel, touches on category one (the way it was) in that it re-creates vividly the last hours of a great poet of antiquity. But its real subject is that poet's painful choice between private vision and public responsibility. Though he harks back to an age in which the artist—he mentions Aeschylus specifically—felt no discontinuity between private perception and the demands of a public art, Virgil does not seem to think of himself as the first artist to wrestle with this problem. If he did, one would classify this novel as an example of category three, the turning point. Since resistance to the idea of state art is in fact a modern phenomenon, *The Death of Virgil* belongs to category four, the distant mirror. Mirrors, however, reverse images; consequently Broch, who began this novel in a concentration camp, contrives to reflect an evil dictatorship of the twentieth century in a benign dictatorship of the first. Broch's Virgil must reconcile his conception of art as something personal and private with his public role as servant of the state. He finds the private artist's coldly accurate perception of truth often at odds with the "moral fictions" that sustain a great empire. If Virgil, despite his mental reservations, retreats before the predictable arguments of Augustus Caesar on this point, the reader attentive to the specular dimension of the conflict understands that the problem adumbrated by the dying poet does not admit of courtly capitulation in the age of Hitler.

But making and defending categories does not take one far in the more important task of defining the problematic component of historical fiction—the history—and gauging its value vis-à-vis the narrative art that converts it into literature. Contemporary novelists seem to recognize the amphibious character of history; they know it for a discipline that, however venerable, has yet to define itself adequately. Texts on the philosophy of history—Aristotle, Hegel, Croce, Collingwood—can easily be deconstructed to reveal the anxiety of both historians and philosophers over the question of epistemological credentials, the question of whether to construe history as science or art. As Hayden White points out, "continental European thinkers—from Valéry and Heidegger to Sartre, Lévi-Strauss, and Michel Foucault—have cast serious doubts on the value of a specifically 'historical' consciousness, stressed the fictive character of historical reconstructions, and challenged history's claims to a place among the sciences."[10] But historians, especially in the twentieth century, aspire nevertheless to the enormous prestige of science, a kind of exclusive club only recently opened to those who do not discourse in mathematics.

History cannot escape imprecision because source material, frequently incomplete or slanted, must undergo interpretation by historians who, unlike physicists or chemists, can never neutralize or obviate the effects of their own subjectivity. According to the historian Marc Bloch, however, science can no longer vaunt itself on the certainty and precision with which it describes physical reality. "For certainty," says Bloch, the scientists "have . . . substituted the infinitely probable; for the strictly measurable, the notion of the eternal relativity of measurement. . . . We find it far easier to regard certainty and universality as questions of degree." Bloch favors calling history "a science in its infancy" that, "having grown old in embryo as mere narrative, for long encumbered with legend, and for still longer preoccupied with only the most obvious events . . . is still very young as a rational attempt at analysis."[11]

The references here to "mere narrative" and "obvious events" hint at the direction historical methodology, and especially

French historiography, would take in the decades after Bloch, for recent historical writing—Fernand Braudel is the name most often associated with this development—eschews the chronicling of epiphenomenal wars and coronations to concentrate on daily life in the past among the vast majority of persons seldom touched by the events formerly construed as history. Yet in leaving behind the house of art and sundering their allegiance to Clio, historians risk emasculating their field, causing a loss of identity in a formerly independent discipline with a tradition of its own. Marrying at last into the prestigious scientific family so long aspired to, history may find itself, like psychology and sociology, patronized as a poor relation.

But if history spurns art, art has not spurned history. Artists, however, tend to be unimpressed by the posturing of historians avid for autonomy, and their evaluation of raw history— as opposed to history refined and transfigured by art—can be quite harsh. One such artist, Feuchtwanger, is in fact a renegade historian. He died before completing *The House of Desdemona,* his book on the historical novel, but his detailed notes for the uncompleted parts indicate his disbelief in what Harold A. Basilius, his translator, refers to as "authoritative, objective, scientific history." Basilius adds that the author saw "scientific' history" as "a snare and a delusion" and "history and historiography" as "wish projections of certain periods, and cultures, and individuals."[12]

Less strident is Robert Graves, one of the most indefatigable of historical iconoclasts. Graves writes history as well as historical fiction and does not hesitate to engage historians on their own ground. As the apologist for a unique, mythographic approach to history, he has devoted much energy to exposing the betrayal, in the remote past, of the supreme, three-personed deity called the White Goddess, genius immemorial of natural matriarchal order. The West, repudiating matriarchy, replaced the White Goddess with a pantheon dominated by male gods, and the West has been at odds with the natural world ever since. An eagle in the dovecotes of historical assumption, Graves calls into question the premises of Western tradition and the integrity of its chroniclers, guilty of conniving at and even promoting a fundamentally erroneous reading of cultural origins.

Graves gives a kind of paradigmatic expression to the principle of historical relativity or unreliability in a witty little poem about perceptions of a famous battle. What happened when Persian met Greek at Marathon?

The Persian Version

Truth-loving Persians do not dwell upon
The trivial skirmish fought near Marathon.
As for the Greek theatrical tradition
Which represents that summer's expedition
Not as a mere reconnaissance in force
By three brigades of foot and one of horse
(Their left flank covered by some obsolete
Light craft detached from the main Persian fleet)
But as a grandiose, ill-starred attempt
To conquer Greece—they treat it with contempt;
And only incidentally refute
Major Greek claims, by stressing what repute
The Persian monarch and the Persian nation
Won by the salutary demonstration:
Despite a strong defence and adverse weather
All arms combined magnificently together.

Historians speak earnestly of the operation of "judgment" on "evidence," but Graves's poem suggests the unlikelihood of any resultant objectivity. Here the same evidence—an encounter between a Persian "reconnaissance in force" and Greek defenders with a weather advantage—yields different history to the exercise of Western and non-Western judgment: the Greeks transform the Persian reconnaissance into a major invasion culminating in a battle crucial to the course of Western history, while the "truth-loving Persians" obscure an inglorious episode with euphemistic rhetoric. Graves's irony operates on both versions of history, and he implies that even art—"the Greek theatrical tradition"—offends against simple truth. But the reader who recalls that the Persians were to invade Greece again, and in full force, may recognize a distinction between ordinary historical falsehoods and those created or abetted by art. In the great struggle between civilization and barbarism a decade after Marathon, the victories at Salamis and Plataea went to the nation shaped by the more potent myths, the more cogent historical fictions. These, Graves intimates, are fostered less by history than by the artistic treatment of history.

Graves's iconoclasm reveals primarily a distrust of history's claims to objectivity and a preference for the undisguised myth-making of imaginative literature. Yet history too deals in story and myth. The historian presents not the past but a version of the past, for history, like imaginative writing, involves a selection of detail, a determination of emphasis, a narrational shaping. "All historians," as J. Hillis Miller points out, "have been aware that the narrating of an historical sequence in one way or another involves a constructive, interpretive, fictive act."[13] History and fiction, then, have affinities, and in many languages the words for story and history coincide. Italian *storia*, French *histoire*, Spanish *historia*, Russian *istorya*, German *Geschichte*—all demonstrate the linguistic tendency to obscure the distinction between veracious and imagined narrative. Thus the non-English writer must at times introduce a foreign word to avoid ambiguity, as for example in Schabert's phrase *"Die story als Deutung für die Geschichte."* Most of these languages retain the Latin form—*historia*— more or less intact, but in Italian and English the archaic form has undergone aphaeresis, the dropping of an initial syllable. The English word *history* was originally as ambiguous as its cognates in other languages; "in early use," according to the

O.E.D., the word denoted a narrative of events "either true or imaginary."

English is remarkable in retaining both the archaic and aphaeretic forms and in their evolving toward a semantically convenient distinction. Among native speakers of English, however, this circumstance may generate unconscious resistance to the idea of a family resemblance between history and fiction. R. G. Collingwood, who traces assertions of this resemblance from Dilthey and Simmel to Benedetto Croce, attempts to defend history against the kind of leveling relativism that denies its autonomy. Thus an early essay by Croce, "History Subsumed under the Concept of Art," makes him nervous. In their focus on the singular and the specific, says Croce, history and art reveal their essential identity and their incompatibility with science, which focuses on the general. Collingwood himself concedes "the resemblance between the historian and the novelist," noting that each depends on imagination and that "each aims at making his picture a coherent whole."[14] But he argues that "all history," unlike fiction, "must be consistent with itself" and that "the historian's picture," which "stands in a peculiar relation to something called evidence," differs from the novelist's in that it "is meant to be true."[15]

Collingwood's attempts to distinguish the historical imagination from the literary get him into trouble, as Avrom Fleishman has pointed out. "The chief distinction," says Fleishman, "is the familiar one between imagination and fancy," but in fact the imagination of the novelist differs from that of the historian "not in kind but in degree."[16] Collingwood's views regarding the superior verity of the historical product, for which he finds support in the later Croce, also invite challenge, for the truth at which literary art levels, the truth of the universal in human experience, is hardly less valid or consistent than that of history. The necessity of focusing exclusively on the actual may prove a liability for the historian, who seeks the same truth the artist seeks yet is constrained to deal with singular fact rather than something imagined and universal. Collingwood's asseverations seem especially dubious in the rarefied poststructuralist environment—an atmosphere in which language, the historian's medium no less than the novelist's, is no longer conceived of as something corresponding to or coterminous with objective reality. As Terry Eagleton explains, "The hallmark of the 'linguistic revolution' of the twentieth century, from Saussure and Wittgenstein to contemporary literary theory, is the recognition that meaning is not simply something 'expressed' or 'reflected' in language: it is actually *produced* by it."[17] Inevitably colored by the language in which they receive expression, both the evidence relied on by historians and the truth to which they aspire remain mockingly fluid and elusive. Thus history achieves at best a kind of superior moral imagining—itself subject to possibly devastating linguistic analysis.

The historian resists the idea that this superior moral imagining may find its most reliable expression in fiction, yet such a proposition might be the only way to resolve the perennial problem of differentiating history and fiction, the problem that exercised Collingwood and, before him, historiographers and estheticians from Croce back to Aristotle. Collingwood's desire to view history as science rather than art complicates the question. In attempting to differentiate history's truth-quotient from that of art, however, he merely varies a distinction that goes back at least to Coleridge, who suggests in chapter 14 of *Biographia Literaria* that one might distinguish history ("science") from art ("poetry") by considering whether "truth" or "pleasure" was the "*immediate* end" of the practitioner. But this formulation proves unsatisfactory, at least with regard to literature, whose immediate end, as classically formulated (e.g., by Horace) is at once to delight *and* instruct. Where one sometimes, as a secondary reward, takes pleasure in history, one always learns (about the universals in human experience) from literature. Whether or not art "subsumes" history, it seems the more comprehensive human experience, and the novelist invades the historian's domain more often and more successfully than vice versa. The reader, then, who wants to know what really happened at the Battle of Waterloo may learn more from Hugo, Stendhal, or Thackeray than from Michelet or John Keegan, for the novelist routinely transcends imagined material to speak with great authority about the past.

Even the popular historical novel instructs as it delights. Popular writers, as a matter of fact, sometimes instruct too much. One recognizes second-rate historical fiction not by its devotion to mindless pleasure but by the failure of its author to transmute mere facts into something of ideational consequence and to achieve the proper balance between historiographic and artistic considerations. The inferior historical novel is positively gravid with information; the inferior historical novelist fails to subordinate raw history to art.

As one of the most lively manifestations of the form, the popular historical novel deserves at least brief attention. Only the best popular novels—those, for example, of Mary Renault—can advance the argument for fiction's epistemological superiority to history, but even the worst can illustrate the strange family resemblance between the fictive and the historical. A novel like Gary Jennings's *Aztec* (1980), neither literature nor pure hack work, exemplifies both the strengths and weaknesses of popular historical fiction. It also happens to lend itself to comparison with a work of history on the same subject. Jennings's novel and William Hickling Prescott's *History of the Conquest of Mexico* actually complement each other, for the work of fiction focuses on the Aztecs and ends with the coming of their conquerors, in contradistinction to the work of history, which focuses, after a brief sketch of Indian civilization, on the Spaniards and their extraordinary campaign to subjugate Montezuma's empire. The books also complement each other as narratives. Each has a clear point of view—that of the Aztecs on the one hand, that of the conquistadores on the other. Each has a protagonist—the Aztec Mixtli, the Spaniard Cortes—whose fortunes provide narrative impetus. Each has an orderly structure: that of a single life in *Aztec,* that of the quest in the historical work. Both books, in other words, are fictive. One is a *Bildungsroman* with aspirations to tragedy; the other is an epic. As history, however, the books diverge, especially as regards the portrayal of the Spaniards—vicious opportunists in one, resourceful heroes in the other. Again one encounters an irremediable relativism; as with the Graves poem, two judgments of the same evidence produce two versions of history. Yet as fictions—literary or historical—both books are true. From the assumptions of two radically different cultural climates (*Conquest* was written nearly a century and a half before *Aztec,*) each author tells the truth sanctioned by his age: where Prescott makes a statement about human heroism (that of the Spaniards), Jennings shows that an indigenous culture has a special and splendid vitality whose leeching by colonialism is nothing less than rape. One naturally thinks the twentieth-century view superior, that is, "truer," but one must avoid worshiping what Bacon called the Idols of the Theatre, for immersion in the values of one's age makes objectivity difficult. Perhaps the modern anthropological ethic embraced by Jennings, which enjoins respect for and tolerance of "primitive" cultures, should be expanded to promote tolerance of allegedly unenlightened historical thought as well. By accepting the idea of multiple historical truths in place of the ever-elusive definitive version of the way things were, contemporary thinkers might free themselves from the treadmill of historical relativism. One resists giving the palm for historicity to *Aztec* and having done with the matter, in part because *Conquest* makes the better novel. Macaulay remarks that "a perfect historian must possess an imagination sufficiently powerful to make his narrative picturesque,"[18] and Prescott, a superb stylist, knew instinctively the value of vivid narration. *Aztec*'s author, by contrast, seems not to know whether he wants to write a work of fiction or an anthropological and historical treatise. He takes pains to introduce as much information about the Aztecs and other pre-Columbian peoples into the novel as possible, and at times all sense of forward movement lapses as an episode designed solely to illustrate this or that cultural curiosity is narrated. Thus he neglects the necessary subordination of factual to fictive.

Fortunately this necessary subordination does not elude all popular novelists, whose ranks, after all, include such fine storytellers as Margaret Mitchell, Mary Stewart, and Rafael Sabatini. Some of these also deserve respect as serious writers, writers whose work, in addition to showing literary merit, proves interesting as a mode of fictive history. Mary Renault, for example, stands up well to critical analysis at the same time that she boasts a large popular following. Renault never allows her meticulous knowledge of ancient customs and landscapes to overwhelm narrative. A kind of euhemerist, she accounts for mythological events, frequently supernatural, in terms of plausible human experience in historical time. Thus she aims at something quite different from the literary treatment of legend that, according to Erich Auerbach, an ancient author like Homer undertakes.[19] At the same time she conveys a strong sense of the palpable reality, to the ancients, of religious beliefs and customs despised and ridiculed over the centuries of Christian hegemony. Ancient religion figures as an important presence in most of her novels, something eminently cogent and real, and one senses on the author's part a profound respect, even a yearning, for ancient forms of belief. The narrator in the typical Renault novel is clearly a believer in the mysteries touched on.

Renault never exploits ancient religion for mere shock value, nor does she ever patronize modern religion. She never descends, even implicitly, to the kind of Christian-baiting that mars Jennings's *Aztec*, where the religion that supplanted the Aztec pantheon figures exclusively as a study in greed, hypocrisy, and cant—a convenient vehicle for mulcting the aboriginal Mexicans. Whatever the merits of this view, Jennings makes the point too stridently. He also lays himself open to charges of a different kind of hypocrisy when he attempts at once to apologize for Aztec religious practices and to exploit them as a means of titillating the reader.

One sees the same divergence in these authors' handling of sexual practices in the historical milieux they re-create. The author of *Aztec* punctuates its thousand or so pages with an ultimately rather ridiculous litany of incest, lesbianism, necrophilia, sodomy, castration, rape, rape-sacrifice, rape-sacrifice-cannibalism, and so forth. These sensational features vitiate an often vivid and even reliable introduction to the Aztec world; they spoil the novel as serious fiction. In Renault's novels, by contrast, sex figures more plausibly and more tastefully. In *The Last of the Wine* (1956), *Fire from Heaven* (1969), and *The Persian Boy* (1972), Renault's sensitive and intelligent approach to sex in the ancient world enables her to treat even the potentially sensational subject of homoeroticism in such a way as to lose neither amorous pathos nor the heterosexual reader. In the closing sequence of *The King Must Die* (1958), the first of her two books on the Theseus legend, she handles an equally difficult subject in the euhemerized account of the hero's abandonment of Ariadne on Naxos (occasioned, according to the myth, by Ariadne's affair with Dionysus). With no lapses in taste, Renault depicts the Dionysian revels and their effect on Theseus, who turns from Ariadne in disgust on seeing the thing she clutches in her insensate hand after a night of drunken abandonment. The author does not identify the fearsome thing, but one imagines a gobbet of flesh (perhaps, indeed, a particularly intimate piece of flesh)—all that remains of the maenads' surrogate Dionysus. These details sound sensational, but Renault handles them with restraint.

Surprisingly, Renault's euhemerism does not diminish her heroes. The legendary Theseus and the historical Alexander become human yet do not lose their mythic stature. The ancient world, for this author, remains mythopoeic, and her treatment of it exemplifies the idea central to this discussion, the idea of a fictive as opposed to a literalist conception of history. Thus in her hands the historical novel demonstrates its viability as a medium for probing the past.

To go further and argue that fiction can present the past more authoritatively than history, one must dispose of a vulgar error regarding the value of historical thinking. Santayana's remark about the fate of "those who cannot remember the past" has become a cliché, the delight of shallow journalists and pedagogues. Such sciolists never pause to question Santayana's dubious premise. If they did, they would discover that knowledge of the past does not in fact promote mastery of the present or the future. Though individuals can gain insight into historical currents and the shores to which they bear us, history is the aggregate experience of more than the historically knowledgeable few. These individuals, moreover, seldom occupy positions from which to direct or influence events. "What experience and history teach is this," says Hegel: "that people and governments never have learned anything from history, or acted on principles deduced from it."[20]

Had he lived in the twentieth century, however, Hegel would have witnessed "people and governments" acting on historical principle, applying to problems in Berlin and Korea the lesson learned about appeasement in World War II. But in the complexity of international power struggles, any such lesson becomes rapidly obsolete. In Israel and Vietnam, for example, the principle of non-appeasement yields only muddle and tragedy. Ironically, the precepts history offers one generation seldom agree with those embraced by previous generations. The Vietnam generation, faced with another Munich, will likely act according to the wrong set of historical principles. Some American schoolchildren learn from their study of the past that traits like self-reliance, sacrifice, and hard work made their nation prosperous and powerful, whereas others learn that the national prosperity originated in the unfettered depredations of rapacious capitalists, slave-owners, dispossessors of Indians, exploiters of labor, and despoilers of the environment. The lessons of history seem always to admit of radically different interpretations, and simple historical truth remains forever obscure. One does not therefore repudiate history or cease to study it; one does, however, jettison naïve notions about learning from the past. History is the societal analogue to the examined life, and one studies it as a way of fostering, on the one hand, national or cultural identity and, on the other, a sympathetic understanding of other national or cultural identities.

The rationale of history, then, coincides with that of art, for each promotes a cultural self-knowledge commensurate with and complementary to that personal self-knowledge traditionally viewed as one of the major objects of humanistic study. But every culture expresses itself more definitively through its artists than through its historians. Homer and Sophocles do more to define their civilization than do Herodotus or Thucydides, and Mark Twain and Walt Whitman capture the American spirit better than does Francis Parkman. Artists, after all, speak to the cultural memory with greater authority than do historians. Artists provide the myths by which any cultural body defines itself, the myths that historians mistakenly seek to unravel. Thus history makes its greatest contribution when it supplies the creative artist with raw material, for the kind of historical knowledge described here, the kind with the greatest validity, concerns the rational judgment of the historian much less than the moral and imaginative discrimination of the artist.

One must think of such knowledge as fictive and evolutionary rather than objective and immutable, and one must remember than art, not history, remains the best approach to it. Yet history and art, especially literary art, do not always exist as separate entities. History is always fictive, and literature is often historical. In fact, many of the books most closely associated with the cultural identity of the West demonstrate the remarkable affinity of historical consciousness and fictive imagination. Books like *The Iliad, The Aeneid, The Divine Comedy,* and *War and Peace,* in other words, are historical fictions.

Like the creators of these fictions, the contemporary historical novelist has an advantage over writers constrained to represent the past without benefit of creative license. To gauge the extent to which the novelist surpasses the historian, the extent to which literature delivers more, epistemologically, than does historiography, one must approach historical fiction with a critical method designed to facilitate meaningful discrimination rather than ideology or mere taxonomy. The critical approach introduced in the foregoing and further illustrated in the rest of this book promotes discrimination among the four basic modes of the historical novel at the same time that it encourages recognition of contemporary historical fiction's multifarious relevance to the age that produces it. In the examples of this fiction adduced here, and in those analyzed more fully in the following chapters, one views the past from the perspective of an age unique in the annals of history, an age in which the idea of apocalypse has acquired a new and terrible meaning.

This book began with encounters on my part with some novels that seemed exemplary fictions of history—exemplary because of the artistic and historiographical acuteness of the authors. I found that these novels fell conveniently into one or more of the four categories introduced earlier in this chapter. For the reader who remains puzzled about the rationale behind the categories (Why four? Why these four?), perhaps this would be a good place to iterate that the four categories are not imagined to be absolute or definitive. They do, however, serve to classify a wide variety of historical fictions; moreover, they define a temporal spectrum with the present at its center. Historical fiction, in other words, is one of the means whereby the present can know itself, know the forces that have created such a dangerous age, and this relevance to the present, a consideration for the historical novel in any age (as Feuchtwanger argued), is especially important in our own. Contemporary historical novelists conceive of history—past and future—as something whereby they can judge and assess and understand the present. A present grasped as part of a historical continuum may prove a malleable present, prolegomenon to a livable future.

I have chosen eight works—two from each of my categories—to explore the meaning of history in contemporary fiction. These include Yourcenar's *Memoirs of Hadrian* and Barth's *The Sot-Weed Factor* as examples of The Way It Was, Hoban's *Riddley Walker* and Atwood's *The Handmaid's Tale* as examples of The Way It Will Be, di Lampedusa's *The Leopard* and Thomas's *The White Hotel* as examples of The Turning Point, and Faulkner's *Go Down, Moses* and Eco's *The Name of the Rose* as examples of The Distant Mirror. Why these eight? These books, produced by authors aware that the greatest art addresses moral issues, invite their readers to reflect on the currents and forces of history from a moral perspective. These works provide insights into the moral life of humanity in the past and in the present.

They also reveal changing literary perceptions of history. The modernist writer like Pound or Eliot views history as a repository of cultural standards. Its legitimacy is not particularly in question, and it remains a stable contrast to a current cultural fragmentation. Other moderns view history as collective psychological fantasy or oneiric vision; thus history is the mythic dream of Humphrey Chimpden Earwicker or the nightmare from which Stephen Dedalus desires to awaken. Joyce, the creator of H. C. E. and Stephen, takes an interest in the way history and myth interrelate, even celebrates history as myth, because he embraces the modernist idea of myth as instinctual truth, something that defines the human condition.

But where Mauberley observes the mottoes on sun dials, his successors deconstruct them. Pound would say that time flies, Derrida that it figits. According to the postmodernist view, the accuracy or inaccuracy of history is a problem only for the naïve. One can know only the "truth" that one's language equips one to know: language speaks us, rather than the other way around. Thus an independent, objectively verifiable historical reality does not exist independently of the language with which one speaks of it, and even myth remains problematic.

If all the authors represented here nonetheless assert that the past, having shaped a dangerous present, must be known, all seem implicitly to say that the past can only be known imaginatively and that the most reliable explorer of the past is the one best able to integrate facts into a living imagined reality—again, not the historian but the historically informed artist. They seem also to know or intuit that the conundrums of postmodernist thought become moot or academic when the organism—or the race—is in extremis. The prospect of being hanged concentrates the mind wonderfully, says Dr. Johnson. By the same token the prospect of annihilation means that one ought to do more than play games with language, and so the contemporary historical novelist exploits the technical license or opportunities afforded by both modernist and postmodernist esthetics to address issues that cannot be dismissed as merely linguistically structured. One can assert that reality does not exist independently of or anterior to language, but in fact the bomb exists whether language says it does or not. Historical fictions, however sophisticated, must finally allow some provisional truce with Wittgenstein, De Saussure, Pierce, and the other architects of our painful new understanding of the relationship between language and phenomenal reality.

Thus the context in which one should judge these works is moral as well as epistemological, for the contemporary historical novel differs from the historical novel of other periods quite simply in that the past assayed has issued in a present in which, as Faulkner said in his Nobel Prize acceptance speech, we expect at any moment to be blown up. The apocalyptic tinge of much contemporary fiction is the very sign and emblem of the concerns that, with greater or lesser consciousness, motivate writers who recognize acutely that life under the gun, once the comparatively rare experience of individuals under sentence of death, citizens of towns under siege, or populations threatened by pestilence, is now the condition of existence for humanity at large. The changed historical circumstances of our era lead these writers to project into the past and into the future, in symbolic terms, the one great question of the present: human survival. These writers execute variations on an apocalyptic theme.

There is a difference in the historical novel in an age of anxiety (an age in which the anxiety is more justified than in any previous age so characterized) and the historical novel in a more stable or less justifiably anxious age—an age that could construe history as part of its stability or as the standard against which to measure some new instability. Perhaps every age perceives its own anxiety as somehow definitive, but only since 1945 have we known precisely the shape that apocalypse would take. We look to history now to provide clues for understanding, gauging, addressing the more absolute instability of our nuclear present.

To summarize: in setting up and exploring four categories of contemporary historical fiction, the author of this book argues (1) that his schema will be effective if its components prove unified, prove to delineate a temporal continuum, with past and future centering on the present, (2) that the past, if it can be known at all, can be known best by historically informed artists, and (3) that the thermonuclear contingency to which a number of these artists respond in their various ways distinguishes their work from that of their predecessors, historical novelists of other periods, who seldom attempted to define their enterprise as genuinely crucial to the continued viability of their present.

A final point, again an iteration. Not all of the authors discussed here are postmoderns, for not all estimable contemporary fiction is postmodernist. Modernism remains fitfully viable, and simple realism has never dried up altogether (it is a river that goes underground only to reemerge as the Arethusa of minimalism or the recently modish fiction of rich, affectless urban and suburban youth). Although I write from a postmodernist thesis concerning history, I have generally reserved postmodernist esthetics to the appropriate fictions, except occasionally in the light of some special interpretive need. The eight novels read closely in the chapters to come, at any rate, illustrate the variety of historical fiction since World War II, from the psychological realism of Yourcenar to the traditional modernism of di Lampedusa to the genuinely postmodernist self-referentiality of Barth and Eco to the technical and philosophical eclecticism of Hoban, Atwood, and Thomas. Like Beethoven between classicism and romanticism in music, Faulkner is the amphibium here, for he exploits myth like a modern yet simultaneously subverts or deconstructs it like a postmodern. Eight historical novelists, eight esthetic postures, eight bands in the spectrum of novelistic practice in the latter part of the twentieth century.

2

The Way It Was

THE FIRST CATEGORY of historical fiction properly accommodates only the work of novelists healthily skeptical about history as a mode of knowledge, novelists sensitive to the unreliability of language, the difficulties of labeling reality objectively. Consequently this category, however numerous its aspirants, proves less crowded than one might initially expect. The least naïveté about history on the part of a writer will generally suffice to force that writer's work into another category, one more congenial to historical romanticism. Writers capable of a genuinely mythopoeic romanticism, however, sometimes produce work that fits in here, for those who take an interest in history as myth— one thinks of Joyce or García Márquez—merely approach the way it was from their own unique perspective. They succeed to the extent that they embrace myths of true universality, and often they speak with great authority of a collective instinctual past.

Authors who embrace egregious myths, on the other hand, produce only popular historical romances, in which readers encounter not the way it was but a distant mirror of their own fantasy lives. Whatever the merits of *Gone with the Wind*, for example, it does not belong in a category reserved for novels that scrupulously re-create historical actuality. Its author, Margaret Mitchell, fails to make the Southern myth universal or to treat it with the saving, if poignant, irony of a William Faulkner. Yet though she misses the reality of the antebellum South, she succeeds—and even anticipates the later Faulkner—as a novelist of historical process. The fantasy of aristocratic manners in her novel gradually gives way to greater realism, as the harsh actualities of Reconstruction supplant the genteel, flyblown fiction of Southern chivalry. Just as Faulkner chronicles the displacement of an older order by the rapacious Snopes clan, Mitchell depicts a new bourgeois ethic becoming the only recourse for a prostrate culture. Thus her novel, though unreliable as a window on the way it was before the war, succeeds as meditation on a historical turning point.

Novelists, then, may achieve historical actuality less often than they think, and only those who continually analyze their own assumptions about language and their own tendencies to romantic thinking can hope to bring the past completely alive. Two writers who practice this kind of self-examination, Marguerite Yourcenar and John Barth, have produced historical novels that reflect the difficulties of capturing the truth about the past in language. Yet both Yourcenar, in *Memoirs of Hadrian,* and Barth, in *The Sot-Weed Factor,* affirm the possibility of forcing language to yield up secrets about the reality it tends to distort. Barth creates a narrator whose witty and ironic language calls attention to itself; the extreme elegance of Yourcenar's narrator, Hadrian, works the same way. In many contemporary fictions such self-reflexiveness merely illustrates the larger referential inadequacies of all language, thereby undermining all attempts to grapple linguistically with reality. But the self-reflexiveness of the language in Yourcenar and Barth seems rather to function as an ever-present reminder that one can get at reality only by becoming self-conscious about the medium through which one encounters it.

Yourcenar's *Memoirs of Hadrian* and Barth's *The Sot-Weed Factor,* both novels in which a protagonist achieves self-knowledge, exemplify the kind of historical fiction that takes its reader into the very mind of the past. In each, the theme of the examined life, ostensibly explored in terms of a single mind and heart, gradually takes on cultural and historical dimensions. In coming to know themselves, Yourcenar's Hadrian and Barth's Ebenezer Cooke encounter or inventory their own respective cultures. As they proceed—the one deliberately, the other accidentally—toward self-knowledge, the reader comes to know Rome in the second century and America in the seventeenth. Each story evolves into what Janet Whatley, commenting on Hadrian's narrative, calls "a résumé, a *summa* of a certain stage of culture."[1] Thus the examined life in these novels becomes identified with history itself, the examined past.

The Secret of the Springs: *Memoirs of Hadrian*

The reader who would know the feel of Roman life in the second century finds in Yourcenar's *Memoirs of Hadrian* an extraordinary feat of literary, spiritual, and mental archeology. Yourcenar makes the past live through her literary skill and through the exercise of an imagination disciplined by scrupulous scholarship. By focusing the novel on one man's lifelong pursuit of order, liberty, self-knowledge, and the good life, she makes his story a cultural history of politics, society, and thought in ancient Rome. She brings to life a Roman emperor almost two thousand years dead, and with him the myths, the science, the mores, the philosophy, the very consciousness of an age long past. She overcomes the disparities between ancient and modern cultural attitudes. She shows her reader the way it was.

Memoirs of Hadrian stands up well in comparison with other modern and contemporary novels set in the Roman world, including Graves's *I, Claudius* and *Claudius the God*, Broch's *The Death of Virgil*, Robert DeMaria's *Clodia*, John Williams's

Augustus, Hersey's *The Conspiracy,* Wilder's *The Ides of March,*
and Vidal's *Julian.* Yourcenar matches Williams for psychological precision, and she matches Graves for erudition. Indeed, her erudition is less eccentric, and one suspects a
comment on Graves when her Hadrian hints that Suetonius—
Graves's chief source for the *Claudius* novels—may have distorted the history he was charged with recording. Though
less technically innovative than Broch, Yourcenar achieves
substantially more control, precision, and economy. In her
prose, finally, and in her direct sensuous apprehension of a
bygone reality, she outclasses all these other writers.

Though Vidal, Williams, and Hersey all follow Yourcenar
in the epistolary structure of their novels, none manages the
acuteness of her psychological portrait. By casting her novel
in the form of an autobiographical letter from the Emperor
Hadrian to Marcus Aurelius, his adoptive grandson and a
future caesar himself, she enables the reader to experience
the mental life of the refined and hellenized ruler who did
much to consolidate Rome's fabled status as "eternal city."
Early in his letter Hadrian promises Marcus Aurelius "a recital
stripped of preconceived ideas and of mere abstract principles; it is drawn wholly from the experience of one man, who
is myself. I am trusting to this examination of facts to give me
some definition of myself, and to judge myself, perhaps, or
at the very least to know myself better before I die."[2] Hadrian's
personal goal mirrors the goal of both history and art: knowledge of the human reality. Yourcenar, through Hadrian, intimates a relationship between self-knowledge and knowledge
of the past. One of the things that makes *Memoirs of Hadrian*
a good historical novel is the interweaving in it of psychology
and history, personal self-knowledge and cultural self-knowledge, the manifest psychological and spiritual rewards of the
one enriched and made yet more meaningful by the other.

Hadrian offers an instructive contrast to that other aged
monarch, King Lear. Lear "hath ever but slenderly known

himself" (I.i.296–97), as one of his vicious daughters remarks, and Shakespeare's drama demonstrates, among other things, the ramifications of such culpable and dangerous nescience. Lear's ignorance on this point reflects what seems a generalized ignorance among the characters of the play with regard to the past, or at least the civilized past, of the kingdom they inhabit. Thus no one—not even the sensible Kent—thinks to advance the argument of history against Lear's proposed division of a kingdom. Lacking both personal and collective self-knowledge, Lear and his realm easily revert or regress to a savage state—from which "history" must begin all over again.

Unlike Lear, Hadrian maintains contact with a cultural and personal past. He is a man of historical sensibility, like his imperial predecessor Claudius. But in contrast to Claudius, who could do little more than study history, Hadrian actually directs it. As Yourcenar conceives of him, he is that rarity, the thinker who can also lead.

He can also write. The emperor's prose discovers an accomplished man of letters, a modest poet, a discriminating lover of literature. He produces a shapely narrative, with well-turned paragraphs and sentences that hover at the distant periphery of epigram. Every expression combines what Chaucer calls "solas" and "sentence."

But Hadrian's stylistic virtues generate difficulties. In conferring upon her narrator these literary gifts, which complicate his task of self-examination, Yourcenar complicates her own task of historical re-creation, which depends greatly on the emperor's credibility. Hadrian aspires to candor in his narrative yet cannot help the tendency of his polished prose to gainsay all that might make him seem less than exemplary. One becomes suspicious of such an artful narrator. One notices, for example, his remarkable ability to reveal his virtues without seeming proud and his flaws without seeming vicious. At times, after all, Hadrian cloaks actions that might seem vicious or unbalanced in language so measured and reasonable as to forestall opprobrium, and only by acts of rigorous discrimination does the reader perceive a disparity between the thing reported—the endless and extravagant memorials to Antinous, say—and the elegant terms of the reporting. Throughout the narrative, in fact, Hadrian affects a tone implying passions long since banked.

The point is not that Hadrian means to deceive. One can recollect and report a violent action or a violent grief in tranquility, but sometimes one can belie an emotion's original violence by the artful language in which one describes it. The problem—it is really Yourcenar's—concerns narrative technique: how to circumscribe the tendency of a rhetorically sophisticated narrator to compromise psychological and historical accuracy. Yourcenar, the translator into French of Henry James and Virginia Woolf, handles this technical challenge with great resourcefulness. She creates in Hadrian a narrator just unreliable enough to remain human. She reports in her "Reflections on the Composition of *Memoirs of Hadrian*" that as her fictional emperor took on autonomous life—as the characters of a good writer properly do—she retained the necessary detachment. "At certain moments, though very seldom, it has occurred to me that the emperor was lying. In such cases I had to let him lie, like the rest of us."[3] Thus the reader encounters Antinous, for example, "through the emperor's memories, that is to say, in passionately meticulous detail, not devoid of a few errors" ("Reflections," p. 334). Even when the emperor does not lie consciously, the ideal of psychological accuracy dictates that he make mistakes or color certain events with his own mild prejudice.

Yourcenar's refusal to make the emperor a paragon, a Roman King Arthur, argues a judicious and discriminating approach to recapturing the way it was. Though she perceives Hadrian as "a very great man" (p. 341), she seeks to give her readers a real person whose essential honesty and wisdom do not preclude occasional mistakes, poor judgment, and moral lapses. Her emperor, however admirable, remains a human being, subject to the distortions of character that inevitably accompany power. Thus he admits to striking Antinous; he exiles Favorinus for his sharp tongue and Juvenal for mocking a favorite actor; Suetonius he forces into retirement, and Apollodorus he has executed as part of the Servianus faction. Most shocking of all, perhaps, he drives a stylus into the eye of a contentious scribe in a fit of pique. Some readers find this last detail simply incredible—an odd lapse on the part of both author and character. Jean Blot, a French critic, complains that "this act remains impossible, unrealistic, gratuitous. The gentleman of the *Memoirs* is constitutionally incapable of this kind of brutality."[4] But the inclusion of this incident is of crucial importance to balancing the insidious effects of the narrator's elegant prose. It forces the reader, in a moment of empathic mortification, to recognize other objectionable acts in their true light, acts for which allowances have perhaps too willingly been made. Between the shock value of this incident and the surprising number of dubious acts it causes to come suddenly into focus, Hadrian—and behind him Yourcenar—corrects for the tendency of good writing to neutralize confessional revelations.

Hadrian's candor regarding the number and the occasional severity of his lapses, then, has the effect of compensating for his artful presentation of them. His admissions ultimately witness to his essential honesty and integrity, for he could easily have passed over these embarrassing actions. His forthrightness in such matters makes one believe him when he disclaims the villainies imputed to him by his enemies—when, for example, he says that he did not poison his wife Sabina, that he does not prepare his own food out of fear, or that he did not order the deaths of "three intriguing scoundrels and a brute" (p. 100) who threatened his position after the death of Trajan.[5] Both his real and imputed lapses, on the other hand, weigh less in the scale than his gestures of kindness and mature restraint—pardoning the slave's attempt on his life, for example, or declining the Senate's gestures of empty fawning ("the long series of honorary appellations which is draped like a fringed shawl round the necks of certain emperors"—pp. 103–4). Hadrian's civilized distaste for bloodletting, whether in the coliseum or in Parthia, would compensate for much more villainy than that with which the emperor manages to charge himself. One forgives any number of minor sins in a man who sanely turns his back on meaningless and counterproductive wars of conquest.

The emperor prefers to invest his energies in consolidating the peace and conserving the heritage of the past. As he remarks on his restoration of the tomb of Epaminondas, Hadrian feels the need "to commemorate . . . a time when everything, viewed at a distance, seems to have been noble, and simple, too, whether tenderness, glory, or death" (p. 158). He has ordered tombs, monuments, shrines, temples, and public buildings refurbished or rebuilt throughout the empire, and this work symbolizes the more abstract and awesome task of refurbishing Rome itself—its institutions, its power, its security, its ideals, its splendor, even its Hellenic pedigree. All of these had suffered under Tiberius, Caligula, Nero, and the rest of the mad or inverted or merely incompetent rulers between Augustus and Nerva.

"I have done much rebuilding. To reconstruct is to collaborate with time gone by, penetrating or modifying its spirit, and carrying it toward a longer future. Thus beneath the stones we find the secret of the springs" (pp. 126–27). These remarks describe historical fiction no less than conservationism, for the author of an historical novel—this one, for example—also engages in an act of reconstruction, of collaboration with time gone by. Yourcenar seeks to uncover the vital origins of her own moribund culture. She, too, seeks the secret of the springs.

In addition to his other acts of cultural conservation, Hadrian builds libraries and orders books copied and recopied, for "each man fortunate enough to benefit to some degree from this legacy of culture seemed to me responsible for protecting it and holding it in trust for the human race" (p. 217). Yourcenar, herself an accomplished classical scholar, a beneficiary of Hadrian's sense of cultural responsibility, does her part to preserve and pass on the special vitality of the ancient world, to effect in some small measure the reinvigoration of a culture whose classical antecedents seem to lie in ruins. But to disinter the values of antiquity, she must first disinter a whole set of perceptions common to that world but now alien. She accomplishes this end primarily through an act of psychological reconstruction. Focusing on one man's psychological reality, she re-creates the mind of Hadrian and thereby re-creates Hadrian's time as well. The reader looks into that mind as into a mirror angled to catch the light of a remote age.

Occasionally, however, the mirror reflects the age of the reader. As noted in the preceding chapter, a historical novel will commonly function in one primary and one secondary mode; in this one the primary attention to the way it was does not preclude secondary reflections in a distant mirror. Thus Hadrian, with various degrees of conscious prevision, can from time to time address posterity and even show a later century its own face. He imagines at one point "a hypothetical empire governed from the West, an Atlantic world" (p. 137), and he sounds even more prescient when he describes the puritan work ethic and the materialistic and antlike societies of the future: "I can well imagine forms of servitude worse than our own, because more insidious, whether they transform men into stupid, complacent machines, who believe themselves free just when they are most subjugated, or whether to the exclusion of leisure and pleasures essential to man they develop a passion for work as violent as the passion for war among barbarous races. To such bondage for the human mind and imagination I prefer even our avowed slavery" (p. 115).

These touches alone represent mere glances toward the twentieth century, rather than an actual mirroring of the present in the past. The real mirroring is more a matter of atmosphere, for in her depiction of the autumnal civilization of Hadrian's Rome, the author invites the reader to recognize a later civilization, also past its prime. In her "Reflections on the Composition of *Memoirs of Hadrian*," Yourcenar explains that the novel, after a number of false starts beginning as early as the 1920s, really began to come together in her mind late in 1948, when "everything that the world . . . had gone through" seemed to illuminate her reading of ancient source materials on Hadrian, to cast "upon that imperial existence certain other lights and shades." She felt a special affinity with the long-dead emperor and his age, because "the fact of having lived in a world which is toppling" (p. 327) gave her a real appreciation of an age and a civilization that had to suffer a like dissolution of old values, old certainties, old sources of strength. "Both Plutarch and Marcus Aurelius knew full well that gods, and civilizations, pass and die. We are not the first to look upon an inexorable future" (p. 333).

But these features merely enhance the creation of an author whose primary energies serve the end of a faithful capturing of the past in its own unique character. Yourcenar realizes the difficulties of getting at historical truth, but she does not assume that it must therefore remain forever out of reach. In her "Reflections" on the novel she emphasizes the necessity of scrupulous research animated by an imagination capable of filling gaps with authority: "Learn everything, read everything, inquire into everything," she declares. Fill "hundreds of card notes," call before the mind's eye both people and actions, and recognize that divergent texts do not call each other into question but rather represent "different facets, or two successive stages, of the same reality, a reality convincingly human just because it is complex" (pp. 330–31). She aspires to "constant participation, as intensely aware as possible, in *that which has been*" (p. 328), and she refuses "to suggest, as is too often done, that historical truth is never to be attained, in any of its aspects. With this kind of truth, as with all others, the problem is the same: one errs *more* or *less*" (p. 330). She recognizes that Hadrian himself seeks the truth, no less than the writer who aspires to present him accurately. True to her Roman orientation, she even invokes Pontius Pilate, whom the Western world has been conditioned to think singularly blind on the subject, as a wise man in matters of truth: "He who seeks passionately for truth, or at least for accuracy, is frequently the one best able to perceive, like Pilate, that truth is not absolute or pure" (p. 340).

Notwithstanding her respect for the usual kinds of historical research, Yourcenar places special emphasis on a kind of linking up with the mind of the past, and she reflects that "some five and twenty aged men, their withered hands interlinked to form a chain, would be enough to establish an unbroken contact between Hadrian and ourselves" (p. 321). She suggests with this figure the essential identity of history and personal memory. She elaborates by pointing out the "historical" aspects of a writer like Proust:

Those who put the historical novel in a category apart are forgetting that what every novelist does is only to interpret, by means of the techniques which his period affords, a certain number of past events; his memories, whether consciously or unconsciously recalled, whether personal or impersonal, are all woven of the same stuff as History itself. . . . In our day, when introspection tends to dominate literary forms, the historical novel, or what may for convenience's sake be called by that name, must take the plunge into time recaptured, and must fully establish itself within some inner world [p. 329].

To know the past, this author implies, one must enter a representative mind of the past, live in that "inner world." But the attainment of such historical empathy remains problematic because of the extrinsic mental baggage accumulated over the centuries. The most cumbersome of this baggage is the set of religious and cultural assumptions intervening—and strengthened, down through the ages—between ancient Rome and today. When the Supreme Pontiff, the Vicar of Christ, supplanted the Pontifex Maximus (an event actually imagined by Hadrian), an enormous change in values took place. Julian, the fourth-century Byzantine emperor who tried, too late, to halt the Christian transformation, allegedly died murmuring *"Vicisti Galilæe,"* and only the occasional Gibbon, who associated the rise of Christianity with the decline and fall of Rome, or Swinburne, who translated Julian's last words in the famous line "Thou hast conquered, O pale Galilean," has registered the toll of Christian hegemony, given adequate expression to what the world lost by the new dispensation's displacement of the old.

Even the waning of Christianity in the modern world has done little to restore an older set of attitudes or perceptions in matters spiritual. Consequently, Yourcenar must take strong measures to bring home the radically different worldview of Hadrian and his age. She allows the emperor to express opinions about Jews and Christians—mere common sense to the cultivated Romans of his day—that run shockingly counter to the received views of a later age. Hadrian, nonetheless, speaks as a religious man—but a religious man in the Roman tradition of thoroughgoing religious tolerance. He has little sympathy with all forms of fanaticism and intolerance. Receiving an apologia from one "Quadratus, a bishop of the Christians" (p. 220), Hadrian reads it thoughtfully and concedes the value of the solace that Christianity affords to simple and poor folk. "But I was aware, too, of certain dangers. Such glorification of virtues befitting children and slaves was made at the expense of more virile and intellectual qualities; under the narrow, vapid innocence I could detect the fierce intransigence of the sectarian in presence of forms of life and of thought which are not his own, the insolent pride which makes him value himself above other men, and his voluntarily circumscribed vision" (p. 221).

The Christians at least render unto Caesar the things that are Caesar's. The Jews, on the other hand, cultivate a really monumental intransigence. Their resistance to the rebuilding of Jerusalem leads to blood-shed on a scale that appalls and sickens the "pacifically inclined" (p. 240) Hadrian. The costs of the savage conflict in Palestine, as the emperor recounts them, make grim reading: "In those four years of war fifty fortresses and more than nine hundred villages and towns had been sacked and destroyed; the enemy had lost nearly six hundred thousand men; battles, endemic fevers, and epidemics had taken nearly ninety thousand of ours" (p. 249). Hadrian reasons that only fanatics, "sectarians so obsessed by their god that they have neglected the human" (p. 35), could resist the *Pax Romana* so long and at such cost.

Hadrian overstates the fanaticism of the Jewish rebels. As Yourcenar remarked to Patrick de Rosbo, "He is incapable of admitting . . . that these people do not desire the benefits of Greco-Roman civilization."[6] He also fails to consider how zealously he and his countrymen might resist another Carthaginian invasion of Italy. But in expressing his contempt for religious absolutism, Hadrian does not, as at least one critic has hinted, become the mouthpiece for an anachronistic and monstrous anti-Semitism. To impute anti-Semitism in the modern sense to either this character or his creator implies an odd expectation that the author will impose on historical material an inappropriate modern perspective. Yourcenar, writing only a few years after the opening of the death camps and the first modern Palestinian war (1948), takes certain risks here to establish the profound difference between the way ancient Romans thought about religion and the way those influenced by the Judeo-Christian heritage think about it.

One should note, however, that Yourcenar ironically undercuts her narrator when he speaks of "leaning against the trunk of a leafless fig tree" (p. 248) to observe the Roman assault on Bethar, the last Jewish stronghold. The oblique reference to an earlier Jew's least sensible gesture, the cursing of the fig tree, would seem to have something to do with the senselessness of the present bloodshed. But Hadrian probably remains unaware that he has touched on a famous incident in the New Testament, an incident traditionally held to symbolize the fate of the old Judaic dispensation at the coming of a new order. According to biblical interpreters, the fig tree cursed by Christ represents the tree of Judah, inherently unripe for miracle. In Yourcenar's context, the tree no longer vital enough for the new dispensation is ironically associated with Romans and Jews alike. Both face superannuation by crescive Christianity.

The toll of the Jewish war also figures in the novel's central myth—a myth so familiar to Hadrian and his correspondent as to require little direct reference. In writing of his life as a progression from early vigor and happiness to declining health and vitality, Hadrian recapitulates the Ages of Man, and the presence of this myth in his narrative, resonant with but distanced from its Judeo-Christian and psychoanalytic congeners, provides further evidence of Yourcenar's having immersed herself in psychological givens that differ from those of her own age. Yourcenar's subtle exploitation of the myth contributes to the accuracy of her historical reconstruction, so that the reader experiences not only the events of the past but also its half-conscious mythic thinking. This mythic thinking shapes Hadrian's narrative. From his accession to power and his relationship with Antinous to the dissolution of love and peace, Hadrian follows the archetypal pattern of slow wasting established in the cosmology of Hesiod and Ovid.

According to the myth, the world began in an age of Gold, then declined successively to ages of Silver, Bronze, and Iron, with attendant changes in tutelary deities. Saturn ruled in the Golden Age, Jupiter in the Silver, and lesser gods thereafter. The terrestrial environment and its human inhabitants also changed. During the Golden Age, humanity lived peacefully in a kind of perennial spring, but subsequently the climate became harsher, the human beings more warlike and knavish.

Hadrian's recollections of the years with Antinous elicit the few direct references to this myth. "When I think back on these years," he declares in the chapter entitled "Saeculum Aureum," "I seem to return to the Age of Gold" (p. 156). Subsequently he describes this period as "truly an Olympian height in my life. All was there, the golden fringe of cloud, the eagles, and the cupbearer of immortality" (p. 163). The eagles belong iconographically to Rome, over which he reigns, and to Olympian Zeus, or Jupiter, with whom he identifies, and he recognizes his cupbearer, his Ganymede, in Antinous. But according to Hesiod, such voluptuousness—Hadrian even notes the anagrammatic relationship of *Roma* and *Amor*—belongs to the Age of Silver, not the Age of Gold. Hadrian, identifying with Jupiter, is actually at one remove from the Golden Age. Ironically, the emperor fails to see that the process of decline has already begun, that his real Golden Age had slipped by during his successful defense of the Dacian frontier, his rise to power, his wise treaties, his early, judicious rule. Then was he Saturnlike, enjoying "the virgin gold of respect" (p. 103), untouched as yet by the passing years because Saturn, qua Kronos, is master of time.

After Saturn and Jupiter comes Mars, and with him the Age of Bronze. In this age, says Ovid, "men were of a fiercer character, more ready to turn to cruel warfare" (*Metamorphoses*, I).[7] Hadrian enters his Age of Bronze in the Jewish war, which seems in the narrative to follow hard upon the death of Antinous. The emperor understands that this war, with its multiple cruelties and endless bloodshed, represents a terrible decline from what has gone before in his life and in his reign, and he begins to glimpse an elemental process at work, eroding civilization itself. In a bleak moment he catalogues the cultural slippage: "I was beginning to find it natural, if not just, that we should perish. Our literature is nearing exhaustion, our arts are falling asleep; Pancrates is not Homer, nor is Arrian a Xenophon; when I have tried to immortalize Antinous in stone no Praxiteles has come to hand. Our sciences have been at a standstill from the times of Aristotle and Archimedes; our technical development is inadequate to the strain of a long war; even our pleasure-lovers grow weary of delight" (p. 243).

As Hadrian himself grows weary of delight, he enters the Age of Iron and even identifies with Pluto, its grim deity. Ovid says of the Iron Age: "friend was not safe from friend, nor father-in-law from son-in-law, and even between brothers affection was rare. Husbands waited eagerly for the death of their wives, and wives for that of their husbands." Thus at the end of his narrative Hadrian speaks with greatest frankness about the hostility between himself and his wife Sabina, and almost casually he orders the execution of his brother-in-law and grandnephew, Servianus and Fuscus. He even recapitulates his identification with the various deities associated with the Ages of Man: "men . . . no longer compare me, as they once did, to serene and radiant Zeus, but to Mars Gradivus, god of long campaigns and austere discipline. . . . Of late this pale, drawn visage, these fixed eyes and this tall body held straight by force of will, suggest to them Pluto, god of shades" (p. 286).

More painful to Hadrian than his personal griefs are the signs by which he recognizes Rome's fate, recognizes that "catastrophe and ruin will come" (p. 293). The Romans restore order on one frontier after another, but gradually the defenses crumble: "I could see the return of barbaric codes, of implacable gods, of unquestioned despotism of savage chieftains, a world broken up into enemy states and eternally prey to insecurity. . . . Our epoch, the faults and limitations of which I knew better than anyone else, would perhaps be considered one day, by contrast, as one of the golden ages of man" (p. 243). Thus the myth at the heart of *Memoirs of Hadrian* operates on several levels: one sees it in Hadrian's life, in the decline of the Roman Empire, and, most chillingly, in the decline over the centuries from Golden antiquity to the present Age of Iron. Part of the power of this myth, like the myth of Eden and its loss, lies in its ability to capture and reflect a sense of the progressive decay that time visits on individual human beings and on nations. It even anticipates the entropic decline posited by modern physicists.

Considerations of this kind prey on the mind of the emperor at the end of his reign because he has devoted his life to the promotion and consolidation of order. Hadrian's pursuit of this ideal constitutes the most important thematic thread in the novel; the prominence of the theme reveals how fully Yourcenar understands the man and the age that she sets out to present with fidelity. She recognizes, for example, that Hadrian's love of order springs from his regard for Greek culture no less than from the Roman values he must, as Caesar, preserve and protect. As Jacques Vier has remarked, Hadrian embodies "the perfect accord of the Greek genius and the Latin genius."[8] Thus he delights in contributing to the dissemination of the Greek heritage, and he labors to accelerate the grafting of the older culture onto its successors. He dreams, early in his career, "of Hellenizing the Barbarians and Atticizing Rome, thus imposing upon the world by degrees the only culture which has once for all separated itself from the monstrous, the shapeless, and the inert, the only one to have invented a definition of method, a system of politics, and a theory of beauty" (p. 74).

Yet despite his own Hellenism, Hadrian remains a true Roman, for his vision of order goes beyond anything the

Greeks ever achieved or even imagined. Alexander, after all, subjugated but did not stabilize, and *The Republic*, that most comprehensive Greek statement on the subject of political order, seems conceived exclusively on the scale of the city-state. Only a Roman could dream of *tellus stabilita*, and Hadrian, true to his heritage, wants an abiding imperial peace: "I could see myself as seconding the deity in his effort to give form and order to a world" (pp. 143–44). This passion of Hadrian's extends to his most mundane imperial duties—he fosters a solid and capable civil service bureaucracy to ensure that poor rule will not undermine stability—and even to his casual observations: "Pompey, in endeavoring to bring order to this uncertain world of Asia, sometimes seemed to me to have worked more effectively for Rome than Caesar himself" (p. 185). But readers probably find most attractive Hadrian's refusal, in the name of greater security and order, to pursue wars of imperial expansion. "I dreamed of an army trained to maintain order on frontiers less extended, if necessary, but secure. Every new increase in the vast imperial organism seemed to me an unsound growth, like a cancer or dropsical edema which would eventually cause our death" (pp. 70–71). Hadrian's Wall, the most famous relic of this enlightened attitude, survives to this day in England, an "emblem of my renunciation of the policy of conquest" (p. 137).

One must work to create and maintain order because it does not flourish in the natural state. Hadrian, a contemporary of the astronomer Ptolemy, seems to distinguish between sub-lunary and cosmic spheres. He hints at the distinction in the opening pages, where he mentions his interest in the possible meaning contained in "the random twitter of birds, or . . . the distant mechanism of the stars" (p. 26). Here the translation, presumably with the approval of Yourcenar, clarifies a point left ambiguous in the original French. *Babillage,* "babbling" or "chatter," becomes "*random* twitter," the adjective implying the disorder of the sublunary sphere. Thus in the English translation Hadrian differentiates stars and birdsong: the one is mechanical, remotely orderly, and accessible to the astronomer; the other is "random" or orderless, yielding at best problematic messages to haruspices. Sublunary life, in other words, progressing from organic to inorganic and back to organic, amounts only to a crude approximation of order, and from moment to moment life tends to wallow in disorder. Only in moments like the one in which he lies out under the Syrian stars all one night can Hadrian affirm that "disorder is absorbed in order" (p. 147). Elsewhere he speaks of "the order of the universe" (p. 110) as of something divine, a referent for all human aspirations to harmony.

But wherever one achieves order on earth, it must dissolve sooner or later into chaos. "One has always to begin over again" (p. 249), says Hadrian. "Nature prefers to start again from the very clay, from chaos itself, and this horrible waste is what we term natural order" (p. 244). Nevertheless, Hadrian remains as impressed by the human capacity to rebuild as by the tendency toward dissolution. "Catastrophe and ruin will come; disorder will triumph, but order will too, from time to time. Peace will again establish itself between two periods of war" (p. 293). Whatever the fate of the actual political entity he has served, the emperor reflects, the *idea* of Rome will survive, a beacon in the realm of the attainable ideal. "Rome would be perpetuating herself in the least of the towns where magistrates strive to demand just weight from the merchants, to clean and light the streets, to combat disorder, slackness, superstition and injustice, and to give broader and fairer interpretation to the laws. She would endure to the end of the last city built by man" (p. 111).

For Hadrian, the ideal of order subsumes a number of other philosophically related goals, goals definable only through a sustained inquiry into the good life. This inquiry, another part of the Greek legacy to Roman civilization, leads the emperor to reflect on the relative value of pleasure versus duty, freedom versus discipline, and the life of the senses versus the life of the mind. With remarkable lucidity he analyzes everything from his own sexuality to his official function and the sacrifices it entails. As Hadrian explores the political and ethical philosophy of the age, he completes, as it were, an inventory of his own mind, and Yourcenar, the presence behind this voice out of the remote past, completes her picture of a bygone intellectual reality.

Philosophically, Hadrian represents a curious mixture of stoic and hedonist, and here again, in the coexistence of a tropism for pleasure and a tropism for duty, one sees the rich flowing together of Greek and Roman traditions. The emperor's hedonism finds its definitive expression in a kind of polymorphous sexuality. Homosexual in the great passion of his life, he moves on the periphery of Roman tolerance, apologist for a relationship the Greeks, in an earlier age, would have viewed as natural. Yet he actually describes himself as bisexual, intimating that only the shallowness of women in second-century Rome has precluded their becoming his lovers more often. The one exceptional woman he has known, Plotina, is unavailable to him as a lover (or so Yourcenar interprets a relationship that Hadrian's enemies viewed as sexual). Nevertheless, he does encounter in her a genteel variety of hedonism, for she "leaned toward Epicurean philosophy, that narrow but clean bed whereon I have sometimes rested my thoughts" (p. 81). If Hadrian inclines toward embracing pleasure more frankly, he does so on reflection and on principle. In his most direct apologia for his life, the emperor rebukes the "so-called wise, who denounce the danger of habit and excess in sensuous delight, instead of fearing its absence or its loss." He replies, too, to the puritans of every age who see early pleasures requited in later sorrows: "My own felicity is in no way responsible for those of my imprudences which shattered it later on; in so far as I have acted in harmony with it I have been wise. I think still that someone wiser than I might well have remained happy till his death" (p. 164). He compares himself, finally, to Alcibiades, "that great artist in pleasure" (p. 165).

If Hadrian tends to speak of his hedonism more often and more directly than of his stoicism, one should remember that he addresses Marcus Aurelius, famous even as a youth for his sobriety and indifference to pleasure. Hadrian offers this earnest young man an eloquent paean to an alternative philosophy. But the attentive reader discovers indications of philosophical balance on the emperor's part. Part of the evidence presents itself in the composition of the imperial circle, for Hadrian keeps about him not only beautiful youths like Antinous, Celer, and Diotimus but also a "circle of Platonist or Stoic philosophers"[9] led by Chabrias. He gives further proof of philosophical duality in his arrangements for the succession. He chooses first Lucius Ceionius, a hedonist, then Antoninus Pius and Marcus Aurelius, a brace of stoics. In fact, he obliges Antoninus to adopt Lucius's son along with Marcus Aurelius, as if to insure the continued presence of a hedonist counterweight in the succession.

The courtliness and civilized discourse of the emperor notwithstanding, one may still resist or despise some of the practices and attitudes for which he apologizes. But all resistance vanishes, at least among readers who value freedom, when Hadrian addresses himself to political questions. Yourcenar makes her narrator the spokesman for a philosophy that anticipates the reasoning of the eighteenth-century architects of political liberty in France, England, and America. Thus one hears echoes of "Life, Liberty, and the Pursuit of Happiness" and "*Liberté, Egalité, Fraternité*" when Hadrian introduces his own ringing triad of political desiderata. This triad, however, undergoes a revealing modification in the course of the narrative. Hadrian speaks first of "*Humanitas, Libertas, Felicitas*" (pp. 111, 112), but at the end, having surrendered his own personal happiness and no longer buoyed by pleasant recol-

lections, he speaks of *"humanity, liberty,* and *justice"* (p. 293).
The substitution of *iustitia* for *felicitas* hints at a revision dictated by sobering experience, a transition from the hedonism
of youth to the stoicism of age. Humanity and liberty, on the
other hand, he embraces with lifelong consistency, though
fully aware of the faults of the one and the dangers of the
other.

Hadrian's regard for liberty begins with his own sense of
freedom and its value—a sense he calls the "one thing" that
makes him "superior to most men":

[Others] fail to recognize their due liberty, and likewise their true
servitude. They curse their fetters, but seem sometimes to find them
matter for pride. Yet they pass their days in vain license, and do not
know how to fashion for themselves the lightest yoke. For my part
I have sought liberty more than power, and power only because it
can lead to freedom. What interested me was not a philosophy of
the free man (all who try that have proved tiresome), but a technique:
I hoped to discover the hinge where our will meets and moves with
destiny, and where discipline strengthens, instead of restraining, our
nature [pp. 42-43].

Observations like these reveal a man who knows how "to com-
mand, and what is perhaps in the end slightly less futile, to
serve" (p. 39). They express, according to Michel Aubrion,
"the whole doctrine of classicism" and provide "the key to the
character and to the novel, the key, too, to the entire *oeuvre*
of Marguerite Yourcenar, to her philosophy and to her aes-
thetic."[10]

In *Memoirs of Hadrian,* then, the reader experiences the way
it was in the Roman Empire of the second century. Yourcenar
depicts Rome's pleasures, political intrigues, and wars. Most
of all she depicts, in the representative and empathic mind
of her narrator, Rome's mental life, and she achieves psychological mimesis of a very high order. In the act of reconstruction, according to Hadrian, one collaborates with time gone

by to uncover the secret of the springs. Yourcenar reconstructs a rich classical world to uncover a spring, a source of ideas and values, that flows around many obstacles into all subsequent Western culture. In "Reflections on the Composition of *Memoirs of Hadrian*," she describes setting out to "do, from within, the same work of reconstruction which the nineteenth-century archaeologists have done from without" (p. 226), and surely Clio smiles on the result, a book in which history and fiction blend with pathos and grace.

Clio Swived: *The Sot-Weed Factor*

In Greek mythology, Zeus fathered the nine muses on Mnemosyne, goddess of memory. One imagines the goddess feeling a special fondness for Clio, muse of that collective memory called history. The inclusion of Clio among the muses suggests that the ancients viewed recording the past as something related to the production of tragedy, comedy, epic, the dance, sacred music, and lyric poetry—that they saw it, in other words, as an art among arts. Indeed, with the example of Homer fresh in their minds, the ancients would have known that historical thinking originates in verse and tale. Ebenezer Cooke, the hero of John Barth's *The Sot-Weed Factor*, remarks that no one would remember the Trojan war and the heroic deeds it occasioned if Homer had not sung them. A later poet, Byron, notes the fate of those neglected by the bard: "They shone not on the poet's page,/And so have been forgotten" (*Don Juan*, I, lines 36–37). Barth's Eben, himself a poet, recognizes a certain responsibility to history. In the colloquy with the man he takes for Lord Baltimore, he notes the poet's primitive function as historian. Though he compares the historian to the poet invidiously, and though he notes the poet's tendency to improve on graceless fact, he clearly conceives of the poet as, in effect, a kind of superior chronicler. In his suit for a poetic commission from Lord Baltimore he offers to become the bard of Maryland—a poet with obligations to Clio no less than to Calliope. He becomes the novel's archetypal historian as well as its archetypal poet, and as such he resembles that other artistic chronicler of the past, the novel's author. Barth, like his character, produces a mock-epic colonial record entitled *The Sot-Weed Factor,* and even in the detail of the twin sister the author projects himself in his character. Barth, too, seems to have an acute sense of the affinity between literary art and recording the past—even though he finds the label "historical novelist" uncongenial.[11]

Barth slyly quotes a reviewer who calls the poem by Ebenezer Cooke "a refreshing change from the usual false panegyrics upon the Plantations."[12] The words apply equally to the novel in which they appear. Cooke's poem, written late in the seventeenth century, satirizes colonial society; Barth's novel similarly satirizes various pieties expressing America's historical perception of itself. One senses in Cooke's unsparing account of life in the new world—even discounting for satiric license—something of the naked truth about the rampant guile, sharp dealing, and utter commercial rapacity that much have constituted much of the colonial experience. Barth therefore mines the poem for many of the incidents in his novel: the unpleasant ocean crossing, the initial contact with the loutish colonials in blue scotchcloth, the canoe ferry, the planter's board, the encounter and postprandial colloquy with the hoydenish swinemaid, the journey on horseback with the planter's son, the uproarious workings of colonial justice, the painful "seasoning" undergone by new arrivals from Europe, the acrimonious game of lanterloo (in which allegations of unchastity fly thick), the visit to the woodsman, and the dealings with shysters, quacks, and other charlatans.

Barth found in the original *Sot-Weed Factor* a piece of primary material on which to base a revision of the glorious annals of the colonial period. One should not label the author an epigone, however, for he converts the clumsily versified and disjointedly episodic poem into a complexly ordered and elegantly plotted fiction. Thematically, too, the novel goes far beyond the poem, chiefly in Barth's development of certain suggestive details supplied by Cooke. The factor in Cooke's poem, for example, wonders what could have created America's disagreeable inhabitants and concludes, in a passage that Barth cites in the novel, that only "erring Nature," unsupervised by deity, could have produced the outré Maryland colonials. The Indians, by contrast, are so fearsome that only Satan could have made them. The factor even imagines the new world as the place of the first murderer's banishment: "The Land of Nod,/Planted at first where vagrant Cain/His brother had unjustly slain" (ll. 34–36).[13] Barth seizes on the idea of mighty but dubious forces at work in the new world; reversing Cooke's trope of America as the infamous Land of Nod, he opts for the more familiar myth of America as Eden and constructs, in the tradition of Cooper, Twain, Fitzgerald, and Faulkner, a symbolic story of the American Adam's innocence and fall.

Barth was embarrassed to see his novel described, on the cover of an early edition, as "a moral allegory cloaked in terms of colonial history." As he explained to an interviewer, "I mentioned the word *allegory* to somebody off the cuff, and then they cheated and put it on the cover of the book."[14] David Morrell, responding to Barth's diffidence in this matter, calls the book "not so much allegorical as symbolic."[15] But Barth wrought better than he knew—or at least better than he cared to claim publicly. His novel *The Sot-Weed Factor* is in fact highly allegorical, for its characters and action, as will be seen, not only function at a literal and concrete level but also discover, at another level, a coherent structure of abstract meaning.

Barth reimagines the American political myth in the interests of truth (a thing not necessarily congruent with "fact") and national self-knowledge. Treating certain episodes of

American history ironically, he converts them into a revisionist fable. But Barth's revisionism goes beyond the mere debunking of jingoist pieties. Thematically and generically, his novel constitutes a meditation on a number of historical questions, along with their philosophical, anthropological, and literary corollaries. Thus Henry Burlingame remarks at one point that history, like a snake, sees only motion and is consequently ill-equipped to perceive "eternal verities" (p. 172)—the province of philosophy and literature. Burlingame here echoes Aristotle in chapter 9 of the *Poetics*: "Poetry . . . is a more philosophical and a higher thing than history: for poetry tends to express the universal, history the particular."[16] Bertrand Burton makes the point even more strikingly: "Your poet need never trouble his head to explain at all: men think he hath a passkey to Dame Truth's bedchamber and smiles at the scholars building ladders in the court" (p. 220).

These hints receive further substance at an ironic moment later in the story when Eben discourses on "sundry theories of history—the retrogressive, held by Dante and Hesiod; the dramatic, held by the Hebrews and the Christian fathers; the progressive, held by Virgil; the cyclical, held by Plato and Ecclesiasticus; the undulatory, and even the vortical hypothesis entertained, according to Henry Burlingame, by a gloomy neo-Platonist of Christ's College, who believed that the cyclic periods of history were growing ever shorter and thus at some non-predictable moment in the future the universe would go rigid and explode" (p. 681). The author here provides a broad hint of his own thematic program, for the plots and subplots of his novel seem to illustrate one theory of history after another. Eben delivers this little lecture, for example, at a moment when he has just reenacted the adventures of Captain John Smith and the first Henry Burlingame among the Indians. Presently he will reenact his own adventure with pirates, thereby demonstrating cyclic recurrence even within the brief span of his personal experience.

These repetitions, however, prove not purely balanced cycles but rather corkscrew turns of a vortical history—events hastening in shorter and shorter cycles to some desperate pass. Just as Eben's second encounter with pirates is more desperate than the first (this time he leaves his womenfolk behind when he escapes), so the second encounter with the savages of Bloodsworth Island takes place in a context of imminent colonial apocalypse, for the Indians and escaped slaves contemplate a bloody rising. Moreover, Barth invites the reader to compare these models of history with the "progressive" model that Eben also cites and that most Americans grow up embracing without question. But if America, with its wealth and power, can exemplify the way humanity has progressed since the seventeenth century, it can also, in its vulgarity and materialism, exemplify a spiritual decline over the same period. In a novel set in the seventeenth century yet breathing twentieth-century philosophy from every page, Barth comments on both perceptions and expects of his reader a willingness to reflect on the forces that went into creating the American present. Given the subversive multiplicity of historical perspective in the novel, the reader who perpends the direction of time's arrow in America and Western history may well conclude that the progressive assumptions so central to the way Americans think about their country have long since ceased to reflect any credible Virgilian paradigm of national destiny.

Barth critiques even the chiliastic tendencies of American social reform, for the imminence of racial cataclysm—left unresolved at the end of *The Sot-Weed Factor*—refers as much to our age as to that of Eben and Henry. Barth wrote just as America's social conscience had awakened to the plight of the nation's minorities, especially blacks and Indians. But Barth does not idealize the novel's oppressed races, nor does he assume an easy moral superiority to their exploiters. In fact, through Eben, he ascribes the roles of oppressed and oppressor to "accidents of history" (p. 545) rather than to racial characteristics (here he echoes Faulkner's Isaac McCaslin, who recognizes in "accidents of geography" the origins of racial injustice). Barth does not, however, excuse colonialism or racism, and he does hint at the virtues of various integrations. The most noble characters in the book, the sons of the Tayac Chicamec, are the products of intermarriage between red and white; by the same token, the most cohesive amd purposive political unit joins red and black. But the author is quite cool-headed about his blacks and Indians. Indeed, he makes his point all the more effectively by inviting the reader to embrace Quassapelagh, Drepacca, and even Charley Matassin as stereotypical noble savages, only to reveal in these characters subsequently the same congeries of contradictory passions to be found in his white characters. Moreover, in one of the novel's most graphically symbolic images, the sexual encounter of Captain John Smith and the Indian maid Pocahontas, he makes the prurient eagerness of the princess and her people quite plain. One should recall, too, that this cultural violation mirrors the more or less literal rape of Father FitzMaurice by the Indians.

But more gets violated in this story than a priest or an Indian maid and the land she represents. Barth swives Clio too, and with her that most shrinking virgin of all: the naïve, sensitive, idealistic American whose innocence, at least with regard to history, makes him or her the most tight-kneed of the lot. Generations of Americans, ignoring the likely sexual component of such a relationship, have accepted Smith's intimation that Pocahontas loved him for his manly beauty, for his virtue, and for the dangers he had passed. But as Richard Noland points out, Barth's version of the encounter between John Smith and Pocahontas "burlesques the writing of American history and suggests that much of it may be more fancy than fact and that the facts would be subversive of many orthodoxies."[17] Ideally, then, the Pocahontas story as Barth tells it will strike the reader more as a dispensing with euphemism than as a shocking liberty with the historical record. Indeed, given the ultimate ramifications of the cultural encounter chronicled in the famous story of the English colonist and the aboriginal princess (I refer to the subsequent fate of the Indians in America), the question of any literal violation in 1607 becomes academic.

For a historian, the cavalier attitude to fact indulged in the present speculations would be unthinkable. The historian cannot arrange or modify facts to square with some scholarly thesis, however unimpeachable the theory of history thereby demonstrated. Yet few object to the manipulation of rough material on the storyteller's part, and one notes just here—at the risk of a truism—the really significant difference between novelist and historian. By the same paradox that obtains generally in fiction (that the artist tells truth by lying), the historical novelist can—by judicious (sometimes egregious) departures from fact—provide more insight into historical truth than the historian constrained by fact. The point bears emphasizing because several critics argue that Barth merely undermines history without attempting seriously to improve its accuracy.[18] The more judicious Tony Tanner, on the other hand, simply notes that "Barth loses no opportunity to promote the question: how can we tell 'history' from the various and multiple 'fictions' or versions of it which are available and which have been promulgated from time to time?"[19] But if Barth undermines conventional ideas of history, he does so, I would argue, the better to write superior history, the kind made possible by an escape from the tyranny of meaningless facts.

The tension in Barth's novel between history and fiction, along with the playful demonstrations of mutually exclusive theories of history, should be kept in mind as one explores Barth's allegory—or rather allegories—of the fall and redemption of humankind. As already noted, this allegory has its precedents as an American literary theme, but it appears in *The Sot-Weed Factor*, as in Faulkner's *Go Down, Moses*, as a critique of the tendency to embrace the kind of "dramatic" historical vision exemplified by the Christian myth and the Christian view of the human struggle over time. This struggle the Christian views as linear: it begins with creation and ends with apocalypse. The incarnation, the moment at which the human and the divine intersect, is an event unique in time. But for a modern writer with profoundly skeptical proclivities, armed with the findings of both physical and cultural anthropologists, such a view of history can only seem inadequate. History may well prove ultimately linear, but the trajectory from big bang to entropic heat death suggests nothing transcendental. Hence the theistic account of history serves Barth only as a target for parody, an object of irony, and one must test all conclusions against this point to avoid going astray in assessing the role of Christian allegory in *The Sot-Weed Factor*.

One should also note that Barth ingeniously—and mischievously—doubles the allegory. He develops it first, in the main plot, in terms of the white settlers in the new world. He develops another version, in the Burlingame subplot, in terms of the aboriginal Americans and their natural paradise. Thus Barth anatomizes colonialism and its evils at the same time that he explores the classic question of humanity's essential baseness or nobility—the question with which one traditionally associates the names of Hobbes and Rousseau. Like Conrad he depicts his colonists encountering their own savagery, and like Faulkner he finds versions of original sin among Indians as well as whites.

Like Spenser, moreover, Barth marries his religious allegory to an allegory of national identity. The observant reader recognizes Ebenezer Cooke, early in the story, as a representative figure. A third-generation American at his birth in 1666, he springs from a family that evidently goes back to the colonial genesis. Eben's grandfather must have come with the first Maryland colonists, who arrived and founded St. Mary's City in 1634. But the major symbolic dimensions of Eben's story really begin to emerge when he returns to the new land after many years in England and promptly becomes the main character in a little morality play. As the innocent, Adamic everyman, he suffers a fall, forfeits his estate, and subsequently toils long and hard to regain his patrimony. Eben and his fellow sufferers—his sister Anna, his servant Bertrand Burton, his mentor Henry Burlingame et al.—strive to serve the good and to secure a merciful justice in a vast theater dominated by two mighty figures of ambiguous virtue and evil. Lord Baltimore is Yahweh, his colonial "creation" usurped by various demonic forces under the aegis of the satanic John Coode, a hater of "government itself" who "loathes . . . any kind of order" (p. 137). Various thrones, powers, and dominions lieutenant these two: Captain Mitchell plays Beelzebub to Coode; Governor Nicholson seems a kind of Archangel Michael. Like the dread entities they stand for, the two mighty opponents seem never actually to reveal themselves to mortal eyes. A rueful Henry Burlingame admits: "I ne'er have met the man who hath seen John Coode face to face, nor, despite his fame and influence and the great trust he hath placed in me, have I myself ever seen Lord Baltimore" (p. 487).

But Barth reserves extensive detail for the mortal end of his allegorical scale. Thus the story's Adam has a twin sister, with whom he shares a relationship as strange and curious as that of humanity's first parents—who were, after all, as much siblings as spouses. This Adam defines himself as virgin and poet, terms expressive, in his view, of some human essence (Barth may have had in mind Shelley's remark that poetry, "the expression of the imagination," is "connate with the origins of man"). As virgin and poet, Eben avers, he is "not man but Mankind" (p. 60). When this erring Adam loses his estate, he cries "How like a paradise Malden seems to me, now I've lost it!" (p. 440) and becomes, like so many others in the new

world, a "redemptioner." Lapsed, he must encounter the fallen
world, for which the once lovely but now poxed Joan Toast
is the perfect symbol. "The world hath used you hardly," says
Eben; "I am its very sign and emblem" (p. 468), she replies.
He goes in dread of his "father's wrath" (p. 451) and describes
himself as "sick unto death" (p. 439). The ironic echo of the
Gospel of St. John (11:4) identifies Eben at this moment as a
moribund Lazarus, awaiting resurrection. The phrase also
recalls that anatomist of despair and first existentialist, Sören
Kierkegaard. Unlike the Danish philosopher, who made the
"leap of faith," Eben must deal with despair in a manner more
congruent with later existentialist philosophy, for the novel's
religious allegory, always ironic, never translates to personal
religious comforts for the characters.

The most subtle aspect of this allegory, its identification of
original sin, receives various definitions in both the main plot
and the subplot. Eben falls in at least two senses, according
to what one might call a morality of deed and a morality of
motive (a distinction he himself introduces in a conversation
with John McEvoy). He falls in deed when, judging by appearances, he surrenders his estate to villains; he falls in the
second, more truly culpable, sense when he deserts and robs
the hapless Joan Toast. But these lapses leave one unclear as
to what, allegorically, the author identifies as original sin. Barth
refuses to make the primal transgression in his fable obvious,
perhaps because he considers this kind of moral convenience
objectionable. Instead he directs the reader's attention, at three
widely separated points in the story, to germinal errors that
seem to approximate original sin. The recognition of these
errors filters through Eben's consciousness in moments of
insight—the first on Bloodsworth Island, where Eben and his
friends find themselves prisoners of a savage alliance bent on
overthrowing white rule, the second and third at Malden,
where the sight of his mother's grave fills the hero with guilt

and where, in the book's closing pages, he expresses a yearning for atonement. Eben first begins to grapple with the idea of original sin as he awaits execution on Bloodsworth Island and recognizes in himself a strange kind of sacrificial victim. He realizes that "as an educated gentleman of the western world he had shared in the fruits of his culture's power and must therefore share what guilt that power incurred" (p. 545). As noted previously, he understands that the roles of exploiter and exploited are "accidents of history," but this consideration does not encourage him to rationalize his position as exploiter. Rather he sees himself as a member of the race—the human race—that exploits itself. Recognizing his kinship with the exploiters and the exploited, he identifies simultaneously with both and translates the identification into familiar theological terms: "In sum, the poet observed, for his secular Original Sin, though he was to atone for it in person, he would exact a kind of Vicarious Retribution; he had committed a grievous crime against himself, and it was himself who would soon punish the malefactor" (p. 545). The allegorical drift here, with Eben identified with the New Adam as well as the old, has been prepared for earlier, in the epiphanic description of the hero lying ignominiously in a corncrib manger, swaddled only in "hose and drawers" (p. 405). On Bloodsworth Island now—the name, one notices, hints at Paschal sacrifice—Eben recognizes the essential humanity of Adamic transgressor and redemptive scapegoat alike. It is another "epiphany." He understands, in other words, that the mythic figures of Adam and Christ project only the range of human potential—not the scheme of human transgression and divine mercy posited by Christian belief.

Eben's next insight comes when he, Bertrand, and McEvoy, made to swim for it by pirates, wash ashore at Cooke's Point. There he sees the grave of his mother, whose bitter epitaph translates the Hebrew *Ebenezer*: "*Thus far Hath the Lord/Helped*

Us." Eben's misery and guilt—Anne Bowyer Cooke died giving birth to him and his sister—threaten to overwhelm him at this moment, and McEvoy remarks: "Go to, 'tis like the sin o' Father Adam, that we all have on our heads; we ne'er asked for't, but there it is." Eben, however, rejects the philosophical dodge implied in McEvoy's theology: "Such fables hurt too much beside the truth" (p. 694). He seems to have perceived the full implications of "Thus far hath the Lord helped us," and he pauses in horror before the equally abhorrent possibilities of *dio boia,* the hangman god, and *deus absconditus,* the absentee god. But he also endures another Adamic epiphany: from his mother to his present companions and family, many have suffered and will continue to suffer because of him. His pain at "the general condition of things"—the phrase refers specifically to the plight of Eben and his immediate circle but hints also at the universal suffering of humanity—derives less from the fact of loss than from "the responsibility for it." Again he sees himself as original sinner, the one who causes the suffering of the innocent who come after him: "The fallen suffer from Adam's fall, he wanted to explain; but in that knowledge—which the Fall itself vouchsafed him—how more must Adam have suffered!" (p. 695).

The last of Eben's insights, at once simplest and most ambiguous, shows him yearning for atonement. Though he desires some kind of crucifixion, some opportunity for a redemptive sacrifice, he replies oddly to his sister's assertion—"Thou'rt the very spirit of Innocence"—of his Christlike qualities. He reproaches himself for "the crime of innocence, whereof the Knowledged must bear the burthen. There's the true Original Sin our souls are born in: not that Adam *learned,* but that he *had* to learn—in short, that he was innocent" (p. 739). The statement reinforces the secular light of the preceding references to original sin. It causes the theme of this long account of innocence and its spiritual toll to come sharply into focus. The author has encouraged the reader to see in Eben the embodiment of an innocence like that of Christ or the prelapsarian Adam, but the meaning of this innocence gets transvalued. As Barth remarks elsewhere, "One should be no great admirer of innocence, in either narratives, individuals, or cultures. Where it's genuine, after a certain age it's unbecoming, off-putting, even freakish and dangerous. Where it's false, it's false. To admire it much is patronizing and sentimental; to aspire to it is self-defeating. Let us admire—in cultures, narratives, and people—not innocence, but experience and grace."[20]

In *The Sot-Weed Factor*, Barth gives the lie to Sir Thomas Gray's fatuous maxim, "Where ignorance is bliss,/'Tis folly to be wise." As Jac Tharpe has observed, Barth promotes "the Platonic dictum that knowledge is virtue, a concept which means that right conduct must be based not on innocence but on knowledge of what right conduct is."[21] In a humanistic defense of knowledge in all its forms, the author even resolves what Arthur O. Lovejoy calls the "paradox of the fortunate Fall"—the idea that the primal human lapse ultimately proves no less providential than disastrous, for it allows a demonstration of God's power and benevolence greater than that manifested in the creation and subverted by Adam's sin. The fall, initially calamitous, is "fortunate" in the end because it leads to Christ's sacrifice and the redemption of humanity.[22] But Barth shows the fallacy in the theological premise: innocence is in fact ignorance, and ignorance is vicious. The fall, because it promotes knowledge, can *only* be fortunate. Human beings, says Barth, must free themselves of the Christian ambivalence toward knowledge and recognize in ignorance alone the root of their flawed condition, the true primal sin. Thus Eben, who attempts to perpetuate his innocence, deserves not praise but blame, for without knowledge one suffers and causes others to suffer.

Eben acquires experience almost as painfully as Shakespeare's Othello, another of the great naïfs of literature. The

Moor, too, is humankind in the aggregate, torn between good and evil alternatives, an innocent reasoning but to err. Othello's plight is nowhere more clearly allegorical than when he likens himself to "the base Indian" who "threw a pearl away/ Richer than all his tribe" (V.ii.351–52). The comparison provides new-world associations relevant to *The Sot-Weed Factor,* whose protagonist also throws away something of inestimable value and eventually comes to recognize a cosmic folly. Like Othello, Eben renders judgment without knowledge and thereby guarantees a miscarriage of justice. His other major lapse compounds the error. Deserting Joan Toast, he avoids the consummation, the knowledge, that is every person's responsibility—knowledge of the world Joan symbolizes. Each of these lapses involves a failure—indeed, an active repudiation—of knowledge, for in priding himself on his virginity, Eben embraces a culpable nescience.

Barth's transvaluation of innocence, and by implication its archetypal representatives, allows the recognition, on the part of the reader, of a further ironic twist to the allegory—a twist that reveals again the author's ultimate focus on history, especially as theistically misinterpreted. In giving Eben's birth year as 1666, Barth disregards the usual dating—1670 or 1672—of the real Ebenezer Cooke's birth. The author no doubt wanted his hero born in a more portentous year, that of the great London fire and the other prodigies chronicled in Dryden's *Annus Mirabilis.*[23] But the year also held apocalyptic expectations for Christendom, which saw in its last three digits the dreaded number of the beast, the false messiah of Revelation. Thus Barth hints that the archetypal innocent in his parable, the ostensible embodiment of prelapsarian Adam and Christ, is in fact, from a humanistic perspective, a monster. As the personification of a false ideal of innocence, Eben proves less Christ than Antichrist; his career suggests that the world embraces to its discredit the ethic he represents. Barth shows all human superstitions coming back to humanity itself—and with great cogency in this instance, inasmuch as the obscure wording of Revelation in the description of the beast invites interpretation in simple humanistic terms: "Here is wisdom. Let him that hath understanding count the number of the beast: for it is the number of a man; and his number is Six hundred threescore and six" (13:18). One thinks of the beast as a supernatural entity, some satanic lieutenant, but the biblical author's phrase ("the number of a man") focuses expectation on the human sphere. In the birthdate of the all-too-human Eben, apologist for a seductive but monstrous ideal, Barth takes the author of Revelation at his word.

In his satirical meditations on history as conceptualized by the faithful, Barth includes even Armageddon. The apocalyptic battle that follows the advent of the beast and the Second Coming of Christ figures in *The Sot-Weed Factor* as the expected rising of Indians and escaped slaves. In fact, the whole Indian subplot doubles or complements the main plot's allegory of innocence and its fate in the American Eden. A summary of this subplot, especially as Henry Burlingame enters into it, will make for greater clarity in what follows, for pieces of the puzzle of Burlingame's paternity appear at widely scattered intervals in the novel, making comprehension on the part of the reader somewhat difficult. One should note, for example, that the events crucial to Burlingame's destiny—the encounters between Indians and whites in Maryland—occur at intervals of a generation or two throughout the course of the seventeenth century. The first of these encounters, the expedition up the Chesapeake by Captain John Smith and company in 1608, eventuates in the abandonment of Henry Burlingame I, who assumes the Ahatchwhoop throne and sires Henry Burlingame II, better known as the Tayac Chicamec, on Queen Pokatawertussan. Chicamec rules the Ahatchwhoops in 1634, the year that Lord Baltimore's Catholics come to his newly chartered state. The missionary Father Joseph FitzMaurice, driven into remote country by a hurricane in

September of that year, falls among the Ahatchwhoops and suffers a martyr's death. Obliged to sleep with the unmarried women of the tribe before his execution, he sires the beautiful half-breed on whom Chicamec in turn fathers three sons: Matassinemarough, known as Charley Matassin; Cohunkowprets, known as Billy Rumbly; and Ebenezer Cooke's friend and tutor, Henry Burlingame III, known by many names. Aged, increasingly vindictive, and allied now with Drepacca and the escaped slaves, Chicamec still rules the Ahatchwhoops in 1694, the novel's present, when Eben and his companions fall into his hands on Bloodsworth Island.

The tangled skein of this chronicle becomes, in Barth's hands, a secondary burlesque of the Christian myth. The first Henry Burlingame becomes for the Indians of subsequent generations the "heavenly father" (pp. 569, 571) or "heavenly spouse" (p. 572), at once the dynastic founder or celestial ancestor common to primitive cultures and a parody of God the Father. He even promulgates a sacred mystery, the "Rites of the Holy Eggplant." His unwitting prophet is his enemy John Smith, whose *Secret Historie* becomes the Indians' Bible, *The Book of English Devils*. This document, like Christian scripture, proscribes certain demonic forces. Just as some Christians find in the Bible the authority to view the "colored" races as the impure descendants of Cain, the catechists of *The Book of English Devils* view as evil all with white skins. The Indians disregard the racial background of Henry Burlingame I but learn from him to hate other representatives of his race. Thus they murder Father FitzMaurice, the next white person who falls into their clutches. Instead of accepting the good Jesuit as their deliverer, the Indians make him the devil in their developing religion, regarding his bloodline as a source of evil over the generations. They view Chicamec's adoption of the priest's posthumous daughter as "a mighty sin against the gods." Nevertheless, "reared as a princess among the Ahatchwhoops," this "child of the Devil" (p. 571) eventually becomes the bride of Chicamec and the mother of his errant sons. Chicamec and his people assume that the failings of these sons derive from their tainted blood. But the infant Henry Burlingame III, whom the Indians expose to the elements as an "English Devil" (p. 573), proves like Moses an antitype of the divine savior. This reversal of allegorical roles figures in the main plot as well. The title of one chapter, for example, invites a recognition of Burlingame's diabolical status: "If the Laureate Is Adam, Then Burlingame Is the Serpent" (p. 398). But as the character who nudges Ebenezer and Anna Cooke toward knowledge, the character who proves to have served, in Governor Nicholson, the cause of peace and order in the new world, Henry Burlingame scarcely deserves his satanic reputation. Indeed, if Barth means to invert the orthodox valuations of innocence and knowledge, then the serpent in the garden becomes the serpent of wisdom, a savior.

Thus Barth provides him with the exotic genealogy of a Christ, for he descends from paternal grandfather Henry Burlingame I, the "heavenly spouse," and from maternal grandfather Joseph FitzMaurice, who arrives among the Indians in a boat bearing the sign of the dove. A would-be deliverer, Father FitzMaurice perishes on a cross, at least in the mythopoeic version of Father Smith, who even imagines the martyr saying "Forgive them, for they know not what they do" (p. 362). Despised and rejected by those he comes to save, Father FitzMaurice is allegorically the first, historical Christ—and he lives again in Henry Burlingame III, the Christ whose Second Coming coincides with expectations of apocalyptic violence. Burlingame's immediate family is also mythic. His father, Chicamec, is a figure of strict Old Testament justice, a cruel Jehovah prepared to wreak a terrible vengeance on humanity—his prisoners on Bloodsworth Island—unless his son or sons prove willing to redeem the condemned.

Governor Nicholson is also in some sense Burlingame's

father—a moral and political father who balances the vengeful Chicamec as the New Testament God of justice tempered with mercy balances the awful deity of inflexible Mosaic law. Governor Nicholson may strike some readers as a technical flaw in the novel. He appears, thinly drawn, late in the action and seems too much the "god on wires" (p. 452) Eben wishes for at one point (he has his origins, according to Harry B. Henderson, in "the Great Man" who appears in the novels of Sir Walter Scott to effect narrational resolutions).[24] But as a humanistic alternative to the paranoid superstitions invoked in the central religious allegories, Governor Nicholson must not shine too brightly. Barth realizes that depicting law and reason dispelling the dark fantasies of the theistic worldview risks misrepresenting the prospects for enlightenment in an age of religious zealotry. The action of *The Sot-Weed Factor* takes place at the close of the seventeenth century, and Governor Nicholson functions as an understated harbinger of the century to come, the Age of Enlightenment, when reason would begin to displace superstition. He represents the emergence of a new political and moral promise in the colonies, one associated with the transition from the age of Hobbes to the age of Rousseau; he heralds, too, the age of Washington, Jefferson, Franklin, and Adams—and the new state they would found.

Like *Beowulf* or *The Tempest*, *The Sot-Weed Factor* ends with a repudiation of supernatural props. The revels ended, Barth, like Prospero, breaks his staff and quietly excuses his characters from further allegorical duty. No longer required to represent an embattled archetype of Christian innocence, Ebenezer Cooke lives on at Malden, chastened and poxed, in what Freud would call "ordinary, everyday unhappiness." No longer Satan and Yahweh, the villainous John Coode and "that shadowy figure presumed to be at the other pole of morality, Lord Baltimore" (p. 751), become themselves again, too, figures of history who once engaged in a political struggle. But Coode, like his more plausible moral antagonist Henry Burlingame, retains a certain ambiguity. He resists demythologizing and remains enigmatic, as if to hint at the residuum of unaccountable evil in the human breast. The mere abandonment of supernatural explanations, Barth implies, does not resolve the mystery of human evil.

In approaching Barth's religious allegory, then, the reader susceptible to myths and structures must proceed cautiously, recognizing the irony and the iconoclasm. A novel that parades its allegorical features so enticingly invites one to discover familiar patterns, to embrace known mythopoeic material. But the tendency of human society, primitive or civilized, to embrace theistic fictions that vary relatively little from culture to culture is one of the novel's major satiric targets. The reader who comes away with the notion of having encountered the latest demonstration of certain timeless religious truths (or, for that matter, the reader who leaps to conclusions based on racial stereotypes, whether positive or negative) has fallen into the same error as Barth's European and Indian characters. Such a reader has failed to see that the real "savior" in Barth's cosmology is whoever can promote peace and live free of illusion, without recourse to superstition.

According to pious surmise, human history is a divinely authored drama—a tragedy in the garden of Eden, a comedy at Easter. But history unfolds as no such shapely drama, says Barth. Existence is at best black comedy, that conflation or hybrid of the nihilistic and the comic that promotes laughter in defiance of the abyss. Yet in *The Sot-Weed Factor* Barth mitigates the unsparing bleakness of his earlier novels. Having written, in *The Floating Opera*, a "nihilistic comedy" and in *The End of the Road*, a "nihilistic tragedy," Barth rounds things off with a novel of existential possibility. Though he does not abandon nihilism altogether, he banishes absolute metaphysics to the background. If ultimate realities give the lie to all brave existential posturing in the end, they need not be embraced prematurely, and in the interim the right kind of existentialist—Henry Burlingame, for example—can deliver himself and his friends from immediate destruction and perhaps do other worthwhile things on the stage of the world. In Burlingame Barth makes up for his dyslogistic portrayal of Joe Morgan, the rigid existentialist in *The End of the Road*. Morgan recognizes the necessity of provisional ethics, but he fails to recognize the necessity of allowing the provisional rules—not to mention the provisional self—to evolve, to mutate along with contingency itself. Burlingame is Joe Morgan with flexibility, a sense of humor, and a gift for irony.

In Burlingame, *The Sot-Weed Factor*'s existential linchpin, the reader recognizes the ultimate irony of all the allegorical labels in the novel. With great brilliance and with little overt anachronism, the author gives Ebenezer Cooke, with his largely seventeenth-century sensibility, a mentor with a twentieth-century view of things. "What is . . . man's lot?," he asks Eben rhetorically:

He is by mindless lust engendered and by mindless wrench expelled, from the Eden of the womb to the motley, mindless world. He is Chance's fool, the toy of aimless Nature—a mayfly flitting down the winds of Chaos! . . .

Once long ago we sat like this, at an inn near Magdalene College—do you remember? And I said, "Here we sit upon a blind rock hurtling through a vacuum, racing to the grave." 'Tis our fate to search, Eben, and do we seek our soul, what we find is a piece of that same black cosmos whence we sprang and through which we fall: the infinite wind of space. . . .

Why is't you set such store by innocence and rhyming, and I by searching out my father and battling Coode? One must needs make and seize his soul, and then cleave fast to't, or go babbling in the corner; one must choose his gods and devils on the run, quill his own name upon the universe, and declare, "'Tis *I*, and the world stands such-a-way!" One must *assert, assert, assert*, or go screaming mad. What other course remains? [pp. 344–45].

As Frank McConnell has pointed out, Barth's novel "is nothing less than an attempt to imagine the primal collision of human consciousness with the circumambient void which is the origin of all philosophy."[25] Burlingame has seen the ultimate cosmic meaninglessness and recognized that the course of his life—not to mention the course of history—is a matter of existential choice, constrained only by accidents of cosmic circumstance. Consequently, he makes new choices of himself with ease; proto-existentialist, shape-shifter, and supreme *eiron*, he chooses his identity at will.

To know himself fully, Burlingame must voyage into the heart of darkness. His story, a Telemachiad, concerns a journey toward the father, a journey from civilization to savagery; indeed, inasmuch as his is really a twentieth-century sensibility, he enacts a cultural retrogression of staggering proportions, an expedition into the human past, a journey through history. Burlingame's fate remains uncertain at the end because human fate is uncertain. We have in our time come to know our savage hearts, and we have grappled with the passing of the gods. Whether we shall reconcile our savagery with our existential possibilities remains to be seen—as does Burlingame's fate among the Indians on his mission to preserve civilization.

In setting, style, and subject, *The Sot-Weed Factor* brings together the seventeenth, eighteenth, and twentieth centuries, and this breadth of direct and indirect historical reference serves the author as a basis for something more than scatter-shot iconoclasm. Barth is impatient with theories about the past and debunks them, notably when he satirizes, in his ironic allegory, the Christian attempt to read into the events of history a supernaturally ordained order. He also satirizes the genre in which he writes. As Leslie Fiedler observes, *The Sot-Weed Factor* "looks like a full-scale historical novel and is in fact a travesty of the form."[26] But to travesty a literary form in which history figures does not mean to travesty history itself. Barth, I think, respects the past and does his best to present its reality truthfully. Though certainly calling a number of historical "orthodoxies" into question, Barth does not undermine them indiscriminately. If he lampoons the myth of heroic Captain Smith and compassionate Pocahontas, if he presents the colonial scene as more brutal and rapacious than is commonly allowed, he seems at the same time disinclined to subvert historical perceptions of the next century, when according to the collective memory something admirable and splendid emerged in America.

The fact that history offers not the past but versions of the past does not daunt the best historical novelists, for they know that art exists to speak with precision about history and other forms of human experience resistant to analysis and description. Thus Barth's statement about history involves more daring than is recognized by critics who see in his novel an elaborate demonstration of the unreliability, even the absurdity, of any and all historical narrative. Such critics unwittingly assume that the resources available to the artist do not differ from the resources available to the historian. They assume that fiction is as fallible as history—as if it were just another social science. Though they see that Barth in his novel asks if the past can be known, they do not hear the affirmative answer. We can know the past, says the author of *The Sot-Weed Factor*, but only through art.

The past recaptured, however, is not the past made orderly. Writers who succeed at re-creating the past—writers like Barth and Yourcenar—do not balk at representing the disorder of history. It figures explicitly in Barth's satire, implicitly in Yourcenar's reflections on the inevitable destiny of states and their human servants. Barth subjects the myth of colonial origins to revisionist scrutiny and undercuts theories of history from antiquity into the nineteenth century. Yourcenar, through Hadrian, projects a bleak yet heroic view of historical process.

Each of these writers makes clear the disparity between the mental life of the past and that of the present, and each overcomes received ideas about history to show readers the actual look and feel of the past. They demonstrate that historical fictions devoted chiefly to historical verisimilitude can and indeed must be highly sophisticated. Yourcenar captures the way it was by immersing herself in the inner life of a person out of the past.[27] She struggles to escape—and to help her readers escape—the mental habits of the present and the recent past the better to think historically. Barth, more daringly, introduces twentieth-century ideas into a description of life in the seventeenth century and thereby clarifies the differences in values, mores, and thought itself from age to age. Both Barth and Yourcenar unfold a relationship between the examined life of a protagonist and the examined life of a whole culture. Thus they demonstrate that history, however disorderly, remains meaningful. History can still enable humanity to know itself and its condition, and in the historical novel, especially the type devoted to recapturing the way it was, history often finds its most legitimate realization.

3

The Way It Will Be

"IF YOU WANT a picture of the future," says a character in Orwell's *1984*, "imagine a boot stamping on a human face—forever." Where Orwell envisions simple dystopia, other literary oracles serve up Eloi and Morlocks, entropic heat-death, human anthills, and nuclear Armageddon. These authors have in common a preference for the somber robes of Cassandra over the pigtails of Pollyanna. They see unpleasantness in the future.

A few of these writers have made narrative speculation about tomorrow something more than the usual pasteboard fantasies of science fiction. Many science-fiction novelists understand technology and its future configurations, but their work lacks literary significance because they fail to focus on the human response to all the hardware. Better artists produce fictions of the future that meet the criteria for literature. These works rise above the norm because extravagant auguries about physics, engineering, and chemistry figure less prominently than does rigorous thinking about biology, psychology, and sociology—in short, the human side of the future. Occasionally these novelists address themselves to those broader events in the human aggregate that constitute history. They imagine the way it will be.

In doing so, they make this category of historical fiction one that contains all the others. Like authors who depict the way it was, authors who depict the way it will be can aim quite simply at an ideal of unsensational verisimilitude. They can also depict a future shaped by some turning point imagined as happening in the reader's present—some technological breakthrough, say, or some catastrophic war. More distal turning points also figure, but they tend to introduce variations on the last category of the historical novel, the distant mirror. In fictions of this type, the future recapitulates the past or satirically mirrors the present.

Great novels about the future fall into a spectrum from less to more concerned with history per se. History plays almost no part, for example, in Anthony Burgess's *A Clockwork Orange* (1962) or Nikolai Amosoff's *Notes from the Future* (1970). Burgess's novel is really a piece of sociological extrapolation. The author glances at history only in the vague suggestion (in the density of Russian loan words in the argot of the youth gangs) that communist influence will wax strong on the British working class. He gives the phrase "dictatorship of the proletariat" a grim new meaning, for the youth gangs seem to have the ordinary, law-abiding citizenry very much on the defensive. History plays an even more oblique role in *Notes from the Future*. Here an imagined clinical technique to lower body temperature enables the narrator, who suffers from a fatal disease, to "hibernate" from 1970 until 1991, at which time medical science offers a cure for his malady. The author's sketchy account of life late in the twentieth century yields almost no vision of political or historical currents. Doubtless Amosoff had little desire to envision a future acceptable to his Soviet censors; consequently he tells a story so focused on the individual sensibility as to make the book's movement into the future almost an arbitrary plot development. *Notes from the Future* is really neither a historical novel nor science fiction;

it is an old-fashioned psychological novel, a "novel of con-sciousness," tricked out with a little technology.

Less well written but more historically acute is Pierre Boulle's popular *Planet of the Apes* (1963). Critics struck by the credulous traveler who narrates this novel have occasionally compared it with *Gulliver's Travels*. Set on another planet in a distant future, the story is a thinly disguised satire on the urban and industrial society of earth in the nineteenth and twentieth centuries. Boulle imagines that on the ape planet (virtually identical to earth) humanity degenerates and the lower pri-mates rise to take the place of their erstwhile masters in the evolutionary chain. But because of the well-known simian pro-clivity to imitate, ape society evolves into a travesty of human society. The novel's satiric targets include economic institu-tions (one scene takes place at the simian stock market), science (researchers' egos and lust for vivisection receive no quarter), and sport (a hunting scene, with human game, recalls the extravagant hunt in Jean Renoir's *The Rules of the Game*). The scientific and cultural satire reaches its climax when the apes go through their own wrenching version of a Darwinian rev-elation about their biological and historical past. This devel-opment foreshadows the surprise of the novel's ending, for when the narrator returns to his native planet he finds that, in the immense amount of time that has elapsed on earth during his interstellar travels, the human species on terra has itself been superseded by apes.

The biological and evolutionary future receives further at-tention in *Inter Ice Age 4* (1970), by the contemporary Japanese novelist Kobo Abé. In a genre often judged by the inventive-ness authors bring to their hardware, this novel features tech-nology that almost always leaves the reader a little unsettled, slightly disgusted, or curiously violated. These sensations are all part of the novel's ultimate statement about the future, which will be what it will be, says Abé, regardless of what it does to our sensibilities. But here again, the novel concerns history only in part; indeed, it takes its readers into the future—as opposed to a technologically sophisticated present—only toward the end.

Though the flyleaf says it is "set in the next century, as the polar ice caps begin to melt, threatening to submerge the continents and destroy all terrestrial life," the novel for the most part seems set in the present. An internal reference to Alexei Kosygin as a contemporary Soviet leader makes the period of at least the first part of the novel the late 1960s. But sophisticated technology—chiefly computers that are able to interview the dead, to think like human beings, and to predict the future—creates a futurological ambience. The future appears unequivocally only at the end, in a vision of things to come when human beings have of necessity—given the melting of the polar ice cap—modified themselves physically to live under water. The "aquans" of this later era dwell in the sea, preserve terran culture in museums, and probe the exotic underwater ruins of great cities like Tokyo.

The novel focuses on a computer scientist, Professor Katsumi, who resists the ruthlessness of the future's planners. Although new developments owe much to the genius of Professor Katsumi, he faces liquidation for his reactionary scruples. The author invites one's sympathy for this humane scientist yet declines to sentimentalize his end. As Abé says in a postcript, "The future . . . is . . . cruel by virtue of being the future."[1] It may very likely be uncongenial to the most cherished values of the present.

Though historical currents, as such, do not figure prominently in the book, the vision of the future with which it ends is informed by an awareness of history—or rather of prehistory. The novel concludes with an ironic scene that reflects and reverses a scene from the remote biological past; the author hints at a continuity that he then proceeds to demolish.

Before his necessary elimination, those against whom Professor Katsumi has rebelled allow him a vision of the future and of his son's place in it (the child had been aborted, but aborted fetuses have been secretly used for modification as aquan prototypes). In this future, terran culture exists only as a dim memory, a vague biological embarrassment. But one boy, a misfit, at once the son and the distant descendant of Professor Katsumi, yearns for the land, patches of which still remain. He travels to a remote coast and struggles onto the strand. The reader—and Professor Katsumi, presumably— expects this heroic gesture to inaugurate a new cycle of terran existence, which originally began when water dwellers struggled up a shore and adapted to life on land. But the boy simply perishes on his beach. Cruelly the author thus underscores his idea of a future radically different from the present, a future that reflects both the present and the remote past only to mock them.

Abé, like the other novelists considered thus far, does not make ideas about history really central to his representation of the way it will be. But with Orwell's *1984* one comes to a novel imbued with a tragic sense of history's vulnerability to manipulation in an unscrupulous future. Although the year that gives the novel its title has come and gone, *1984* has not lost its sting. The ultimate totalitarian state continues to hover on the political horizon, and the horrors described by Orwell seem still to furnish criteria by which to judge the benightedness of any given regime that terrorizes its own citizens. Orwell's great fiction of totalitarian terror does not "date" because its vision is broadly stylized and allegorical. It will always be an accurate roadmap to dystopia.

Although his novel reflects an acute knowledge of history as the product of human passions, warped economic systems, and the *Wille zur Macht*, Orwell paradoxically imagines the death of any authentic sense of the past. History perishes of its absolute fictionalization in a state that has acquired the power actually to preempt the past, to shape history to its own ends. Winston Smith, the novel's hero, spends his days revising historical documents at the Ministry of Truth, a great hive in which bureaucrats rewrite history on a daily basis. Smith and his colleagues routinely destroy originals and in their place substitute forgeries that reflect current policies or political pieties. One regards with civilized horror the idea that a totalitarian regime can institutionalize its own warped and biased version of history. But the true horror lies less in that regime's power to dictate an official version of history than in its power to destroy and counterfeit history's very sources, so that informed descriptions of the past become impossible to produce at the same time that imaginary versions of the past approach infinity. The necessary diversity of historical interpretation thus shifts toward a condition of appalling pliability. In this vision of lawless proliferation, one sees the cancer of history.

In contrast to the idea of an infinitely malleable past is the idea of a tragically irrecoverable past, as after nuclear war. Such a loss structures *Riddley Walker*, by Russell Hoban, and *A Canticle for Leibowitz*, by Walter M. Miller, Jr. Both authors imagine human history after a nuclear conflagration that makes for centuries of backwardness, mutations, and other suffering; they imagine that one disastrous consequence of nuclear catastrophe would be a campaign on the part of the survivors to root out all that might remain of what Hoban's characters call "clevverness." During this orgy of anti-intellectualism, which Miller calls the Simplification, angry mobs systematically hunt down and slay the intelligent and the educated—those presumed to have brought the world to such a desperate pass. Miller wryly notes the tendency to exacerbate and hasten the lapse into a dark age. But because Miller is at pains to make his postholocaust history a mirror of the history that went before, he calls the nuclear war the Flame Deluge and makes it reminiscent of such great human calamities as the biblical flood and the fall of Rome. He makes the ages that follow the Simplification analogous to the great periods of modern Western history. Thus the three sections of his novel correspond to the Middle Ages, the Renaissance, and the age of technology. The story ends with the return of nuclear war, this time with the trappings of New Testament apocalypse rather than Old Testament deluge. *A Canticle for Leibowitz* is finally an allegory of human history from primal transgression to apocalyptic salvation.

Hoban, too, sets up a distant mirror in the future. But his choice of a first-person narrator precludes the kind of historical perspective available to Miller. In this regard, Miller is more ambitious than Hoban, but not necessarily as accomplished technically. Obliged to divide his narrative into three inadequately connected sections, Miller relies on an omniscient narrator, and thus the book unfortunately lacks a single human protagonist to unify it. The main character is history, a mere abstraction. Miller's theme, moreover, comes uncomfortably close to pietism. He brilliantly captures humanity's tragic limitations but fails to convince the skeptical reader that Christianity remains undiminished as the universal solution to the human condition. The author embraces a dated Catholicism and even wrestles absurdly with the question of Jewish guilt (the novel predates Vatican II).[2] He has since admitted that the novel's Catholic orientation was, from his own point of view, highly provisional.[3]

Miller attempts to anchor his vision of historical circularity in the transcendent idea of the Christian God: all cycles will eventually be subsumed in the timeless divine order. Hoban by contrast faces the possibility that history will ultimately prove meaningless, and *Riddley Walker* seems the more rigorously honest book. Although both Hoban and Miller present a double vision of history, Hoban treats the future with greater sophistication. Miller contrasts a secular vision of history with a largely obsolete religious one, but Hoban creates a more complex and instructive tension between two sets of polarized alternatives: he contrasts primitive and modern conceptions of historical time at the same time that he contrasts an idea of history as the unfolding of some numinous purpose with the starker and more modern idea that human events transpire in an existential void.

The Terror of History: *Riddley Walker*

Winston Churchill, commenting on the atomic bomb, remarked that "the stone age may return—on the gleaming wings of science." In *Riddley Walker,* Russell Hoban imagines Churchill's prophecy as fulfilled and looks to the moment in the postholocaust future when humanity, well into its second Iron Age, begins once again to pursue knowledge that will destroy it. Hoban conceives of history as something tragically lost in this blighted future, and in part his story concerns a culturewide yearning to know the more splendid past. He imagines a primitive society surrounded by evidence of its more civilized origins. Thus two antithetical conceptions of past time—primitive and civilized—coexist within the novel and constitute a dialectic in terms of which Hoban examines "the terror of history"—Mircea Eliade's phrase for the suspicion or conviction that history answers to no transcendent rationale.[4]

In the Iron Age of *Riddley Walker,* the characters know about the advanced civilization that preceded them and half-remember that civilization's idea of history as a sequence of discrete events, the etiology of the present. At the same time, however, they embrace a mythic model of history, one more appropriate to their unsophisticated culture. This second mode of historical consciousness, which Eliade calls "archaic" or "primitive," involves the periodic repudiation or transcendence of what civilized humanity construes as historical time, achieved by frequent reenactments of the "archetypal" gestures of gods or heroes in a golden, nontemporal age. These reenactments, which commonly take place in ritual, restore the human community to a cultural dawn, obliterating the intervening time and canceling any spiritual debts. Human experience, then, has temporal substance only to the extent that it partakes of a time-swallowing mythic paradigm. Eliade refers to this idea of periodic reversion to a timeless beginning as the myth of the eternal return.

The idea that "history," with its inevitable human lapses, can be canceled out or redeemed might seem the exclusive province of primitive societies. Eliade notes, however, that the myth of eternal return also finds expression in advanced societies—in ideas like Nietzsche's doctrine of eternal recurrence or in cyclical models of history like Vico's *corsi* or the theories of the "Great Year" found in Plato and in Eastern philosophy. The myth of eternal return has even become congenial to science, as one sees in the theory of a great cosmic cycle from "big bang" to "big crunch."

In advanced societies the myth of return sometimes coexists with the nominally more modern conception of history as a linear sequence of events, the kind of one-way street in time posited in the Marxist vision of a historical progression from feudalism to the rise of the bourgeosie to the disintegration of capitalism and the triumph of the proletariat. A similar insistence on the linear model characterizes Christianity, with its doctrine of a beginning (the creation), a middle (the incarnation), and an end (the apocalypse). But the promise of a clean slate, the squaring of Adam's accounts by Christ the heavenly accountant, reveals the presence of a myth of return at the heart of Christianity. Divine sacrifice cancels original sin and returns the Christian to a condition of primal innocence.

One seldom, at any rate, sees the linear conception of history in any kind of pure form in *Riddley Walker*. It tends to be qualified by some more archaic idea of historical time, as will be seen presently in an examination of the novel's language, its Iron Age setting, and its most prominent plot feature (the quest to reinvent gunpowder). These features discover a congruity with the past, a historical circularity, that inevitably calls the linear idea of history into question. The idea is present, however, as a vestigial awareness on the part of a society whose ancestors embraced it, and it is present in the mind of the readers who are, after all, precisely those ancestors. But the distinction between circular and linear historical models matters less than the distinction between perceptions of history as the expression of some transcendent or divine will or as something essentially meaningless, however self-perpetuating. Unfortunately, says Hoban, echoing Eliade, humanity in its sophistication proves less and less able to interpret history—whether linear or cyclical—as the reflection of any vast but coherent purpose. As one contemplates the bloody ebb and flow of human events, the appalling historical record of mass killing and meaningless bloodshed, one may begin to recognize intimations of a blind, oppressive, random-yet-deterministic mechanism. One experiences the terror of history. This perception, widespread in the age for which Hoban writes, complements the metaphysical Angst first described by Heidegger and central to modern existentialist philosophy. In terms of modern historicism, humanity attempts to define itself and thereby creates history—but history always, in the end, betrays those who make it.

Such is the gist of what the much less intellectually privileged Riddley Walker comes to recognize in the fifth millennium, for he can think in both the mythic terms of his primitive world and in the historically linear terms of an advanced civilization. He even glimpses the tragic significance of his age's spiritual impoverishment, living as he does in a time when such religion as exists is largely inchoate. Beyond those "spirits of the corn and wild" that Frazer identifies as common among primitive societies, Riddley's people have only a vague perception of "Aunty," a kind of degenerate triple goddess of night, birth, and especially death. Riddley, however, makes up for the fleabitten spirituality of his world by his intelligence; he achieves a series of brilliant insights into the human condition in his age and in the reader's.

Riddley lives in a backward age indeed, an age in which human life exemplifies the Hobbesian formula: nasty, poor, brutish, and short. He lives, in two senses, in an Age of Iron. It is an Iron Age in comparison with the golden age of high technology and it is an iron age in the archeological sense. This imagined Iron Age of the future, of course, mirrors the actual Iron Age of the past—the Iron Age in England, that is, which began about 500 B.C., much later than in the Near East. Hoban dates Riddley's era in such a way as to make its distance from the present—apparently a little less than twenty-five hundred years—approximately equal to the distance from the present of the original Iron Age. Thus Hoban implies a great cycle—Iron Age to Iron Age—of five thousand years. It is, however, a cycle unredeemed by a larger cosmic significance.

Hoban would probably know about the existence (in Hampshire, one county over from Riddley Walker's Kent) of the Butser Ancient Farm Research Project, where archeologists have re-created an Iron Age farm as it might have looked in 300 B.C. According to Peter J. Reynolds, the experiment's director, "Celtic society was initially one of farmers, with a warrior elite and a small class of priests and artisans."[5] Hoban seems to have imagined a moment corresponding to a slightly earlier period, when a few last settlements of hunter-gatherers (the "fentses" and "moving crowds" of the novel) held out against absorption by the agricultural settlements (the "forms") and their warrior elite (the "hevvies" and the Ram). The iron of this Iron Age seems largely to consist of found iron, the remnants of the more advanced civilization now vanished, rather than iron mined and smelted. Thus the people of Riddley's day, though backward, have probably managed to avoid the more radical regression to a Stone or Bronze age. They have, at any rate, the essential Iron Age technology: they produce the charcoal necessary to fuel fires hot enough to melt iron.

Humanity, moreover, is poised to advance. Already an agricultural order seems to absorb more and more of the human energies once expended on hunting and gathering. The death of the last wild pig, with which the story opens, represents the passing of wilderness and even heralds the accelerating displacement of animistic religion (the Big Boar and the Moon Sow) by more sophisticated cults like that of Eusa. But civilization flourishes with knowledge that in the end proves destructive. Humanity in Riddley's time "roadits" toward the more civilized order that its own past record makes ambivalent. This point comes into focus in the particular advance whose pursuit structures most of the novel: the reinvention of gunpowder. The reader knows, with Riddley and certain of the other characters, that in time the 1 Littl 1 will lead to the 1 Big 1, as humanity plays its own version of "Fools Circel Ninewise," the children's game based on a benighted ritual. An image of the foolish aspirations of Goodparley and his lieutenants, the game comes at last to represent history itself.

Like its setting, the novel's language manages at once to reflect primitive or mythic paradigms and to demonstrate a linear idea of history. Hoban surely knows that a language would change more radically in twenty-five hundred years than what he shows the reader. Riddley's idiom, then, must be understood as a brilliantly stylized version of the English language as it would exist in the fifth millennium. The condition of language in Riddley's milieu, in other words, should not be taken as a realistic depiction of linguistic principles, but rather as a metaphor for the scale of human disaster. A cataclysm that halts all other forms of social vitality—so Hoban asks his reader to imagine—would arrest or at least severely retard the evolution of language itself.

Yet however apparently "degenerate" in its spelling, punctuation, and vocabulary (all seem to have suffered a kind of radiation sickness),[6] the language here reflects, with great expressiveness and subtlety, the world in which it exists. One thinks, reading it, of a Cockney Huck Finn whose supposedly debased dialect proves surprisingly suitable for profound observation of the social scene and the human heart. In fact, the reader encounters a genuinely poetic idiom, an illustration of Johann Gottfried von Herder's famous contention that the language of primitive humanity is naturally and essentially poetic, that human beings must become civilized to speak prose (linguists have come to similar conclusions in studying street language and the language of the oppressed generally). The paronomasic possibilities of language seldom harnessed in writing make for apt linguistic evolutions—as teachers of Freshman Composition realize when they read in student papers that "we live in a doggy dog world." In *Riddley Walker* this principle yields some equally suggestive mutations—for example, the idea that the "soar vivers" [7] of nuclear holocaust find themselves "living on burrow time" (p. 203).

In addition to being intrinsically poetic, the language of this novel is a satiric index to the jargon of the twentieth century—especially that of technology, fossilized in the droll locutions and vocabulary of Riddley and his mates. Some of these survive in formulaic or ritualistic phrases, often largely divorced from any real meaning ("spare the mending" for "experimenting," "tryl narrer" for "trial and error," "many cools" or "party cools" for "molecules" and "particles"). Others continue to signify something, though speakers remain largely ignorant of original referents. One says "I program" to mean "I figure" or "I think"; the preterite, "programmit," can also mean "fated."

"Pirntout" (i.e., "printout") means "conclude," and "glitch my cool" means "bother or trouble me." "Input" now has a largely sexual meaning. After "doing the juicy" repeatedly, the "Bloak as Got on Top of Aunty" does not have much "input" left.

Although Hoban makes the technology that eventually brought disaster the most important feature of this language, he achieves some of his most telling satire and historical commentary with political terms from Old Time. Medicine men of this age go around "clinnicking and national healfing" (p. 141). The chief political figure of Inland (island, in-land, England) is called the Pry Mincer, a title that hints marvelously at what the common folk always impute to politicians: invasions of privacy, sexual inversion, and habits of circumlocution. This archetypally unsavory person works out of the "Mincery," where Iron Age bureaucrats no doubt slice things pretty fine. In transitional periods, a "care maker Mincery" (p. 202) probably does little to reassure a nervous populace.

A care maker Mincery would do little to alleviate the terror of history, relief from which requires a belief that history answers to some divine purpose. In *Riddley Walker* humanity gropes—vainly, for the most part—for some such transcendent rationale to order its relationship to the past and to the future. Hoban re-creates the mythical value systems of primitive humanity for his vision of the future, but he ironically intimates that, given the circumstances, such value systems must lack an adequately developed spiritual or sacral dimension. The Eusa cult, more a piece of government propaganda than an authentic religion, exists as a convenient tool of the Ram, and one cannot help thinking of Orwell's mendacious Ministry of Truth when Goodparley, that would-be Big Brother, attempts to justify his new aspirations by reshaping the Eusa story. He seeks, thereby, to rewrite history.

Thus Riddley's people lack a myth adequate to their spiritual needs. The Eusa story, a degenerate or factitious myth of the fall and of endless punishment, is unbuttressed by myths of creation or redemption; consequently it offers little to those who embrace it. In the Eusa show, as in any primitive ritual, participants unify themselves with a mythic original, for "the time of any ritual," according to Eliade, "coincides with the mythical time of the 'beginning' " (*Myth*, p. 20). Normally, says Eliade, the "annihilation" of the time intervening between the original and its ritual repetition is a desirable thing, because humanity will have lapsed or sinned or otherwise erred in the interim. Ritual squares the spiritual accounts of the people and returns them to a pristine condition, to the golden time of beginnings. But in observing a ritual that collapses the time between Eusa and themselves, Hoban's characters return not to a golden age but rather to hell itself, that other locus classicus of timelessness. Thus the rituals associated with Eusa, the chief mythic figure of Riddley Walker's age, merely revalidate an idea of infernal bondage. At the same time, the mythic perception of time and history functions imperfectly, so that these primitives remain acutely aware of their imprisonment in history. The Mincery, in fact, with its year-counting, preserves an idea of history as a linear progression, an idea that is one of the badges of its ambiguous superiority to the primitives out in the countryside who themselves dream of recovering the greatness of their ancestors materially—not merely in hallowed gestures. Thus the two historical models, linear and cyclical, exist in a debased form, and one glimpses a tragic destiny in humanity's inability to recapture either in its original vitality.

Part of Hoban's genius is to have imagined the mythic life of Riddley Walker and his people with such thoroughness that the primal myth colors the interpretation of all experience. Here again one recognizes a pattern described by Eliade: "In the particulars of his conscious behavior, the 'primitive,' the archaic man, acknowledges no act which has not been previously posited and lived by someone else, some other being who was not a man" (p. 5). Moreover, "among primitives, not only do rituals have their mythical model but any human act whatever acquires effectiveness to the extent to which it exactly *repeats* an act performed at the beginning of time by a god, a hero, or an ancestor" (p. 22). In Riddley's world, persons continually comment on themselves and on events as archetypal reflections of the *Eusa Story* or of the other, complementary fables whereby this race hands on its collective wisdom from generation to generation.

The characters whose experiences reflect the *Eusa Story* most obviously include Goodparley, Lissener, Belnot Phist, and Riddley himself. Goodparley, for example, is, like Eusa, instrumental in inventing a terrible "new" technology of destruction; having been tortured like Eusa, he ends—again like the archetype—with his head on a pole. Riddley, on the other hand, reenacts the story most comprehensively—and most redemptively. He, like Eusa, undertakes a quest with hunting dogs (dogs that actually hunt for themselves, in this instance), and he, too, finds his quarry—a terrible knowledge—in the heart of the wood that is in the heart of the stone (i.e., among the treelike stone pillars of the ruined Canterbury crypt). Here he even hallucinates the dogs walking on their hind legs, as in the Eusa story.

Riddley's knowledge, and the quietist ethic he forges from it, makes the story something of a morality play. Riddley matures as a wise and admirable man in the course of his adventures, but only after dodging various temptations along the way. Hoban projects these temptations in the guise of Riddley's "moon brothers," the psychological doubles who include Abel Goodparley, Lissener, and possibly Belnot Phist. Riddley has both the "follerme" or charisma that would make him a success at politics, like Goodparley, and a measure of the psychic ability that would make him a magus, like Lissener.

Like Lissener, too, he loses a father to the insane machinations of the Ram, but inasmuch as a momentary lapse on Riddley's part may have cost the life of his father, he shares the Oedipal guilt of Goodparley, who attempted to murder his foster father Granser. Riddley becomes a fugitive, again like Goodparley, after a harrowing initiation at the time of his twelfth naming day. He threads his way between the positions represented by these two, swayed now this way, now that—until he repudiates both as dangerous alternatives.

Riddley has little difficulty resisting the appeal of the unscrupulous Goodparley, but the heteroclite spirituality of Lissener, the Ardship of Cambry, poses a more subtle temptation. Warped by his desire for revenge against those who put every succeeding Ardship to the torture, Lissener suffers disfigurement within as well as without—as Riddley eventually realizes when he discovers the Ardship's connivance in the torture and mutilation of Goodparley. As for the effete Belnot Phist, "some kynd of brother may be even a moon brother like the other 2" (p. 146), Riddley learns from him that they perish first who play power games without sufficient ruthlessness and guile.

Riddley fends off these tempters like Thomas Beckett in Eliot's *Murder in the Cathedral*. Indeed, his spiritual agon reaches its climax in the ruins of Beckett's church. Riddley's transcendence of the temptations around him, in other words, seems linked to his pilgrimage to what comparative religionists call the holy center, the omphalos or world navel that defines the world of primitive humanity, orienting it and making it real. "Being an *axis mundi*, the sacred city or temple is regarded as the meeting point of heaven, earth, and hell," says Eliade (p. 12); "the center . . . is preeminently the zone of the sacred, the zone of absolute reality" (p. 17). Riddley's "senter," both city and temple, is Cambry, once known as Canterbury, and he undergoes a profoundly religious experience as he approaches it. But as noted previously, the traditional sacralization is, in this blasted future, imperfect and degenerate, and thus in the holy center he finds only evidence of human viciousness and a strange figure he calls Greanvine, emblem of an idea of human life as mere shabby mechanism, something scarcely removed from the vegetable world.

To gauge the significance of this failure of the numen will require consideration of several points, all relevant to the question of historical redemption and the prospects for escape from the terror of history. One must, for example, identify the historical Eusa. One must also probe with Riddley and his creator the role of the artist in a world potentially or actually destroyed by nuclear war. Lastly, one must consider the myth of the Waste Land in *Riddley Walker,* especially as it complements Hoban's version of the fall.

Hoban weaves into his narrative an elaborate and creative myth of original sin, for the inhabitants of Riddley's world, "soar-vivers" all, labor under a universal sense of guilt, the result of their collective emotional response to a condition of endless punishment and suffering. Based on a misreading of the legend of St. Eustace and imperfect memories of the nuclear age and its excesses, the *Eusa Story* is a Blakean myth of the primal error as a fall from unity into division, from a human unity with nature, that is, to the human exploitation of nature, the transgression focused in the splitting of the atom. This last detail reveals the historical component of the Eusa myth. Eusa's identification with St. Eustace is essentially a red herring. The fortuitous preservation of the saint's legend gave shape to a story that quickly modulated, in a process that Eliade (pp. 39–48) describes as common among unsophisticated peoples, from simple historical record to myth. The real antitype of Eusa is the country responsible for splitting the atom and thereby giving the division and alienation of modern society a basis in physics itself. Eusa, one realizes, is the eponymous projection of "USA," the United States of America, the nation that, as the first nuclear power, gave a whole new meaning to the terror of history.

As history became myth, it blended with a much older idea of human transgression, one that Riddley intuits in a trancelike moment in the ruined crypt of Canterbury Cathedral. There he discovers a version of the Tree of Knowledge and the idea of its baleful fruit. In his story, as a consequence, he rigorously scrutinizes different kinds of knowledge, from the destructive science pursued by politicians like Abel Goodparley and Erny Orfing to the mythic and cultural lore transmitted in the tales and fables frequently transcribed for the reader. Hoban ultimately focuses on Riddley's growing insight into the human condition—insight that enables him to distinguish various kinds of appetitive knowledge from real wisdom, *scientia* from *sapientia*. In a sense, then, Riddley produces a scriptural record, a kind of wisdom book or neo-Ecclesiastes freighted with a lesson about the vanity of human wishes. Riddley puns throughout on the phrase "hart of the wood," but the most resonant of his punning variations are "heart of the wood" and "heart of the would." At the heart of something one finds its most characteristic or essential part; at the heart of a wood or forest, that ancient symbol of error, one encounters moral night. Thus Riddley's narrative, with its recurrent motif of heads on poles, ultimately concerns the human heart of darkness, construed as the heart of human volition, the human "would." "You see what Im saying," says Riddley, "its the hart of the wud its the hart of the wanting to be" (p. 165).

Riddley's first interpolated story, "Hart of the Wood," introduces this theme in terms of a primal loss of innocence. Mr Clevver, whom an earlier age called the devil, strikes a hideous bargain with an archetypal couple. He will help them cook and eat their child—and thus survive—if they will give him the child's heart. Thereafter, the heart of the child, commonly taken to represent a quintessential innocence, belongs to Mr Clevver and the powers of darkness. In other words, Mr Clevver gives knowledge—how to build a fire (these things begin simply)—for the human heart of innocence. But the fable also exists to transmit the secret of producing charcoal, a necessity for smelting iron or making gunpowder, and Mr Clevver intimates that the knowledge of fire-making will later serve these very ends. Moreover, "when they bern the chard coal ther stack wil be the shape of the hart of the chyld" (p. 4). Charcoal is produced by burning wood without air; in primitive times a stack of wood would be fired after being partially covered with earth. What remained after the fire smoldered out would be charcoal. The people of Riddley's time have come to think that the earthen and wooden lumps on the earth somehow resemble hearts—a perception the myth "explains." "Seed of the berning," then, "is Hart of the Chyld."

The sacrifice of the child figures also in Punch and Judy. Riddley wonders, even as he takes his leave of the reader, "Why is Punch crookit? Why wil he all ways kil the babby if he can? Parbly I wont never know its jus on me to think on it" (p. 220). The point, of course, is that Punch represents erring, concupiscent humanity. He is another version of the parents who barter their child to Mr Clevver, and indeed, the devil is a stock figure in the Punch and Judy show. Humanity, like Punch, "kills the babby" over and over again, without ever really meaning to give in to whatever terrible and nameless appetite prompts such cruelty.

Glumly, Riddley remarks: "Wel Im telling Truth here aint I. That's the woal idear of this writing which I begun wylst thinking on what the idea of us myt be" (p. 117). He comes eventually, like Conrad's Marlowe, to a recognition of the essential human reality: "Whats so terbel its jus that knowing of the horrer in every thing. The horrer waiting. I dont know how to say it. Like say you myt get cut bad and all on a sudden there you are with your leg opent up and youre looking at the mussl fat and boan of it. You all ways knowit what wer unner the skin only you dont want to see that bloody meat and boan. Never mynd" (p. 153). The dying Kurtz puts it more economically: "The horror! The horror!"

Riddley recognizes the one constant in human experience. In both the Eusa show and the Punch and Judy show he recognizes the same figure of evil, whether called Mr Clevver or Mr On The Levvil (rhyming slang for the devil). Riddley's entire narrative concerns his gathering realization that humanity's pursuit of knowledge tends to lead it only to Bad Time. By the end of the story, he has seen the future, and it frightens him. At the same time he achieves a two-tiered recognition of the danger, the moral morass, of power. "THE ONLYES POWER IS NO POWER" (p. 167), he decides. Later he amends this formulation: "I sust that wernt qwite it. It aint that its *no* power. Its the not sturgling for Power thats where the Power is. Its in jus letting your self be where it is. Its tuning in to the worl its leaving your self behynt" (p. 197). In other words, the individual must abandon self to the great totality of the universe, to be at one with it. Riddley's most profound insight, and the moral heart of the novel, expresses this perception in historical terms that remind the reader of the familiar problems of modern civilization. He stands in the crypt of Canterbury Cathedral:

[I]t come to me what it wer wed los. It come to me what it wer as made them peopl time back way back bettern us. It wer knowing how to put their selfs with the Power staon youwd be moving with the girt dants of the every thing the Big 1 of the Master Chaynjisl Then you myt have the res of it or not. The boats in the air or whatever. What ever you done wud be right.

Them as made Canterbury musve put their selfs right. Only it dint stay right did it. Somers in be twean them stoan trees and the Power Ring they musve put their selfs wrong. Now we dint have the 1 nor the other. Them stoan trees wer stanning in the dead town only wed los the knowing of how to put our selves with the Power

the Power in the stoan. Plus wed los the knowing whatd woosht the
Power roun the Power Ring [pp. 161–62].

Riddley's thoughts here focus the theme of the novel. Postholocaust humanity will yearn for the wonders of the past,
but only the wisest will see that the real loss—the loss that, as
it were, contained the physical catastrophe—was the fall from
oneness with that "girt dants."

The oneness became a manyness, and the central myth of
Riddley's people—that of Eusa and the Littl Shyning Man—
reflects a radical deterioration at the heart of things. The fated
protagonist of the *Eusa Story* pries into the secrets of nature,
searching for and violating the 1 Big 1, the unity of creation.
Stalking the atom, that little shining man, and splitting it apart,
he discovers the great secret and the great catastrophe, the
principle of nuclear fission. But in splitting the atom, pres-
umptuous humanity made a disastrous bargain with the very
principle of division, as one sees in the Littl Shyning Man's
lament under Eusa's interrogation (which prefigures the brutal "qwiries" to which the Pry Mincer subjects the Ardship of
Cambry): "The Littl Man the Addom he begun tu cum a part
he cryd, I wan tu go I wan tu stay. Eusa sed, Tel mor. The
Addom sed, I wan tu dark I want tu lyt I wan tu day I wan
tu nyt. Eusa sed, Tel mor. The Addom sed, I wan tu woman
I wan tu man. Eusa sed, Tel mor. The Addom sed, I want tu
plus I want tu minus I wan tu big I wan tu littl I wan tu aul
I wan tu nuthing" (p. 32).

Riddley's story of a world lapsed from oneness into twoness
contains numerous variations on dualities and sundered pairs:
one encounters such cultural pairs as Goodparley and Orfing
and Goodparley and Lissener, not to mention provisional pair-
ings like Goodparley and Granser, Riddley and Lissener, Riddley and Goodparley, Riddley and Orfing. Other such features
in the story include "form" and "fents," Punch and Judy, the

Punch and Judy show and the Eusa show, and the two halves of Riddley's dog pack. The "Greanvine" figure that Riddley finds seems naturally to seek its partner, too—now Eusa, now Punch. All of these pairs hark back to the mythic idea of the sundered pair as expressed in Eusa and his wife, Eusa's two sons, Eusa's two dogs, and of course Eusa's victim, the Littl Shyning Man, whose splitting in two created a catastrophic pattern.

The story of the Littl Shyning Man resembles the myth that Socrates expounds in the *Symposium*: the original One whose division creates a whole world of desire, the very principle of male and female. Eusa pulls the Littl Man apart "lyk he wuz a chikken" (p. 32) and thereafter, in the Eusa show, the figure for the Littl Man is "qwite a piece of work. . . . The way hes made hes all wood hes got a woal varnisht wood body with parper arms and legs and riggit with wires so he comes in 2 or slyds back in to 1. Hes the only figger there is with a cock and balls. Like it says in the *Eusa Story* when he comes in 2 his cock and balls theyre on his lef side his head and neck theyre on his right" (p. 206). These halves, suggestive of the division between mind and body that perenially interferes with human wholeness, invite a stylization that reveals them as the two separate parts of the traditional Taoist symbol of yin and yang:

The fall into disunity eventually brings with it a plague of destruction and ignorance that lasts for generations. Like Oedipus, Abel Goodparley seeks to account for and deal with the plague, little realizing that his researches will bring his own downfall or that they resemble the researches that brought humanity to Bad Time. Goodparley's fate also resembles Gloucester's, in *King Lear,* that archetypal study of the frangible civilizing institutions that protect humanity from hostile nature. Shakespeare, too, examines the consequences of a disastrous division, and Hoban seems aware of the parallels as he points up the Kentish setting, the journeys to Dover, the blinding of a major character, and, most suggestively, the blighted landscape.

Like *Lear, Riddley Walker* is a vision of the Waste Land, and thus it also echoes "Childe Roland," *Waiting for Godot,* and Eliot's famous poem. The world of Riddley Walker and his people, blasted and crippled, struggles grimly to reanimate some lost principle of fruition, to recapture some regenerative spark. Unfortunately, its political master, Abel Goodparley, seeks a too-literal spark: "this here bag of yellerboy myt be the break and thru the barren year with a bang" (p. 129). Goodparley mistakenly thinks that he can redeem the Waste Land with a potent new weapon, gunpowder, or a political weapon like the state-sanctioned centralization seen "when Littl Salting Fents got largent in by Dog Et Form" (p. 56).

This and other references to the aggression against Littl Salting, which bodes ill for the political future, obliquely develop the theme of the Waste Land. In his "connection" or sacerdotal gloss on the unscheduled and highly tendentious Eusa show whereby the Ram attempts to defend the recent aggression, Riddley's father says no more than the Delphic "a littl salting and no saver." Quietly subversive, the connection reflects the sadness of Littl Salting's fate. For want of a "savior," that defenseless community lost its independence, which gave "savor" to existence there. The pun points the reader toward the source of Hoban's image in the Sermon on the Mount (Matt. 5:13) and elsewhere in the Gospels: "Salt is good: but if the salt have lost its savor, wherewith shall it be seasoned?" (Luke 14:34). In the Bible this figure defines an idea of grievous and often irreversible loss, as of the soul to sin; in *Riddley Walker* it serves to comment indirectly on human civilization as a salt that, after nuclear war, will have lost its savor.

The salt without savor, the world laid waste. As in the earliest versions of the myth of the Waste Land, everything is perceived as hinging on the questions that will miraculously restore the moribund land and the blighted human society that subsists on it. Hence the ritual questions that the Pry Mincer asks the Ardship of Cambry: "They jus keap hoaping some time some Goodparley wil ask the right asking and some Ardship wil say a anser whatwl break them thru the barren year" (p. 84). The old magic, however, has dissipated; the Pry Mincer always asks the wrong questions. Riddley, penetrating the Holy Center at Canterbury, arrives at the Chapel Perilous of the myth, but he fails to ask the questions that will restore the Waste Land. No such questions exist.

Like Eliot's poem, the novel contains allusions to and echoes of other great visions of anomie, spiritual paralysis, and cultural blight. The rain that falls almost continually in this novel hints at some terrible meteorological calamity and recalls the ironic reversal of Eliot's theme of aridity by Hemingway in *A Farewell to Arms*. One also encounters Orwell, Beckett, and Burgess here, but the most important allusions and echoes— from Anglo-Saxon poetry at one end of the cultural spectrum, from James Joyce at the other—bracket the novel in such a way as to make it in effect a disquisition on the literary past as well as on other kinds of history.

A number of details in *Riddley Walker* recall Anglo-Saxon poetry and the culture that produced it. As in "The Wanderer," the special horror of exclusion from the community hearth is a given in this story. Eusa suffers this fate, and Riddley, Lissener, Goodparley, and Orfing all share it. The payment of *wergild,* the "man-price" due in ancient times to the relatives of a person killed, figures here as "comping station." As in *Beowulf*, the cosmic numbers three, nine, and twelve seem to receive special emphasis. Beowulf struggles against three infernal antagonists, he slays nine sea monsters, his men despair at the ninth hour, he ends twelve years of depredations by Grendel, he receives twelve gifts, twelve followers run the gamut from betrayal to heroic loyalty in the dragon fight, and so forth. The narrator of *Riddley Walker* embraces a similar numerology, as one sees in the three moon brothers, the three ingredients of gunpowder, the ninefold interrogation of the Ardship of Cambry, the children's rhyme Fool's Circel Ninewise, and Riddley's twelve years.

The novel's dedication, "To Wieland," also glances obliquely at the Anglo-Saxon epic, for the Norse blacksmith-god made Beowulf's armor.[8] A figure like Wieland is especially important in an Iron Age. More gifted and attractive than Vulcan, his classical counterpart, Wieland is closer, perhaps, to Dedalus, the type of the artist. Like Dedalus, in fact, Wieland created his own pinions and soared aloft. Riddley Walker, then, comes to his true calling, and to silence, exile, and cunning, under the aegis of a fabulous artificer; thus Hoban's picture of the human condition in Inland, and his reflections on the artist's obligation to respond to it, recalls the theme and hero of *A Portrait of the Artist as a Young Man*. Nominally a "connection-man," a kind of priest, Riddley flies clear of the nets of family, religion, and country, and moves in the course of his narrative toward being, like Stephen Dedalus, "a priest of the eternal imagination." The ceaseless walking of Hoban's protagonist also reminds one of Joyces's peripatetic hero. Riddley's formula for existential horror—"bloody meat and boan"—even echoes Stephen Dedalus in *Ulysses*: "raw head and bloody bones." Riddley, too, ends in a self-imposed exile, already engaged in forging the uncreated conscience of his race.

As Riddley executes his literary task, the writing of this narrative, and comes to recognize his literary and theatrical calling, his story modulates from *Bildungsroman* to *Künstler-roman*. Like every great artist, Riddley encounters and grapples with the eternal questions of human destiny, the "riddles" humanity has sought to answer since Oedipus confronted the sphinx. As a writer and puppeteer, he is an artist, and the novel concerns the role of art in humanity's struggle to know itself in history and—in Hoban's hypothetical future—to recover a lost human potential. That struggle and the artistic response to it recapitulate certain important moments in the evolution of literary art, especially vis-à-vis the authority of the state. The resurrection of Punch and Judy, for example, calls to mind the restoration of the theaters in seventeenth-century England (when Punch and Judy first came to that country); the resurgence of an independent theater after a long period of authoritarian preemption, by the same token, recalls the gradual secularization of the stage after its early control by the medieval church. In the Eusa show, in fact, one glimpses a reflection of the origins of drama in the religious rituals of ancient Greece (for Eusa is this people's scapegoat, its Dionysus or Orpheus, as well as its primal man).

But as the instrument of the Ram, the half-baked governmental authority to which all Inlanders must do at least lip service, the tragic Eusa show is compromised, and Hoban imagines comedy (Punch and Judy) as its subversive offshoot. At the end the reader sees the authority of the Ram in temporary disarray; though civil authority will reassert itself, one suspects that the subversive art of Riddley and his new "crowd" (they will become an itinerant theater troupe in short order) will continue to survive in the cracks, thereby providing the world with its honest reflection, an alternative to the deranged aspirations of political hacks and the lies or evasions of priests "pontsing for the Ram" (p. 65).

The reader also encounters Riddley as a graphic artist, for he improves and completes the picture of Abel Goodparley he discovers on a wall in Cambry. Someone has depicted the

Pry Mincer as "Greanvine," the mysterious figure that Riddley
has discovered only moments previously. Riddley finds the
Greanvine figure intriguing yet horrific, for it seems to represent the hegemony of mechanical nature over humanity. It
depicts a man with his mouth forced open by emerging "vines
and leaves" (p. 165), a "man dying back into the earf and the
vines growing up thru his arse hole up thru his gullit and out
of his mouf" (p. 168), a man being reclaimed by, lapsing back
into, mere vegetation.

One can turn again to Mircea Eliade for clarification of the
important epiphany that Riddley experiences before this figure. Greanvine represents a "return" that has nothing to do
with transcendence; it can only bring terror to anyone who
yearns, however inarticulately, for the numinous. Eliade takes
pains to distinguish authentic myths of return from the perception or belief that history resembles or is a part of nature,
whose cyclic renewal might suggest a paradigm: "The . . .
'possibilities' of nature each spring and archaic man's possibilities on the threshold of each year are . . . not homologous.
Nature recovers only itself, whereas archaic man recovers the
possibility of definitively transcending time and living in etern-
ity" (p. 158).

Greanvine's, then, is the face of Adam, the universal face
of mortality, and Riddley, despairing, calls it "the onlyes face
there wer" (p. 166). It fits even Eusa's head, thinks Riddley,
who begins to see intelligence itself as mere mechanism (for
Eusa's head was a computer). Only Lissener seems exempt
from the Greanvine face, and Riddley wonders, "What wer it
made the Ardship odd 1 out then?" (p. 166). He does not
answer, but the Ardship seems at once less and more than
human. If his psychic faculties force consideration of the transcendental, his disfigurement and his cruelty make him seem
inhuman. Either way, he gives the lie to Greanvine.

When Riddley finds the graffito of Goodparley qua Greanvine, he understands that someone has made a statement at

once political and metaphysical. In places like Canterbury, one once found paintings of the Dance of Death, the unvarying theme of which was that mortality claims princes and prelates no less than villeins. Whatever their power and whatever their airs, the mighty of this earth are still made in the image of Greanvine. Goodparley, no less than any other human being, is a fallen creature, doomed to existence in time and to kinship with the riotous vegetable world. Under the picture Riddley reads the words "HOAP OF A TREE" (p. 16). He expands the drawing, so that Goodparley is simultaneously the mortal Greanvine and a figure perched among the antlers of the great stag, the hart of the wood. Thus he also becomes the Littl Shyning Man the Addom and the "figure of the crucified savior" in the Legend of St. Eustace. As such, he represents both Adam and Christ, the antithetical figures perched in the heart of the human wood or in the heart of darkness in the "would" at humanity's heart of stone. Riddley's artistic gesture expresses a half-conscious perception of the form divine in every human being—even in the benighted Goodparley. Or perhaps it expresses merely the wish that the human antitype be God rather than Greanvine. The hoped-for tree, though Riddley cannot put all these ideas together, is at once the Tree of Life and the Cross, emblems of a hope still at least dimly familiar to Hoban's twentieth-century audience. But as Hoban sees its dilemma, humanity remains crucified between being cut off from revelation in the future and being obliged to admit its falseness in the present.

Only an idea of transcendence, says Eliade, only faith, can enable humanity to escape the terror of history. The novel contains several prospective but flawed messiahs, including Riddley, Abel Goodparley, Lissener, and perhaps Belnot Phist. All these characters, in the lunar calendar observed by their society (the custom resumes the practice of the ancient Druids), celebrate their naming days at "the second full." If these Iron Age people of the future, like their Celtic ancestors, observe

November 1, the day after Samhain, as the beginning of the new year, then the second full moon would occur some time in December, making these messianic candidates, like Christ, children of the winter solstice. All reenact the passion of Eusa, Adamic scapegoat and primal man.

A second Eusa ought to correspond to the New Adam, the savior who redeems the Old Adam and his progeny, but even in Old Time the myth had ceased to inspire faith. Now no one remembers it at all. Riddley Walker's age lacks a myth of redemption for Riddley or some other messiah to fulfill; no one can put humanity back on the road to spiritual wholeness. Unsparingly honest, the author of *Riddley Walker* invokes Christian symbols but does so with a full recognition of their increasingly tenuous application to human history and the human reality. Admittedly inadequate to restoring the Waste Land, they come to represent what humanity has lost. In the last analysis, Riddley discovers no panacea for the human condition, only the "hope of a tree." Hoban refuses to soften the terror of history.

Puritanism and Patriarchy: *The Handmaid's Tale*

Another novel of the future, another dystopia. One requires considerable reorientation to go from Hoban's neo-Iron Age, millennia hence, to Atwood's neo-puritan age, many of whose inhabitants still remember our own time. In *The Handmaid's Tale* Atwood presents a much more proximate future and roots it in a historical turning point late in the twentieth century, a time of religious and political reaction against hard-won freedoms perceived as moral rot. One notes in the epilogue a hint that the Republic of Gilead exists at the same period as the regime of Iran's Ayatollah Khomenei—an old man in poor health when *The Handmaid's Tale* first appeared. But the author of this novel reflects on history in a number of ways, and in examining it as a historical fiction one undertakes a multiple exploration. The text's multivalence finds expression in an acute meditation on historical witness, historical process, and historical parallelism, not to mention such related topics as the Logos in history, intertextuality as a form of history, and the mind as historical paradigm.

In Hebrew, ironically, Gilead means "Hall of Witness." One ought first, therefore, as a context for other considerations of history, to note this novel's structure as a fictional act of historical witness. The story purports to be a primary historical document—a record of daily life under a latter-day American tyranny. It pays only glancing attention to the leaders and the great public events associated with this moment in history. But as testimony, it has great power and authority.

Authors depicting the way it will be, as I have noted before, can imagine the present as the turning point for one or more major future developments, or they can depict a future mirroring one or more pasts (possibly including the reader's present). In *The Handmaid's Tale* readers encounter a future that looks to their own age as a turning point, the moment when the festering resentment of the fundamentalist right comes to a head and alters the course of history. At the same time, however, this future reflects previous ages of patriarchal or puritan repression. In fact, the story of Atwood's heroine, Offred, takes place in a period that mirrors at once the patriarchal times chronicled in the Old Testament and, only slightly less obviously, the American past of puritanism and the Pilgrim fathers.

The reflection of a puritan age, an age in which a neurotic religious imperative forces personal freedom to the wall, finds expression in small details like the ancient Cambridge church that Offred and Ofglen stroll by after shopping one day, a church where one "can see paintings, of women in long sober dresses, their hair covered by white caps, and of upright men, darkly clothed and unsmiling. Our ancestors."[9] It finds expression more broadly in the story's setting—Boston and Cambridge—and in its echoes of Hawthorne. American puritanism flowered in the Massachusetts Bay Colony, and Atwood, like Hawthorne before her, anatomizes the strange ethos of those who feel compelled to suppress every secular form of joy and pleasure—those motivated, as H. L. Mencken said, by an unreasoning fear that someone, somewhere, may be having fun.

Perhaps more prominent is the parallel between the power structure of Gilead and the Old Testament patriarchy, with its polygamy and its recurrent struggle—Abraham and Sarah, Jacob and Rachel, Joachim and Anna—with the infertility of anile spouses (one of the ironies here is that the Handmaid's mother became pregnant with her at a relatively advanced age). The founders of Gilead cultivate the biblical parallel by calling themselves the Sons of Jacob—after the offspring of that patriarch by Rachel, Leah, and their handmaids. The biblical sons of Jacob became progenitors of the twelves tribes of Israel, but their modern epigones fail conspicuously to be fruitful and multiply—even when, carrying the Old Testament parallel to absurd lengths, they supply themselves with the extra reproductive resources of second-class wives, modern versions of Rachel's handmaid, whom they treat with a bizarre combination of deference and contempt. In basing this fiction on the institution of the handmaid and presenting that institution at parallel, mirroring moments in the past and future, Atwood at once satirizes the fundamentalist doctrine of biblical inerrancy and dramatizes the historical horror of sexual slavery.

The subject of mirroring, of historical parallelism, is complicated by the inclusion of an epilogue crucial to the historical resonance of this novel. In this epilogue Gilead and the narrative of the unnamed Handmaid are viewed from the vantage of two centuries later. So the reader encounters yet another future, and perhaps another mirror. Indeed, if one considers the setting of the epilogue (a scholarly conference held at a university existing in what appears to be an advanced culture of American Indians, with scholars of both sexes present), one concludes easily enough that the epilogue mirrors our own time, no less than the tale proper mirrors a distant puritan or patriarchal time.

In addition, the epilogue is suggestively situated roughly as far from the events in the tale proper as those events are from the drafting and ratification of the American Constitution. For this and for other reasons, the epilogue calls forth strange emotions. The scholarly discussion of the Handmaid's narrative is punctuated by mildly sexist humor: the Handmaid's *tail*, the Underground Frailroad, the joke on "enjoying" the Chair. Coming as they do after such a horrendous story, such witticisms set the teeth on edge. The sexist jokes, and the reader's discomfort at them, are merely a last, refined emphasis on the lessons learned about the meaning of women's freedom in what has gone before. Atwood also introduces this additional historical dimension into the novel to encourage readers silently to supply its complement—to go *backward* two centuries in their minds. The reader who does so—especially the reader who might find the extent of the degradation Atwood has imagined in a proximate future hard to credit—will realize that the utter helplessness and victimization of the narrator and her sisters scarcely belie the historical powerlessness of women, the historical lie of women's being "protected" (the word acquires a painful irony in this tale).

But historical mirroring in this narrative proves less central to it than the argument that American society at the end of the twentieth century may be at a terrible historical turning point. Professor Pieixoto in the epilogue remarks: "As we know from the study of history, no new system can impose itself upon a previous one without incorporating many of the elements to be found in the latter." He supports this remark by suggesting that the "racist policies" of Gilead really institutionalize the "racist fears" (p. 305) of the previous order.

Atwood leaves it to the reader to recognize other aspects of late twentieth-century American culture as transmogrified in Gilead: the growth of censorship, the fury of "pro-lifers," the antifeminist backlash, and the ubiquity, especially in banking, of electronic record-keeping, which facilitates control after the revolution, just as it makes monstrously easy, in the early stages of the new order, the expropriating of accounts and the financial kneecapping of whole elements of society: women, blacks, Jews.

But what about the tacit assumption that the elements exist in contemporary American society to precipitate a fascist revolution? To what extent does Atwood expect one to find her American dystopia credible? The reader who refuses to concede any real prophetic plausibility to the novel misses the contemporary actuality that fuels Atwood's speculation. Revolutions like the one remembered by the Handmaid do not require much popular grounding. Even popular revolutions tend to be effected by a small band of ruthless zealots. Thus Atwood does not insist that her reader think of the revolution that allows the Republic of Gilead to supplant the United States of America as some kind of widespread popular development.

Atwood imagines the end of the United States of America as rooted in the fanaticism of one set of its inhabitants (the Sons of Jacob), in the complicity of another set (the wives, the Aunts), and in the complacency of the rest: the Handmaid and her unvigilant sisters. Not that gender has anything to do with complacency. Though it makes its point in terms of women's experience, the book does not speak exclusively to women. The freedom at stake is more than that narrowly defined form of freedom called call women's liberation. By the same token, the resistance in Gilead is shared by both sexes, by all ages, and by various religious denominations, apparently including Baptists, Catholics, Jehovah's Witnesses, Jews, Presbyterians, and Quakers. Cautious about identifying the actual sectarian affiliations of the Sons of Jacob and those who endorse their usurpation of power, Atwood makes a kind of all-purpose fundamentalism the target of her indictment. The reader can imagine several politically active fundamentalist groups in our time, from the Moral Majority to PTL, as the seedbed for some movement like the Sons of Jacob.

But Atwood does expect her readers to make political connections. Her Sons of Jacob strongly resemble the small but deadly cadres of political—and superficially religious—fanatics scattered here and there in the America of the late 1980s. As Scott Klug shows in a disturbing piece of investigative reporting in the Washington, D.C., *City Paper,*[10] a neo-Nazi named William Pierce, based in Arlington, Virginia, seems to have had some success in unifying political crazies across the country. As a result, considerable contact and mutual influence exist among not only the American Nazi Party and the Ku Klux Klan but also such groups as Pierce's Cosmotheist Community, the Posse Comitatus, the Liberty Lobby, the White Patriots, the Order, and the Aryan Nations, which subsumes the Aryan Youth Movement and the White Aryan Resistance. Members of the Aryan Nations believe, as Klug explains, "that Aryans are the lost tribe of Israel"—a notion that finds oblique expression in the naming of Atwood's revolutionary cabal, the Sons of Jacob (Jacob's sons, as previously noted, became founders and patriarchs of the twelve Hebrew tribes). William Pierce, at any rate, has unified these disparate groups of fanatics in an umbrella organization called the National Alliance (whose mailing list, according to Klug, runs to twelve thousand names). These organizations have bred terrorists who are well armed and well financed. Pierce's novel, *The Turner Diaries,* contains blueprints, as it were, for the assassination of journalists, the bombing of FBI headquarters, the mortaring of the Capitol, and the planting of a nuclear weapon at the Pentagon. The testimony of the Handmaid, who reports that the Sons of Jacob take control by shooting the president and machine-gunning the congress, begins to seem less far-fetched.

Less obvious but more extraordinary among the details that establish the plausibility of the historical turning point envisioned by Atwood are the hints regarding the rise in pornography. To read these hints exclusively as a gauge of twentieth-century American decadence, however, would be to miss the more subtle point. Indeed, Atwood's attitude toward pornography is a complex one and has led to occasional misunderstanding on the part of readers. Atwood is aware that the suppression of pornography is a point on which fundamentalists and feminists can find common cause—but she makes painfully clear what kind of fire the feminist censor plays with. Once the logic of censorship has been accepted, one is defenseless against the less sensible but more powerful ideologue whose index one may—too late—find decidedly uncongenial. Thus Atwood's narrator mentions the suppression of the "Feels on Wheels vans and the Bun-Dle Buggies," along with the "pornomarts" (p. 174), in the same passage as the assassination of the president, the machine-gunning of congress, the roadblocks, the Identipasses, the expropriation of bank accounts— and the suspension of the Constitution.

Atwood—and perhaps her protagonist, too—is no doubt aware that one can define pornography as whatever degrades human beings, for example by treating them as objects. The films shown by the Aunts at the Rachel and Leah or "Red" Centers make the point: the handmaids-in-training see old pornographic movies of "Women kneeling, sucking penises or guns, women tied up or chained or with dog collars around their necks, women hanging from trees, or upside-down, naked, with their legs held apart, women being raped, beaten up, killed. Once we had to watch a woman being slowly cut into pieces, her fingers and breasts snipped off with garden shears, her stomach slit open and her intestines pulled out" (p. 118). Such graphic lessons notwithstanding, Offred seems to feel a humane sympathy for men who, lacking women, might have some need of pornographic diversion. She feels sympathy, for example, for the lower-class paramilitary troops called the Guardians. Denied women, they are forbidden any other sexual outlet: "They have no outlets now except themselves, and that's a sacrilege. There are no more magazines, no more films, no more substitutes" (p. 22).

The suppression of vice, of course, merely makes vice all the more inwardly cankerous. The leadership of Gilead is a cesspool of appalling private obsessions, introduced first in the scene with the lecherous doctor, hinted at throughout the Handmaid's illicit trysts with her Commander, and finally made explicit in the brothel-club called Jezebel's. Thus Atwood's references to the bizarre proliferation of pornography and prostitution in late twentieth-century America are perhaps intended not as routine extrapolation from 1980s trends, a rueful admission of some kind of justification for the outrage of the fundamentalists—but as another kind of extrapolation altogether. She suggests that the relationship between pornography and fundamentalist reaction is not simple cause and effect. Rather, both of these phenomena are twinned effects of another, unstated cause: the neuroses endemic to fundamentalist repression of every stripe. In this regard *The Handmaid's Tale* is a latter-day "Young Goodman Brown"—Hawthorne's classic study of the reptiles bred in the puritan unconscious.

Thus far I have considered features of this novel that link it to the other rubrics of historical fiction: its reflection of historical periods other than the historical period of its setting and its predication on a historical turning point in the reader's present. These features provide the background for the more oblique or abstract historical meanings contained in the novel's exploitation of cultural history as expressed in myth, religion, psychology, and literature. One finds that allusions to the Bible, to Chaucer, to the Waste Land theme, and to the fairy tale Little Red Riding Hood extend the meanings hitherto sketched. These meanings remain largely in the realm of sexual politics, for as Amin Malak observes in his essay on *The Handmaid's Tale*, "dystopias are quintessentially ideological novels."[11]

For example, the psychoanalytic side of the story, contained in parallels between the heroine and Little Red Riding Hood, tends ultimately to concern a feminist agenda. The Handmaid appears early on as "some fairy-tale figure in a red cloak" (p. 9). Cautioned against straying, she threads her way among various horrors to deliver a basket of goodies to the house of an old woman. Indeed, the story features both the benign but cautionary mother and a "granny"—Serena Joy—who shares the heroine's victimization by the wolf. The wolf is the state, its masculine rationality and appetite localized as the Commander, but more broadly the leviathan that swallows every human frailty. It has swallowed Serena Joy only a little less obviously than it has swallowed the Handmaid. The huntsman of deliverance is Nick, the Commander's chauffeur and member of the Mayday underground. In the fairy tale this character cuts open the wolf and delivers Red Riding Hood and her grandmother in a transparent birth fantasy highly relevant to the fertility-obsessions of Gilead.

Like the protagonist of Little Red Riding Hood, Offred lacks a father, and her story can be read as a study in oedipal ambiguities. But the greater significance of the fairy tale here is more broadly mythic. According to Bruno Bettelheim, the red garment is the emblem of Little Red Riding Hood's "sexual attractiveness,"[12] and similarly the Handmaid's red dress suggests her nubility, her sexual maturity, her readiness for impregnation. It is perhaps to be linked, then, with the flowers (they tempt Red Riding Hood, too) that she continually notices as the landscape's ironic comment on the desperate pass to which human reproductive viability has come (she defines them as "the genital organs of plants"—pp. 82, 153). If one asks why Atwood supplies a fairy-tale armature for the structure of this novel, and what it has to do with history, one finds that she is at pains to render this fiction historically significant by reference not only to Old Testament and puritan antecedents to the world she imagines here but also to the universal history of the mind, as contained in the unconscious—and classically given expression in dreams and works of the imagination.

Atwood opts for a child's story as her subtext (rather than, say, something out of Greek tragedy) because she sees the liberation of women as something quite recent, so that women collectively—and historically—can be viewed as passing from childhood into adolescence, where they risk the kind of folly that tempts every child: to dawdle, to collect flowers, to miss the terrible danger all around. In other words, women at the end of the twentieth century risk losing all that their mothers gained for them by treating too casually the freedoms they have inherited, taking them for granted or—worse—consolidating them irresponsibly by flirting with the fascist ideology of censorship. "As for you," the Handmaid remembers her feminist mother's reproach to her Laodiceanism: "you're just a backlash. Flash in the pan. History will absolve me" (p. 121). *The Handmaid's Tale* is the chronicle of that historical absolution.

One finds an intertextual and broadly historical dimension to this feminism in the novel's rich Chaucerian echoes, notably those that invoke the Wife of Bath. Chaucer specifies only red hose for the Wife of Bath, but in paintings she appears all in red. The Handmaid's uniform, also the harlot's red, seems intended to remind the reader of this convention. The Wife, like the Handmaid, lives in a world given over largely to men. She, too, must defend herself against the charge of technical adultery. In her tale, the central male character is a rapist, a chivalric renegade, who has a choice—like the Handmaid's Commander—between a faithful but old and unattractive spouse and a faithless but desirable one. The rapist in the Wife's Tale becomes a sympathetic figure at the end, and similarly there is a movement within Atwood's narrative from the chivalric institution that paradoxically promotes rape (of Handmaids by Commanders) to the martyrdom of the alleged rapist who perishes in the "particicution" (Atwood's coinage) at the end of the story. The Wife, invoking "experience and noon auctoritee," pits her experience of life and desire against the authority of masculine fiat, the tradition of misogynist writings, and patriarchal prerogative. It is the same for the Handmaid.

The Wife, again like the Handmaid, must survive in an era in which women are for the most part powerless, an era in which women must define themselves functionally—as housekeepers, cooks, breeders, or chatelaines. But the Wife's profession—cloth-making—at once makes her an anomaly (she has a career) and links her to that long line of mythic and historical women who escape idleness by making, shaping, or ornamenting cloth. Eve, Philomela, Matilda, Gretchen, the Lady of Shalott, the Wife of Bath—they spin, they weave, they sew, they knit. But this archetype, paradoxically, links her not to the Handmaid but to a sister manqué, Serena Joy. The Commander's wife devotes considerable time to knitting, and the Handmaid imagines her, with her endless knitting of scarves, as a kind of Penelope: "Sometimes I think these scarves aren't sent to the Angels at all, but unraveled and turned back into balls of yarn, to be knitted again in their turn" (p. 13).

Professor Pieixoto credits a colleague with giving the narrative its intentionally Chaucerian title, and the broader Chaucerian features also contribute importantly to meaning. Like the narratives in *The Canterbury Tales*, this one derives its title from the vocation of its teller. Like the General Prologue to *The Canterbury Tales*, this novel gives its readers something of a cross section of the society of its day. Like the poet who begins his narrative with a famous description of spring, invoking the season as an index to the spiritual condition of humanity in general and his pilgrim characters in particular, the author of *The Handmaid's Tale* allows her seasonal setting—the novel's action begins in spring and continues through summer—to enhance the meaning of her story.

But modern and contemporary writers, led by Eliot in *The Waste Land*, invariably make the season of renewal an ironic comment on the sterility of human life in an age that has seen the relentless debunking of all myths of rebirth. Atwood's seasonal setting, with flowers—those floral emblems of fertility—continually in bloom, underscores the poignance of the human infertility that, according to Professor Pieixoto, seems to have resulted from social and ecological folly:

Need I remind you that this was the age of the R-strain syphilis and also of the infamous AIDS epidemic, which, once they spread to the population at large, eliminated many young sexually active people from the reproductive pool? Stillbirths, miscarriages, and genetic deformities were widespread and on the increase, and this trend has been linked to the various nuclear-plant accidents, shutdowns, and incidents of sabotage that characterized the period, as well as to leakages from chemical- and biological-warfare stockpiles and toxic-waste disposal sites, of which there were many thousands, both legal and illegal—in some instances these materials were simply dumped into the sewage system—and to the uncontrolled use of chemical insecticides, herbicides, and other sprays [p. 304].

As in *Riddley Walker*, what issues is a Waste Land of creeping sterility and—as in the Eliot poem—mechanical sexuality, and the spiritual blight that accompanies these afflictions.

One requires little prompting to see the terrible "salvaging" and "particicution" at the end of the novel as versions of the various unfructifying sacrifices canvased in *The Waste Land*. The triple salvaging, with its central malefactor and two flanking figures, parodies the triple execution on Calvary. This time, however, the three criminals executed are female instead of male. The authorities follow this ghastly spectacle with the "hands-on" execution of an alleged rapist—really a member of the Mayday underground. This death, like the deaths that preceded it, is an archetypal sacrifice: the angry Handmaids become frenzied maenads enacting the sparagmos that would, under a different dispensation, renew fertility (I have had occasion previously to mention Mary Renault's handling of this topos in *The King Must Die*; just as Renault's Ariadne is last seen clutching a grisly piece of her surrogate Dionysus, Atwood's pathetic Janine is last seen wandering away from the bloodbath in a dazed state, clutching a wisp of the victim's blond hair). Like other modern and contemporary exploiters of Waste Land mythography, Atwood avoids affirming any efficacy in the sacrifice, but she does insist that any archetypal victims be female as well as male. From the vantage of the epilogue, moreover, she reminds the reader of the hope that the Handmaid is pregnant by Nick—and allows the reader to know that Gilead passes, perhaps as a result of events precipitated by the martyrdom of Mayday members like the nameless particicution victim and Ofglen, who commits suicide rather than implicate her fellow conspirators. Perhaps, then, the sacrifice *is* efficacious.

One perceives the particicution as an enormity, the very gauge of Gilead's benightedness. But like the institution of the Aunts, it reveals how psychologically resourceful the shapers of totalitarianism can be. They know, for example, that "the best and most cost-effective way to control women for reproductive and other purposes was through women themselves" (p. 308), as one learns in the epilogue. Here, too, one learns just how astute the particicution is, that "steam valve for the female elements in Gilead. Scapegoats have been notoriously useful throughout history, and it must have been gratifying for these Handmaids, so rigidly controlled at other times, to be able to tear a man apart with their bare hands every once in a while" (pp. 307–8). They know, too, that women's rage, denied other outlets, will find expression in madness and suicide. When the Handmaid hides a match and contemplates a grandly destructive self-immolation (p. 292), one recognizes the reference to the madwoman in Mr. Rochester's attic in *Jane Eyre*, an image that has become associated, in modern literature, with women's rage and despair.[13] The narrator in Atwood's novel recurs obsessively, in fact, to the subject of suicide and hints repeatedly at her struggle with the terrible temptation that carried off the previous Offred and—albeit for different reasons—eventually carries off Ofglen as well.

At the same time that they provide a harmless "steam valve" or two, the authorities in Gilead try to ensure that the legitimate steam valve of knowledge remains unavailable. In this imagined future state, women are denied literacy. The architects of Gilead forbid women to read or—for the younger generation—to learn to read. Men have laid exclusive claim to the Word. Western civilization, from the Greek heroic age on, has been largely patriarchal and "logocentric"; the central myth of the christianized West has been "the Word made flesh"—that is, the incarnation of a deified masculine rationality. The male consolidators of Gilead capitalize on this traditional definition of the Logos. They lock their Bibles away from those whose bondage it is suborned to justify, for they know that knowledge of the Word is power. Such censorship makes all the easier the rewriting of texts to political ends, inserting improvements, for example, in the Beatitudes (p. 89) or, incongruously, appropriating a suddenly useful bromide from Marx and Bakunin: *From each . . . according to her ability; to each according to his needs*" (p. 117; the phrase is so well known that one can read it without catching the pronoun shift from her to his).

But *The Handmaid's Tale* is also the Word, also "writing," albeit produced on magnetic tape, produced in defiance of the ban on female literacy. The Handmaid's story, moreover, is a powerful *literary* record, the symbolic recognition for which may be the "relief ornament in the shape of a wreath" (p. 7) that gets mentioned repeatedly. This ornament, over her bed, is symbolically the kind of wreath awarded for literary accomplishment, but it suggests other things as well. The richest symbol in the novel, it is an "eye" (pp. 37, 52, 97), as well as "a frozen halo, a zero" (p. 200). It is, in other words, the zero to which her life has been reduced, a life under constant supervision by the baleful eye of masculine authority. As halo it recognizes her martyrdom, her "witness" to an idea of human integrity greater than that allowed by the founders of the Republic of Gilead. Most basically it is a wreath of plaster flowers, and more than once, as noted previously, the reader hears that flowers are really the genital organs of plants (pp. 82, 153). But the artificiality of *plaster* flowers makes one think of the artificial sexuality of the woman whose bed they encircle. The wreath is finally an empty clock face (p. 200), under which the Handmaid echoes the damned Mephistopheles in Marlowe's *Dr. Faustus*: "this is time, nor am I out of it" (p. 37). The substitution of "time" for "hell" reminds one that hell is timeless and perhaps that our century looks forward to the emergence of some ultimate, irreversible species of totalitarianism, under which that form of time called history will calcify. Atwood's Handmaid, at any rate, is the historian who records her times under a sinister and surreal emblem of unreadable time.

History, notoriously, is "his story" not "her story," and Atwood's future history takes this maxim into consideration even as it patently rehearses a woman's historical testimony. Yet in that testimony, witness to the horror of the Republic of Gilead, the female historian proves extraordinarily subversive, merely by giving voice to what has been ordered to remain voiceless. The repressed in history returns as witness, subject is subverted by object, self by other. For a fiction set at such a slight remove from the reader's present, *The Handmaid's Tale* proves a remarkably complex historical meditation.

4

The Turning Point

READERS WHO DESIRE to understand history as process often find themselves drawn to novels that focus on some crossroads of the past. Such readers look for the origins of important political and social developments, the catalytic events and personalities that, in the beaker of history, cause the present to precipitate. George Core, however, has suggested that "the historical element" in fiction works most effectively when "deliberately muted so far as particulars go." Otherwise, "the novelist loses control and history takes over. In consequence the good novelist is careful not to put major historical figures in the center of the stage. In the same way, unless he is a superb craftsman who is utterly in control, he had best steer away from major historical events—from letting those events play too great a role in his fiction."[1]

These dicta would seem to pose problems for authors interested in the most significant moments of the past, authors wanting to enter history at this or that point crucial to its subsequent course. But in fact the validity of these principles depends on the nearness and familiarity of the history a novelist wants to explore. Only the history close to author and reader—close in time and immediate in import—threatens to overwhelm the novelist's art. The more proximate the history, in other words, the more obliquely the author must treat it. The novelist who deals with recent history does best, therefore, to concentrate on the responses of ordinary persons to shifts in their times—and thereby to make the political macrocosm a backdrop, rather than the substance, of the dramatic action.

More remote history, in contrast, lends its major events and personalities quite readily to fiction. Thus a novel with some prominent figure of the ancient world as protagonist tends to generate fewer artistic problems than one about, say, a nineteenth-century figure well known to readers. One can, after all, think of several first-rate historical novels with Roman emperors as protagonists; one can think of few in which an American president takes a central role. The distinction seems valid even within the work of a single writer. Gore Vidal, for example, succeeds better with *Julian* than with *Lincoln*.

But wherever located in the past, the turning point fascinates writers. Indeed, novels based on those moments when the bark of history corrects its course constitute what may be the most important category of historical fiction. A category with abundant and varied examples, it subsumes even the projections of alternative history produced by science-fiction and fantasy writers who speculate on the shape the present would take if events had fallen out differently in the past. Ward Moore's *Bring the Jubilee* (1952), for example, goes beyond what Thurber does so amusingly in "If Grant Had Been Drinking at Appomatox": it depicts the consequences of a Southern victory in the American Civil War. Other writers, like Philip K. Dick in *The Man in the High Castle* (1962) or Norman Spinrad in *The Iron Dream* (1972), imagine the fate of the world after a Nazi conquest of the Allies. Such fictions— they have obvious affinities with the reverse-historical novels treated in the preceding chapter—fit in here because they depend wholly, for their dramatic development, on some freshly imagined turning point or other. Too, they concern the past (sometimes grading into an imaginary present), rather than the future.

But alternative history remains ghettoized as fantasy, and only historical fiction that concerns a real past and its authentic turning points enjoys much critical approbation. Writers of these more respectable turning point novels include both popular and serious practitioners. In *The Angkor Massacre* (1983), for example, the French journalist turned popular novelist Loup Durand depicts the fall of Cambodia to the Khmer Rouge, and with it the passing of European influence in that part of the world. In *The Silver Darlings* (1941) Neil Gunn chronicles the decline, in the nineteenth century, of the independent herring fisheries in his native Scotland. In *The Inheritors* (1955) Nobel laureate William Golding imagines that period in the paleolithic age when *Homo neanderthalensis,* pressed by *Homo sapiens,* began to face extinction. Two American writers, Bernard Malamud and E. L. Doctorow, imagine the birth of a revolutionary consciousness early in the twentieth century. In Malamud's *The Fixer* (1966), an oppressed Jew discovers his vulnerability to history and embraces political activism on the eve of the Russian Revolution. Similarly Doctorow, in *Ragtime* (1975), isolates the moment in turn-of-the-century America when blacks, women, and workers began actively to resist serfdom and peonage in all their forms.

In these examples one sees that an author can construe a historical turning point negatively or positively—can, that is, emphasize the passing of the old or the emergence of the new. Readers encounter both approaches in the novels of Mary Renault, who characteristically explores the way profound historical change transforms a moribund culture. Broadly speaking, her characterization of historical change as desirable or undesirable depends on whether it constitutes an advance toward or a retreat from the great periods of ancient Greece and Macedonia. Turning points that bring a golden age closer receive epic treatment at her hands; those resulting from the betrayal of ideals associated with such an age, on the other hand, are conceived in largely tragic terms.

In *The Last of the Wine* (1956) Renault describes, in elegiac tones, the concluding years of the Peloponnesian War and the passing of the Periclean golden age. Onc of the crucial episodes of this novel concerns a portentous bout between two pankratiasts at the Isthmian Games. The contestant with the perfect body celebrated in classical sculpture loses to the contestant with the physique of an ape. In sport and in war, the reader discovers, the bestial contenders will prevail hereafter. This recognition foreshadows the novel's ultimate burden: the giving way of traditional Athenian ideals to political discord within and Lacedemonian totalitarianism without.

Renault abandons the elegiac mode in *The King Must Die* (1958), which concerns the displacement of the earth mother as the Mediterranean world's central religious figure. With this displacement, the one lamented by Robert Graves in *The White Goddess*, society shifted from a matriarchal to a patriarchal organization. Renault, however, finds this shift admirable, for it heralds the great age of classical civilization. She presents five Mediterranean states in the novel, from humble Troizen and Naxos to rising Athens, transitional Eleusis, and doomed Crete. Two of these have already embraced the masculine sky gods, relegating the mother goddess to the religious periphery. Of the three matriarchies examined, two crumble at the challenge posed by patriarchal alternatives, so that by the end of the story four-fifths of the Hellenic world have made the transition, which proceeds pari passu with the Achaean challenge to Minoan hegemony. Thus in *The King Must Die* Renault achieves a splendid fictional treatment of perhaps the most momentous historical turning point of all.

But in the twentieth century humanity may face an ultimate turning point. The fictions analyzed in what follows—Lampedusa's *The Leopard* and Thomas's *The White Hotel*—concern a more proximate history and thus speak more directly to a modern reader's interest in or curiosity about history as it impinges on the present. Between them, these novels trace the sociological and psychological roots of the modern world, especially as these roots have issued in the political violence of the age. In *The Leopard* the reader sees an ancient Sicilian aristocracy giving ground before an unscrupulous and newly rich middle class. The author implies that the rapacious and largely unprincipled society that emerges from this struggle is the one that will embrace fascism and may yet embrace Marxism. The phenomenon of fascism, especially the psychology behind its ethic of violence against the individual (not to mention violence against unfavored racial categories), receives further attention in *The White Hotel*. The author of this novel focuses on the intimate struggle of a young woman for psychological health. But Lisa Erdman's painful victory over repression reflects the vastly more destructive dislocations occasioned by a whole society's coming of age psychologically. The two levels of the novel's action interrelate in the character of a fictionalized Sigmund Freud, who sketches in the psychological profile of his age in the course of treating one of its representative figures.

Entropic Stasis: *The Leopard*

Readers of *The Leopard* respond with pleasure to the evidence, from page to page, of a literary craftsmanship nothing less than architectonic. The author, Giuseppe Tomasi di Lampedusa, explores a major turning point in the history of modern Italy with subtle emphasis on the way social realities qualify naive assumptions about historical change. The complexity of Lampedusa's historicism emerges in his balancing of characters who enact or express the millenarian expectations of the Risorgimento against characters who cynically suggest that the more things change in Italy, the more they remain the same. But those immersed in the dialectic of liberal dream and conservative cynicism, says the author, miss the actual slippage attendant on this particular turning point. Unmoved by the myth of emergent national unity, Lampedusa laments the decline of a culture; he charts the course of social and historical entropy.

The author chronicles the changes that took place in 1860 and 1861 when Victor Emmanuel, ably lieutenanted by Garibaldi, united the petty kingdoms of Italy under a single crown. Almost as historically significant as the upheaval that took place at the end of the eighteenth century in France, the reunification of Italy brought with it democratic ideas and institutions, but as one sees in Lampedusa's account of the plebescite at Donnafugata (a miniature study in the political corruption that has since plagued Italian democracy), the hopes and ideals of the new order could not forestall disillusionment. The author argues, as Furio Felcini notes, "the failure, on the social and political plane, of the Italian Risorgimento."[2] Historical circumstances, however, figure in the novel largely as background, for Lampedusa treats changes in the political sphere only as they make themselves felt in the social sphere. He therefore sketches in all gradations of the social scale in nineteenth-century Sicily: effete aristocrats like the Salinas, embattled churchmen like Father Pirrone, parvenus like the Sedàras, petty bourgeois and decent peasants like Don Fabrizio's retainers at Donnafugata, and even degraded peasants like Peppe 'Mmerda, dung-redolent father-in-law to Don Calogero Sedàra.

The drama that emerges concerns the inevitable capitulation of the aristocratic Don Fabrizio to the social-climbing of the opportunistic Sedàras. This family moves, in three generations, from the peasantry to the middle class to the new elite of money and liberal politics—all in the course of Don Fabrizio's life. The wealth, power, and influence of the Prince decline proportionately, and he stoically observes the crumbling of his world. He has his faults, but he remains admirable as the twilight of the old order gives way to night. A perfect gentleman, he never succumbs to the temptation to behave ungraciously to the despicable Don Calogero, with whom he must perforce negotiate a mésalliance.

This marriage, between his nephew Tancredi and Don Calogero's daughter Angelica, becomes the central symbol of a new Sicilian order and thus a thematic focal point in the story. Don Fabrizio, who understands what is afoot with cold-eyed clarity, sees the larger significance of Tancredi's poverty and opportunism, as well as that of Angelica's social climbing. Though he perceives that "neither of them was good, each full of self-interest,"[3] he does not impede the match, for he understands that it is done—for his own doomed class, at least—faute de mieux. He knows, as Dr. Johnson once said, that it does a man no good to whine.

But the major task of analysis falls to the narrator, who knows the future and reminds the reader of it from time to time in an ironic aside: "Those were the best days of the life of Tancredi and Angelica, lives later to be so variegated, so erring, against the inevitable background of sorrow. . . . Those days were the preparation for a marriage which, even erotically, was no success" (p. 188). Yet however cynical, the narrator seems willing to give youth, beauty, and ardor their due. He is, in other words, very like Don Fabrizio himself, and thus his evocation of the engagement—though punctuated with reminders that these young people are hardly paragons of any of the standard virtues, along with hints that their marriage will not run smoothly—unfolds with a simple yet affecting lyricism. Charged, too, with erotic energy, the narrator's account of this courtship draws readers into the amorous scene and makes them as resistant to the voice of sober or cynical experience as are the lovers.

At the same time, however, one recognizes that Angelica and Tancredi represent their respective classes, each approaching the imminent union with a calculation that—at a personal level and at the national, political level—dooms the match. Angelica, the newly rich bourgeoise, has determined to secure for herself the perquisites of rank. Tancredi, the impoverished aristocrat, offers to barter an old name for a sufficiently grand dowry. When he embraces Angelica, he does so with an "atavistic" sense of possession: "he really felt as if by those kisses he were taking possession of Sicily once more, of the lovely faithless land which the Falconeris had lorded over for centuries and which now, after a vain revolt, had surrendered to him again, as always to his people, its carnal delights and its golden crops" (p. 178). Don Ciccio Tumeo, the Prince's retainer, comes closer to the truth when he calls the marriage "unconditional surrender. It's the end of the Falconeris, and of the Salinas too" (p. 143).

The turning point seen in the alliance of Sedàra and Falconeri has its reflection among the peasantry, for the changes in the Italian social picture embrace all classes. A sense of the ultimate connectedness of the various social and political factions emerges in chapter 5; Father Pirrone visits his birthplace and straightens out a family quarrel, arranging the marriage of his pregnant niece, Angelina, and his cousin, Santino. Some readers have faulted this episode as a lapse in the novel's unity, but the seeming *divagazione*, as the Italian critics call it, actually functions as a comic analogue to the main plot, which it burlesques point for point. Thus the gentry of the main plot has its peasant equivalent in the family of the late Don Gaetano Pirrone, landowner and paterfamilias. Don Gaetano's brother Turi, who considers himself cheated out of part ownership of an almond grove, feuds with the luckier half of the family and may even encourage his son Santino to get Angelina "in trouble." The upshot of this less-than-ingenuous courtship is the re-alliance of the two sides of the family—the smug haves and the pushy have-nots. The marriage—another mésalliance—provides a comic recapitulation of the match between Tancredi and Angelica. Each courtship takes place in the St. Martin's summer of 1860, and each involves a cousin. An uncle—Don Fabrizio, Father Pirrone—plays a major role in the successful conclusion of nuptial negotiations. Each story involves somewhat hypocritical notions about chivalry and honor—most comically in the Vergaesque "rustic chivalry" of Vincenzino, the pregnant girl's father, more seriously in Tancredi's nun-raping jest, which sows the seeds of both his own and his cousin Concetta's later unhappiness. Father Pirrone, son and nephew of the feuding brothers and chief architect of the reconciliation, sums up the events he has witnessed: "that brutish love-affair come to fruition in St. Martin's summer, that wretched half almond grove reacquired by means of calculated courtship, seemed to him the rustic poverty-stricken equivalent of other events recently witnessed" (p. 242).

The author includes this episode as a commentary on the prospects for economic justice in Sicily. Father Pirrone says of the aristocracy: "If, as has often happened before, this class were to vanish, an equivalent one would be formed straight away with the same qualities and the same defects" (pp. 231–32). But any such revolution would have to be effected in the dubious manner seen in San Cono: someone—only the vernacular will do here—would have to get "screwed." In the main plot, the moribund aristocracy gives ground not to some idea of democracy or economic justice but to a rapacious middle class that will benefit in its turn from economic inequality. In the San Cono subplot, by the same token, the reader sees that the outcome of any attempt at redistribution of wealth would be either to make poverty universal (the almond grove cannot support all of those with a claim to it) or to rearrange—superficially and inadequately—the patterns of haves and have-

nots. This second alternative is the more likely. Though Santino and Angelina gain half an almond grove, it may well
prove too little to support them. Turi, on the other hand,
gains nothing but the satisfaction of posthumously squaring
accounts with his brother. The financial status of Angelina's
parents, meanwhile, remains unchanged only because Father
Pirrone gives up his patrimony to placate his brother-in-law—
a gesture that recalls the sacrifices the church at large is being
compelled to make in the revolutionary world beyond San
Cono. Social and economic change, Lampedusa suggests, seldom results in a more just order—at least in Sicily.

This vision receives elaboration at every turn, for the author
seldom misses the opportunity to undercut the shallow optimism of the age's liberals, those who support Garibaldi and
the Piedmontese. Don Ciccio Ferrara, the Palermo accountant,
speaks to Don Fabrizio of "glorious new days for this Sicily
of ours" (p. 45), and Russo, one of the Prince's larcenous
vassals, looks to the liberal millennium with dewy eyes: "Afterward . . . we'll have liberty, security, lighter taxes, ease,
trade. Everything will be better" (p. 47). Yet even this enthu-
siast interjects a paradoxical qualification: "Honest and able
men will have a chance to get ahead, that's all. The rest will
be as it was before" (pp. 47–48). Don Fabrizio sifts these
sentiments and thinks: "all will be the same. Just as it is now:
except for an imperceptible shifting around of classes" (p. 48).

The idea that change tends to prove superficial seems to
typify the history of this island so often invaded over the
centuries, and to such scant effect. The author may expect
his readers to reflect that the central political event of the
novel, the landing of the Garibaldini in 1860, resembles the
invasion of Sicily by the Americans and British in 1943. Indeed, as Archibald Colquhoun notes, Lampedusa considered
concluding his novel with "a . . . chapter to be based on the
actual arrival of the American troops."[4] That the novel does

not end this way suggests a disinclination on the author's part to tïp the scales too far in the direction of a cyclical vision of history, for in the last analysis he allows the reader to see that the proposition "things remain the same in Sicily regardless of social or political change" must be understood in a larger context. Such stasis remains ultimately entropic, for every change takes the nation further from the ideals of humanity, service, and noblesse oblige that characterize the old aristocracy at its best. By the end, the author introduces an oblique reference to this idea of cycling toward entropic collapse in the remarks of Colonel Pallavicino at the Ponteleone ball. In an augury of the new nation's lapse into fascism and its prolonged flirtation with communism, Pallavicino observes that though the red shirts have had their heyday and their minor setbacks, "they'll be back again. When they've vanished, others of different colors will come; and then red ones again" (p. 270).[5]

Lampedusa, then, takes the tragic view of Italian politics, which he conceives in a strange double vision, a paradox: things remain the same, yet they get worse. The paradox receives its definitive expression in Tancredi's remark in defense of his own acquiescence in the new order: "If we want things to stay as they are, things will have to change" (p. 40). This pronouncement takes on ironic meanings as "things" develop. The ironies, in fact, are multiple, and only half-grasped by Tancredi himself. Tancredi thinks he can circumvent the forces of change, but he misconstrues the sameness of the future. He sees, like Don Fabrizio, that for all the dislocations, the elbowing aside of one class by another, the end result seems merely another version of the status quo ante. Though those in a dominant position have changed, power and wealth remain unevenly distributed. He fails, however, to recognize the accompanying moral slippage. In the replacement of a chivalric myth (and its attendant ethos) by an ethic of political chicanery, the moral justification for such inequalities as will always dog economic institutions becomes even less defensible. In the name of progress, civilization loses ground.

The ironies of political change, as Lampedusa conceptualizes them, extend back through Italian history to Machiavelli, the quondam liberal who wrote a famous manual for princes and called for the reunification of Italy three centuries before Garibaldi and Victor Emmanuel. When Don Fabrizio, who prefers a position forthright and aboveboard in his dealings with family, peers, and social inferiors, feels "vexation at having to conduct delicate negotiations . . . with the use . . . of precaution and cunning alien to his presumably leonine nature" (p. 119), he forgets the lesson of Machiavelli: a prince must combine aggressive and bold policy with more cunning, less forthright, behavior. The prince, in other words, must combine the political virtues of the lion and the fox. But necessity is a good teacher, and eventually Don Fabrizio becomes the true Machiavellian prince, a blend of the pardlike attributes of his family emblem and the vulpine craft necessary to survival when the hounds of social and political change begin to bay.

The author quite deliberately rejects the older symbolism of the medieval beast fable, in which the fox, Renard, represents a resourceful middle class that tends to have its way with the aristocratic lion. Thus Don Calogero is repeatedly characterized as at best a jackal with vulpine aspirations. When he arrives to negotiate the marriage contract between his daughter and Tancredi, "he would have looked like a jackal had it not been for eyes glinting intelligence; but as this intelligence of his had a material aim opposed to the abstract one to which the Prince's was supposed to tend, this was taken as a sign of slyness" (p. 145). In a conversation with a fellow aristocrat who has made his peace with the Renards of their world, the Prince will reflect: "We were the Leopards, the Lions; those who'll take our place will be little jackals, hyenas" (p. 214).[6]

The fellow aristocrat, Chevalley, visits Don Fabrizio to encourage him to accept a seat in the new senate, to "collaborate." The Prince, refusing, delivers a small lecture about the meaning of Sicilian conservatism, and here, according to Olga Ragusa, "the public themes of the historical novel . . . reach their acme."[7] Chevalley tries to invoke the plight of Sicily's poor, but the Prince knows that the poor they always have with them. One of the clearest expressions of the gulf between liberal and conservative—a gulf hardly limited to nineteenth-century Sicily—occurs in the juxtaposed thoughts of these two men: "Chevalley thought, 'This state of things won't last; our lively new modern administration will change it all.' The Prince was depressed: 'All this shouldn't last; but it will, always; the human "always," of course, a century, two centuries . . . and after that it will be different, but worse'" (p. 214).

Yet Don Fabrizio also expresses the profound human yearning for order, stability, and continuity. He imagines a more positive stasis that would not be merely the ironic by-product of superficial change. This yearning finds expression in his interest in astronomy, for like Yourcenar's Hadrian he looks to the heavens for an example of perfect order. An amateur astronomer of some repute, he thinks of the stars as "incapable of producing anxiety" (p. 102). The precision of the calculations that can predict stellar movements is for the Prince "a triumph of the human mind's capability to project itself and to participate in the sublime routine of the skies" (p. 54). When he leaves the ball at the Palazzo Ponteleone, Don Fabrizio decides to walk home, desiring "to draw a little comfort from gazing at the stars. There were still one or two up there, at the zenith. As always, seeing them revived him; they were omnipotent, and at the same time they were docile to his calculations; just the contrary to human beings, always too near, so weak and yet so quarrelsome" (p. 272). Ironically, he has missed the import of another unsettling remark by Pallavicino, who observed earlier in the evening that "even fixed stars are so only in appearance" (p. 271).[8]

The same holds for the polestar—including the symbolic one in the "constellation of family miniatures" (p. 200) at Donnafugata. "In the center of the constellation, acting as a kind of polestar, shone a bigger miniature; this was of Don Fabrizio himself" (p. 201). But just as Polaris enjoys only a seeming immunity to time and chance, so must the secure station of Don Fabrizio prove subject to decay. He, too, faces eventual dislocation; he, too, drifts toward dissolution.

All of the novel's astronomical images illustrate or comment ironically on developments in the human sphere. These images range from the pointed—"the sun was back on its throne like an absolute monarch kept off it for a week by his subjects' barricades" (p. 111)—to the casual: a reference to Tancredi's eye "in temporary eclipse" (p. 67), say, or to San Cono's "planetary" distance from the "Palermo sun" (p. 219). But gradually the idea of astronomy, the order of the heavens, coalesces in the image of "always faithful" Venus, Don Fabrizio's sensuous lodestar: "When would she decide to give him an appointment less ephemeral, far from carcasses and blood, in her own region of perennial certitude?" (p. 273).

This question, which concludes the sixth chapter, receives its answer at the end of the seventh, when Don Fabrizio dies in a scene reminiscent of that depicted in Greuze's *Death of the Just Man*, a copy of which had caught the Prince's eye in the library of the Ponteleone palace years earlier. Among those gathered around his bed, the Prince notices the mysterious figure of "a young woman, slim, in a brown traveling dress and wide bustle, with a straw hat trimmed by a speckled veil which could not hide the sly charm of her face" (p. 291). Only the dying Don Fabrizio sees her, for "it was she, the creature forever yearned for, coming to fetch him . . . . When she was face to face with him she raised her veil, and there, modest, but ready to be possessed, she looked lovelier than she ever had when glimpsed in stellar space" (pp. 291–92). This vision, however, issues from the fevered mind of a dying man, and in embracing Venus under such circumstances he becomes neither Mars nor Adonis. A sterile Anchises perhaps, he sires no new Ilio-Italic hero. In yearning for Venus, as in imagining that the asteroids he has discovered will "spread the fame of his family through the empty spaces between Mars and Jupiter" (p. 19), he dreams of becoming an Olympian, but the days for such heroic translations into the heavens are past.

Their passing has been hastened by Garibaldi, twice associated with the humorless husband of Don Fabrizio's mythological beloved. When the Prince first makes the comparison, he dismisses the ill-favored god and his human counterpart as "a cuckold" (p. 61). But in the myth Vulcan has the last laugh on Venus and her lover, whom he humbles by netting them in flagrante delicto. Thus at the end, Don Fabrizio must admit that "that fellow Garibaldi, that bearded Vulcan, had won after all" (p. 286).

The allusions to Vulcan and Venus fit into a larger pattern of mythological imagery that complements the astronomical references and contributes to the theme of decline. The author introduces this pattern in the opening scene's "Rococo dining room" (p. 15), on the ceiling of which gods and goddesses gamely elevate the Salina coat of arms. But the story to come will reveal that this coat of arms, along with its Olympian retainers, is already passing into desuetude. Scenes from mythology also decorate the floor. The images on the floor gradually emerge in the course of this scene, as priestly soutane and the dresses of pious women withdraw. Though this room belongs, for twenty-three and a half hours a day, wholly to its mythological guardians and what Lampedusa elsewhere calls their "rude energy" (p. 60), the reader soon learns that the gods and the family here celebrated pictorially exist only on sufferance, eclipsable at any time by a newer faith and a newer social order.

In the novel's conclusion, which takes place in the same room, the reader hears nothing of these gods and goddesses, and one wonders if perhaps they have suffered the same fate as those in the "mythological scene" effaced for the chapel created by the three pious sisters. Only the cockatoos and monkeys seem to remain—symbols of vanity and the world's evil. The gods and goddesses seem already to have gone the way of those on the ceiling of the ballroom at the Palazzo Ponteleone, who "thought themselves eternal; but a bomb manufactured in Pittsburg, Pennsylvania, was to prove the contrary in 1943" (p. 258). As John Gilbert has shown in his examination of "the metamorphosis of the divine in *Il Gattopardo* and its accompanying theme of demythification," the author represents the decay of a world by means of abundant examples of old gods, old heroes, and old values slipping into superannuation: "They are no longer immune, as were the gods of old, to the impact of reality, to the effects of time and history."[9]

This kind of decay has its classic expression in the breakdown of those myths of sacrifice and rebirth celebrated in the ancient world—myths glanced at explicitly when, early in *The Leopard*, Don Fabrizio wonders about the miserable death of the man whose corpse he has found in his garden. Lampedusa, a cultured and well-read man, would have known the lines from *The Waste Land*: "That corpse you planted last year in your garden,/Has it begun to sprout?" Eliot's bizarre image, an allusion to the mythic scapegoat-god whose sacrifice brings annual fructification, contributes to a meditation on the spiritual deadness of a cultural environment in which sacrifice proves meaningless. In Lampedusa's hands this motif of the unredemptive sacrifice makes its contribution to another version of spiritual inadequacy. The soldier in Don Fabrizio's garden, his disembowelment suggestive of sparagmos, is a surrogate for the dying and reviving god—for Dionysus, say, to whom the leopard is sacred. The soldier supposedly dies "for the King, who stands for order, continuity, decency, honor, right; for the King, who is sole defender of the Church, sole bulwark against the dispersal of property" (p. 22). But Don Fabrizio cannot convince himself of the efficacy of the sacrifice. The sacrifice fails, the king fails, and a world perishes.

The decline of an ancient order, overtly treated in the més-alliance of Tancredi and Angelica, in the rise of the Sedàras, and in the play of astronomical and mythological imagery, receives its most subtle expression in the tone of the narrator. The reader encounters extraordinary control in every aspect of the author's narrative technique—most notably in the re-sourceful handling of the center of consciousness, Don Fabrizio. Lampedusa never allows the narration to go slack, for even when he departs from Don Fabrizio he supplies a sur-rogate or a successor. Thus Father Pirrone becomes a credible stand-in for the main character in the narrational sidetrip to San Cono; and in the visit to the three sisters at the end, the reader remains close to the Prince's successor, Concetta, last member of the family to show anything like the old spirit. In chapter 4, the perceptions of Don Fabrizio, emphasized at the beginning and the end, effectively bracket the scenes with Tancredi and Angelica, so that one follows them on their amorous rambles through the palace at Donnafugata as if in the mind of that pile's feudal lord.

The narrational mastery reveals itself also in such details as the narrator's incremental self-assertion and in the increas-ingly insistent references to a modern perspective. Self-effac-ing through the first third of the novel, the narrator suddenly, in chapter 3, tosses in an analogy from modern jet travel. Subsequently, the narrator's asides and comparisons take in Freud, suburban transportation in the twentieth century, tu-berculosis researcher Robert Koch, and the Soviet film-maker Eisenstein. The narrational intrusions, by no means gratui-

tous, all take as their tenor some "revolutionary" manifesta-
tion: psychoanalysis, modern travel and medicine, the cinema,
and Soviet Russia. Thus form and content interweave as moments in a story about historical change—radical historical
change—are illustrated with reference to radical changes in
psychology, transportation, disease control, art, and later history. The postponement of the narrator's self-assertion, along
with the emphasis on twentieth-century analogues, has the
effect of seeming suddenly to accelerate the decline in the
fortunes of the Salinas. One begins the novel with a sense of
temporal proximity to Don Fabrizio, but gradually he becomes
a person of the past. The reader comes to recognize in the
narrator a contemporary, a person in whom knowledge, nos-
talgia, and a saving irony allow a last flicker of an old Sicilian
greatness.

This narrator has much in common with his creator, last
of a family that, like the Salinas, dates back to before the
crusades.[10] The Lampedusa who lives into the middle of the
twentieth century seems to project himself, in the narrator,
as the last scion of the Salinas—perhaps as that same "Paolo
Corbera di Salina" who narrates "The Professor and the Mermaid." But perhaps the narrator's relationship with the family
of the protagonist is best characterized as what Stephen Dedalus would call consubstantial rather than consanguineous.
Don Fabrizio's thoughts never run to grandchildren (only a
nephew), and he mentally refers to himself as "the last of the
Salinas" (p. 285).

Characteristically, the narrator emphasizes the humorous
and the ironic in the scenes and actions described: embracing
Don Calogero, the Prince becomes "a huge violet iris with a
hairy fly hanging from a petal" (p. 149), and indeed Don
Fabrizio's dealings with the dreadful Don Calogero seldom
transpire without some comic aside on the part of the narrator.
But this narrator favors simple humor less than irony—the
irony, for example, of describing the earnest activity in an ant

pile in terms that discover the social and military pretensions of two-legged creatures. The ironic tone carries special meaning, given the modern perspective of the narrative, for irony dominates the literature of an age that has seen the devaluation of all the "big words"—the grand abstractions like glory, honor, *patria*—by which humanity once conferred dignity on its aspirations. A Hemingway character, in a famous passage in *A Farewell to Arms*, debunks "the words sacred, glorious and sacrifice . . . . I had seen nothing sacred, and the things that were glorious had no glory and the sacrifices were like the stockyards at Chicago if nothing was done with the meat except to bury it." Artists in a world in which these words have lost their meaning find the range of literary expression diminished. In an earlier age, when the validity of certain ideas (of noblesse oblige, for example) went unquestioned, the story of the Salinas would have been heroic, the story of their decline, tragic. But epic and tragedy require a worldview long since exposed as fraudulent. The modern world values nothing so much as irony in its literature—that same irony Northrop Frye calls "the non-heroic residue of tragedy."[11]

One finds striking, in this regard, the observations about irony in the work of Giambattista Vico, the Italian philosopher known for his theory of historical cycles. Language becomes ironic, Vico suggests, toward the end of a given *corso*, or great cycle. As Hayden White interprets Vico, "irony is the mode of consciousness which signals the final dissolution. . . . Underlying this mode of speech is a recognition of the fractured nature of social being, of the duplicity and self-serving of politicians, of an egotism which governs all professions of interest in the common good, of naked power (*dratos*) ruling where law and morality (*ethos*) are being invoked to justify actions."[12] Lampedusa, then, sees his characters in a cultural twilight, which he describes with relentless irony. He names the Prince's nephew, for example, after a heroic character in

Tasso's *Gerusalemme liberata*. This original Tancredi was a crusader, like that Salina ancestor who fought at the siege of Antioch late in the eleventh century, but the novel's Tancredi takes up arms in a more dubious cause. His heroism has little legitimate scope, and his Angelica, named for the pagan heroine of Ariosto's *Orlando Furioso*, eventually cuckolds him.[13]

The archetypal cultural decline mapped by Vico figures in Lampedusa's treatment of the historical macrocosm as well as in his meditation on the microcosmic fortunes of one great family over time. Vico, borrowing terms from Egyptian cosmology, describes the phases within a given historical cycle as "the age of gods, the age of heroes, and the age of men."[14] Lampedusa recalls the age of gods in allusions to the mythological deities that once held sway in Italy, and in references to the Salinas's splendid past he evokes the age of heroes. But he mentions the ancient glory of the Salinas only to underscore its present vitiation in the age of men, the age that heralds the disintegration that precedes the Viconian *ricorso*. For Vico, this disintegration came with the fall of Rome, but Lampedusa seems to see that event as only the end of the age of heroes, with subsequent history as the age of men. Vico does not, incidentally, characterize the age of men as an age of unremitting squalor, for in its early part it includes the rise of humanistic, democratic, and libertarian ideas. Thus Lampedusa associates this phase with the period between the Renaissance and the Risorgimento: splendid at first, squalid toward the end. But where a naive observer might mistake Italy's reunification for the beginning of a new and promising cycle (as its promoters in fact did), the less sentimental Lampedusa, privileged to have witnessed the fascist debacle and thinking more rigorously about the sweep of history, recognizes in the creation of modern Italy the true waning of the Viconian age of men. With its self-deception, its inflated rhetoric, its phony balloting, and its pretensions to a renewed greatness, the Risorgimento merely sets the stage for the disintegration of the Mussolini era, itself a prelude to the era of the Red Brigades.

The novel ends with a symbolic gesture, the discarding of the stuffed carcass of Bendico, Prince Fabrizio's favorite canine companion. As in Malcolm Lowry's *Under the Volcano,* the corpse of a dog, flung on a midden, focuses the pathos of a miserable and largely futile passing in the novel's last line and last image. This act of disencumbrance climaxes the pathetic sequence of events in which the elderly sisters' large, private collection of relics has come under the scrutiny of the church, whose representative finds that he can certify only five items as authentic. One realizes along with the still spirited Concetta that what little remains of the old Salina glory is, like the discarded relics, mostly rubbish. The dog, so full of life and energy in chapter 1, is "nest now of spiderwebs and of moth" (p. 305) and dead some forty-five years. When a servant flings the carcass out the window, the pathos of the moment briefly gives way to a last bitter irony, hinted at in the description of its transit from window to trash heap: "During the flight down from the window his form recomposed itself for an instant; in the air one could have seen dancing a quadruped with long whiskers, and its right foreleg seemed raised in imprecation" (p. 320). Bendico has become the shabby simulacrum of a proud family's ancient symbol. The dancing gait, the raised paw, the whiskers (great danes do not have whiskers)—all point to a momentary transmogrification from ridiculous canine to proud feline. Thus arrives the long-delayed moment of the leopard's final dissolution, a dissolution postponed for decades by the pretensions of the old Salina ladies. Its paw lifted in "imprecation," the leopard seems to depart with a curse, perhaps on those who have failed to preserve its ancient grandeur, perhaps on a world indifferent to its passing. From *"mortis"* in the first line to "dust" in the last, the novel has been the story of a death, a postponed dissolution—that of the family symbolized by the leopard for more than a thousand years. But in the end, what flies through the air to the trash heap is not a leopard but a malodorous stuffed dog, the more fitting emblem, perhaps, of the family in its decadence, its squalid perishing.

The image also focuses the theme of the turning point, for it concentrates and telescopes the transition from splendor to squalor—or rather allows in the moment of squalor's triumph an ironic glimpse of the former splendor. Yet this emblem of decline subsumes more than the deterioration of a single family. It represents the progressive rot in the social fabric of Italy itself. Lampedusa, then, reveals just how rigorously a novelist can think about and represent history, and Giorgio Bassani rightly praises this author for a "wideness of historical vision joined with the most acute perception of the social and political reality of contemporary Italy, the Italy of today."[15] The author of *The Leopard*, in other words, demonstrates an understanding of the inexorability with which the past shapes the present. The root of the word "entropy" means "a turning," after all, and Lampedusa knows the relationship between turning points and the principle of historical entropy. He knows, too, that lies in and about the past must take their toll in the years that follow.

Abreaction of the West: *The White Hotel*

Lies in and about the past also receive attention in D. M. Thomas's *The White Hotel*, the story of a woman whose struggle for self-knowledge and self-mastery parallels a similar struggle on the part of civilization as a whole. Thomas makes the mind of his heroine, Lisa Erdman, an emblem of modern consciousness. He imagines her the patient of Sigmund Freud and hints that her psychoanalysis proceeds at the same rate as the larger psychological liberation that Freud effected in

Western culture. But just as Lisa undergoes an "abreaction," a harrowing release of repressed emotions, so civilization must pay the price of its own dark compact with repression. Thomas suggests that civilization undergoes a collective abreaction in the war that began only seven days after the death of Freud, the war that claims Lisa Erdman as one of its earliest victims.

Thomas seeks the turning point of the twentieth century in the psychoanalytic genesis of the century's violence. Yet if *The White Hotel* concerns the currents of twentieth-century history, it also concerns a great many other things—or rather it brings together a great many things as part of its historical inquiry. To deal adequately with this novel, at any rate, one must avoid forcing its historicism. I mean, therefore, in my discussion of Thomas's achievement, to go beyond the strict confines of the present study's subject matter. But what I have to say about the historical insights of this novel will, I think, be t.ıe clearer and more cogent for the broader approach, for these insights emerge in part from the author's calculated subversion of twentieth-century science and metaphysics, and in part from his handling of a venerable theme: the multitudinous ways in which appearance and reality diverge. The author realizes these ends through a complex layering of fictive elements: he deploys several narrative voices, he doubles or mirrors his plot details, he introduces echoes of myth, and, most importantly, he chronicles the entire course of his central character's psychoanalysis.

With its gradual penetrating of the psyche's elaborate and destructive defenses, psychoanalysis is an ideal structural device for a fiction concerning appearance and reality. The Freudian therapist deals with a world of deceptive appearances that he or she must pierce before reaching psychological bedrock. Indeed, the system resembles those forms of philosophical idealism based on the idea—it has roots in Christian, Gnostic, and Neoplatonic thought—that imperfect sensory apparatus make direct apprehension of a hidden reality difficult. But Freudian psychoanalysis does not countenance an ultimately transcendental reality. Freud rejected all forms of supernaturalism. Though he saw that the unconscious lies beneath many layers of repression, he resolutely refused to believe that the psychic mechanisms he studied might have ontological or epistemological analogues. Thus in his writings he often refers to a positivistic "reality principle" that the healthy mind must recognize and accept. For this principle Freud favored a Greek word, *ananke*, and his fictional counterpart in Thomas's novel puns on it when he makes "Anna G."—he would pronounce the "G" hard—the case-history pseudonym for Lisa Erdman.

But at the same time that he exploits the formal convenience of Freudian procedure, the author of *The White Hotel* subverts the positivistic (not to mention male-centered) assumptions of Freudian theory. Undermining these assumptions, Thomas undermines the vaunted empiricism of science itself and thereby makes possible an exciting new esthetic. Because modern art has tended to reflect the secularism of modern science, an artist like Thomas, who calls into question scientific premises, provides himself latitude for a spiritualized art rare indeed in the twentieth century. Consequently, *The White Hotel* proves something of a refreshing anomaly, for it promotes a myth of the human spirit's resilience without shirking consideration of the Holocaust, so reductive of human pretensions to spiritual distinction.

Thomas adopts the onion-peeling technique of psychoanalysis because it demonstrates with great cogency the gulfs between appearance and reality, but as one sees in the fluid symbolism of the white hotel itself and the train journey to and from it, the author also reveals the fallibility of the system's rational and empirical biases. The white hotel, setting for the erotic fantasies produced by Lisa Erdman as part of her psychotherapy, is the embodiment of truth's ambiguity. Lisa's analyst first describes the white hotel as a general symbol of the mother's body, then speaks more specifically of "the haven of security, the white hotel—we have all stayed there—the mother's womb."[16] But like many Freudian hypotheses (as the real-life Freud understood), this one falls short of complete accuracy. The patient comes to see that the white hotel in fact represents her life in its entirety—a view the narrator endorses in the elegiac remarks about the escalating genocide in which Lisa Erdman dies: "a quarter of a million white hotels at Babi Yar" (p. 251). By the end of the novel, then, the reader recognizes the white hotel as corporeal existence.

Lisa arrives at the white hotel by train. As a symbol, the train journey one interrupts to sojourn at the white hotel metamorphoses repeatedly until its real significance emerges. When Thomas's fictional Freud interprets Lisa's dream of debarking from a train *in the middle of nowhere* (p. 102) as a fantasy of death, he forgets that the fantasies of the white hotel *begin* with a train journey. He fails, in other words, to recognize in the train symbol a hint of an existence that precedes corporeal life and continues after it. In the fantasy with which the novel ends, Lisa and her fellow sufferers debark from their train "in the middle of nowhere" (p. 257) once again, only to find their lives continuing in an astral Palestine. Lisa's death at Babi Yar has been described in the chapter entitled "The Sleeping Carriage," and one sees readily enough that the image of the sleeping carriage refers to death—as it does in Nabokov's "Spring in Fialta." But when the passengers in Thomas's sleeping carriage debark in the hereafter, the reader comes to understand that in life human beings are sleeping travelers, only vaguely aware of transit and often ignorant of their ultimate destination. In death they awake and return to the reality that corporeal life temporarily obscures.

Lisa's train fantasies fit into a larger pattern of mental attributes beyond the purview of traditional psycholoanalysis.

Though the character based on Freud helps Lisa resolve her oedipal fixation and its numerous complications, he never altogether relieves his patient's fear of bearing children, her shortness of breath, or the pains in her breast and pelvis. By the same token, he never really accounts for the recurrent fantasy of bodies falling through the air. These symptoms and fantasies refer less to Lisa's childhood traumas than to her tragic fate at Babi Yar. Like the train fantasies, they are the manifestations of her prescience.

Freud was prepared to believe in the existence of this phenomenon, but he made relatively little effort to make a place for it in his system—an odd omission in one who otherwise balked at no strangeness of the mind.[17] The fictional Freud writes to Lisa: "My experience of psychoanalysis has convinced me that telepathy exists. If I had my life to go over again, I should devote it to the study of this factor" (p. 196). This passage is based on a letter the real Freud wrote—from Bad Gastein, interestingly enough—to a man soliciting his support for parapsychological research: "I am not one of those who dismiss *a priori* the study of so-called psychic phenomena as unscientific, discreditable or even as dangerous. If I were at the beginning rather than at the end of a scientific career, as I am today, I might possibly choose just this field of research, in spite of all difficulties." Freud concludes this letter with a characteristically tough-minded statement about the implications of clairvoyance: "I am utterly incapable of considering the 'survival of the personality' after death even as a scientific possibility."[18]

Though his novel does not include that statement, Thomas seems to have conceived *The White Hotel* as a reply to it. He offers a poetic vision that comprehends more than the Freudian system, for the careful reader discovers that psychoanalysis accounts for only half of Lisa Erdman's psychic reality—the half that exists in the past. Lisa's analyst fails to realize that many of her symptoms and fantasies refer forward as well as backward; indeed, some make sense only as clairvoyant responses to the future. Collectively, these symptoms and fantasies offer a key to her instinctual identity at both ends of life's spectrum. The novel's Freud views the white hotel, for example, as paradisal, but for him such a paradise can exist only in the past, as is seen when he introduces his case history with a reference to "Anna G.'s" childhood as a paradise from which she would be expelled by her mother's death (pp. 99, 108). His colleague Hanns Sachs, a loyal disciple, also sees the white hotel as paradisal: the *"phantasy strikes me as like Eden before the Fall—not that love and death did not happen there, but there was no time in which they could have a meaning"* (pp. 10–11). In emphasizing the timelessness of life at the white hotel, Sachs comes a little closer to the truth than does his master. The idea of timelessness bears on Lisa's prescience, since one way of accounting for foreknowledge is to assume that on some plane the ostensive future event has already happened. The idea of "now" gives up some of its pretensions to uniqueness and absoluteness. Thus from the white hotel of her corporeal existence Lisa looks simultaneously backward to the womb and forward to the afterlife, glimpsing Eden in her past and the Promised Land in her future. Again, corporeal existence partakes of a larger continuum.

Yet one errs to assume that D. M. Thomas despises either psychoanalysis or its creator. Though "Freud comes out . . . looking considerably less authoritative than when the book started," as Mary F. Robertson notes,[19] the startlingly authentic simulation of Freudian case history seems a labor into which Thomas poured not the contempt of the satirist but the enthusiasm of an admirer. If the admirer has reservations, he nevertheless allows the character based on Freud to provide Lisa Erdman, whose symptoms he only half grasps, with substantial assistance in recovering psychological health. Lisa's past, after all, is of great importance to the novel's plot, and it is unlocked—for her and for the reader—by psychoanalysis. Lisa must come to terms with her personal reality, a reality unfaced since childhood. Many of the details in "Don Giovanni" and "The Gastein Journal," the fantasies she produces as part of her psychotherapy, present the traumatic events of her childhood symbolically. Characters in these fantasies turn out to be dramatis personae in the drama of her life; events in the fantasies like the storm, flood, and fire eventually reveal themselves as symbolic renderings of moments in her past, especially those associated with learning of her mother's infidelity and terrible death. Lisa's analyst, with his grasp of the way the repressive forces of the mind encode painful memories, recognizes and treats symptoms generated by— on the one hand—an unbearable knowledge of maternal impurity and—on the other hand—a disabling conviction of personal unworthiness.

Every child, according to Freud's theory of the Oedipus complex, must adjust to maternal betrayal. At some point in childhood one realizes that a third party—the father—has a prior claim to the mother. Lisa's oedipal phase is profoundly complicated by a bizarre situation: the father has himself been supplanted by a lover—or rather by two lovers, since Lisa's mother participates in a ménage à trois with her twin sister and brother-in-law. Lisa's family, with an adulterous mother, a lesbian aunt, and their incestuous arrangement, seems designed to illustrate a famous Freudian thesis concerning maternal appearance and reality. In two of his best-known papers, "A Special Type of Object Choice Made by Men" and "The Most Prevalent Form of Degradation in Erotic Life,"[20] Freud notes and discusses the neuroses growing out of oedipal convictions regarding the purity—or impurity—of the mother. He points out that confusion about the sexuality of women in general and of one's mother in particular leads to the neurotic classification of women as either pure or impure—mothers or harlots.

The ambivalence about maternal sexuality, which in Lisa Erdman manifests itself as confusion about personal purity as well, is behind Thomas's making Lisa's mother a Mary, named after the Virgin, and her aunt a Magda, named after the archetypal prostitute. Thomas gives his heroine names that compound the confusion on this score. Both Elizabeth and Anna are names of women close to the Virgin—her cousin and her mother. But mere nominal propinquity does not satisfy; it expresses at once the wish for and the remoteness from the ideal. Lisa's famous psychotherapist comments on her overdetermined response to a question about masturbation: "I might, her attitude implied, have been asking the question of the Virgin" (p. 100). Lisa's eventual acceptance of the sexual reality behind this pose, not to mention the sexual reality behind her false icon of maternal purity, constitutes a major advance in her progress toward psychological health.

The analyst describes his patient's self-discovery as something analogous to Venus's looking into a mirror and seeing Medusa (p. 8). In his case history he describes Lisa's mother as a Ceres who proves a Medusa (p. 142)—a figure the patient herself adopts (p. 192) when she realizes the extent of her mother's duplicity. The Medusa references, more than a colorful way of characterizing the initial horrors of self-knowledge, provide further light on Lisa's condition. As the real-life Freud suggests in "The Infantile Genital Organization of the Libido," the myth of Medusa projects infantile theories concerning castration of the mother. The ghastly head represents "the genital of the mother"; Freud comments, too, on the significance of the head's being associated with the virgin goddess, for "Athene, who carries the head of Medusa on her armour, becomes by virtue of it the unapproachable, the woman at sight of whom all thought of sexual desire is stifled."[21] Lisa, then, makes progress in resolving her oedipal problems, especially the neurotic desire to be the unapproachable virgin, only when she confronts her most primal fears and misbeliefs. The preceding considerations are adduced to demonstrate that Thomas understands Freudian theory and does justice to the psychoanalytic method—at the same time that he politely suggests that there are more things in heaven and earth than are dreamt of in Freud's philosophy. To be sure, he risks much when he counters Freudian skepticism with speculation about clairvoyance and personal immortality. He risks the contempt of readers who share Freud's impatience with spiritualist mumbo jumbo. But the subtlety with which Thomas undermines the empirical biases of a materialistic age (Freud represents that age perfectly) goes far toward making his case, for he reminds the reader forcefully of reality's multifariousness—what William James called its "buzzing, blooming confusion." One realizes in due course that empiricism may be as likely to lead to error as various forms of philosophical idealism, which at least start from a recognition of the universality with which appearances disguise reality. Thomas therefore renders the teeming surface of deceptive reality and provides clues to take the reader under that surface.

For this reason one encounters an extraordinary number of narrative voices in the novel, even without counting Lisa's ventriloquism in the letters and cards from guests at the white hotel. Frau Erdman produces three types of document: a poetic, freely lyrical fantasy, a fantasy-journal, and some letters to her analyst. The novel's Freud also contributes a number of documents; in addition to letters to fellow psychoanalysts (some of their letters appear too), he produces an exhaustive and ingenious case history, then corresponds with his subject. The last half of the novel (parts 4–6) is the work of an anonymous narrator who takes the reader to the furthest reaches of Lisa Erdman's psychic reality. At several points, to enrich his catalogue of narrative voices, Thomas blends in actual documents (for which he has had to fend off charges of plagiarism): real letters or parts of letters from Freud and his colleagues, and Dina Pronicheva's testimony as it appears in Anatoli Kuznetsov's *Babi Yar*.[22]

The narrative technique nicely suits the novel's special problems of characterization and plot. The "documents," real and imaginary, help to preserve the story's sense of and roots in actuality, for the author has set himself the task of making some sense, if possible, of Babi Yar and its congeners—real history that, though it has generated authentic testimony, has resisted civilized understanding. But the complexity of narrative technique functions most effectively in allowing the reader to participate, as it were, in one woman's battle for psychological equilibrium and self-knowledge. Thus the reader, initially at a level of understanding scarcely more privileged than that of the patient herself, proceeds from hysteric fantasies to the deductions of a master psychoanalyst and the wrenching emotional recognitions—the abreaction—induced by his treatment. As Lisa abreacts, she gains the strength to improve on her analyst's necessarily tentative conclusions. Only after her mind and, up to a point, her body have been healed does the reader proceed more deeply into the mystery of Lisa Erdman. The ultimate level of truth concerns not her body or her mind but her soul, her spiritual reality. This level, inaccessible to her doctors, yields up its secrets only to an artist: the creator of *The White Hotel*.

The author complicates the reader's perception of Lisa's mental and spiritual complexity by a strategy of doubling, mirroring, and paralleling of narrative detail. The novel resembles one of those boxes in which a single toy soldier and an arrangement of mirrors present the eye with a rank of soldiers receding to infinity; to do justice to *The White Hotel*, however, one must imagine such a box with several peepholes, extra mirrors, and a large number of objects for multiple reflection. One sees a good example of this mirroring technique in the handling of Lisa's crucifix, which resembles certain of her fantasies in that it provides a key to both her past and her future. Freud, in the novel, finds the crucifix an invaluable clue to the veracity of his patient, who fumbles with it whenever she departs from the truth in her sessions with him. Eventually he learns that she associates it with the discovery that destroyed forever "the ikon of her mother's goodness" (p. 134). The crucifix had belonged to Lisa's mother, who, angry at familial opposition to her marriage, had torn it from her neck on the day of her wedding. Her twin sister, Lisa's aunt, had continued to wear a crucifix, and this fact eventually forces Lisa to admit, to her analyst and to herself, the identity of the woman naked in the summer house with Uncle Franz on a distant day in Odessa. Though analysis uncovers the buried memory that generates her anxiety, the analyst cannot know that her fumbling with the crucifix and her frequent references to her mother's violent removal of it derive also from her foreknowledge that the same corpse robber that kicks her in the breast and pelvis at Babi Yar will also rip the crucifix from her neck. In the end, in "the camp," the crucifix helps mother and daughter overcome their mutual reticence, the mother saying that Lisa's having kept it pleases her.

The kind of doubling seen with the crucifix receives its most exhaustive treatment in the many character relationships that mirror each other throughout the novel. A number of these reflect the crucial early relationship between Lisa and her mother, the relationship terminated so painfully. In Saint Petersburg, for example, Lisa comes to depend on "Madame R." as on a mother, but in the classical oedipal pattern a third party, a father figure, claims the mother and supplants the child. The pattern remains, though attenuated, after Lisa, in analysis, resolves her oedipal fixation. In Vera Serebryakova Lisa finds another Madame R., another mentor and surrogate mother, though now the relationship does not crumble at the introduction of a husband, Victor Berenstein. In fact, Lisa soon demonstrates her psychological maturity by becoming a Madame R. herself: she makes Lucia, her understudy in Milan, her protégée. Subsequently, she becomes a literal surrogate mother to little Kolya, the child Vera dies giving birth to. But as these replicating relationships recede toward infinity, the mirroring becomes more mysterious, for Vera Serebryakova's fall in Milan seems to echo Lisa's fall in Saint Petersburg, and when Lisa marries Victor little Kolya becomes in some sense the baby Lisa lost in the accident at Madame R.'s dance studio.

Lisa's relationship with Vera and Victor is the most harmonious triangle in a novel that teems with them. Whether in actual relationships within the action of the story or in allusions to such relationships in literature and music, love triangles are everywhere in *The White Hotel.* Lisa, for example, performs with Victor in *Eugene Onegin,* whose action includes a particularly famous triangle, and she later casts the letter accepting Victor's offer of marriage in the form of Tatiana's letter to Onegin. The novel opens, similarly, with Sandor Ferenczi's letter to his beloved "Gisela," a married woman. In that letter, moreover, he reports on a suggestive dream of Freud's, *"in which his sister-in-law (Minna) was having to toss bundles of corn at harvest time, like a peasant, while his wife looked idly on"* (p. 5). The dream hints at something long suspected of the real-life Freud: that he had an affair, like Lisa's Uncle Franz, with his sister-in-law. The fictional Freud remarks at one point that in the summer of 1921 he had met Lisa Erdman, by then his former patient, while vacationing at Bad Gastein "with another member of my family" (p. 143). Later in the novel (p. 182) Lisa reveals that the "member of the family" was indeed Minna. Lisa had been at Bad Gastein at least once before, on the visit that inspired "Don Giovanni" and "The Gastein Journal," and part of the eroticism of these fantasies may derive from a prescient awareness or anticipation of her analyst's philandering.

The proliferating love triangles contribute to one's sense of the difficulty of sorting erotic realities from their manifold deceptive appearances. In addition, along with the novel's other doubled and mirrored elements, the triangles discover a world of fictive artifice, a Joycean demonstration of the possible convolutions of artistic order. But Thomas hints that the perceptions, repressions, and experiences of his heroine reflect, as microcosm, an order more than merely esthetic. He thereby distances himself from those twentieth-century artists who admit to or even insist on the distinction between art and life as the distinction between order and disorder. Forster expresses this idea succinctly in *Two Cheers for Democracy*: "A work of art . . . . is the only material object in the universe which may possess internal harmony."[23] Other writers, from Beckett to Nabokov and from Woolf to Thomas Pynchon and William Gass, have made similar statements—in their work if not in direct pronouncements. Thomas, however, has affinities with the older type of artist whose work reflects a larger, external, divine order. By structuring his novel as a psychoanalytic case history, by multiplying narrative voices, and by doubling characters and plot details, the author of *The White Hotel* creates an interlocking, cohesive whole, and this esthetic harmony gradually reveals itself as an image of the larger order of which one's individual life and experiences are a part.

But from the vantage of most individuals, the larger harmony remains obscure. Lisa wonders, in the crucial passage of a letter to her analyst, "whether life is good or evil" (p. 192). The question, central to the novel, occurs to her when she reflects on something she had witnessed in childhood, the primal scene that forever complicates the story's Ur-triangle, Lisa's Oedipus complex. She had come upon her mother, aunt, and uncle making love on a yacht—a scene that, having made an indelible impression on her mind, reappears in the fantasy of herself, the young man, and Madame Cottin at the white hotel and, in more distorted form, in the fantasy of herself, Alexei, and a rival on another yachting weekend. Of the primal scene itself she recalls that one woman, her mother, grimaced while the other, her aunt, smiled. Much later Lisa realizes that even in these facial expressions appearance misrepresented reality: "*the grimacing woman, joyful; and the smiling woman, sad*" (p. 192). But in Lisa's tortured unconscious, mirrors appear within mirrors: she reports the sense of a "reflection" in the scene, because her aunt and her mother were twins, mirror images of each other. Later she develops a mirror phobia; having seen Venus and Medusa reflecting each other, she had despaired of determining which was the reality and which was the specular illusion. But much truth inheres in the impression she retains of "*good and evil coupling, to make the world*" (p. 192). Some ghastly marriage between good and evil would seem to have taken place in a world that can produce, in the same age, a healer like Freud and a tyrant like Hitler.

This idea of the interdependence of good and evil, along with its fearsome realization in the novel, may reflect the controversial Freudian theory of a death instinct that gradually balances and cancels out the libidinal energies of the life instinct. Freud came to believe that the individual psyche, becoming increasingly enamored of its own dissolution, yearns at last to embrace Thanatos. The fictional Freud, believing that Lisa Erdman's writings "lend support" (p. 8) to this hypothesis, sees his patient as "someone in whom an hysteria exaggerated a *universal* struggle between the life instinct and the death instinct" (pp. 128–29). Yet ironically he does not recognize the figure who embodies Thanatos in the white hotel fantasy. Together, he and Lisa identify most of the persons in the fantasy, but neither accounts satisfactorily for the young man with whom Lisa imagines amorous abandonment. Patient and analyst run through a fairly extensive list of possibilities, beginning with the initial identification as Freud's son and proceeding through the men who play roles in Lisa's life. According to the case-history summation, "the young man is from time to time (or even at the same time) Anna's father, brother, uncle, her lover A, her husband, and even the unimportant young man on the train from Odessa" (pp. 141– 42). Lisa herself eventually concludes that she had based the phantom lover on "*a very young impertinent waiter*" (p. 183) at Bad Gastein; repressed ardor and a fevered imagination elevate this supernumerary to the status of wish-fulfillment Don Juan, the "Don Giovanni" who gives his name to the lyric fantasy with which the novel opens. But the mystery and potency of the young man, not to mention the intensity of the erotic fantasy woven around him, would seem to invite further consideration; one suspects, indeed, that he reifies the death instinct.

The idea of a strange affinity between love and death has figured prominently in Western culture for centuries. The Renaissance notion that every orgasm shortens life by some small degree, not to mention the Renaissance pun on the verb "to die" (the pun itself refuses to die), survives in the idea Lisa's analyst finds so intriguing: orgasm as "*la petite mort*" (p. 129). Thus the long, drawn out, lubricious affair at the white hotel has its bizarre fulfillment when Lisa Erdman dies in parodic intercourse. Bayoneted through the vagina, she "jerked back and relaxed, jerked and relaxed" (p. 249) in a ghastly simulacrum of erotic transport. Her end, another version of "good and evil coupling, to make the world," conflates love and death in the novel's single most appalling image.

The mysterious symbioses under consideration here—good and evil, love and death—also figure in myth, which the author of *The White Hotel* exploits to make even more resonant the probing of illusion and truth in the mind of Lisa Erdman and in the world with which she grapples. Myth resembles artifice in that its prominence in twentieth-century literature reflects largely secular purposes; its role as structural device, for example, has displaced its older role as an expression of the sacred, what Freud's rebellious disciple Jung called the *numinosum*. Unlike most moderns (one would have to except Lawrence), Thomas exploits both the structural and spiritual resources of myth. In the "Author's Note" he defines myth as "a poetic, dramatic expression of a hidden truth," and he finds such truth not only in "the great and beautiful modern myth of psychoanalysis" but also in classical and Christian myths. The most prominent of these, the Christian or quasi-Christian myth of the afterlife with which the novel ends, risks an outrageous pietism, but Thomas avoids Christian apologetics by allowing allusions to other, complementary classical myths to precede and qualify the message of the conclusion.

As noted previously, both Lisa and her psychotherapist refer to familiar figures of mythology like Ceres, Venus, and Medusa to illustrate the workings of her unconscious. Though largely incidental, these allusions should alert the reader to other possibilities, for Thomas associates his heroine with the earth mother and with her priestess, Daphne. One sees her affinity with the earth in her surnames, Erdman and the initial "G." The "G," as pronounced in German, becomes one of the names of the Greek earth mother, Ge. "Ge" happens to be the title of a poem by Thomas that appears in the early collection *Two Voices*.[24] In this poem he imagines the "Crone goddess" as a slatternly creature living in a dark basement (space) illuminated by a single light bulb (the sun). Abandoned and desperate, she eyes a newly erected radio-telescope intended to listen for extraterrestrial communication. "A watched phone," however, "never rings." The "potent stranger-god. . . . called maybe when she lay un-/conscious, or will try her unrecorded number at random when the dead receiver hangs dead from its wire. . . ." Inasmuch as Ge is literally the earth, the poem appears on the page in circular form. Published thirteen years after the poem, *The White Hotel* suggests that

Thomas continues intrigued with the earth mother, for the flood and fire that recur in the fantasies of Lisa Erdman are proverbially the first and last great ordeals of the earth and its inhabitants.

The earth goddess with whom Thomas associates Lisa most directly is Cybele, sometimes described in mythology as the daughter of Ge. Cybele's lover Attis castrated himself under a pine tree, which became sacred to the goddess. Lisa has an affinity with pine trees; on her visit to Odessa with Victor and Kolya she finds in the scent of pines an intimation of immortality. The novel ends, too, with a reference to the mythic tree: "she smelt the scent of a pine tree. She couldn't place it. . . . It troubled her in some mysterious way, yet also made her happy" (p. 274). Lisa's Attis may be the courtly Richard Lyons, whose amputation is a symbolic displacement of Attis's wound.

But Thomas associates Lisa most consistently with Daphne, the earth mother's priestess, rather than with the earth mother herself. Both "Don Giovanni" and "The Gastein Journal" begin with the fantasy of flight, Lisa's psychic anticipation of Dina Pronicheva's escape from the death pit at Babi Yar. In the fantasy the desperate woman imagines being turned into a tree, as Daphne was when she fled Apollo; her wrestling with the iron ring of a trapdoor in the ground recalls her mythic allegiance to the earth. According to some versions of the myth (those of Pausanias and Apollodorus), Daphne is not turned into a tree but rather spirited away to Crete, where she becomes Pasiphaë. Lisa, of course, will be similarly spirited away to Palestine, where she, too, undergoes a name change, adopting her mother's maiden name. Her existence beyond nominal death recalls the symbolism of the laurel's never-fading foliage. Like the laurel, the pine she smells at the end is an evergreen, an emblem of immortality.

Like so many elements in the novel, the myth has a double reference. It refers backward to Lisa's therapy and forward to her fate. As a hysteric, Lisa flees all the things represented by Apollo: healing, self-knowledge, surrender to Eros. He is also the divine patron of her psychic gift. But she also flees a literal rape, consummated terribly at Babi Yar, where she succumbs to the Nazis' "Apollonian" rationale, the idea of imposing order on the chaos of Europe.

With myth, then, as with narrative technique, Thomas adds further strands to the fictive web that reproduces at once the world of phenomenal appearances and the complex realities they veil: realities of history, realities of consciousness, and realities of the spirit. Thomas hints at these realities in the novel's epigraph:

> We had fed the heart on fantasies,
> The heart's grown brutal from the fare;
> More substance in our enmities
> Than in our love . . .

These lines, from Yeats's "Meditations in Time of Civil War," introduce a novel that, like the poem itself, concerns the enmities of the twentieth century and the failures of love. Moreover, in balancing "fantasies" against "substance," Yeats addresses the theme of appearance and reality that will figure centrally in the book. The poet laments the dominance of enmity over love; love's seat is the heart, and if it is not fed on something more substantial than fantasies, it starves, grows "brutal." D. M. Thomas, like Yeats, invites readers to consider the effects of unnourishing fantasies. Lisa had fed her heart on such fantasies—narrowly defined maternal and personal virtues— and she had paid the price of a severe hysteria. Her heart had grown brutal, and she had been unable to enjoy a normal affectional life. But more destructive still are the fantasies that afflict whole societies—fantasies of nationalism and guilt and racial hatred. The heart of Western humanity received no sustenance whatsoever from such "fare," and so love faltered, allowing brutality to come into the ascendant.

The personal and public referents of the epigraph merge in the experiences of the novel's heroine, for Lisa Erdman's life touches certain of the important shaping events of the twentieth century. The author places her in Odessa during the abortive revolt of 1905, a trial run for the Russian Revolution of 1917, and in Kiev for one of the earliest and most horrible of the Nazi atrocities. In between, her life touches that of Sigmund Freud, who created, as Auden suggested, the very tenor of modern consciousness. Her father and second husband suffer in the political agony of Russia; her first husband, an Aryan anti-Semite, contributes to the political agony of Germany. Because her life seems to coincide with carnage throughout the twentieth century, one is tempted to see in Lisa an entity like Pynchon's V., the mythic woman who personifies the age's violence and its cumulative disorder. But Lisa symbolizes something at once vaster and more intimate: she is the soul of humanity in modern times. Freud was aware that the phases of the individual's development could serve as a paradigm for the phases through which whole civilizations pass,[25] and Lisa's growth toward self-knowledge, which culminates in psychic maturity and wholeness accompanied by the painful and violent release of repressed emotions, parallels that of Western civilization in the twentieth century. She enacts the moment in Europe's rise to consciousness when an important advance in self-knowledge (the advent of psychoanalysis) coincides with the unleashing of incredible repressed violence, for the intellectual and cultural growth of the West in a sense culminates in the insights of Freud—himself the product of that civilization—and in the catastrophic violence of the culture-wide abreaction that began within a week of his passing.

The reader attentive to these aspects of the novel's meaning will understand the realities of history and consciousness that

Thomas reveals and relates. The reader will also be prepared to venture with Thomas into the possibility that realities of the spirit also exist and can also be uncovered by those adept at winnowing what is from what seems. Thomas suggests not only that World War II was the abreaction of the West but also that the victims of the war, especially the innocent civilians systematically murdered as a result of the Nazi *Vernichtungsbefehl*, must be viewed as the century's sacrificial holocaust. One should remember that "holocaust," which has become the public's thoughtless word for Nazi genocide, refers specifically to a burnt offering, a religious sacrifice, and the Final Solution, Thomas suggests, reenacts the ultimate holocaust— the crucifixion. Thomas's heroine notices that, according to the testimony of the Turin shroud, the crucified Christ was laid out with "the hands placed becomingly over the genitals" (p. 168); subsequently she notices the same modest gesture among those stripped and led to execution at Babi Yar: "she saw that, as the men and women were led through the gap, they all without exception clasped their hands over their genitals. . . . It was the way Jesus had been buried" (pp. 242–43). As the representative victim, the one who focuses the horror of that atrocity, Lisa focuses, too, the sacrificial, Christlike identification. The child of a Mary and of an indeterminate father, this innocent who dies horribly yet lives becomes what she calls another of Freud's patients, "a kind of Christ figure of our age" (p. 193). Part of the irony of the novel, then, lies in Lisa's gradual shift toward the agnosticism espoused by her mother. She muses sadly, for example, over the shroud of Turin, which simply convinces her that Jesus died. She no longer believes in the resurrection and remarks that if a visit to Turin and its famous relic can destroy that much of her faith, a visit to Rome would make an atheist of her. The author, however, arranges for her to go beyond Rome: on the eve of Babi Yar, she prepares for a trip to the Holy Land that not even death itself can forestall.

But the fantasy of Lisa's translation to the hereafter hints at redemptive possibilities the reader may find difficult to credit. Set in a kind of half literal Palestine, half afterlife, the concluding sequence seems a shameful retreat from a responsible facing of unsavory but inescapable horrors, and many readers can accept it only as a piece of calculated irony.[26] An essential critical question about *The White Hotel*, then, is this: Do the religious implications of the conclusion spoil the novel, given the dramatic force of the events and actions that would seem to give them the lie? Is D. M. Thomas, to rephrase the question more simply, what Freud would dismiss contemptuously as a "mystic"?

Thomas's words ask the reader, provisionally at least, to believe in the soul and its survival after death. As he concludes the account of Lisa's terrible suffering, he prepares the reader for what follows by saying: "But all of this"—the horrors of death at Babi Yar—"had nothing to do with the guest, the soul, the lovesick bride, the daughter of Jerusalem" (p. 253). He may mean these words quite literally, and one can read the novel, with its stunning mimesis of one woman's psychological complexity, as an argument that, just as layer upon layer of repression swaddles inner psychic reality, just as the primal, "polymorphous" stirrings of the id can be glimpsed only through the most elaborate—and frequently conjectural—analysis, so beneath the deadening layers of mundane experience might one discover a little ontological surprise: something equally primal and truly aboriginal, something at home, really, only in the timeless hereafter, which it occasionally allows one to glimpse.

But the word "soul" can be merely a rhetorical convenience, time-honored shorthand for "the human essence." Even Freud, in the novel, avails himself of this convenience. In a letter to Lisa he concedes that analysis can never peel away all the psychic layers. "I call to mind a saying of Heraclitus: 'The soul of man is a far country, which cannot be approached or explored"' (pp. 195–96). The author repeats this statement as he reflects on the settling bodies at Babi Yar, remarking that every one of these persons had led a life as complex and as meaningful as the one he has tried to render in something like full detail. Perhaps, then, a broader, more figurative interpretation of the word "soul" would not misrepresent the author's point. One comes thereby to an understanding that the soul of Lisa Erdman, which does not perish, represents the spirit of humanity, which forges on past every individual death.

Thus to concede to D. M. Thomas his imaginative conceit— what Freud dismisses as "the 'survival of the personality' after death"—need not involve the reader in orthodoxy. Like the author of the Immortality Ode, who invokes the Neoplatonic idea of a prenatal existence, Thomas can exploit a myth without—to paraphrase Wordsworth—recommending it to faith. In Thomas's imagined afterlife, in fact, one sees little in the way of transfiguration. Souls arrive in this hereafter with all their afflictions: armless, scarred, burned, emotionally wounded. The problems of life, especially between individuals, do not disappear, though the atmosphere seems conducive to a general healing. (The reader learns of the therapy of Peter Kürten, the psychopath, and Lisa hopes that the understanding she comes to with her mother will be followed by a similar rapprochement with her father.) Thomas makes no mention, finally, of the deity one might expect in an astral Palestine. The great rose that Lisa and her mother see in the sky may recall the *Paradiso,* but where Dante imagined a rose composed on angels, Thomas describes merely the effects of sunlight through dust.

In imagining his characters "emigrating" to another plane, one in which they can try—with better hope of success—to resolve their life problems, Thomas may have been influenced by the Russian poet Marina Tsvetayeva, whose life span (1892–1941) mirrors that of his heroine (1890–1941). Tsvetayeva's views on life and death complement those of the author, who sums them up in "Poem of the Midway": "I know from your poetry/what you think of God, love,/and your life—that suburb/of a town you're exiled from."[27] Simon Karlinsky, in his *Marina Cvetaeva: Her Life and Art*, notes that this poet often imagines in her work a flight from the agony of the modern age.[28] Such a formulation, as long as one intended no imputation of escapism, might describe Thomas's novel as well, but one can also interpret it as an expression of optimism about the ultimate meaning of the darkest and bloodiest hours of a century whose climacteric, World War II, may yet result in a general cultural advance. According to the moving vision of D. M. Thomas, the soul of humanity in the twentieth century, which perishes horribly in the death camps, rises phoenixlike from the ashes, chastened by a terrible knowledge but ultimately indestructible. The reader may therefore understand "the camp" to which Lisa and her fellow-sufferers travel as an idealized Israel,[29] civilization's superego, where European culture can at last reach maturity. There the survivors gather to build anew, to redress the ills defined in that phrase from the novel's epigraph: "More substance in our enmities/ Than in our love." Thus, though one begins *The White Hotel* with Yeats's bleak lines, one comes in the last chapter to the more sanguine words of Canticles: "Many waters cannot quench love, neither can the floods drown it" (p. 261).

In *The White Hotel*, then, D. M. Thomas takes the reader by degrees into the unconscious of Lisa Erdman and gradually converts the psychological life of his heroine into a symbolic treatment of human consciousness in the modern era. The effect of psychological complexity is heightened—at the same time that it is symbolically extended—by tantalizing echoes of myth and by diverse narrative voices. The author casts much of the novel as a case history in which dreams, fantasies, and childhood memories double and mirror each other in an ultimately cohesive design. The mirror of mirrors, however, is the book itself, a *speculum mundi* in which one sees reflected the individual and collective life of a troubled age.

The novel also reflects truth, for the author inventories, in the minds of men and women and in the history of the twentieth century, the subtlety and cunning with which appearance masks that complex abstraction called reality. The word "reality" denotes something enigmatic in the extreme, and the simple verbal label, in isolation, seems to generate its own irony, to decay like a radioactive element, to shade over into its ostensible antithesis. Indeed, Nabokov describes it as "one of the few words which mean nothing without quotes."[30] But the author of *The White Hotel,* a literary artist of extraordinary gifts, treats the subject so insightfully as to dispense with the qualifications and the epistemological failures of courage implicit in those quotation marks. By focusing on the perhaps supernal mysteries of the human psyche, Thomas persuades us of the possibility, at least, of an alternative to the dreary metaphysics of the twentieth century.

5

The Distant Mirror

MANY DISCUSSIONS OF historical fiction center on the assumption that historical novelists find irresistible the temptation to project into the past the concerns of the present, and certainly one would be hard-pressed to cite many historical novels that manage entirely to sidestep contemporary relevance. But by the same token historical novelists produce genuine "distant mirror" fictions as rarely as they produce purebred examples of "the way it was." One can, then, nearly always see brief reflections of the present in historical fiction; to discover a more sustained and comprehensive image of the present in a novelist's imagined past, however, can prove an uncommon and rather exhilarating experience.

T. H. White's *The Once and Future King* and Tolkien's celebrated *The Lord of the Rings* provide interesting, if problematic, examples of this kind of fiction. In White's novel the bloody and morally complex interaction of might and right in Arthurian England can be read as an analysis of or commentary on similar issues in the Second World War, in which the author, a conscientious objector, had refused to serve. The war also figures allegorically in the Tolkien trilogy. Though only by courtesy historical, its setting is recognizably an archaic, factitiously legendary England. More to the point, its action, in which the plucky and unmistakably British hobbits and their friends take on the forces of darkness, is again the mighty struggle of England and its allies against the Axis.

Contemplating these fictions, one realizes that the desire to mirror the present in the past finds expression most easily in a skewed or legendary or fabulous history more amenable than real history to the allegorical projection of the present. The fashioning of a distant mirror fiction with real history, in fact, requires not only acute knowledge of the past but also an eye for striking and often not immediately obvious historical symmetries. Writers as diverse as Ishmael Reed and John Fowles have explored this fictive territory. Reed, in *Mumbo Jumbo* (1972), offers an account of the 1920s Harlem Renaissance that "reflects" the resurgence of black pride in the 1960s and 1970s; the political context also contributes to the parallel, with Harding and Coolidge recognizable as distant-mirror images of Nixon and Ford. Fowles, in *The French Lieutenant's Woman* (1969), complicates his meticulous recreation of Victorian England with a relentlessly postmodernist narrative technique. Though he "mirrors" twentieth-century feminism and male anxiety in his main characters, he is much more interested in subverting the conventions of narrative in the Victorian novel with the self-conscious and self-reflexive techniques common to the contemporary novel. He plays with the reader's expectations of authorial omniscience and draws attention to the artifice at every turn. He forces recognition of his own—and the reader's—twentieth-century perspective on the historical fiction he presents. Though the past of *The French Lieutenant's Woman* mirrors the present very strangely, it mirrors it with surprising thoroughness.

Sometimes, however, the distant mirror does not reflect the present per se. Shūsaku Endō, a Japanese Catholic, sets *The Samurai* (1982) in the seventeenth century and decribes the mysterious workings of divine grace among Spanish missionaries and the Japanese converts, skeptics, and apostates with whom they interact. But as he admits in his preface, Endō treats history as essentially incidental to the spiritual theme that he universalizes. Thus his novel proves a kind of distant mirror hybrid, its history functioning simply to promote detachment on the part of a reader perhaps reluctant to accept the novelist's message. The spiritual drama set in the seventeenth century, at any rate, "reflects" the spiritual agon of any age.

Though also historically heteroclite, D. H. Lawrence's *The Man Who Died* (1929) provides a more striking example of a fiction whose action, set two thousand years in the past, exists chiefly to hold a mirror up to the present. The novel is a brilliant critique of the origin of Christianity from the perspective of the culture that Christianity is in large measure responsible for shaping. The story concerns the resurrection of Jesus Christ, which Lawrence accounts for without recourse to supernaturalism. "They took me down too soon,"[1] says the man who died. Lawrence's Christ realizes that he had erred in attempting to impose a set of ideas on others and he eventually sees that he had omitted the most crucial part:

"I asked them all to serve me with the corpse of their love. And in the end I offered them only the corpse of my love. This is my body—take and eat—my corpse—"
A vivid shame went through him. "After all," he thought, "I wanted them to love with dead bodies. If I had kissed Judas with live love, perhaps he would never have kissed me with death. Perhaps he loved me in the flesh, and I willed that he should love me bodylessly, with the corpse of love—" [pp. 89–90].

Jesus repudiates all that he has been and sets out alone to find himself. Eventually he experiences sexual love with a priestess of Isis, and in this shocking consummation Lawrence symbolically imagines two of the most powerful and humane religions of the ancient Mediterranean world encountering and enriching each other.

Conspiring against this reborn Christ are Romans, slaves, and the priestess's mother—all of whom behave with the modern pettiness, intolerance, and bourgeois narrowness with which Lawrence himself had repeatedly to struggle. But when the Romans come for Jesus again, he escapes, unwilling to be passively executed again. He has at last come to understand the splendor of life in the flesh, of being a man. He leaves with a promise to return in the spring to his pregnant lover, and thus Lawrence renews and enhances the seasonal fertility myth at the heart of the mystery religions.

One must admit that Lawrence simply disregards history in this historical fiction. Though he incorporates the gospel accounts, including the *noli me tangere* scene and the encounter with the disciples on the road to Emmaus, he radically revises the only received record of events after the crucifixion. He allows the story to move away from its "authorized" version toward something as parable-like as the teachings of its protagonist. In *The Man Who Died* Lawrence gives definitive expression to his long-standing disagreement with Christianity. He confronts his own age with its unwholesome shaping by and complicity with a religion that has notoriously denied the body and the holiness of sexual love to glorify a bloodless ideal of intellect and faith. The body, says Lawrence, has been crucified for centuries by a civilization now hopelessly abstract, sick, and overintellectualized.

More historically conscientious than Lawrence are the authors of the two books whose analysis will constitute the chief focus of this chapter: Faulkner's *Go Down, Moses* and Eco's *The Name of the Rose*. Faulkner's novel is an extremely sophisticated version of a type of historical fiction, the chronicle-novel, that seems infrequently to achieve greatness. The history in such novels tends to be superficial, but they lend themselves to the same categories as other historical novels: the way it was, the turning point, the distant mirror, and even, in the hands of the more ambitious science-fiction writers, the way it will be.

Faulkner, at any rate, is almost unique in his ability to impose form on the chronicle of a single family over several generations. Eco's *The Name of the Rose,* on the other hand, focuses an extraordinary variety of twentieth-century concerns in its fourteenth-century compass. The history here is by no means window-dressing, but neither is it the novel's real raison d'etre. Ultimately in Eco's story we confront again the terror of history probed in *Riddley Walker* and come—in our end may be no beginning after all—to that vision of apocalypse that figures with disturbing frequency in the historical fiction of this age.

Through a Glass Darkly: *Go Down, Moses*

Since its publication in 1942, critics have less and less frequently described *Go Down, Moses* as a collection of stories.[2] One recognizes it now as a series of linked fictions—a Pointillist or Imagist novel, so to speak; with a unified thematic focus. Its antecedents and congeners include *Dubliners* and perhaps *Winesburg, Ohio,* but in its greater unity it seems to have made the transition from linked stories to modernistically fragmented novel. The fragmentation proves thematic as well as structural, for one glimpses the landscape of this fiction—to borrow a figure from Conrad—through rents in a fog. The "landscape" here, the social and historical reality of the South, appears, fades, and appears again in the fog of misconceptions on the part of Southerners who romanticize their region and non-Southerners who fail to grasp either the real dimensions of Southern guilt or the real dimensions of Southern integrity. Beyond the regional focus, however, the reader encounters a more universalized or more purely archetypal theme of guilt and innocence.

Go Down, Moses represents a remarkable approach to the problem of handling history fictively—especially the problem of demonstrating the specular congruence of past with present. Faulkner glances, to be sure, at "the way it was," for when Isaac McCaslin sweeps away the cobwebs and probes the old ledgers in the plantation commissary, he discovers simple historical fact about his family's past; he also discovers the ultimate historical "turning point," at least in archetypal terms, for in the chronicle of land ownership and slavery, as in the destruction of the wilderness in his own lifetime, he perceives a reenactment of the fall, the loss of the American Eden. But the greater power of Faulkner's novel derives from its rigorous and unsparing examination of relationships between the races, then and now, in the American South—relationships that parallel or "mirror" each other, shocking detail for shocking detail. Faulkner adumbrates the historical violation of human beings in the past, in the sins of Carothers McCaslin, and in the present, in the banal evil of Roth Edmonds's sexual irresponsibility. The possibly incestuous miscegenation of Carothers McCaslin and that of his great-great-great-grandson Roth Edmonds become the twin foci of this examination, with Isaac McCaslin in moral orbit around them. The two strains of the fiction emerge in parallel, and the reader comes to understand the present in terms of the distant mirror Faulkner unveils in the past.

What, then, does Faulkner see as the salient features of the present, and to what extent does he replicate them in the glass of Southern history? In the present, Faulkner reveals a society impaired by the fact that one element in it has disenfranchised and disinherited its companion element. Divided between a privileged class and a serf class, the society Faulkner presents in the present differs only superficially from the society he reveals in the past. The black race in the novel's present, like the black race in the past, subsists sans land, wealth, franchise, or education. Its very blood compromised, it must accept into its pariahhood the half-caste bastards gotten on it by still-arrogant white masters. With characteristic irony, Faulkner suggests that this race retains no small moral integrity, not to mention the native cunning to make the best (and sometimes even get the best) of a bad bargain with the Man, whether he present himself as a salesman of metal detectors or as the local landowner and sharecropper slumlord.

The novel's title suggests that the suffering of the black serfs has its historical and even archetypal dimensions. The spiritual "Go Down, Moses" gives expression to black identification with the plight of the Hebrews in bondage to Pharaoh. In its refrain, God ordains deliverance: "Go down, Moses, way down in Egypt's land, tell old Pharaoh to let my people go." If none of the black characters in the book ever aspires to the office of Mosaic deliverer, several make calculated gestures of resistance. Moses, after all, began his career as deliverer by killing an Egyptian, so the motif of violence against the oppressor, as will be seen, figures repeatedly in the novel.

The book's whites may seem its "Egyptians," but they suffer their own moral bondage. Once molders of a powerful culture, they now manage only white supremacist posturing or, at best, the impotent moral gestures of an Ike McCaslin. They, too, require a savior; indeed, one critic characterizes the entire novel as "a plea for a deliverer."[3] Ike McCaslin, like the biblical Moses, comes to a recognition of literal brotherhood with the oppressed and sunders his uneasy alliance with pharaonic power. Most critics, however, see in Ike a failed messiah. At most, as Alfred Kazin says, Ike fully accepts "that slavery was a curse" and "lightens himself of its burden." Though "he becomes his own redeemer,"[4] he becomes no one else's.

Ike's humility contrasts with the extravagant conception of personal honor embraced by Faulkner's other whites. Though Faulkner represents the white Southern ethos as fundamentally flawed, he notes that it generates, over time, a spectrum of moral qualms: old Carothers McCaslin's $1000 legacies, his sons' attempts at manumission, and the conscience-ridden gestures of his grandson, who not only goes to great lengths to distribute the legacies to his black cousins but also declines his own much vaster but irremediably tainted legacy: the McCaslin plantation, symbol of the Southern land unjustly passed on to the white McCaslin progeny, unjustly sold by those aboriginal and no more noble Americans, the Indians. One crux of this novel, as will be seen, is whether Ike's principled "relinquishment" represents the arrest as well as the culmination of this progressive enlightenment. Ike's gesture has no impact on the society in which he lives, and he has no son to carry the torch of interracial justice into the future.

Given the double focus on a parallel past and present, one would expect some complementary relationship between the first story and the last. These are apparently at the two ends of the book's temporal spectrum: object and mirrored image, anchors for the fluid treatment of time that obtains in several of the other stories. Except for its brief introduction, which seems to locate the entire story—indeed, the entire sequence of stories—in the mind of the aged Isaac McCaslin, "Was" deals exclusively with an earlier day. Set significantly in 1859, the last moment when the old order could be viewed intact, it is the comic yet disturbing account of a triple pursuit—of Tennie Beauchamp by Tomey's Turl, of Tomey's Turl himself by his white halfbrothers, and of Theophilus McCaslin ("Uncle Buck") by Sophonsiba Beauchamp. "Go Down, Moses," on the other hand, is wholly about the present, when Southern blacks have learned to go North to embrace "getting rich too fast"[5] and to run disastrously afoul of the law.

How, then, do "Was" and "Go Down, Moses" reflect each other across the eight decades between them? What connects the comic tale of antebellum courtship and the sad story of Samuel "Butch" Beauchamp's obsequies? The connection would seem to be in what Faulkner calls the "human solidarity and coherence" (p. 380) that qualifies, perhaps even redeems, the moral horrors of past and present. The actual substance of "Go Down, Moses," as Arthur Mizener first pointed out, is the consideration, trouble, and expense to which the white community goes to comfort an old black woman,[6] and this sense of community finds its reflection in the antebellum past of "Was." Faulkner recognizes the enormity of white brothers owning and chasing a nominally black sibling, but eventually he will allow the reader to discover that the McCaslin brothers have already, at the time of this story, begun to free their slaves, including Roscius, Fibby, and Thucydides. Their intention to free the others will be realized violently and prematurely by the "stranger in Washington" (p. 271) and his Emancipation Proclamation. More important, however, is the absence of actual malice among the principles of this story. Aside from Hubert Beauchamp's remark that Turl will think himself in trouble with a "buck hornet" once Buck McCaslin catches him, one hears nothing of Turl's being punished, and indeed Turl intimates at one point that he and Sophonsiba Beauchamp have made common cause. As Cleanth Brooks points out, "Tomey's Turl . . . controls the situation from beginning to end" and is authorially "accorded full dignity."[7] The whole episode is, amazing as it may seem, a *family* affair— as is, I think Faulkner always implies, the entire Southern "problem."

The best symbol of Faulkner's integrated vision of past and present may be the mansion in which the McCaslin slaves dwell. The mansion is another and more concentrated symbol of the Southern land then and now, for the great house has been compromised terribly by the fact that the vile institution of slavery built it. Its owners, who cannot live in the house, make it the nominal prison of their slaves; and thus has it always been in the great, ramshackle edifice of Southern culture. Home to a subject race that fills yet does not own it, the South is a splendid mansion rendered uninhabitable by the circumstances of its building. The house also augurs the future, from Reconstruction (when uncouth former slaves briefly displace their former masters in positions of power and authority) to the present, when, as the reader learns in "Go Down, Moses," black gangsters "live in millionaires' mansions" (p. 364) in Chicago.

In addition to the winning of Tennie Beauchamp by Tomey's Turl, "Was" concerns the preliminary courtship of a faded travesty of Scarlett O'Hara (Sophonsiba) and an old bachelor (Buck McCaslin) who nearly runs out of marital dodges when he inadvertently offends against a chivalric code that requires marrying a woman one has compromised. The reader's respect for this code dwindles with the recognition that one can gamble one's way out of the situation—in a poker game whose participants, as Annette Benert points out, bet "the marriage of one player's sister" against "the ownership of the other player's brother."[8] Uncle Buck and Sibbey, at any rate, are burlesque symbols of white manhood and womanhood in the old South. Thus the first phase of their courtship, related in "Was," takes place in 1859, on the eve of the war that forever qualifies Southern pretensions to chivalry; they proleptically embody the vitiation that will follow the war. One can scarcely believe that Uncle Buck and Sophonsiba enjoy each other when, some years later, they do marry. Perhaps they finally accept each other and even procreate as a result of what the war has shown them—something that their son, who will fail to procreate, never quite manages to see.

The unromantic union of his parents distantly mirrors the yet more effete marriage of Ike McCaslin, and in this parallel, as in the interweaving of elements in "Was" and "Go Down, Moses," one sees the novel's most prominent structural feature. As is common in modernist texts, parallels in motivic detail become patterns, which in turn reveal meaning. The motivic detail interrelates culturally and historically, allowing ironic connections between the black experience and the white experience, between men and women, and—especially—between past and present. Consider, for example, the motifs of marriage, sterility, violation, prostitution, and suicide. Faulkner inflects all of these historically, and they become the chief parallels of past and present.

One node of meaning in the book—a kind of structuralist "code"—is the polarity of chastity and promiscuity introduced satirically in the hubbub over the compromised virtue of Sophonsiba Beauchamp. What Sophonsiba comically fears (and all her wailing does not convince one of her actual sincerity) is violation—which is precisely the fate of her black neighbors. Part of the irony here has to do with the fact that the fevered concern for her virginity evinced by herself and her brother scarcely disguises their desire that she rid herself of it in matrimony. Uncle Buck is nearly obliged to marry Sophonsiba just to preserve appearances—a circumstance echoed historically in the "arranged marriages" of the pregnant Eunice to Thucydides and of Sam Fathers's mother (pregnant with him at the time) to another black slave. Sophonsiba's desire for a home of consequence, whether with her brother Hubert on the plantation she insists on calling Warwick, or with her reluctant suitor Theophilus McCaslin on his plantation, mirrors that of her son's bride, who goes to great lengths in her turn—again the power of sex becomes the means of persuasion—to oblige a man to go along with her desire for social and economic distinction. What Faulkner glances at here is the fundamental prostitution that can exist in marriage. In fact, he once told a student that the morality of Ike's wife made her little better than a prostitute.[9] These marriages, entered into under the shadow of one kind of impure motive or another, ironically parallel more overt instances of prostitution or near-prostitution: the relationship between Hubert Beauchamp and his black mistress or that between Roth Edmonds and the woman he pays off in "Delta Autumn." When this woman meets Ike McCaslin, he even suggests that she, too, like her slave-ancestors, make an appearance-saving marriage.

If Ike, like Roth, considers a technically interracial marriage unthinkable, he would be hard-pressed to affirm a racially acceptable alternative, for in the world of this novel white men and white women do not have satisfactory marriages. Ike feels a physical passion for his wife, but it is contaminated—one thinks of Salinger's Seymour and Miriam Glass—by spiritual distance and contempt. Zack Edmonds seems to regret the loss of his wife, but the relationship is not presented in sufficient detail for the reader to get the idea that white marriages can be meaningful. Looking to the other marriages, one sees whore-mongering in the first generation (old Carothers McCaslin and his venery) and comically reluctant courtship in the second (Carothers's son Theophilus and Sophonsiba Beauchamp). These passionless marriages hint at the larger vitiation of this society.

In significant contrast, real passion for a wife, as well as the pain of losing a wife, is rendered only in terms of the black experience: the novel opens with the risk-taking in the name of love of Tomey's Turl, who eventually wins his bride over all the obstacles that his and her owners can put in his way. Lucas Beauchamp, by the same token, risks a terrible fate to preserve the virtue of his wife. Even the pathetic Fonsiba remains loyal to her ineffectual scholar-husband. "Pantaloon in Black" offers an oblique addition to this pattern. Its protagonist, Rider, literally cannot go on living after the death of his wife (in contradistinction to the similarly bereaved Zack Edmonds in the flashbacks of "The Fire and the Hearth"). Rider, unlike Lucas, does not lose his wife to a white man, but the white attitudes that perpetuate the bitter comedy of race relations again figure prominently. The insensitive deputy sheriff (he thinks Negroes incapable of proper connubial feelings: "they ain't human") and his testy wife are merely the banal avatars of Carothers McCaslin—or of his sons, who could plot manumission even as they defended the idea that Tomey's Turl, at once their nephew and their brother, was also somehow their property, a domestic animal to be hunted down like some errant horse or pig.

Somewhere between the sterility of white marriages and the passionate commitment of black marriages (Faulkner slyly inverts the racist stereotype in this detail), there is the haunting spectrum of black-white relationships, intermarriage, "miscegenation." One notes the recurrence, throughout the novel, in the past and in the present, of miscegenation or the threat of miscegenation. The sin of Carothers McCaslin (if Ike can be trusted on this point—a question to be taken up presently) was miscegenation compounded by incest. Ike thinks of Carothers McCaslin as "that evil and unregenerate old man who could summon, because she was his property, a human being because she was old enough and female, to his widower's house and get a child on her and then dismiss her because she was of an inferior race" (p. 294). Old Carothers's transgression mirrors and focuses that of Roth Edmonds and "the girl," his part-Negro cousin. Although the conscious intentions of Zachary Edmonds remain problematic when he brings Molly Beauchamp into his home after the death of his wife, one is inclined to respect the bitter recognition, on the part of Molly's husband, that whatever the initial reasons for this woman's going to the house of the newly widowed Edmonds, violation is likely sooner or later to follow. Lucas faces Edmonds down, threatens his life, risks the horrible fate of the black man who kills a white man, and manages to achieve a certain moral ascendancy over his adversary—an ascendancy uneasily sustained, in the next generation, with Zack's son Roth, Lucas's feudal lord in the present.

Lucas, in other words, risks the fate of Rider, who perishes horribly to pursue his wife into the other world. Indeed, the chief irony of "Pantaloon in Black" is that it is the account of a lengthy and complicated suicide. Rider, overcome by the loss of his wife, begs her ghost "lemme go wid you, honey"

(p. 141). Hard at work, "he could stop needing to invent to himself reasons for his breathing" (p. 145). He seems actually to court the disaster that eventually transpires: killing Birdsong and dying at the hands of the mob.

One insists on the suicidal element in Rider's death because self-murder is a motif in the book that can easily pass unnoticed. This motif provides another way in which past mirrors present. Eunice, according to Ike's surmise, feels the incestuous violation of her daughter so keenly that she drowns herself; her death occurs exactly three months into Thomasina's pregnancy—it occurs, that is, just as the pregnancy becomes actually visible. Rider and Samuel "Butch" Beauchamp commit suicide indirectly by killing whites, and Lucas makes clear his willingness to take the same extreme measure. The classic explanation of suicide is Freud's theory that it constitutes violence that cannot, owing to various repressions, be directed against an appropriate target—but which nevertheless must have expression, and so is turned against the self. Faulkner's blacks take their own lives both directly (Eunice, who as woman and slave early in the nineteenth century has no legitimate outlet for her rage and sorrow, is the book's single straightforward suicide) and indirectly (Rider, Samuel, and, potentially, Lucas Beauchamp). Faulkner's subtle emphasis on suicide should be recognized as poetic license, since in fact black suicide rates have historically been quite low, at least in comparison with whites. The historical development of black rage, however, is unmistakable: its target—though never, for a host of sociological reasons, altogether exempting the self—comes increasingly to be the white oppressor. Samuel, associated explicitly with the biblical Benjamin, is called "the slain wolf," reminding us of the prophetic words of his father Jacob on his deathbed: "Benjamin shall ravin as a wolf" (Genesis 49:27). One marvels at the prophetic powers of Faulkner himself, who manages to cap his story of black and white relationships in the past and present with an augury of their relationships in the future. Writing at a time when the social victimization of Negroes was second only to the time of their actual enslavement, Faulkner anticipates by a decade the birth of the civil rights movement in *Brown vs. Board of Education* (1954) and by a generation its flowering—at times in violence that took its toll on the self (in Rochester, in Watts)— in the 1960s.

If Faulkner can make the past mirror the present of the book's writing and publication, as well as the future that his later readers would inhabit, he can also make his distant mirror at times a transparent medium, a window into a yet more remote past. The transgression of Carothers McCaslin and the accompanying blight on the land "reflects" not only the ongoing transgressions of white Southerners in the twentieth century and the attendant blighting of the land, but also the primal transgression in Eden. As in Eden, the point is that innocence perishes. Ike McCaslin discovers the passing of innocence in the violation of human beings and of the land itself. In his painful initiation, he enacts the coming of age of an entire culture.

The spirit of the land that, for him, symbolizes Eden is the splendid beast Old Ben, whose passing focuses several of the novel's themes, especially with regard to history. Myra Jehlen, who argues that "Faulkner was obsessed by history," suggests that this preoccupation dictates the symbolic treatment of Old Ben. "Paradoxically, given its pre-historic status, that 'shaggy tremendous' beast whose march across time is 'a corridor of wreckage and destruction' that no one and nothing seems able to stop, embodies history itself."[10] But one resists the characterization of Faulkner as *obsessed* by history. Though he took the keen interest in history and genealogy characteristic of many Southerners, his greatest interest, as Jehlen also and more legitimately suggests, was that broader thing, culture. Old Ben's death, at any rate, does not put an end to history— which keeps on keeping on, though in increasingly Beckettian futility and exhaustion. Consequently most critics agree that Old Ben embodies not history but wilderness—"the big woods, bigger and older than any recorded document" (p. 191). Thus one recognizes in the bear a principle—destructive, yes, but also redemptive—of vitality in nature against which human civilization must define itself, despite the paradoxical risk that human civilization will, by defeating the wilderness finally and absolutely, rob itself of the testing ground or conditions necessary to its continued health.

One can contrast, say, Robert Frost's view of nature. His pastoralism notwithstanding, Frost saw nature as an amoral, indifferent force problematically kept at bay by human labor, ingenuity, and vigilance. And when the human guard slips—whenever the farm stands unoccupied too long—the wilderness "coalesces" (to borrow and subvert Faulkner's word) and reclaims its own. Faulkner, from his different regional perspective, is closer to someone like E. M. Forster, who ruefully remarks that he had once conceived of the sea as something ultimately inviolable by humanity—only to realize later how vulnerable it had in fact become to human pollution.[11] Faulkner, similarly, sees nature at last defeated by human industry and rapacity, by the "onslaught of axe and saw and loglines and then dynamite and tractor plows" (p. 354).

Though Lynn Altenbernd places this spoliation in the context of the mythic American experience ("an ironic necessity in human affairs requires the fullest realization of the dream shall destroy the source of the dream"),[12] Faulkner explicitly distinguishes the wilderness and its genius from that record of human civilization we call history. His protagonist, as W. R. Moses argues, is a person who inherits a mythic perception of the world and of time yet must grapple with the antimythic implications of history.[13] His story, then, will concern human civilization—and history—impinging on the hitherto timeless wilderness. Faulkner's conceit is to associate this intersection with the fall of Adam—an event traditionally seen as the birth of time, the beginning of history.

In part 4 of "The Bear" one sees this history as it emerges from primary documents. Carl E. Rollyson notes that Faulkner normally presents history as something that exists in the memories of the aged: "the commissary books . . . constitute Faulkner's one extended attempt to deal with the type of evidence that is the stuff out of which historians fashion their version of the past."[14] As paradigmatic historian, Ike interprets and provides narrative shape to the cryptic, cramped, and ill-spelled ledger entries that reveal to him his real heritage. He undertakes his research and makes his discoveries at age sixteen, immediately after the last, successful hunt for Old Ben. Faulkner "juxtaposes," to use the word he favors, Ike's discovery of racial guilt and the passing of the perfect, Edenic wilderness—which begins to crumble (with the death of the bear and Sam Fathers) even as he recognizes its value and meaning. Thus Ike superimposes a vision of primal guilt on a vision of primal innocence, and thus he conflates all of human history.

But is Ike's history accurate? Can one not fault him for his too-ready conclusions of his grandfather's villainy? Should the reader not question his reliability—at least regarding the motivation of Eunice's suicide? Though the reader has only Ike's fevered, perhaps already biased, imagination as evidence of Carothers McCaslin's miscegenation and incest, I would argue that the reliability question is a red herring. To be sure, Faulkner encourages his readers (here and in *Absolom, Absolom!*) to recognize the unreliability of history, to recognize that history exists in various versions, no one of them definitive. Nevertheless, like his character Ike McCaslin, Faulkner expects history to be *accountable*—accountable, that is, to the present, with its racism and injustice and tragic human suffering. As Gary D. Hamilton argues, "the author is very much concerned with showing how that which was determines that which is."[15] Isaac McCaslin may or may not err in interpreting the meaning of specific details in the documents he pores over and analyzes, but he does not fail in the all-important task of composing a version of the past that correlates with the facts of the present. To this extent he is a reliable historian.

One must remember that virtually all of the great central fiction here—"The Bear"—is historical. History figures not only in those ledgers, going back to the late eighteenth century, but also in the central action of the story, which transpires between Ike McCaslin's tenth and twenty-first birthdays—from 1877 or 1878 to the turn of the century. And like the history contained in the ledgers, this history—of nineteenth-century hunters—is a distant mirror of the present as presented in "Delta Autumn" and "Go Down, Moses." But in the present, there has passed away a glory from the earth. The wilderness has shrunk, it lacks the numinous genius that presided over the initiation of young hunters in the past. And Ike, his heart and mind and conscience still acute, recognizes in the destruction of the wilderness (along with the sins of attempting to own land or persons) an analog to or even a reenactment of original sin. He imagines that "man, and the game he would follow and kill," must have elicited from God the statement: "The woods and fields he ranges and the game he devastates will be the consequence and signature of his crime and guilt, and his punishment" (p. 349).

This picture of wilderness purity always smaller and farther away suggests a world of larger meanings, almost a metaphysics. Faulkner intimates that the condition of modern humanity is existentially meager and shrunken. As Sartre observes in his essay "Time in Faulkner," this author "uses his extraordinary art to describe a world dying of old age, with us gasping and choking in it."[16] The greatheartedness and vitality of the past are moribund—the hunters cheat, they kill does and fawns, seemingly indifferent to the acceleration of the wilderness decline they thereby become guilty of. And the does and fawns are explicitly linked to human women and children—traditionally to be shielded and protected but now seemingly as targetable as men.

Not that Faulkner engages in historical Arcadianism. After all, Eunice and Thomasina and the infant Sam Fathers and his mother were all "does and fawns" victimized by predatory, thoughtless power. Then and now remain devastatingly parallel in this respect. The past mirrors the present darkly indeed. This congruence, this specular dimension to history (at least negative history), in part dictates Faulkner's treatment of time in this book. Past and present alternate in the minds of the characters (chiefly McCaslin's: again, as the opening of the book makes clear, his is the novel's ground-consciousness) and in that of their creator, who is aware that time-and-consciousness, at least in the persuasive analysis of the philosopher Henri Bergson, is ultimate reality, the *Urstoff* itself. R. W. B. Lewis has diagramed the back-and-forth temporal movement of "The Bear" and emphasized the centrality of Ike's sixteenth year—the year he witnesses the passing of Old Ben and discovers the secret of the ledgers.[17] But one must not miss the focus on Ike's agonized "now"—Ike who has only the past and an increasingly attenuated present, since the future holds only proximate death. Sartre charges Faulkner with conceiving of humanity without a *consciousness* of the future; Sartre's reflections on "time in Faulkner," however, mainly concern *The Sound and the Fury* and are of limited value to a consideration of *Go Down, Moses*, for implicit in the book's title, and in Ike's gesture with the horn, are the consciousness of and hope for the future the absence of which Sartre sees as the peculiar affliction of Faulkner's humanity.

At the end of his life—at the time of "Delta Autumn"—Ike continues to wrestle with what he had discovered in the ledgers so many years earlier. He must come to terms with his failure to redeem himself and his land, his failure to be either the

Mosaic or the Christlike deliverer. His reflections center on his recognition of the archetypal meaning contained in the destruction of the wilderness as well as on the loss of his wife and, with her, his hopes for a son. Ike's relationship with his wife, complicated by his attempt at a redemptive gesture ("relinquishment"), seems to have culminated in his own personal fall.

In part 4 of "The Bear," Ike discusses history, ethics, and religion with his cousin Cass Edmonds, to whom he attempts to justify his resolution to arrest the generational and cumulative progress of the primal guilt, the curse on the land. In "Delta Autumn" Ike thinks back to

that day and himself and McCaslin juxtaposed not against the wilderness but against the tamed land, the old wrong and shame itself, in repudiation and denial at least of the land and the wrong and shame even if he couldn't cure the wrong and eradicate the shame, who at fourteen when he learned of it had believed he could do both when he became competent and when at twenty-one he became competent he knew that he could do neither but at least he could repudiate the wrong and shame, at least in principle, and at least the land itself in fact, for his son at least: and did, thought he had: then (married then) in a rented cubicle in a backstreet stock-traders' boarding-house, the first and last time he ever saw her naked body, himself and his wife juxtaposed in their turn against that same land, that same wrong and shame from whose regret and grief he would at least save and free his son and, saving and freeing his son, lost him [p. 351].

Ike never quite recognizes in the attempt to escape guilt the attempt—hopeless, foredoomed—to escape the human condition. He must choose literally between progeny and his impossible ideal of escape from guilt, for his wife apparently leaves him over his intransigence.

Ike's greatest failing is that he effects no significant redressing of the injustice. At best he makes a gesture, he sets an example. Perhaps one would be naïve to expect him to distribute his patrimony among the unjustly disinherited. He knows that they are in no condition to benefit from such an act of justice, and he knows that he and they both still live in a society that would view such a gesture as a profound threat. Oedipa Maas, protagonist of Thomas Pynchon's *The Crying of Lot 49*, in a similar moment (she has also been sensitized to the unjust distribution of property), makes clear the social and even legal pressures that preclude independent redress of injustice:

What would the probate judge have to say about spreading some kind of a legacy among them all, all those nameless, maybe as a first installment? Oboy. He'd be on her ass in a microsecond, revoke her letters testamentary, they'd call her names, proclaim her all through Orange County as a redistributionist and pinko, slip the old man from Warpe, Wistfull, Kubitschek and McMingus in as administrator *de bonis non* and so much baby for code, constellations, shadow-legatees.[18]

Isaac McCaslin may see the injustice done in the land and may embrace a Christlike abnegation, but his gesture comes to naught. Indeed, the Christ parallel is deceptive: unlike Christ himself, who abandoned carpentry to begin his ministry, in which he gave up his life, Isaac turns from his father's business—the plantation—to the quietistic and inconsequential practice of carpentry. Christ's celibacy, moreover, was freely chosen; Ike's is the ironic consequence of his messianic calling.

His unhappy marriage curiously focuses Ike's relation to the land, to his patrimony, and to history. Ike's wife tries with her body to blackmail him into entering into his inheritance. She correlates one possession with the other, one "entry" and the other. Ike apparently sees his wife completely nude only once, and on this occasion temporarily surrenders his moral position under the influence of a powerful erotic temptation.[19] The passage that describes this scene hints at Ike's perceptions of his wife's mysterious and unsettling subtlety, a depth profound and—to him—unattractive. "*She already knows more than I with all the man-listening in camps where there was nothing to read ever even heard of. They are born already bored with what a boy approaches only at fourteen and fifteen with blundering and aghast trembling*" (p. 314). The problem—which generates subtle hints that the behavior of Ike's wife is literally meretricious—is that she apparently overcomes her extreme modesty as an ultimate plot to persuade her husband to come into his (now their) inheritance. The reference to the "movement . . . one time older than man" (p. 314) refers merely to making room for Ike on the bed (this movement is "one time older than man" in that it precedes the act that will bring him to conception and birth). With another such atavistic movement ("one time more older than man"—p. 315), she disengages herself after intercourse. The point of these locutions is to hint at Ike's perception of having been somehow victimized by some primal female duplicity—all ironic in that he seems not to include his own weakness in the indictment.

Like Byron's Spanish lady who, "whispering 'I ne'er will consent'—consented," Ike goes down fighting: "I can't. Not ever. Remember" (p. 314), he asseverates, referring to his refusal to inherit. But he is overwhelmed by the urgency of "the steady and invincible hand and he said Yes and he thought, *She is lost. She was born lost. We were all born lost* then he stopped thinking and even saying Yes" (pp. 314–15). From our ironic perspective, the two manage only to come into the "inheritance" of duplicity that subverted Eden. But perhaps more central to the action is the fact that Ike, overcome by desire, succumbs to his own moment with the apple, his own moment of prostitution. In a parody of Molly Bloom's great affirmation on a similar occasion, he gurgles yes to his wife's reiterated demands. He evidently reneges on this concession, but he has nevertheless sold out. His is the major moral compromise.

Or so he seems to think, years later in "Delta Autumn," when he awakens from reveries on this decades-old regret to

confront another love affair complicated by racial injustice—
the same racial injustice that had irremediably complicated
his marriage. As Michael Millgate observes, "the point at which
all the threads of the novel seem to cross, at which the whole
pattern of the book emerges with final and absolute clarity,
is that of Ike's encounter with Roth's mistress."[20] Does Ike live
up to the moment he encounters "the girl"? This question,
like that of Ike's relinquishment, remains critically controversial. Millgate, for example, believes that Ike makes a very
poor showing on this occasion, and other readers find Ike
obtuse and embarrassingly racist ("You're a nigger!"). But
anyone aware of attitudes in the novel's present must realize
that Ike merely gives expression to a lifetime's understanding
of racial dynamics. He speaks as realist when he dismisses
hopes for the kind of racial accommodation attempted by Roth
and the girl. He is only superficially wrong when he says,
"*Maybe in a thousand or two thousand years*" (p. 361).

Though interracial marriage would be seen even in the
South within a few years, the likelihood of its being really
accepted remains quite remote. Ike is not, then, giving vent
to some personal, crotchety, unreconstructed, hypocritical racism, and one knows from his musings about his wife and the
son he never had that he has not, contrary to the angry charge
leveled at him by the granddaughter of Tennie's Jim, forgotten what love is. He sees in Roth's bastard the son he never
had and makes the gesture he will never be able to make with
a son of his own loins. I remain convinced that the gift of the
symbolic horn is something great-spirited. Though the wilderness code seems more and more degenerate (this is one
point of the doe-killing business), it lives in the heart of Isaac
McCaslin and may be recoverable once the primal, racial guilt
is more broadly accepted and atoned for. Though the South
must continue to enact the tragedy of its blighted heritage,
must continue its generational expiation, it remains a place
where the sense of community and the concept (if not always

the reality) of personal honor continue to thrive and to matter. As numerous apologists have argued, the South has the moral capital of great suffering, and great suffering is redemptive.

Ike's story, then, this book, concerns the discovery, by one preternaturally sensitive to history itself, of a distant mirror in the past. As part of that discovery Ike encounters—"for the millionth time," as Stephen Dedalus says—the powerful polar opposites of innocence and guilt: Edenic wilderness on the one hand, the sins of landownership, of commercialism, and especially of slavery on the other. The kind of historical fiction typified by *Go Down, Moses* has a natural tendency toward allegory, or at least toward the archetypal (Faulkner seems too little interested in the Ur-myth as a repository of ultimate meanings for this story to become truly allegorical). Archetypes derive from the repetition of psychologically or culturally important events or images, and history, in that it repeats itself, is innately archetypal. Even a single repetition— the present, which is "reflected" in and thereby must "repeat" the past—is enough to establish pattern and significance.

Thus *Go Down, Moses* enacts the "dialectic of desire and repugnance" that Northrop Frye invokes to define literary art "in its social or archetypal aspect." Frye defines ritual in terms of the same dialectic, and of course Faulkner's great fiction centers on the ritual hunt. But even as hunting tests and trains the hunter, it tempts him to "devastate" the game and the wilderness, and thus to rob himself of the means whereby he defines his human worth against nature itself. This combination of desire and repugnance figures also in the demise of Old Ben, hunted annually in a ritual within the ritual. The social and cultural context of the book—slavery and its legacy or more broadly the racial situation in the South—partakes of the same dialectic and of the same archetypal, if not ritualistic, character. The exploitation of blacks, and especially of black women by white men, recurs archetypally, from the predations of Carothers McCaslin to Hubert Beauchamp's black mistress to the transgressions or near-transgressions of the Edmonds men.

But the archetypal "desire" is not only the sexual desire of white men for black women. It is also present as a powerful wish for black-white community. Frye further defines art as ultimately idealizing, ultimately expressing a collective desire for civilization, for a better world. "The imaginative element in works of art . . . lifts them clear of the bondage of history.[21] *Go Down, Moses* immerses its readers and its main character in history the better to free them from its bondage. It contrives, too, to find an approximation in the past and in the present of the fuller ideal of human community that it manifestly expresses a yearning for in the future

Face to Face: *The Name of the Rose*

Reading Umberto Eco's *The Name of the Rose*, one delights in the author's extensive knowledge of medieval culture: art, architecture, politics, philosophy, theology, superstition, folkways, daily life, cuisine, sexuality. But this erudition and the historical veracity it serves has little to do with the structure of coherence and significance on which meaning in this novel finally depends. Eco re-creates the fourteenth century to shed light on the twentieth; the one finds its reflection in the other in a variety of forms. The discussions of censorship and access to knowledge, for example, reflect the era of the Meese Commission no less than the proscriptions of the medieval church, and the ideological fragmentation of the fourteenth century besets our world as well. The endless and occasionally bloody maneuvering of pope and emperor reminds one of the global division into superpowers some centuries later, and though one normally thinks of communism and Catholicism as diametrically opposed, the medieval church's militant policing of orthodoxy and its single-minded and bloody persecution of heresy and doctrinal adulteration find their complement in the ideological fragmentation of modern Marxism, with Soviet orthodoxy continually challenged by the various Marxist splinter groups that dot the world today and vie with each other for influence, power, and ideological purity as much as they counter "bourgeois" and "capitalist" interests.

Other, better defined images in the distant mirror reveal Eco's out-and-out flirtation with anachronism. William of Baskerville, for example, is a skeptical scientist and prevenient semiotician. His valuation of laughter, democracy, tolerance, reason, scholarship, humanistic learning, and even uncertainty have surprisingly little relevance to the period of the novel's setting. All of these subjects are concerns of the twentieth century gotten up in the clothes of an earlier age. Though one encounters veracious history in *The Name of the Rose*, or at least a veracious historical setting, the novel nevertheless proves the perfect example of a fiction in which the past mirrors the present.

Not that this novel would be out of place in a consideration of "turning point" fictions. The reader senses an air of expectation as one age gives way to another, for the life of the narrator, Adso of Melk, spans the fourteenth century, transitional between the Middle Ages and the Renaissance. The *Zeitgeist* is warping, shifting from faith, superstition, and fanaticism to humanism and powerful civil and secular institutions. The old order must, unfortunately, suffer a near-fatal dissolution before the new dispensation—the Renaissance—can flower. This dissolution finds symbolic expression in the apocalyptic fire that destroys, as it were, the mighty edifice of medieval faith. In a way, the crazed and evil Jorge knows what he is doing in attempting to keep his volume of Aristotle hidden from the world. He himself remarks that the Stagyrite promotes empiricism, involvement with and probing of the concrete realities of this world—things medieval faith had in large measure always tried to ignore or transcend. Jorge's single volume is a powerful symbol of the intellectual energy about to be unchained as the West rediscovers the classical learning long dormant in monastic libraries.

But the fourteenth-century turning point merely reflects a like moment of cultural dissolution in our own time—one fraught with more than symbolically apocalyptic possibilities. Civilization late in the twentieth century seems once again at the point of some painful collapse. The annihilation figured in the fiery cataclysm, and obliquely alluded to by an increasingly agnostic-sounding Adso in the closing pages, is not, ironically, the one apprehended by the monks. It is, instead, a clear augury of the secular, meaningless annihilation everywhere dreaded and expected in the thermonuclear age.

Announcements of the distant mirror at times appear more overtly than the thematic indications hitherto considered. At points Adso's mask slips—or rather Eco's Adso-mask slips—and reveals something obviously aimed at an age much later than Adso's. Even in the introduction one encounters ironic remarks about the alleged irrelevance of Adso's manuscript to our time. "The story of Adso of Melk," says the fatuous scholar (Eco with tongue in cheek), is "immeasurably remote in time" and therefore "gloriously lacking in relevance for our day, atemporally alien to our hopes and our certainties."[22]

One finds Adso's lament at the beginning of his manuscript less ironic but more pointed: "The young no longer want to study anything, learning is in decline, the whole world walks on its head" (p. 15). Such fulminations issue from every "older generation," and indeed these echo Jorge's sermon on the Antichrist (pp. 403–4), delivered two or three generations earlier. But when William remarks that "the learned man has the right and the duty to use an obscure language, comprehensible only to his fellows" (p. 89), one thinks immediately of contemporary criticism and its esoteric language (Eco, a leading semiotician, mocks himself here).[23] When Adso dreams the *Coena Cypriani*, William makes another time-warp observation: "if the day came when someone insisted on deriving a truth even from our dreams, then the day of the Antichrist would truly be at hand" (p. 438). As noted in the discussion of *The White Hotel,* the age of Freud (who derived truth "even from dreams") is also the age of Hitler, closest thing to an authentic Antichrist that the world has yet seen. More broadly, of course, Eco says again that his own era, the age of psychoanalysis, is the "apocalyptic" age par excellence. This age would collectively endorse William's subsequent observation, too: "A dream is a scripture, and many scriptures are nothing but dreams" (p. 438).

Dreams, in the present age, continue millenarian, though as many chiliasts look to *Das Kapital* as to the Bible for their scripture. Indeed, Marxism resembles Catholicism in curious ways. Both are founded in an idea of communal life and a repudiation of lucre, especially disparities of wealth. Both embrace an ideal in the name of which they restrict individual freedom in a variety of ways. Both compromise the ideal and drift into bureaucracy, injustice, paranoia, totalitarianism, and corruption. One has the impression that the perennial splitting-off of heretical offshoots in the period of Eco's novel is intended to remind us of the proliferation of Marxist heresies since the Second World War. Small wonder, then, that the first date one encounters on opening this book is August 1968, when the Soviet Union, modern analogue of Eco's corrupt medieval zealots of orthodoxy, invaded Czechoslovakia, home of a heretical and hence dangerous variation on the True Faith. Thus one understands an enigmatic remark in Adso's peroration as another statement as much about our time as his: "at times it seems to me that the Danube is crowded with fools going towards a dark place" (p. 501).

The proliferation of heresies also suggests the cancerous spread of twentieth-century terrorist factions, where one finds the same fanaticism, the same obsession with obscure ideologies and doctrinal distinctions that cannot be understood by even the most earnest student (as Adso himself finds after the lectures vouchsafed him by Ubertino and William). Ulrich Wyss, describing Eco's novel as an "allegory of today's Italy," places terrorist factionalism in a larger national context. He sees the Fraticelli as Italy's radical left, the Dolcinians as the Red Brigades, the Franciscans as the Communist Party, and the powerful Benedictines as the multinational conglomerates that resist change in the political and economic order.[24] Eco, in an interview, has hinted at the validity of Wyss's parallels: "I am fascinated by the fact that many of the ideological/political groups born in the 'sixties underwent in the last two decades the same problems of many medieval millenarian movements—the way groups polluted each other ideologically, the way dogmatic faith in their own position brought self-destruction to many of them."[25] Eco adds that he began the novel the day Aldo Moro was kidnapped by the Red Brigades, whom he elsewhere calls "those last, incurable romantics of Catholic-Papist origin."[26]

Other mirrors, less obvious, require analysis and interpretation. William's remarks about the psychological side of torture, for example, make him sound almost as if he had done some reading in twentieth-century authors. The inquisitor, he notes, leaves the actual torture to the "secular arm," thus creating a warped perception of the proceedings on the part of "the accused, who, when the inquisitor arrives, suddenly finds support in him, an easing of his sufferings, and so he opens his heart" (p. 374). Perhaps the use of torture has always been this sophisticated, but this particular disquisition seems to come from Orwell, Koestler, Jacopo Timmerman, and other analysts of totalitarianism in the twentieth century, when torture has reached an apogee of sophistication.

Sometimes the ostensibly overt reflection of the twentieth century in the fourteenth-century glass contains extra dimensions of subtlety—especially in the allusions to modern writers.[27] In the hands of a master semiotician like Umberto Eco, in fact, William of Baskerville's story becomes a distant mirror of "intertextuality"—a demonstration piece, that is, of the way one literary text echoes and incorporates other literary texts or types of discourse to become more subtle, more rich, and more ambiguous. Thus Eco bases his action on a popular modern genre, the detective story, and deliberately imitates the manner of Sir Arthur Conan Doyle. In the "investigator," William of Baskerville, and in his sidekick, Adso of Melk, one recognizes Sherlock Holmes and Dr. Watson.

Joyce and Nabokov are also present—chiefly in the novel's hidden schema, for Eco has conceived the mighty duels between Pope John and the Emperor Louis, between Bernard Gui and Michael of Cesena, and between Jorge, abetted by the abbot, and William, abetted by Adso, as a double chess game. The only hint of this appears in the scholarly introduction, in the reference to "a Castillian version," in Italian for some reason, of a Russian book whose author allegedly quotes at length from Adso's lost manuscript. Entitled *On the Use of Mirrors in the Game of Chess,* this book presumably concerns mirroring moves, but its author, one Milo Temesvar, seems to have been taken with the description in Adso's manuscript of the labyrinth, its central chamber disguised by a distorting mirror. Perhaps the penetration of that distorting mirror made Temesvar think of Lewis Carroll's *Through the Looking-Glass,* another fiction based on a chess game.

Adso's narrative, like chess, features crowned heads, aristocrats, prelates, and pawns. In it two separate chess games mirror each other. In one, those supporting the emperor oppose those supporting the pope. In the other, those who seek justice in the abbey oppose those who defend or benefit from the corrupt system run by Jorge and the abbot. Although there are more names in the story than the number of men in chess, both of the games here seem to feature the same thirty-two characters. These include the emperor and the pope as kings and William of Baskerville as the white queen. The black queen can be either Jorge or Bernard Gui, depending on which game is being analyzed. The major pieces that flank the king and queen on the chessboard, the bishops, knights, and rooks, are the imperial and papal ambassadors. All the rest are pawns.

In both games, then, the two sides are basically the sympathetic characters (those serving the emperor, along with the handful of innocent or less culpable monks) versus the unsympathetic characters (those serving the pope, along with the truly corrupt monks). The sixteen men on the "white" side include the emperor, Michael of Cesena, Ubertino of Casale, William of Baskerville, and Adso, along with the simpler and more innocent monks and lay brothers: Aymaro, Nicholas, Alinardo, Salvatore, and Remigio. Bit players in the imperial legation round out the sixteen: Brother Arnold of Aquitaine, Brother Hugh of Newcastle, Brother William Alnwick, the bishop of Kaffa, Berengar Talloni, and Bonagratia of Bergamo. On the "black" side are the pope, Bernard Gui, the abbot, the monks Jorge, Adelmo, Venantius, Berengar, Severinus, Malachi, and Benno, and the papal legates Lawrence Decoin, the bishop of Padua, Jean d'Anneaux, Jean de Baune, the bishop of Alborea, and Cardinal del Poggetto.

This labyrinthine reticulation of schematic meaning hints at the presence of a last major literary presence here: Jorge Luis Borges. Eco borrows Borges's manner in the Introduction and plays on the name of the Argentine writer in the name of his villain, Jorge of Burgos. The description of Fra Dolcino's followers, who abandon themselves to evil to accelerate the apocalypse, calls to mind the Histriones, the heretics in Borges's "The Theologians." (Some, says Borges, called the Histriones Speculars, from their habit of replacing images of the Lord with mirrors, or from their esoteric doctrine concerning a separate mirror-world of inverted reflections.) But the major inspiration from Borges, as several reviewers and critics have pointed out, is the idea of a labyrinthine library, symbolically coterminous with the universe. Eco gets the idea for his library from the one in Borges's "The Library of Babel." Both libraries have mirrors, both have books that prove indecipherable. Each author presents a narrator who, in Adso's words, imagines that a book in the labyrinth contains his own "present story" (p. 241). Each author also invites speculation about a book of books, a key to the mystery embodied in the library as a whole. Both imagine a kind of ultimate librarian, whose divine or demonic character is assayed. *The Name of the Rose*, in other words, is "The Library of Babel" at book length.

It is also, as should be clear by now, a historical novel with an extraordinary density of twentieth-century referents. Thus Eco makes the sensibility of his hero, William of Baskerville, essentially unmedieval. Like all the other artful anachronisms of atmosphere, temper, and personality in the novel, this aspect of William's character is managed with great deftness and subtlety. William seems spiritually bruised by his experience as inquisitor and imperial legate, and his exposure to the fledgling science of Roger Bacon and the finely honed logic of William of Occam has also promoted his skepticism. But the reader gradually perceives something stronger and more modern in William's growing inability to reconcile faith and reason. William's skepticism comes out repeatedly in his discussions with Adso. His explanations of heresy, for example, seem "correct," yet one cannot ignore the subtle, tendentious admixture of irony (Ubertino's parallel explanations lack the irony and come out as absurd hair-splitting and special pleading). The irony reveals a corner of William's heart that he cannot express openly, lest he become fair game for some zealot like Bernard Gui. Adso makes the perfect foil to William, and Eco ingeniously preserves the narrator's medieval cast of mind, along with his limited grasp of the unthinkable (apostasy). Only toward the end does he face some of the faith-sapping implications of William's hints. Eco, with great brilliance, manages to have his historicism both ways. By allowing Adso to remain a man of the fourteenth century (even when he experiences love or the cosmic disorder William speaks of), Eco preserves intact the historical illusion—even while everything of any import in the story proves to mirror an age six centuries later than the ostensible period of the action.[28]

Eco contrives, too, to make his medieval science and philosophy seem to mirror the thought of modern physicists like Einstein and Heisenberg. William agonizes over the problem of discovering scientific laws that will reveal order in the universe, for, as even Adso sees, such laws undermine the principle of divine omnipotence. God bound by the laws of physics is not God. Though the problem tends toward a faith-endangering paradox, it remains protoscientific, thoroughly medieval. But as William discusses the thought of William of Occam, he seems to slip the intellectual bonds of the Middle Ages, to transcend those Idols of the Theater of which a later philosopher would speak, the habits of thought dictated by the age in which one lives:

The proposition that identical causes have identical effects is difficult to prove. A single body can be cold or hot, sweet or bitter, wet or dry, in one place—and not in another place. How can I discover the universal bond that orders all things if I cannot lift a finger without creating an infinity of new entities? For with such a movement all the relations of position between my finger and all other objects change. The relations are the ways in which my mind perceives the connections between single entities, but what is the guarantee that this is universal and stable? [pp. 206–7].

This is a version of the uncertainty principle, the principle that in observing a thing one affects it (so that, as one popularizer pointed out, one cannot investigate darkness by shining a light into it). Though it begins with the simple discovery that an investigator cannot know both the location and the velocity of a subatomic particle, the ramifications of this radical uncertainty include the gradual or abrupt undermining of the empirical science founded by Aristotle, furthered, after a lengthy hiatus, by Roger Bacon and his disciples, brought to fruition in the splendid clockwork universe described by Newton, and transformed into intellectual gospel by the eighteenth century. William, then, is at once a medieval philosopher and a modern scientist. His presence in the novel invites the reader to look forward not only to the beginnings of modern science in the Renaissance but also to its culmination in new and terrifying perplexities in the reader's own age, when uncertainty about the simplest physical reality seems merely to complement religious, social, political, and historical uncertainties. William's thought summarizes the science of his own age at the same time that it anticipates the subsequent evolution of science. Thus his quest ironically recapitulates the entire history of science. The universal laws he seeks will in time be sufficiently codified to present the investigator (William's suggestive title) with a clock-work universe and a clock-maker god—a pale version of the omnipotent being celebrated and feared by medieval faith. Such a god need no longer be concerned with creation; indeed, such a god might be dead, as the nineteenth century (again anticipated by William) was eventually to realize.

To the extent that William of Baskerville and his philosophical brethren really belong to the fourteenth century, they need not concern themselves with the problems of general and special relativity, quantum theory, and the "particle zoo." They have enough to consider with the world and its place in the cosmos, and William's investigation in this story is recognizably a probe into the micro- and macrocosm as represented in the abbey and its labyrinthine library. The abbey, a multivalent symbol, suggests, first, the human body, with its centers of cerebration, spirituality, and appetite. In its microcosmic diversity, and even without permanent women residents, it resembles a model of human society, a little city-state. The larger symbolism of the abbey and its labyrinthine library is perhaps the most obvious. Adso notes early on that "architecture, among all the arts, is the one that most boldly tries to reproduce in its rhythms the order of the universe" (p. 26). The abbey may, says William, be a "speculum mundi" (p. 120). An exchange between William and Adso hints at the relationship between the labyrinth and the world. "How beautiful the world is, and how ugly labyrinths are," says Adso. Not slow to see the symbolism of the place, William replies: "How beautiful the world would be if there were a procedure for moving through labyrinths" (p. 178). The abbot proves an unwitting developer of this symbolism when he says, "The library was laid out on a plan which has remained obscure to all over the centuries, and which none of the monks is called upon to know" (p. 37). Even old Alinardo sees the symbolism: "Hunc mundum tipice labyrinthus denotat ille. . . . The library is a great labyrinth, sign of the labyrinth of the world" (p. 158). William, on hearing evidence of the human and spiritual diversity within the monastery, declares: "The abbey really is a microcosm" (p. 196). When William and Adso penetrate and map the library, they find it—before Columbus, by the way— "laid out and arranged according to the image of the terraqueous orb" (p. 320).

As the abbot notes when he orients William and Adso to the rules of the abbey, especially as regards its fabulous collection of books, the library embodies more than "a terrestrial labyrinth." It also represents "a spiritual labyrinth" (p. 38) because it contains secular works as well as sacred, falsehood as well as truth. It is, then, like any library, a powerful symbol of epistemology itself, and Eco places it on a high hill that calls to mind John Donne's conceit for the pursuit of truth as an arduous, uphill struggle:

> On a huge hill,
> Cragged and steep, Truth stands, and he that will
> Reach her, about must and about must go,
> And what the hill's suddenness resists, win so. . . .

But the desire for knowledge can be warped, can be simply a lust and thus sterile, says William, who notes just this perversion in Benno, who, unlike Roger Bacon (who sought knowledge to better the lives of others), wants merely to exercise his intellectual pride (a danger for William, too, as more than one character suggests). Benno thirsts for knowledge, but his intellectual curiosity does not make him some kind of appealing Jude Fawley. He will bar others from knowledge if such censorial complicity will secure his own access, and thus like the rest of the abbey's jealous librarians he conspires to make books "dumb," to "bury" them. What a travesty in a repository that "has more books than any other Christian library" (p. 35), for "the good of a book lies in its being read" (p. 396).

Though couched in medieval terms, the theme of knowledge in the book, along with the running debate on censorship, seems most cogent when interpreted in modern terms. To be sure, much of the discussion concerns the alleged desirability of keeping knowledge the province of the qualified clergy—a subject that exercises few today, for the church has long since given over its opposition to vernacular scripture and liturgy (though it still maintains an index of works that good Catholics should avoid). But in the idea that some knowledge is so dangerous that it must be kept from all except certain select guardians, one glimpses one or two ambivalent modern parallels.

In the theme of censorship the thrust is most recognizably modern. For the problem is the classic one: Who will guard the guardians? The censor here—Jorge—guards knowledge as potentially destructive, in his view, as an atomic bomb. But William and Adso see this knowledge, however destructive in the short term, as potentially redemptive. Eco discovers in censorship a question less of morality than of power. Jorge has acted as much to maintain and consolidate control over the monastery as to spare Christendom a dangerous endorsement of laughter.

One errs, however, to take a simplistic, libertarian view of the censorship assayed in this novel, for the indiscriminate dissemination of knowledge poses real danger. When William reports that his master Roger Bacon worried that "the secrets of science" might "pass into the hands of . . . some" who "could use them to evil ends" (p. 87), one hears a comment more clearly aimed at the modern era than at the Middle Ages. Few would quarrel with the proposition that a thermonuclear device in the hands of a terrorist group—or even some tin-pot dictator—would represent a completely evil dissemination of knowledge. Ironically, the reader's recognition that the knowledge guarded by Jorge at once constitutes a destructive potential in his own eyes and symbolizes the modern technology of destruction—knowledge that could in fact be too widely disseminated among the unqualified or uninitiated—precludes an easy taking of sides on the censorship issue. Civilization has come full circle—I think this is Eco's point—from an indefensible control of knowledge, to a promotion of knowledge and education as a universal good, to a recognition that there exists, after all, knowledge from which we must be protected. Though one would insist on a distinction between one kind of knowledge and another (a technology of destruction should be guarded, but not an idea or set of ideas like those to which Jorge bars access), the primal, Edenic lesson remains disturbingly valid.

But ultimately the knowledge examined in this novel concerns a technology of destruction less than the terrible recognition of cosmic absurdity, and the novel asks if we can live with such knowledge. Within the restraints necessary to his setting and his characters, Eco adumbrates the grim knowledge that has always awaited both the logician and the empirical investigator. Eventually Adso's faith falters. In his postscript, he seems to describe something between mysticism ("divine shadow," "ineffable union") and despair (death as desert, a lapsing into "uninhabited divinity"). This preserves the pietism necessary to Eco's historical setting, but it also describes the only options remaining for religious sensibility in the twentieth century's godless day. At a crucial earlier moment, Adso has himself flirted, moth to flame, with apostasy: "Isn't affirming God's absolute omnipotence and His absolute freedom with regard to His own choices tantamount to demonstrating that God does not exist?" (p. 493). After such knowledge, what forgiveness?

But if humanity must give up meaning and God, there yet remains laughter, which will counter despair and promote survival. The story's modern slant emerges in the fact that its villains—Jorge of Burgos, Bernard Gui—prove consistently to lack a sense of humor. Jorge calls laughter "the Luciferine spark" and compares it to the fear-dispelling gift of Prometheus. He would refuse this gift, for he considers fear (the fear of God) salutary. A more modern temper, however, would define fear as a form of degradation. Fear of the tyrant, for example, merely consolidates injustice, and if a later age repudiates the very idea of God as the ultimate tyranny, it will need—or at least fall into—a laughter-weapon to keep the dark at bay. (And is not the frosty laughter of irony—William's characteristic vein—the definitive mood of the twentieth century?) Jorge even augurs the fate of belief in the modern age when he imagines "one day" when "someone could say . . . I laugh at the Incarnation" (p. 477). But at least on that day one can also laugh at the abyss that remains after one has let go of God.

Thus far, I have noted a variety of images of the modern age in Eco's fourteenth-century *speculum*: Eco's discourses on political and religious fragmentation, on torture, and on knowledge and censorship all bear on his age as much as or more than on the age ostensibly under discussion. These specular features are enhanced by the curious interconnections between Adso's manuscript and the modern, "framing" narrative regarding encounters with, transcriptions of, and references to that manuscript. As usual with framing narratives, this one establishes credentials for a story that may pose problems of credibility by linking it narrationally to someone closer to and more trusted by the reader. James invites the reader of *The Turn of the Screw*, for example, to accept the governess's narrative by framing it twice, so that the reader "hears" it from no fewer than three narrators, two of whom—the most proximate—seem sufficiently trustworthy to make their own credulity credible. In the same way, Eco persuades us of the authenticity of the fourteenth-century story and postpones a bit our recognition of its contemporary affinities. But recognize them we do, for ultimately the chief function of the scholar who speaks in the frame would seem to be to introduce and establish the contemporary perspective on the events Adso will narrate. Some of these touches are quite subtle. The scholar, who has a way of stumbling on some amazingly outré texts, may remind one of the similarly serendipitous Borgesian narrator, and thereby prepare one for the discovery that the main narrative's central conceit—library as microcosm—comes from Borges. Similarly, the peripatetic and doomed love affair this author recounts has a decidedly Nabokovian flavor—indeed, one thinks of that other wandering lover, that other Umberto, Nabokov's Humbert Humbert. But does our scholar meet a lover of a different sex?[29] He hints, or perhaps *she* hints, at yet another mirror image for the inverted passions in Adso's story. One notes, in this connection, that Adso's manuscript, which concerns the inaccessibility of a rare manuscript, is itself hard to locate—or rather relocate. Ironically, access to old manuscripts would seem as problematic in the twentieth century as in the fourteenth. Indeed, even in a technological age, with the immense resources of academic libraries and legions of scholars, great chunks of the written past can still disappear.

One can note in passing that in some ways Adso's manuscript parallels that of Aristotle. Both survive only as reconstructions; both are lost in the original. Adso narrates a memoir or history, not criticism like Aristotle. But Adso's narrative is from the reader's viewpoint a fiction, with possibilities for both the tragedy and the comedy analyzed by Aristotle. That the story is one of cosmic futility, disorder, and meaninglessness, however, reveals its "modern" inability to rise to tragedy; its "black" comedy, by the same token, is a modern hybrid that Aristotle's age would not have found congenial.

The author seems at pains, at any rate, to reverse the credibility established in the frame, to undermine confidence in the authenticity of Adso's manuscript by describing a suspicious web of references (seldom agreeing with each other) to an original no longer to be found. Eco provides this oddly detailed provenance for the story—this checkerboard of sources and texts—to remind the reader of the multiplicity and frequent unreliability of the "signs" by which one "reads" experience. As Terry Eagleton remarks in sketching the structuralist background to semiotic theory, "art estranges and undermines conventional sign-systems, compels our attention to the material process of language itself, and so reverses our perceptions."[30] Eco's work functions precisely in this fashion, and without the semiotic didacticism one might fear. He does, however, provide a number of exempla in the course of the novel. In the opening pages, for instance, when Adso speaks of "signs of signs" yet declines to speculate on the larger "design" of the tale—a collection of signs—he will narrate, one knows to prepare for a lesson in semiotics. Presently William is performing a little semiotic demonstration with Brunellus, the abbot's errant horse, preparatory to working on the more complex series of signs surrounding the murders in the monastery. To this end he frequently expatiates on signs of all sorts—for example, "Venantius's prints in the snow" or the pictures of unicorns in bestiaries. "If the print exists, there must have existed something whose print it is." But slippage can occur, for at times one must speak of an "impression . . . left in our mind: it is the print of an idea. . . , sign of a sign" (p. 317). Thus William can define a book as "made up of signs that speak of other signs, which in turn speak of things" (p. 396).

The expectation that a sign refers ultimately to some concrete "thing" would seem to be a point at which the author denies his character full semiotic knowledge, the better to preserve, in some measure, his credibility as a fourteenth-century thinker. This attempt to find in signs and in language a reliable index to the phenomenal world motivates Eco's central character. It figures, for example, in William's attempts to make an etymological connection, in his learned remarks to the imperial and papal ambassadors, between Latin *nomen* (name) and Greek *nomos* (law). Though William makes a political point (he wants to suggest that God's encouragement of Adam to give things names—*nomina*—implies as well a divine tolerance of certain democratic possibilities—that is, a system of laws—*nomoi*—devised by humanity), he makes it in terms that reveal his desire to see language as potentially a key to what King Lear calls "the mystery of things." At this point in the story William clings to the hope that law and name will prove related, that one can learn the names—the signs, that is—sufficiently well to find in language itself the Logos, the supreme rationale of the cosmos. He seeks the ultimate system of names or signs that will discover the laws of the universe, for he wants language to function as reality-probe. He does not yet recognize in language a reality-maker.

William's remarks about names and naming, and his interest in signs generally, help the reader to grapple with Eco's mysterious title, in which twentieth-century semiotics and the realist-nominalist controversy of the Middle Ages converge. Speculation on the rose and its name is proverbial, from Shakespeare ("A rose by any other name would smell as sweet") to Gertrude Stein ("A rose is a rose is a rose"). The word *rose*, however, is polysemic, denotatively and connotatively multifarious: it is the flower, of course, but it is also a mystical emblem, a woman's name, a stained-glass window, a symbol of beauty, love, secrecy, and deity. Much of this semantic proliferation is a matter of metaphoric extension from the flower, but in a word this rich one can see the essential plasticity of language, what the semioticians call the play of the signifier.

The word *rose* can be specific or generic, but in semiotics this distinction is not enough. Semioticians describe a "sign" as an entity containing a "signifier" (the written or spoken word—*horse*, for example) and a "signified" (the generic designation—the concept *horse*). A particular horse—Brunellus, say—is called the "referent." This declension of the "sign" is not terribly important in itself—except to the extent that it promotes an understanding of the subtlety of language and the attendant complexities of communication. Such an understanding contributes signally to a grasp of just what language can and cannot do for the metaphysician. William only gradually realizes the inadequacy of his theories of language and of signs. He tends, for example, to think of signs as ontologically subordinate to the things they designate and related to them by simple one-to-one correspondence. He is also constrained to think about language in medieval terms.

A phrase like "the name of the rose," in fact, invites reflection on one of the great philosophical debates of the Middle Ages and the Scholastic philosophers— the existence of "universals." Medieval philosophers defined themselves as realists or nominalists, depending on whether they believed or disbelieved in the existence of universals. The realists saw universals as something like Plato's Ideal Forms—something "real" that would subsume or dictate the incidental form of individual phenomena. For the nominalists, universals were merely convenient concepts—linguistic categories or classes for similar things. The distinction may seem needlessly subtle to the modern mind, but the medieval philosopher considered it a necessary part of conceptualizing a coherent, rationalistic model of the universe. The medieval philosopher—William, for example—needed universals to understand the world rationally. Without them, he was obliged to sunder faith from reason, theology from philosophy. William knows William of Occam and makes use of his "razor" ("one should not multiply explanations and causes unless it is strictly necessary"—p. 91), and he knows, presumably, about "Terminism," Occam's *linguistic* resolution of the realist-nominalist controversy in favor of the latter: only individual things exist.[31] Archrationalist and nominalist, William is forced unhappily to the conclusion that the universe subsumes merely a collection of disparate things, a buzzing, blooming confusion without order.[32]

So what is the significance of "the name of the rose"? The serious, essential questions raised in this novel suggest that "rose" refers to the mystical symbol of truth and beauty and ultimate reality that Yeats often invokes. For Yeats, as for every mystic, the rose is, in medieval terms, a realist universal. But the novel and its hero call into question the existence of such a universal, and thus of order in the universe. If such an order existed, its name (*nomen*) and the law (*nomos*) it bodied forth would be knowable. Not for William, not for Eco. William's insistence on rational models stands as perhaps the strongest illustration of the modern temper beneath his medieval exterior. Were he really a man of his age he would have no difficulty—call it the "negative capability" of the Middle Ages—in allowing theology and philosophy, faith and reason, their separate spheres. William's final, elegiac pronouncements suggest that he concludes his investigation perilously close to apostasy, and behind him Umberto Eco seems to admit that the Rose—what Yeats called "the symbolic heart of things"—must remain unnamed, shrouded in ambiguity.

By the end of his story Adso, too, flirts with agnosticism. This narrative, like the Bible, begins with "in the beginning" and ends with a vision of apocalypse. But after "in the beginning" Adso says "was the Word," so that he echoes the beginning of the Gospel according to Saint John as well (whose echo of Genesis is also deliberate; we are again immersed in intertextuality). The Word is the Logos, the divine principle of order in the universe, but the story unfolds as an account of the discovery of the *absence* of that principle of order.

Much is said in the novel about difference. Adso earnestly attempts to define the differences between doctrines endorsed by the Holy "Roman" Church and those—often confusingly similar—condemned as heretical. Adso's quest for orthodoxy is treated with some irony, but the attempt to recognize differences is sound semiotic practice. Signs are defined, according to semioticians, by their differences from other signs. One knows a "bar" for a place to drink because it is not bat, car, tar, or boar. To master the language, one masters the differences. Adso, a dutiful novice, seeks to master the sign system, the language, of the Catholic Church. But Adso also believes in an ultimate signified for all language, a point at which word coincides with *ens*. Adso mistakenly laments William's dwindling ability to grasp differences, but this inability reveals that William is recognizing the problem of the multiplicity of language; it foreshadows William's eventual realization that no ultimate language exists, no supreme set of signs reveals an orderly cosmos. The analysis of differences, then, leads *away* from an encounter with or validation of the Logos.

Though less pietistic than Adso, William, too, starts with an expectation that he can probe signs to their phenomenal bedrock. He takes pride in having trained himself to look for and interpret signs, whether of an errant horse named Brunellus, of the subject matter of an absent book, of a monachal psychopath, or of order in the universe. To solve the problem or mystery of the murders, William must perform on a larger scale the act of cryptography that is the breaking of Venantius's code—the whole book in miniature. He must discover the system of signs whereby the murders become meaningful. But William learns—painfully—that sign systems invite us to discover in them meanings we expect to find or otherwise find congenial.

Thus the reader enters, in this novel, a world of deceptive appearances. If one has illusions about monasteries as places of piety, chastity, labor, and quiet worship, one soon finds a tangled web of petty jealousies and murderous fanaticism. One of William's first discoveries, for example, is that among the intellectual monks, those who work in the scriptorium, there exists a kind of homosexual cabal; the coarser kitchen staff, on the other hand, smuggle peasant women into the monastery at night for regular debauches. Thus the unraveling of the mystery brings with it shocks to the reader's expectations that complement similar shocks to William's intellectual pride. William is influenced by a remark of Alinardo's and thinks he sees a pattern of apocalyptic allusions in the series of deaths. But the pattern in fact begins with nothing more than a homosexual monk's suicide and is only later embraced by the opportunistic Jorge. "Alinardo had told me about his idea," says Jorge, "and then I heard from someone that you, too, found it persuasive." "So then," admits William, "I conceived a false pattern to interpret the moves of the guilty man, and the guilty man fell in with it" (p. 470). The signs, in other words, complicated by secondary mysteries and red herrings, invite an erroneous interpretation—that they somehow represent an apocalyptic sequence. But the reader—with William—eventually learns that the sequence, and the apocalyptic symmetries, is in fact a mixture of psychopathology and accident shaped by pattern-making tendencies in the mind.

Jorge's acts and their accidental ramifications are what semioticians call a *parole*—a set of "speech acts" that ought to be grounded in a controlling sign-system, a grammar or *langue*. William tries to discover this grammar, and in doing so recapitulates his search for the grammar of that other sign-system, the universe. But neither proves intrinsically coherent, neither discovers an orderly or sensible realm of essential truth or reality. The point is that various minds—William's, Jorge's, the reader's—latch onto random facts and "read" them, impose a pattern on them that reflects only a limited grasp of the way signs work to create reality. William, with all his wisdom and caution and awareness of this very principle, still falls into the trap of language and so concludes ruefully:

I have never doubted the truth of signs, Adso; they are the only things man has with which to orient himself in the world. What I did not understand was the relation among signs. I arrived at Jorge through an apocalyptic pattern that seemed to underlie all the crimes, and yet it was accidental. I arrived at Jorge seeking one criminal for all crimes and we discovered that each crime was committed by a different person, or by no one. I arrived at Jorge pursuing the plan of a perverse and rational mind, and there was no plan, or, rather, Jorge himself was overcome by his own initial design and there began a sequence of causes, and concauses, and of causes contradicting one another, which proceeded on their own, creating relations that did not stem from any plan. Where is all my wisdom, then? I behaved stubbornly, pursuing a semblance of order, when I should have known well that there is no order in the universe. (p. 492)

When Adso loyally points out that he has nevertheless solved the mystery, William insists that it is a meaningless triumph: "The order that our mind imagines is like a net, or like a ladder, built to attain something. But afterward you must throw the ladder away,[33] because you discover that, even if it was useful, it was meaningless" (p. 492). William at last achieves the full insight of twentieth-century semiotics.

William and Adso do not learn their bitter lesson alone. We, too, have been seduced into perceiving a meaning (the apocalyptic sequence) that is merely the result of the codes we are equipped with, which we mistake for tools of universal perception. Eco intimates that, given the dangerousness of the modern world, a failure to recognize our imprisonment in language, along with a tendency to project linguistically determined assumptions onto a reality uncongenial to them, will lay us open to the cataclysmic possibilities symbolized by the conflagration with which the novel ends. William, in his confrontation with Jorge, calls the blind monk "the Devil," which he defines as "arrogance of spirit, faith without smile, truth that is never seized by doubt" (p. 477). Later he is the Antichrist (p. 491), an appropriate actor in the concluding grand drama of apocalypse or "horrid replica of Armageddon" (p. 490). These terms figure ironically now, for he and the reader have come to realize how deceptively "coded" they are. The "apocalypse" eventually brought to parturition—the fiery end of the microcosmic monastery—proves bleakly secular. The "promised end" is only a parody of the end expected by medieval Christianity—it is the very sign and symbol, on the other hand, of the destruction imminent for the world symbolized by the monastery. The cataclysm, ironically, will be largely indistinguishable from the one an ancient linguistic model of reality leads one to expect—except that it will not eventuate in the Second Coming. It is a warning, finally, of the apocalyptic perils posed by the fanatics of a later age. But Eco preaches no sermon. As he said to the interviewer in *Vogue*, "You want me to be a sort of guru, and I refuse the role."[34]

And so, a semiotic object-lesson. But the ultimate semiotic object-lesson concerns history itself, and indeed, as I have argued all along, the signs that seem to say "this is a story of the fourteenth century" are deceptive. They really announce a fiction that drafts twentieth-century perceptions of language to meditate on the twentieth century itself. Eco reminds his readers that they communicate by signs and that in distinguishing signs—in language, in writing, even in the environment—they must resist the naïve assumption that a separate world of concrete reality exists for these signs to report on, gloss, or label. Language does not label reality, it creates it. Eco insists on the crucial importance of a recognition that language is not based on positive, absolute, or essential realities but rather on an arbitrary set of relationships and "differences." On such a recognition depend one's prospects not only for solving mysteries but also for establishing a sound epistemology.

Eco's semiotically cautionary vision of apocalypse provides the right note on which to conclude these reflections on history in the contemporary novel, for the apocalyptic vision proves disturbingly common in the fiction of the nuclear age. Under the distant mirror rubric as well as the other categories, the topos of Armageddon figures in several of the works examined here: *Memoirs of Hadrian, The Sot-Weed Factor, Riddley Walker, A Canticle for Leibowitz.* To these one can add the suggestively titled *The War of the End of the World,* by Mario Vargas Llosa. Like *The Name of the Rose,* it features an unhinged cleric whose eschatological obsessions provide the frame for a tale of gradually escalating and portentous violence.

But perhaps the supreme meditation on apocalypse is *Gravity's Rainbow,* by Thomas Pynchon. Set in the period just before and after the conclusion of World War II, this novel opens in an embattled London, with a dream sequence in which the Crystal Palace, that monument to Victorian assumptions about progress, has sustained a direct hit from a V–2 rocket representing the technological fulfillment of all that the famous Victorian structure stands for. The novel contains more than one such image of technology looping back on itself in a destructive circuit. At several points, for example, Pynchon refers to Kekulé von Stradonitz, the nineteenth-century chemist who dreamed of a serpent biting its tail and came thereby to grasp the structure of the benzene ring, to invent the technology of aromatic polymers, and thus to accelerate the tinkering with nature that may yet reach its climax in the kind of cataclysm Pynchon imagines at the conclusion of *Gravity's Rainbow*. This conclusion provides yet another instance of circularity, for like *Finnegans Wake* the novel ends where it begins, except that the rocket descending on the final page is something vaster and more terrible than the V–2.

Pynchon structures *Gravity's Rainbow* as a movie and even marks chapter breaks with a representation of film sprocket holes. Though the action ostensibly transpires in the months just before and after the end of World War II, it ends as an ICBM, another ironic fulfillment of an earlier technological promise, poises over the theater in which the film is being shown. The viewers (the readers, along with the rest of humanity) watch what is not so much a historical film as the movie of history. In this denouement, Pynchon deliberately and shockingly violates his narrative frame to suggest the fragility of all our fictions of history and the need for our historical fictions to reflect what seems more and more like a historical tropism for apocalypse. In collapsing the years between 1946 and the present, moreover, he demonstrates the incredible rapidity with which a terrible reckoning seems to be overtaking us.

The contemporary historical novelist, then, examines the past in a number of ways and for a variety of reasons. But this novelist works in an age unique in the annals of history, an age in which, for the first time, humanity can envision a do-it-yourself apocalypse. Consequently the imminence of cataclysm (some would say the immanence) figures with greater or lesser explicitness in the serious historical fiction of the age. According to the creators of this body of work, history no longer unfolds with its wonted slowness. If it is a movie, as Pynchon says, it is a movie unreeling from a projector gone haywire in an empty projection booth. It is, as I suggested early on, a scary version of one of those old-fashioned, jumpy newsreels.

These cinematic metaphors resemble the older idea—one can trace it from Heraclitus to Bergson—of time as a river. The contemporary historical novelist explores the headwaters of this river for what they may reveal about singularities in the delta. Some explorers seek simply to describe a stretch of riverscape; others search for the point at which the river acquires a peculiar sedimentary admixture; still others look for meaning in the replication of meanders and oxbows. Those who dwell in the flood plain, meanwhile, anxiously await what may be crucial information from upstream.

Notes
Works Cited
Index

Notes

1. Time Present and Time Past

1. *The Historical Novel,* trans. Hannah and Stanley Mitchell (London: Merlin Press, 1962), p. 168.
2. Darmstadt: Wissenschaftliche Buchgesellschaft, 1981.
3. New York: Oxford, 1974.
4. Avrom Fleishman, *The English Historical Novel: Walter Scott to Virginia Woolf* (Baltimore: Johns Hopkins, 1971), pp. 3–4.
5. *"Le roman et l'histoire,"* Nouvelle revue française, 20 (October 1972) 132. My translation.
6. 5 October 1901, *The Selected Letters of Henry James,* ed. Leon Edel (New York: Farrar, Straus and Cudahy, 1955), pp. 202–3.
7. *The Triple Thinkers: Twelve Essays on Literary Subjects* (New York: Oxford University Press, 1952), p. 114.
8. *An Autobiography* (London: Oxford University Press, 1939), p. 79.
9. *The House of Desdemona, or The Laurels and Limitations of Historical Fiction,* trans. Harold A. Basilius (Detroit: Wayne State University Press, 1963), pp. 129–30.
10. *Metahistory: The Historical Imagination in Nineteenth-Century Europe* (Baltimore: Johns Hopkins University Press, 1973), pp. 1–2.
11. *The Historian's Craft,* trans. Peter Putnam (New York: Knopf, 1953), p. 13.

12. Translator's Foreword, Lion Feuchtwanger, *The House of Desdemona* (Detroit: Wayne State University Press, 1963), p. 7.
13. "Narrative and History," *ELH*, 41 (1974) 461.
14. *The Idea of History* (New York: Oxford University Press, 1946), p. 245.
15. Collingwood, *Idea,* p. 246.
16. Fleishman, p. 6.
17. *Literary Theory: An Introduction* (Minneapolis: University of Minnesota Press, 1983), p. 60.
18. Quoted in Collingwood, *Idea,* p. 241.
19. See *Mimesis: The Representation of Reality in Western Literature,* trans. Willard R. Trask (Princeton: Princeton University Press, 1953), p. 19.
20. *The Philosophy of History.* trans. J. Sibree (1857; reprinted, New York: Willey, 1944), p. 6.

2. The Way It Was

1. "*Mémoires d'Hadrien:* A Manual for Princes," *University of Toronto Quarterly,* 50/2 (Winter 1980–1981) 223.
2. Marguerite Yourcenar, *Memoirs of Hadrian and Reflections on the Composition of Memoirs of Hadrian,* trans. Grace Frick (Paris, 1951; reprinted, New York: Farrar, Straus & Giroux, 1963), p. 21.
3. In Yourcenar, *Memoirs of Hadrian,* p. 340.
4. *Marguerite Yourcenar, Ecrivains d'Hier et d'Aujourd'hui,* 38 (Paris: Editions Seghers, 1971), p. 140. My translation.
5. In Marguerite Yourcenar, *Les yeux ouverts: entretiens avec Matthieu Galey* (Paris: Centurion, 1980), p. 155, the author hints that Hadrian's lies extend to the circumstances of his accession to power. The point is disputed by historians.
6. *Entretiens radiophoniques avec Marguerite Yourcenar* (Paris: Mercure de France, 1972), p. 106. My translation.
7. Quotations from the *Metamorphoses* are from Mary M. Inne's translation (Baltimore: Penguin, 1955).
8. "*L'Empereur Hadrien vu par* Marguerite Yourcenar," *Etudes Littéraires,* 12/1 (April 1979) 32. My translation. The point here is something of a critical commonplace. Yourcenar herself, in the *Entretiens radiophoniques,* calls Hadrian "one of the supreme representatives" of ancient culture (p. 109).

9. Yourcenar, "Bibliographical Note," in *Memoirs of Hadrian*, p. 314.

10. "Marguerite Yourcenar *ou la mesure de l'homme*," *La Revue Générale* (January 1970), pp. 28–29. My translation.

11. In Barth's view, historical novels tend to be devoted to information rather than to the Aristotelian desiderata for literature: "the experience of human life, its happiness and its misery." See Barth, "Historical Fiction, Fictitious History, and Chesapeake Bay Blue Crabs, or, About Aboutness," in his *The Friday Book: Essays and Other Nonfiction* (New York: Putnam's, 1984), pp. 180–92.

12. John Barth, *The Sot-Weed Factor*, 2nd ed. (Garden City, N.Y.: Doubleday, 1967), p. 753.

13. Ebenezer Cook, "The Sot-Weed Factor," in *Early Maryland Poetry; the works of Ebenezer Cook, gent: laureate of Maryland*, ed. Bernard C. Steiner (Baltimore: John Murphy, 1900).

14. John J. Enck, "John Barth: An Interview," *Wisconsin Studies in Contemporary Literature*, 6 (1965) 14.

15. *John Barth: An Introduction* (University Park: Pennsylvania State University Press, 1976), p. 49.

16. Trans. S. H. Butcher (New York: Hill and Wang, 1961), p. 68.

17. "John Barth and the Novel of Comic Nihilism," *Wisconsin Studies in Contemporary Literature*, 7 (1966) 254n26.

18. See, for example, Alan Holder, "'What Marvelous Plot . . . Was Afoot?': History in Barth's *The Sot-Weed Factor*," *American Quarterly*, 20/3 (1968) 596–604; Brian W. Dippie, "'His Visage Wild; His Form Exotick': Indian Themes and Cultural Guilt in John Barth's *The Sot-Weed Factor*," *American Quarterly*, 21/1 (1969) 113–21; Gordon W. Slethaug, "Barth's Refutation of the Idea of Progress," *Critique*, 13/3 (1972) 11–29; and Barbara Ewell, "John Barth: The Artist of History," *Southern Literary Journal*, 5/2 (1973) 32–46.

19. *City of Words: American Fiction 1950–1970* (New York: Harper & Row, 1971), p. 242.

20. "The Self in Fiction, or 'That Ain't No Matter. That Is Nothing,'" in his *The Friday Book*, p. 212.

21. *John Barth: The Comic Sublimity of Paradox* (Carbondale: Southern Illinois University Press, 1974), p. 4.

22. Arthur O. Lovejoy, "Milton and the Paradox of the Fortunate Fall," *ELH*, 4 (1937) 161–79.

23. It is also, as Philip E. Diser points out in "The Historical Ebenezer Cooke," *Critique,* 10/3 (1968) 48–59, the date proposed by Lawrence C. Wroth in his introduction to *The Maryland Muse,* published in *Proceedings of the American Antiquarian Society,* 44 (October 1934).

24. *Versions of the Past: The Historical Imagination in American Fiction* (New York: Oxford University Press, 1974), p. 284.

25. *Four Postwar American Novelists: Bellow, Mailer, Barth, Pynchon* (Chicago: University of Chicago Press, 1977), p. 134.

26. "John Barth: An Eccentric Genius," *New Leader,* 13 Feb. 1961, p. 23.

27. Yourcenar described this technique a number of times, most recently in an interview with Josyane Savigneau—"Yourcenar: *non importa vincere ma essere liberi*"—in the Turin newspaper *La Stampa,* December 29, 1984, cols. 6–7. See also "Reflections," pp. 325, 326, 328–29.

3. The Way It Will Be

1. Kobo Abé, *Inter Ice Age 4,* trans. E. Dale Saunders (New York: Knopf, 1970), p. 227.

2. See Hugh Rank, "Song Out of Season: *A Canticle for Leibowitz,*" *Renascence,* 21 (Summer 1969) 213–21.

3. Letter to the author, May 28, 1979.

4. Eliade introduces this idea at the end of *The Myth of the Eternal Return* (Princeton: Princeton University Press, 1954), pp. 139–62. As will be seen, I rely extensively on Eliade (in, for example, the three paragraphs following this note) in my reading of *Riddley Walker.* I should like to take this opportunity to say that my debt goes beyond my citations; in reading Eliade I have learned much about the way human beings conceptualize history across the cultural spectrum.

5. Quoted in Cullen Murphy, "The Butser Experiment," *Atlantic,* July 1985, p. 23.

6. As Natalie Maynor and Richard F. Patteson note, "most linguists agree that there is no such thing as a 'primitive' language or dialect." See "Language as Protagonist in *Riddley Walker,*" *Critique,* 26/1 (Fall 1984) 20.

7. Russell Hoban, *Riddley Walker* (New York: Summit Books, 1980), p. 121.

8. For more on *Riddley Walker*'s echoes of Anglo-Saxon literature, see Maynor and Patteson, "Language," p. 22.
9. Margaret Atwood, *The Handmaid's Tale* (Boston: Houghton Mifflin, 1986), p. 31.
10. Scott Klug, "Architect of the American Reich," *City Paper* (Washington, D.C.), May 15, 1987, pp. 12, 14, 16–19.
11. Amin Malak, "Margaret Atwood's 'The Handmaid's Tale' and the Dystopian Tradition," *Canadian Literature* (Spring 1987) 11.
12. Bruno Bettelheim, *The Uses of Enchantment: The Meaning and Importance of Fairy Tales* (New York: Knopf, 1976), p. 173.
13. See Sandra M. Gilbert and Susan Gubar, *The Madwoman in the Attic* (New Haven: Yale University Press, 1979).

4. The Turning Point

1. "*The Confessions of Nat Turner* and the Burden of the Past," in *The Achievement of William Styron*, ed. Robert K. Morris, with Irving Malin (Athens: University of Georgia Press, rev. ed., 1981), p. 213.
2. "Giuseppe Tomasi di Lampedusa," in *Letturatura italiana, I Contemporanei*, vol. 3 (Milan, 1969), p. 256. My translation.
3. Giuseppe di Lampedusa, *The Leopard*, trans. Archibald Colquhoun (New York: Pantheon, 1960), p. 259.
4. "Giuseppe di Lampedusa: A Note by the Translator," in *Two Stories and a Memory*, by Lampedusa (New York: Pantheon, 1962), p. 37.
5. Lampedusa seems to have planned a chronicle of these developments in an unfinished novel, a fragment of which ("The Blind Kittens") appears in *Two Stories and a Memory*.
6. For more on animal imagery, see Stanley G. Eskin, "Animal Imagery in *Il Gattopardo*," *Italica*, 39 (1962) 189–94.
7. "Stendhal, Tomasi di Lampedusa, and the Novel," in *Narrative and Drama: Essays in Modern Italian Literature from Verga to Pasolini* (The Hague: Mouton, 1976), p. 20.
8. Sergio Pacifici notes that, "as a serious scientist and mathematician," Don Fabrizio "knows that changes do occur in the 'fixed stars,' but such changes cannot be detected by the naked human eye as they occur over a time span measurable in terms of thousands or millions of years, thus justifying what is aptly called 'permanence in transience.' The prince's only hope is

that all the changes in the sociopolitical order of the South will proceed at the same rate of speed as the stars'" (*The Modern Italian Novel* [Carbondale: Southern Illinois University Press, 1979], p. 75).

9. "The Metamorphosis of the Gods in *Il Gattopardo*," *Modern Language Notes*, 81 (1966) 24, 31–32.

10. According to Archibald Colquhon, the Lampedusas go back to the sixth-century Byzantine emperor Tiberius II ("Giuseppe di Lampedusa: A Note by the Translator," in *Two Stories and a Memory*, p. 21).

11. *Anatomy of Criticism* (Princeton: Princeton University Press 1957), p. 224.

12. Hayden White, *Metahistory: The Historical Imagination in Nineteenth-Century Europe* (Baltimore: Johns Hopkins University Press, 1973), p. 231. I am also indebted to White for reminding me of Frye's definition of irony.

13. Jeffrey Meyers, in "Symbol and Structure in *The Leopard*," *Italian Quarterly*, 9/34–35 (1965) 54, notes a further parallel out of Tasso. In *The Leopard*, Concetta loves Tancredi, who loves Angelica; in Tasso's poem, "Erminia loves Tancredi, who loves Clorinda."

14. Giambattista Vico, *The New Science*, 3rd ed. (1744), trans. Thomas Goddard Bergin and Max Harold Frisch (Ithaca: Cornell University Press, 1968), p. 69.

15. Georgio Bassani, *Prefazione, Il Gattopardo* (Milan: Feltrinelli, 1958), p. 7. My translation.

16. D. M. Thomas, *The White Hotel* (New York: Viking, 1981), p. 143.

17. Freud's important discussions of this subject are in the essays "The Uncanny," trans. Alix Strachey, and "Dreams and Telepathy," trans. C. J. M. Hubback, in Sigmund Freud, *Collected Papers*, ed. Joan Riviere and James Strachey (New York: Basic Books, 1959), vol. 4, pp. 368–435. Firmly skeptical, he argues that what appears to be clairvoyance can usually be accounted for as an unconscious recollection of previous knowledge.

18. "To Hereward Carrington," July 24, 1921, Letter 192, *The Letters of Sigmund Freud*, trans. Tania and James Stern, ed. Ernst L. Freud (New York: Basic Books, 1975), p. 334.

19. "Hystery, Herstory, History: 'Imagining the Real' in Thomas's *The White Hotel*," *Contemporary Literature*, 25/4 (1984) 455.

20. Sigmund Freud, "Contributions to the Psychology of Love," in his *Collected Papers*, vol. 4, pp. 192–216.
21. *Collected Papers*, vol. 2, p. 247n2. See also the posthumous essay "Medusa's Head," *Collected Papers*, vol. 5, pp. 105–6.
22. The material from *Babi Yar*, in particular, has occasioned criticism. Typical are the sour remarks of Martin Amis in his review of Thomas's *Ararat*: "When the reviewers spoke of the transports and crackups they weathered as they checked out of *The White Hotel* ('I walked out into the garden and could not speak,' and so on), it was Babi Yar that had assailed them. The testimony is unbearably powerful; it is the climax of the novel; it is, in plain terms, the best bit—and Thomas didn't write it" ("The D. M. Thomas Phenomenon," *Atlantic*, April 1983, pp. 124–26). But the Babi Yar section of Thomas's novel is not in fact superior to the sustained impersonation of Freud's case-history persona. Anyone who reads these novels side by side must be struck by the fact that Kuznetsov's is highly episodic and disjointed. It does not begin to approach the cumulative power of *The White Hotel*. Perhaps Thomas's borrowings from Kuznetsov, though acknowledged, are unconscionable; it may be that, like the critic who admired the work of Robert Frost but who would not have cared to be in the same room with him, one must distinguish between one's feelings for the tale, however it came to be, and one's feeling for the teller. For a comprehensive discussion (with bibliography) of this controversy and subsequent allegations of plagiarism in Thomas's translations of Russian poetry, see Lynn Felder, "D. M. Thomas: The Plagiarism Controversy," in *Dictionary of Literary Biography Yearbook 1982*, pp. 79–82.
23. New York: Harcourt, Brace & World, 1951, p. 92.
24. London: Jonathan Cape, 1968.
25. Sigmund Freud, *The Future of an Illusion*, trans. James Strachey, in *The Standard Edition of the Complete Psychological Works of Sigmund Freud* (London: Hogarth Press, 1961), vol. 21, p. 43.
26. Some, like Brian Martin, prefer to see the epilogue as a "fantasy for Lisa on the point of death" ("People from the Provinces," *New Statesman*, January 16, 1981, pp. 20–21). More common is the reaction of Thomas Flanagan, who "cannot accept, even as a metaphor, a River Jordan flowing somewhere, beyond the sand pits of Babi Yar" ("To Babi Yar and Beyond," *Nation*, May 2, 1981, pp. 537–39).

27. D. M. Thomas, *Love and Other Deaths* (London: Paul Elek, 1975).
28. Berkeley: University of California Press, 1966. See also Karlinsky's article on Tsvetayeva in the *Columbia Dictionary of Modern European Literature*, 2nd ed. (1980).
29. I am indebted for this idea to my colleague, Donald J. Greiner.
30. "On a Book Entitled Lolita," in his *Lolita* (New York: Putnam's, 1958), p. 314.

5. The Distant Mirror

1. D. H. Lawrence, *The Man Who Died* (New York: Knopf, 1931), pp. 13, 24.
2. Faulkner viewed *Go Down, Moses* as a novel; his publishers added the subtitle "and Other Stories" for the first edition. For a judicious discussion of the points on which this fiction is and is not novelistic, see Michael Millgate, *The Achievement of William Faulkner* (New York: Random House, 1966), pp. 202–3. See also Warren Beck, *Faulkner* (Madison: University of Wisconsin Press, 1976), pp. 344–45.
3. Stanley Sultan, "Call Me Ishmael: The Hagiography of Isaac McCaslin," *Texas Studies in Literature and Language*, 3/1 (Spring 1961) 66.
4. Alfred Kazin, *Bright Book of Life: American Novelists and Storytellers from Hemingway to Mailer* (London: Secker & Warburg, 1974), p. 31.
5. William Faulkner, *Go Down, Moses and Other Stories* (New York: Random House, 1942), p. 380.
6. Arthur Mizener, "The Thin, Intelligent Face of American Fiction," *Kenyon Review*, 17 (1955) 517.
7. Cleanth Brooks, *William Faulkner: The Yoknapatawpha Country* (New Haven: Yale University Press, 1963), pp. 246–47.
8. Annette Benert, "The Four Fathers of Isaac McCaslin," *Southern Humanities Review*, 9/4 (Fall 1975) 424.
9. Ed. Frederick J. Gwynn and Joseph Blotner, *Faulkner in the University: Class Conferences at the University of Virginia 1957–58* (Charlottesville: University Press of Virginia, 1959), p. 275. I am indebted to Brooks, p. 268, for this reference.

10. Myra Jehlen, *Class and Character in Faulkner's South* (New York: Columbia University Press, 1976), pp. 1, 5.

11. E. M. Forster, Introduction to *Two Stories and a Memory*, by Giuseppe di Lampedusa (New York: Pantheon, 1962), p. 16.

12. Lynn Altenbernd, "A Suspended Moment: The Irony of History in William Faulkner's 'The Bear,'" *MLN*, 75 (November 1960) 577.

13. W. R. Moses, "Where History Crosses Myth: Another Reading of 'The Bear,'" *Accent*, 13/1 (Winter 1953) 21–33.

14. Carl E. Rollyson, "Faulkner as Historian: The Commissary Books in *Go Down, Moses*," *Markham Review*, 7 (Winter 1978) 31.

15. Gary D. Hamilton, "The Past in the Present: A Reading of *Go Down, Moses*," *Southern Humanities Review*, 5/2 (Spring 1971) 171.

16. Jean-Paul Sartre, "Time in Faulkner: *The Sound and the Fury*," trans. Martine Darmon, in *William Faulkner: Three Decades of Criticism*, ed. Frederick J. Hoffman and Olga Vickery (East Lansing: Michigan State University Press, 1960), p. 232. For another general discussion of "time (including historical time, tradition, as well as narrative rhythm and pace)," see Frederick J. Hoffman, *William Faulkner* (New York: Twayne, 1961), pp. 24–31.

17. R. W. B. Lewis, *The Picaresque Saint* (Philadelphia: Lippincott, 1958), pp. 197–209.

18. Thomas Pynchon, *The Crying of Lot 49* (Philadelphia: Lippincott, 1966), p. 181.

19. For an astute discussion of "the bedroom scene" in part 5 of "The Bear," see John W. Hunt, *William Faulkner: Art in Theological Tension* (Syracuse: Syracuse University Press, 1965), pp. 163–66.

20. Millgate, *Achievement*, p. 211.

21. Northrop Frye, *Anatomy of Criticism: Four Essays* (Princeton: Princeton University Press, 1957), pp. 106, 347.

22. Umberto Eco, *The Name of the Rose*, trans. William Weaver (New York: Harcourt, 1983), p. 5.

23. For a representative encounter with the "obscure language" of a "learned man" of the twentieth century, see Eco's own *A Theory of Semiotics* (Bloomington: Indiana University Press, 1976).

24. Ulrich Wyss, *Die Urgeschichte der Intellektualität und das Gelächter: Ein Vortrag über Il Nome della Rosa*, Erlanger Studien 41 (Erlangen, Germany, 1983), p. 5. My translation. I am indebted to Bachorski, p. 81, for this reference (see note 28, below).

25. Melik Kaylan, "Umberto Eco . . . Man of the World," *Vogue* (April 1984), p. 330.
26. Umberto Eco, *Travels in Hyperreality: Essays*, trans. William Weaver (New York: Harcourt, 1986), p. 175.
27. I do not mean to suggest that Eco neglects medieval source material. He makes clear in *Postscript to The Name of the Rose*, trans. William Weaver (New York: Harcourt, 1984), that he aimed at scrupulous accuracy in his re-creation of a medieval world. As Louis Mackey points out in "The Name of the Book," *SubStance*, 14/2 (1985) 37, Eco is at pains to quote or allude to a tremendous variety of medieval texts: "Bernard of Cluny, Hugh of St. Victor, the false Areopagite, Brother Tommaso of Aquino, Hildegard of Bingen, Alain de Lille, Bernard of Clairvaux, the bishop of Hippo, a caravan of Arabs, William of Ockham, Roger Bacon, a smiling Stagirite, Meister Eckhart, the Poverello, Isidore of Seville, an assortment of popes and emperors and heretics."
28. For the argument that Adso and William are both "extremely modern, present-day figures," see Hans-Jürgen Bachorski, " *'Diese klägliche Allegorie der Ohnmacht'*: Der Name der Rose *als historischer Roman,*" in *Aufsätze zu Umberto Ecos* Der Name der Rose, ed. Bachorski (Göppingen: Kümmerle Verlag, 1985), p. 82.
29. Teresa de Lauretis raises the same question and notes that in the original Italian, a "strictly two-gendered" language, Eco takes conspicuous care to sustain the ambiguity. "Gaudy Rose: Eco and Narcissism," *SubStance*, 14/2 (1985) 23, 28n17.
30. Terry Eagleton, *Literary Theory* (Minneapolis: University of Minnesota Press, 1983), pp. 99–100. I am generally indebted to Eagleton for information about semiotic theory.
31. In the Middle Ages, as Eco remarks in *Postscript to The Name of the Rose*, "we find a developed theory of signs only with the Occamites" (p. 26).
32. For more on the realist-nominalist controversy and on its relevance to semiotics, see Elke Hentschel, "'Nomina Nuda Tenemus' *oder Zeichen von Zeichen (von Zeichen),*" in *Aufsätze zu Umberto Ecos* Der Name der Rose, ed. Bachorski, pp. 229ff.
33. The statement comes from Wittgenstein. See de Lauretis, "Gaudy Rose," p. 19.
34. Kaylan, "Umberto Eco," p. 330.

Works Cited

Abé, Kobo. *Inter Ice Age 4*. Translated by E. Dale Saunders. New York: Knopf, 1970.

Altenbernd, Lynn. "A Suspended Moment: The Irony of History in William Faulkner's 'The Bear.'" *MLN* 75 (November 1960) 572–82.

Amis, Martin. "The D. M. Thomas Phenomenon." *Atlantic* (April 1983) 124–26.

Aristotle. *Poetics*. Translated by S. H. Butcher. New York: Hill and Wang, 1961.

Atwood, Margaret. *The Handmaid's Tale*. Boston: Houghton, Mifflin, 1986.

Aubrion, Michel. "*Marguerite Yourcenar ou la mesure de l'homme*." *La Revue Générale* (January 1970) 15–29.

Auerbach, Erich. *Mimesis: The Representation of Reality in Western Literature*. Translated by Willard Trask. Princeton: Princeton University Press, 1953.

Bachorski, Hans-Jürgen, ed. *Aufsätze zu Umberto Ecas Der Name der Rose*. Kümmerle Verlay, 1985

———. " '*Diese klägliche Allegorie der Ohnmacht*': Der Name der Rose als historischer Roman." In *Aufsätze zu Umberto Ecos Der Name der Rose*. Ed. Bachorski. Göppingen: Kümmerle Verlag, 1985, pp. 59–94.

Barth, John. *The Friday Book: Essays and Other Nonfiction*. New York: Putnam's, 1984.

———. *The Sot-Weed Factor*. 2nd ed. Garden City, N.Y.: Doubleday, 1967.

Beck, Warren. *Faulkner*. Madison: University of Wisconsin Press, 1976.

Benert, Annette. "The Four Fathers of Isaac McCaslin." *Southern Humanities Review* 9/4 (Fall 1975) 423–33.

Bettelheim, Bruno. *The Uses of Enchantment: The Meaning and Importance of Fairy Tales*. New York: Knopf, 1976.

Bloch, Marc. *The Historian's Craft*. Translated by Peter Putnam. New York: Knopf, 1953.

Blot, Jean. *Marguerite Yourcenar. Ecrivains d'Hier et d'Aujourd'hui*, 38. Paris: Editions Seghers, 1971.

Brooks, Cleanth. *William Faulkner: The Yoknapatawpha Country*. New Haven: Yale University Press, 1963.

Collingwood, R. G. *An Autobiography*. London: Oxford University Press, 1939.

——. *The Idea of History*. New York: Oxford University Press, 1946.

Cook, Ebenezer. "The Sot-Weed Factor." In *Early Maryland Poetry; the Works of Ebenezer Cook, gent: laureate of Maryland*. Ed. Bernard C. Steiner. Baltimore: John Murphy, 1900.

Core, George. "*The Confessions of Nat Turner* and the Burdens of the Past." In *The Achievement of William Styron*. Rev. ed. Ed. Robert K. Morris, with Irving Malin. Athens: University of Georgia Press, 1981, pp. 206–22.

de Lauretis, Teresa. "Gaudy Rose: Eco and Narcissism." *SubStance* 14/2 (1985) 13–29.

de Rosbo, Patrick. *Entretiens radiophoniques avec Marguerite Yourcenar*. Paris: Mercure de France, 1972.

Dippie, Brian W. " 'His Visage Wild; His Form Exotick': Indian Themes and Cultural Guilt in John Barth's *The Sot-Weed Factor*." *American Quarterly* 21/1 (1969) 113–21.

Diser, Philip E. "The Historical Ebenezer Cooke." *Critique* 10/3 (1968) 48–59.

Eagleton, Terry. *Literary Theory: An Introduction*. Minneapolis: University of Minnesota Press, 1983.

Eco, Umberto. *The Name of the Rose*. Translated by William Weaver. New York: Knopf, 1983.

——. *Postscript to The Name of the Rose*. Translated by William Weaver. New York: Harcourt, 1984.

——. *A Theory of Semiotics*. Bloomington: Indiana University Press, 1976.

——. *Travels in Hyperreality: Essays*. Translated by William Weaver. New York: Harcourt, 1986.

Eliade, Mircea. *The Myth of the Eternal Return.* Princeton: Princeton University Press, 1954.

Enck, John J. "John Barth: An Interview." *Wisconsin Studies in Contemporary Literature* 6 (1965) 3–14.

Eskin, Stanley G. "Animal Imagery in *Il Gattopardo.*" *Italica* 39 (1962) 189–94.

Ewell, Barbara. "John Barth: The Artist of History." *Southern Literary Journal* 5/2 (1973) 32–46.

Faulkner, William. *Go Down, Moses and Other Stories.* New York: Random House, 1942.

Felcini, Furio. "Giuseppe Tomasi di Lampedusa." In *Letturatura italiana, I Contemporanei,* vol. 3.

Felder, Lynn. "D. M. Thomas: The Plagiarism Controversy." In *Dictionary of Literary Biography Yearbook 1982,* pp. 79–82.

Feuchtwanger, Lion. *The House of Desdemona, or the Laurels and Limitations of Historical Fiction.* Translated by Harold A. Basilius. Detroit: Wayne State University Press, 1963.

Fiedler, Leslie. "John Barth: An Eccentric Genius." *New Leader* February 13, 1961, pp. 22–24.

Flanagan, Thomas. "To Babi Yar and Beyond." *Nation* May 2, 1981, pp. 537–39.

Fleishman, Avrom. *The English Historical Novel: Walter Scott to Virginia Woolf.* Baltimore: Johns Hopkins University Press, 1971.

Forster, E. M. *Two Cheers for Democracy.* New York: Harcourt, Brace & World, 1951.

Freud, Sigmund. *Collected Papers.* Ed. Joan Riviere and James Strachey. 5 vols. New York: Basic Books, 1959.

———. "Contributions to the Psychology of Love." Translated by Joan Riviere. In *Collected Papers,* vol. 4, pp. 192–216.

———. "Dreams and Telepathy." Translated by C. J. M. Hubback. In *Collected Papers,* vol. 4, pp. 408–35.

———. *The Future of an Illusion.* Translated by James Strachey. Vol. 21 of *The Standard Edition.*

———. "The Infantile Genital Organization of the Libido." Translated by Joan Riviere. In *Collected Papers,* vol. 2, pp. 244–49.

———. *The Letters of Sigmund Freud.* Translated by Tania Stern and James Stern. Ed. Ernst L. Freud. New York: Basic Books, 1975.

———. "Medusa's Head." Translated by James Strachey. In *Collected Papers,* vol. 5, pp. 105–6.

———. *The Standard Edition of the Complete Psychological Works of Sigmund Freud.* Ed. James Strachey. 24 vols. London: Hogarth Press, 1961.

————. "The Uncanny." Translated by Alix Strachey. In *Collected Papers*, vol. 4, pp. 368–407.

Frye, Northrop. *Anatomy of Criticism: Four Essays*. Princeton: Princeton University Press, 1957.

Gilbert, John. "The Metamorphosis of the Gods in *Il Gattopardo*." *MLN* 81 (1966) 22–32.

Gilbert, Sandra M., and Susan Gubar. *The Madwoman in the Attic*. New Haven: Yale University Press, 1979.

Gwynn, Frederick J., and Joseph Blotner. *Faulkner in the University: Class Conferences at the University of Virginia 1957–58*. Charlottesville: University Press of Virginia, 1959.

Hamilton, Gary D. "The Past in the Present: A Reading of *Go Down, Moses*." *Southern Humanities Review* 5/2 (Spring 1971) 171–81.

Hegel, Georg Wilhelm Friedrich. *The Philosophy of History*. Translated by J. Sibree, 1857. Reprinted, New York: Willey, 1944.

Henderson, Harry B. *Versions of the Past: The Historical Imagination in American Fiction*. New York: Oxford University Press, 1974.

Hentschel, Elke. "'Nomina Nuda Tenemus' *oder Zeichen von Zeichen (von Zeichen)*." In *Aufsätze zu Umberto Ecos Der Name der Rose*. Ed. Hans-Jürgen Bachorski. Göppingen: Kümmerle Verlag, 1985, pp. 225–45.

Hoban, Russell. *Riddley Walker*. New York: Summit Books, 1980.

Hoffman, Frederick J. *William Faulkner*. New York: Twayne, 1961.

Holder, Alan. "'What Marvelous Plot . . . Was Afoot?': History in Barth's *The Sot-Weed Factor*." *American Quarterly* 20/3 (1968): 596–604.

Hunt, John W. *William Faulkner: Art in Theological Tension*. Syracuse: Syracuse University Press, 1965.

James, Henry. *The Selected Letters of Henry James*. Ed. Leon Edel. New York: Farrar, Straus and Cudahy, 1955.

Jehlen, Myra. *Class and Character in Faulkner's South*. New York: Columbia University Press, 1976.

Karlinsky, Simon. *Marina Cvetaeva: Her Life and Art*. Berkeley: University of California Press, 1966.

————. "Tsvetaeva, Marina Ivanovna." *Columbia Dictionary of Modern European Literature*. 2nd ed.

Kaylan, Melik. "Umberto Eco . . . Man of the World." *Vogue* (April 1984), pp. 329–30, 393.

Kazin, Alfred. *Bright Book of Life: American Novelists and Storytellers from Hemingway to Mailer*. London: Secker & Warburg, 1974.

Klug, Scott. "Architect of the American Reich." *City Paper* (Washington, D.C.), May 15, 1987, pp. 12, 14, 16–19.

Lawrence, D. H. *The Man Who Died*. New York: Knopf, 1929.

Lewis, R. W. B. *The Picaresque Saint*. Philadelphia: Lippincott, 1958.

Lovejoy, Arthur O. "Milton and the Paradox of the Fortunate Fall." *ELH* 4 (1937) 161–79.

Lukács, Georg. *The Historical Novel*. Translated by Hannah and Stanley Mitchell. London: Merlin Press, 1962.

McConnell, Frank. *Four Postwar American Novelists: Bellow, Mailer, Barth, Pynchon*. Chicago: University of Chicago Press, 1977.

Mackey, Louis. "The Name of the Book." *SubStance* 14/2 (1985) 30–39.

Malak, Amin. "Margaret Atwood's 'The Handmaid's Tale' and the Dystopian Tradition." *Canadian Literature* (Spring 1987) 9–16.

Martin, Brian. "People from the Provinces." *New Statesman*, January 16, 1981, pp. 20–21.

Maynor, Natalie, and Patteson, Richard F. "Language as Protagonist in *Riddley Walker*." *Critique* 26/1 (1984) 18–25.

Meyers, Jeffrey. "Symbol and Structure in *The Leopard*. *Italian Quarterly* 9/34–35 (1965) 50–70.

Miller, J. Hillis. "Narrative and History." *ELH* 41 (1974) 455–73.

Millgate, Michael. *The Achievement of William Faulkner*. New York: Random House, 1966.

Mizener, Arthur. "The Thin, Intelligent Face of American Fiction." *Kenyon Review* 17 (Autumn 1955) 507–19.

Morrell, David. *John Barth: An Introduction*. University Park: Pennsylvania State University Press, 1976.

Moses, W. R. "Where History Crosses Myth: Another Reading of 'The Bear.'" *Accent* 13/1 (Winter 1953) 21–33.

Murphy, Cullen. "The Butser Experiment." *Atlantic* (July 1985), pp. 20–23.

Nabokov, Vladimir. "On a Book Entitled Lolita." In his *Lolita*. New York: Putnam's, 1958.

Noland, Richard. "John Barth and the Novel of Comic Nihilism." *Wisconsin Studies in Contemporary Literature* 7 (1966) 239–57.

Oldenbourg, Zoé. "*Le roman et l'histoire.*" *Nouvelle revue française* 20 (October 1972) 130–55.

Ovid. *Metamorphoses*. Translated by Mary M. Inne. Baltimore: Penguin, 1955.

Pacifici, Sergio. *The Modern Italian Novel*. Carbondale: Southern Illinois University Press, 1979.

Pynchon, Thomas. *The Crying of Lot 49*. Philadelphia: Lippincott, 1966.

Ragusa, Olga. *Narrative and Drama: Essays in Modern Italian Literature from Verga to Pasolini*. The Hague: Mouton, 1976.

Rank, Hugh. "Song Out of Season: *A Canticle for Leibowitz*." *Renascence*, 21 (Summer 1969) 213–21.

Robertson, Mary F. "Hystery, Herstory, History: 'Imagining the Real' in Thomas's *The White Hotel*. *Contemporary Literature* 25/4 (1984) 452–77.

Rollyson, Carl E. "Faulkner as Historian: The Commissary Books in *Go Down, Moses*." *Markham Review* 7 (Winter 1978) 31–36.

Sartre, Jean-Paul. "Time in Faulkner: *The Sound and the Fury*." Translated by Martine Darmon. In *William Faulkner: Three Decades of Criticism*. Ed. Frederick J. Hoffman and Olga Vickery. East Lansing: Michigan State University Press, 1960, pp. 225–32.

Schabert, Ina. *Der historische Roman in England und Amerika*. Darmstadt: Wissenschaftliche Buchgesellschaft, 1981.

Slethaug, Gordon W. "Barth's Refutation of the Idea of Progress." *Critique* 13/3 (1972) 11–29.

Sultan, Stanley. "Call Me Ishmael: The Hagiography of Isaac McCaslin." *Texas Studies in Literature and Language* 3/1 (Spring 1961) 50–66.

Tanner, Tony. *City of Words: American Fiction 1950–1970*. New York: Harper & Row, 1971.

Tharpe, Jac. *John Barth: The Comic Sublimity of Paradox*. Carbondale: Southern Illinois University Press, 1974.

Thomas, D. M. *Love and Other Deaths*. London: Paul Elek, 1975.

———. *Two Voices*. London: Jonathan Cape, 1968.

———. *The White Hotel*. New York: Viking, 1981.

Tomasi di Lampedusa, Giuseppe. *The Leopard*. Translated by Archibald Colquhoun. New York: Pantheon, 1960.

———. *Two Stories and a Memory*. Translated by Archibald Colquhoun. New York: Pantheon, 1962.

Vico, Giambattista. *The New Science*. 3rd ed. (1744). Translated by Thomas Goddard Bergin and Max Harold Frisch. Ithaca: Cornell University Press, 1968.

Vier, Jacques. "*L'Empereur Hadrien vu par* Marguerite Yourcenar." *Etudes Littéraires* 12/1 (April 1979) 29–35.

Whatley, Janet. "*Mémoires d'Hadrien*: A Manual for Princes." *University of Toronto Quarterly* 50/2 (Winter 1980–1981) 221–37.

White, Hayden. *Metahistory: The Historical Imagination in Nineteenth-Century Europe*. Baltimore: Johns Hopkins University Press, 1973.

Wilson, Edmund. *The Triple Thinkers: Twelve Essays on Literary Subjects.* New York: Oxford University Press, 1939.

Wyss, Ulrich. *Die Urgeschichte der Intellektualität und das Gelächter: Ein Vortrag über Il Nome della Rosa.* Erlangen: Erlanger Studien 41, 1983.

Yourcenar, Marguerite. *Memoirs of Hadrian and Reflections on the Composition of Memoirs of Hadrian.* Translated by Grace Frick. New York: Farrar, Straus & Giroux, 1963.

Index

Abé, Kobo, 78–80
Absolom, Absolom! (Faulkner), 181
Adam, American, 55, 61–66
Adams, John, 70
Aeneid, The (Virgil), 26
Aeschylus, 13
Alcibiades, 51
Alexander the Great, 24, 48
Altenbernd, Lynn, 180
America: as Eden, 55, 67, 170
Amosoff, Nikolai, 77
Ancient Evenings (Mailer), 9, 10
Angkor Massacre, The (Durand), 122
Annus Mirabilis (Dryden), 66
Antinous, 36, 37, 44, 45, 51
Antoninus, Emperor Pius (of Rome), 51
Aphaeresis, 17, 18
Apocalypse: 12, 26, 57, 60, 66, 67, 84, 169, 190, 208; nuclear, 2, 29, 76, 81, 82, 83, 88, 93, 191, 192, 212, 213

Apollodorus of Athens, 37, 157
Archimedes, 46
Arethusa, 30
Ariosto, Lodovico, 139
Aristotle, 14, 19, 46, 56, 190, 198, 204
Arrian, 46
Arthur, King, 36
Aryan Nations, 110
Aryan Youth Movement, 110
Atwood, Margaret, 27, 30. See also *Handmaid's Tale, The*
Aubrion, Michel, 52
Auden, W. H., 159
Auerbach, Erich, 22
Augustus Caesar, 13, 38
Augustus (Williams), 34
Aurelius, Marcus, 34, 40, 51
Autobiography, An (Collingwood), 7–8
Aztec (Jennings), 20–22, 23

Babi Yar, 144, 145, 150, 151, 157, 158, 160, 162

Babi Yar (Kuznetsov), 150
Bacon, Roger, 196, 198, 200,
  201
Bacon, Sir Francis, 21, 197
Bakunin, Mikhail, 118
Barth, John, 9, 27, 30, 32, 33.
  See also *Sot-Weed Factor, The*
Basilius, Harold A., 15
Bassani, Giorgio, 141
"Bear, The" (Faulkner), 179–
  82, 183, 184
Beethoven, Ludwig van, 30
Beckett, Samuel, 100, 153
Benert, Annette, 174
Beowulf, 11, 70, 101
Bergson, Henri, 183, 214
Bettelheim, Bruno, 113
Beyle, Henri [pseud. Stendhal],
  20
Bible, 112, 118, 208; Old
  Testament, 69, 106, 107,
  114; New Testament, 70
Biographia Literaria (Coleridge),
  19
Black comedy, 71, 204
Blake, William, 8, 12
Bloch, Marc, 14–15
Blot, Jean, 37
Borges, Jorge Luis, 195–96,
  203
Boulle, Pierre, 78
Boyd, Thomas, 2
Braudel, Fernand, 15
Bring the Jubilee (Moore),
  121
Broch, Hermann, 12, 13, 33,
  34
Brooks, Cleanth, 173
Brown vs. Board of Education,
  179
Burgess, Anthony, 77, 100

Butser Ancient Farm Research
  Project, 86
Byron, Lord George Gordon,
  53, 186

Caesar, Gaius Julius, 48
Caligula, Emperor (of Rome),
  38
Calliope, 54
Canterbury Tales, The (Chaucer),
  115
Canticle for Leibowitz, A (Miller),
  9, 81–82, 212
Canticles, 163
Carroll, Lewis. *See* Dodgson,
  Charles
Chaucer, Geoffrey, 35, 112;
  and *Handmaid's Tale, The*,
  112–14
Chess. See *Name of the Rose, The*
"Childe Roland to the Dark
  Tower Came" (Browning), 99
Chiliasm, 124, 192. *See also*
  Apocalypse
Christianity, 211; in *Memoirs of
  Hadrian*, 42–43, 44
Claudius I, Emperor (of
  Rome), 35
Claudius the God (Graves), 33,
  34
Clemens, Samuel Langhorne
  [pseud. Mark Twain], 25, 55
Clio, 15, 53, 54, 58
Clockwork Orange, A (Burgess),
  77
Clodia (DeMaria), 33
Coena Cypriani, 191
Coleridge, Samuel Taylor, 19
Collingwood, R. G., 14, 18–19
Colquhoun, Archibald, 129

Communism. *See* Marxism
Concentration camps, Nazi, 3, 43
Confessions of Nat Turner, The (Styron), 9
Connecticut Yankee in King Arthur's Court, A (Twain), 7
Conrad, Joseph, 60, 95, 169
Conspiracy, The (Hersey), 34
Cooke, Ebenezer, 54–55, 66
Cooper, James Fenimore, 55
Core, George, 120
Cosmotheist Community, 110
Croce, Benedetto, 14, 18, 19
Crying of Lot 49, The (Pynchon), 185
Crystal Palace, 9, 212
Cvetaeva, Marina. *See* Tsvetayeva, Marina
Czechoslovakia, Soviet invasion of, 192

Dance of Death, 104
Dante, 56, 162
Death of the Just Man (Greuze), 133
Death of Virgil, The (Broch), 12, 13, 33
"Delta Autumn" (Faulkner), 182, 183–84, 185–87
DeMaria, Robert, 33
de Rosbo, Patrick, 43
Derrida, Jacques, 28
Dick, Philip K., 121
Dilthey, Wilhelm, 18
Divine Comedy, The (Dante), 26
Dr. Faustus (Marlowe), 119
Doctorow, E. L., 122
Dodgson, Charles [pseud. Lewis Carroll], 194
Don Juan (Byron), 53
Donne, John, 199
Dos Passos, John, 2
Doyle, Sir Arthur Conan, 194
Dryden, John, 66
Dubliners (Joyce), 169
Durand, Loup, 122
Dystopia, 76, 80–81, 105, 109, 113

Eagleton, Terry, 19, 204
Ecclesiasticus, 56
Eco, Umberto, 11, 27, 30, 168, 169, 212. See also *Name of the Rose, The*
Eden, 46, 71, 179, 186, 188; American, 55, 67, 170
Einstein, Albert, 197
Eisenstein, Sergei, 136
Eliade, Mircea: on history and myth, 93; on holy center, 92; on myth of eternal return, 84, 103; on ritual, 90–91; on terror of history, 83, 89, 104, 105
Eliot, T. S., 27, 92, 99, 100, 116
Endō, Shūsaku, 166–67
End of the Road, The (Barth), 71, 72
English Historical Novel, The (Fleishman), 5
Enlightenment, the, 2, 70
Entropy, 125, 141
Epaminondas, 38
Euhemerism: Eliade on, 93; in Renault, 22, 23–24
Eustace, St., 93, 104
Examined life: history

analogous to, 25, 32–33, 75.
See also *Memoirs of Hadrian*
Existentialism: in Barth, 71–73

Famous Last Words (Findley), 10
Farewell to Arms, A
(Hemingway), 100; compared
with *The Naked and the Dead*,
2–3
Fascism, 124, 130
Faulkner, William, 27, 29, 30,
32, 55, 58, 59, 60, 168, 169.
See also *Go Down, Moses*
Felcini, Furio, 125
Ferenczi, Sandor, 152
Feuchtwanger, Lion, 8, 15, 27
Fiedler, Leslie, 73
Findley, Timothy, 10
Finn, Huckleberry, 88
Finnegans Wake (Joyce), 12, 213
"Fire and the Hearth, The"
(Faulkner), 176, 177
Fire from Heaven (Renault), 23
Fitzgerald, F. Scott, 55
Fixer, The (Malamud), 122
Fleishman, Avrom, 5, 6, 7, 18
Floating Opera, The (Barth), 71
Flying to Nowhere (Fuller), 6
Forster, E. M., 153, 180
Foucault, Michel, 14
Fowles, John, 166
Franklin, Benjamin, 70
Frazer, Sir James George, 85
Freddy's Book (Gardner), 10
French Lieutenant's Woman, The
(Fowles), 166
Freud, Sigmund, 70, 124, 136,
192; on suicide, 178. See also
White Hotel, The
Frost, Robert, 180

Frye, Northrop, 8, 138, 188–89
Fuller, John, 6
Future. *See* Science fiction:
novels of future

García Marquez, Gabriel, 31
Gardner, John, 10, 11
Garibaldi, Giuseppe, 125, 129,
131, 135
Gass, William, 153
"Ge" (Thomas), 156
Gerusalemme liberata (Tasso), 139
Gibbon, Edward, 42
Gilbert, John, 135
"Go Down, Moses" (spiritual),
171
"Go Down, Moses" (story),
172–73, 174, 182
Go Down, Moses (Faulkner), 27,
59, 168; Edenic wilderness
in, 179, 180, 181, 182–83,
184, 188; guilt and innocence
in, 169, 181, 182, 188; Isaac
McCaslin as Christ-figure in,
171, 184, 185; McCaslin
mansion, 173–74; marriage
in, 174, 175–78, 185, 187; as
novel, 169, 224n2; racial
justice in, 171–72; suicide in,
174, 177–79; title, 171
Golden Age, 122, 123; in
Memoirs of Hadrian, 45; in
Riddley Walker, 83, 86, 90.
Golding, William, 122
Gone with the Wind (Mitchell),
31–32
Graves, Robert, 9, 15–17, 33,
34, 123
Gravity's Rainbow (Pynchon), 10,
212–13

Gray, Sir Thomas, 65
Grendel (Gardner), 11
Greuze, Jean Baptiste, 133
Gulliver's Travels (Swift), 78
Gunn, Neil, 122

Hadrian, Emperor (of Rome).
See *Memoirs of Hadrian*
Hadrian's Wall, 48
Hamilton, Gary, 181
Hamlet (Shakespeare), 12
Handmaid's Tale, The (Atwood),
27; and contemporary
fundamentalist right, 109–
10; epilogue, 107–8, 115,
116; flowers in, 113, 119;
historical parallelism in, 106,
107–8; and "Little Red
Riding Hood," 112, 113–14;
Logos, 106, 118, 205, 208;
puritanism and
patriarchalism in, 105, 106,
107, 108, 114, 115;
pornography and censorship
in, 109, 111–12; Serena Joy,
113, 115; and Waste Land
myth, 112, 116–17; wreath
symbol, 118–19
Harlem Renaissance, 166
Hawthorne, Nathaniel, 107,
112
Hegel, Georg Wilhelm
Friedrich, 14, 24
Heidegger, Martin, 14, 85
Heisenberg, Werner, 197
Hemingway, Ernest, 2, 3, 100
Henderson, Harry B., 5, 70
Heraclitus, 161, 214
Herder, Johann Gottfried von,
88

Herodotus, 25
Hersey, John, 34
Hesiod, 44, 45, 56
Historian, poet as, 53–54
Historical fiction: nuclear
anxiety in, 2, 4, 81, 82, 110;
superior to history, 1, 24,
25–26, 28, 30, 59, 74, 75. *See
also* Historical novel
Historical novel, 1; chronicle-
novel as, 168–69; definition,
5–6; genre, 4, 5; Henry
James on, 7; Lukacs on, 3;
popular, 20–24, 32–33;
previous scholarly work on,
4–5; types, 6, 8–13, 26, 27
—The Way It Was, 8, 9, 27,
31–75, 168, 214
—The Way It Will Be, 8, 9–10,
27, 76–119, 168, 214
—The Turning Point, 8, 10,
27, 108–12, 120–64, 168,
170, 190–91, 214
—The Distant Mirror, 8, 9, 10–
11, 27, 32, 39–40, 106, 107–
8, 112, 165–213, 168, 214
Historical Novel, The (Lukács), 4
Historiography, 15, 26, 27. *See
also* History: theory or
theories of
*Historische Roman in England
und Amerika, Der* (Schabert), 5
History: Christian view of, 60,
84; and examined life, 25,
27; modernist and
postmodernist perceptions of,
27–28; and myth, 31; theory
or theories of, 13–20, 56–57,
82–83, 83–85, 86, 90
History of the Conquest of Mexico
(Prescott), 20–22

"History Subsumed under the
Concept of Art" (Croce), 18
Hitler, Adolf, 3, 4, 13, 154, 192
Hoban, Russell, 9, 27, 30, 81,
82, 105. See also *Riddley
Walker*
Hobbes, Thomas, 60, 70, 86
Holocaust, Nazi, 3, 143, 160
Homer, 8, 22, 25, 46, 53
Horace, 19
House of Desdemona, The
(Feuchtwanger), 15
Hugo, Victor, 20

I, Claudius (Graves), 33, 34
Ides of March, The (Wilder), 34
"If Grant Had Been Drinking
at Appomatox" (Thurber),
121
Iliad, The (Homer), 26
"Infantile Genital Organization
of the Libido, The" (Freud),
148
Inheritors, The (Golding), 122
Inter Ice Age 4 (Abé), 78–80
Iron Dream, The (Spinrad), 121

James, Henry, 1, 7, 36, 203
James, William, 149
Jane Eyre (Brontë), 118
Jefferson, Thomas, 70
Jehlen, Myra, 179
Jennings, Gary, 20–23
Jesus Christ, 44, 104, 160, 167–
68, 185
Jewett, Sarah Orne, 7
Jews, 109; alleged guilt of, 82;
Emperor Hadrian's view of,
42, 43–44; paralleled to
Nazis by Steiner's Hitler, 3–4

Johnson, Samuel, 28, 126
Joyce, James, 28, 31, 100, 101,
194
Julian, Emperor (of Rome), 42
Julian (Vidal), 34, 121
Jung, Carl Gustav, 8, 156;
psychology of, 11–12
Juvenal, 37

Kapital, Das (Marx and Engels),
192
Karlinsky, Simon, 163
Kazin, Alfred, 171
Keegan, John, 20
Kekulé von Stradonitz,
Friedrich August, 213
Khomenei, Ayatollah, 105
Kierkegaard, Sören, 62
King Jesus (Graves), 9
King Lear (Shakespeare), 34–
35, 99
King Must Die, The (Renault),
23–24, 117, 123
Kipling, Rudyard, 5
Klug, Scott, 110
Koch, Robert, 136
Koestler, Arthur, 193
Kosygin, Alexei, 79
Ku Klux Klan, 110
Kuznetsov, Anatoli, 150

Lampedusa, Giuseppe di. *See*
Tomasi di Lampedusa,
Giuseppe
Last Man, The (Shelley), 9
Last of the Wine, The (Renault),
23, 123
Lawrence, D. H., 156, 167–68
Lear, King, 34–35, 205
Leopard, The, 10, 27, 123, 124;
astronomy in, 132–33,

221n8; Bendico, 140–41; classical mythology in, 133–35, 139; irony in, 137–39, 140, 141; millennial expectations in, 124, 129; narrational features of, 126, 136–38; political evolution in Italy in, 124–25, 129, 130, 131, 221n5, 222n8; San Cono subplot, 127–29; Tancredi and Angelica, 126–27; theme of entropic stasis in, 125, 130, 132, 141; and The Waste Land, 135–36; and Vico, 138–39
Lévi-Strauss, Claude, 14
Lewis, R. W. B., 183
Liberty Lobby, 110
"Library of Babel, The" (Borges), 196
Lincoln (Vidal), 121
Little Red Riding Hood, 112, 113–14
Logos, 106, 118, 205, 208
Lord of the Rings, The (Tolkien), 165–66
Lovejoy, Arthur O., 65
Lowry, Malcolm, 140
Lukács, Georg, 1, 5, 6, 7, 8; on historical novel, 4

Macauley, Thomas Babington, 21
McConnell, Frank, 73
Machiavelli, Niccolò, 131, Mailer, Norman, 2, 6, 9, 10, 11
Malak, Amin, 113
Malamud, Bernard, 122
Man in the High Castle, The (Dick), 121

Man Who Died, The (Lawrence), 167–68
Marathon, battle of, 16–17
Marina Cvetaeva: Her Life and Art (Karlinsky), 163
Marlowe, Christopher, 119
Marx, Karl, 118
Marxism, 124, 130; and The Name of the Rose, 189, 190, 192, 193; and novel, 4
Massachusetts Bay Colony, 107
Memoirs of Hadrian (Yourcenar), 9, 27, 212; Ages of Man in, 44–47; examined life in, 32–33, 34–35; its historiography, 40–41; parallels with twentieth century, 39–40; Rome in, 33, 46–47; view of religion in, 42–44; Yourcenar's treatment of Hadrian in, 33, 74
—his character, 35, 37–38
—his mind, 39, 41, 50, 74
—his pursuit of order, 47–49, 132
—his reliability and narrative style, 35–37
—his theories of the good life, hedonism, and stoicism, 49–52
Mencken, H. L., 107
Metamorphoses (Ovid), 45, 46
Michelet, Jules, 20
Miller, J. Hillis, 17
Miller, Walter M., Jr., 9, 81–82
Millgate, Michael, 187
Minimalism, 30
Mitchell, Margaret, 22, 31–32
Mizener, Arthur, 172
Modernism, contrasted to postmodernism, 27–29, 30

Montezuma, 20
Moore, Ward, 121
Moral Majority, 110
Moro, Aldo, 193
Morrell, David, 55
Moses, 69, 171
Moses, W. R., 180
"Most Prevalent Form of
  Degradation in Erotic Life,
  The" (Freud), 147
Mumbo Jumbo (Reed), 166
Murder in the Cathedral (Eliot),
  92
Mussolini, Benito, 140

Nabokov, Vladimir, 144, 153,
  164, 194, 203
Naked and the Dead, The
  (Mailer): compared with *A
  Farewell to Arms*, 2–3
Name of the Rose, The (Eco), 11,
  27, 168, 169, 212; abbey and
  its library as symbols, 198–
  200; apocalyptic theme of,
  190, 191, 192, 208, 210, 211;
  apostasy in, 196, 202, 208;
  censorship and knowledge in,
  189, 199–202, 203; chess-
  schema in, 194–95; frame of,
  203–4, 226n29; influence of
  Borges in, 195–96, 203;
  laughter in, 202; medieval
  realism and nominalism in,
  206–7, 226n32; medieval
  sources in, 226n27; meaning
  of title, 206; semiotics in,
  204–7, 208–12
National Alliance, 110
Nazi Party, American, 110
Nazism, 121, 158; compared
  with Hebraism, 4

Nero, Emperor (of Rome), 38
Nerva, Emperor (of Rome), 38
Newton, Sir Isaac, 198
Nietzsche, Friedrich, 84
1984 (Orwell), 9
Noland, Richard, 58
Notes from the Future (Amosoff),
  77–78
Nuclear war, 2, 28–29, 30, 81,
  82, 191, 201. See also *Riddley
  Walker*

Occam, William of, 197;
  Terminism, 207
"Ode: Intimations of
  Immortality" (Wordsworth),
  162
Oedipus, 98–99, 102
Oldenbourg, Zoé, 7
Once and Future King, The
  (White), 165
One Hundred Years of Solitude
  (García Marquez), 12
Order, The, 110
Orlando Furioso (Ariosto), 139
Orwell, George, 9, 76, 80–81,
  89, 100, 193
Othello, 65–66
Outline of History, The (Wells), 9
Ovid, 44, 45, 46

Pancrates, 46
"Pantaloon in Black"
  (Faulkner), 176, 177–78
Paradiso (Dante), 162
Parkman, Francis, 25
Pausanias, 157
Peloponnesian War, 123
Persian Boy, The (Renault), 23
"Persian Version, The"
  (Graves), 16–17, 21

Pierce, C. S., 29
Pierce, William, 110
Planet of the Apes (Boulle), 78
Plataea, battle of, 17
Plato, 56, 84, 207
Plutarch, 40
"Poem of the Midway"
    (Thomas), 163
Poetics (Aristotle), 56
Pompey the Great, 48
Pontifex Maximus, 42
Pontius Pilate, 41
*Portage to San Cristobal of A. H.,
    The* (Steiner), 3–4, 10
*Portrait of the Artist as a Young
    Man* (Joyce), 101
Posse Comitatus, 110
Postmodernism, 166;
    contrasted with modernism,
    27–29, 30
Pound, Ezra, 2, 27, 28
Praxiteles, 46
Prescott, William Hickling, 20–
    22
"Professor and the Mermaid,
    The" (di Lampedusa), 137
Pronicheva, Dina, 150, 157
Proust, Marcel, 41
Ptolemy [Claudius Ptolemaeus],
    48
Punch and Judy. See *Riddley
    Walker*
Puritanism, 50. See also *The
    Handmaid's Tale*
Pynchon, Thomas, 6, 10, 153,
    159, 185, 212, 213, 214

Quantum theory, 198

Ragtime (Doctorow), 122
Ragusa, Olga, 132

Reconstruction, 32, 173
Red Brigades, 140, 193
Reed, Ishmael, 166
"Reflections on the
    Composition of *Memoirs of
    Hadrian*" (Yourcenar), 36,
    40–41, 53
Relativity, 198
Renaissance, 2, 82, 139, 190,
    198
Renault, Mary, 20, 22–24, 117,
    122–23
Renoir, Jean, 78
Republic, The (Plato), 48
Revelation, 66–67
Reynolds, Peter J., 86
Riddley Walker (Hoban), 9, 27,
    81–83, 116, 169, 212; and
    Anglo-Saxon poetry, 100–
    101; Eliade's ideas and, 83–
    84, 85, 89, 90–91, 92, 93,
    103, 104, 105; Eusa cult, 87,
    89–91, 93–94, 96, 97, 98,
    102, 103, 105; Greanvine, 93,
    98, 103–4; "Hart of the
    Wood," 94–95, 104; and
    Iron Age, 83, 85, 86–87, 89,
    104, 105; as *Künstlerroman*,
    102–3; language of, 87–89;
    Mr. Clevver, 94–95, 96;
    oneness and division in, 96–
    99; Punch and Judy in, 95,
    96, 102; religion in, 85–86,
    87, 89–91, 104, 105; Riddley
    like Stephen Dedalus, 101;
    Riddley's psychological
    doubles, 81–82, 85–86, 87,
    89–91, 104–5; theories of
    history in, 82–83, 83–85, 86,
    90; and *The Waste Land*, 93,
    99–100

Risorgimento, 124, 125, 139,
140
Robertson, Mary F., 146
Rollyson, Carl E., 181
Rousseau, Jean-Jacques, 60, 70
Rules of the Game, The (Renoir),
78
Russian Revolution, 159

Sabatini, Rafael, 22
Sachs, Hanns, 146
Saint Joan (Shaw), 10
St. John, Gospel of, 62, 208
Salamis, Battle of, 17
Salinger, J. D., 176
Samhain, 105
Samurai, The (Endō), 166–67
Santayana, George, 24
Sartre, Jean-Paul, 11, 14, 182,
183
Saussure, Ferdinand de, 19, 29
Schabert, Ina, 5, 6, 7
Science fiction, 168; novels of
future, 76–83; weaknesses of,
76. See also *Handmaid's Tale,
The* and *Riddley Walker*
Scott, Sir Walter, 5, 70
Semiotics. See *Name of the Rose,
The*
Sense of the Past, The (James), 7
Sergeant Lamb's America
(Graves), 9
Sermon on the Mount, 99–100
Shakespeare, William, 35, 65,
99
Shaw, George Bernard, 10
Shelley, Mary, 9
Shelley, Percy Bysshe, 61
Silver Darlings, The (Gunn), 122
Simmel, Georg, 18
Smith, Captain John, 56, 57,

67, 68, 74
Socrates, 98
Sophie's Choice (Styron), 6
"Sot-Weed Factor, The"
(Cooke). See *Sot-Weed Factor,
The*
Sot-Weed Factor, The (Barth), 9,
27; apocalypse in, 57, 60, 67,
212; Henry Burlingame I,
56, 67, 68, 69; Henry
Burlingame II/Tayac
Chicamec, 58, 67, 68, 69, 70;
Henry Burlingame III, 61,
71
—devil or savior, 69
—as existentialist, 72–73
—on history, 56
—his paternity, 67
—his Telemachiad, 73;
Christian allegory in, 55, 59–
71, 73; comparison with
Cooke's original poem, 54–
55; John Coode as Satan in,
61, 70–71, 72; Ebenezer
Cooke
—as American Adam, 61–66
—as Antichrist, 66–67
—birthdate, 66
—as Christ figure, 63, 65
—on history, 56
—as Lazarus, 62
—compared with Othello,
65–66; Existentialism in, 71–
73; Father FitzMaurice, 58,
67–68, 69; Indians in, 57–
59, 67–69; innocence and
guilt in, 55, 61–66; Governor
Nicholson, 61, 69, 70;
Pocahontas in, 58, 74; poet as
historian, 53–54; revisionism
in, 54, 55–56; self-knowledge

in, 32–33; theories of history
in, 55–56; Joan Toast, 62,
66; twentieth-century
philosophy in, 57, 72, 75
Sound and the Fury, The
(Faulkner), 183
South, the, 31–32. See also *Go
Down, Moses*
"Special Type of Object Choice
Made by Men, A" (Freud),
147
Spenser, Edmund, 60
Spinrad, Norman, 121
"Spring in Fialta" (Nabokov),
144
Steiner, George, 3, 4, 6, 10
Stendhal. *See* Beyle, Henri
Stevenson, Robert Louis, 5
Styron, William, 6, 9
Suetonius, 34, 37
Sweet Savage Love (Rogers), 1
Swinburne, Algernon Charles,
42
Symposium, The (Plato), 98

Tanner, Tony, 59
Tasso, Torquato, 139
Tempest, The (Shakespeare), 70
Terminism, 207
Terra Nostra (Fuentes), 12
Thackeray, William Makepeace,
20
Tharpe, Jac, 65
"Theologians, The" (Borges),
195
Thomas Beckett, Saint, 92
Thomas, D. M., 10, 27, 123.
See also *White Hotel, The*
Three Soldiers (Dos Passos), 2
Through the Looking Glass
(Dodgson), 194

Through the Wheat (Boyd), 2
Thucydides, 25
Thurber, James, 121
Tiberius, Emperor (of Rome),
38
"Time in Faulkner" (Sartre),
182
Time Machine, The (Wells), 9–10
Timmerman, Jacopo, 193
Tolkien, J. R. R., 165
Tomasi di Lampedusa,
Giuseppe, 10, 27, 30, 123.
See also *Leopard, The*
Trajan, Emperor (of Rome), 37
Trojan War, 53
Tsvetayeva, Marina, 162–63
Turin shroud, 160
Turner Diaries, The (Pierce), 110
Turn of the Screw, The (James),
203
Twain, Mark, *See* Clemens,
Samuel Langhorne
Two Cheers for Democracy
(Forster), 153

Ulysses (Joyce), 101
Uncertainty principle, 197–98
Under the Volcano (Lowry), 140

V. (Pynchon), 6, 10, 159
Valéry, Paul, 14
Vargas Llosa, Mario, 212
Versions of the Past (Henderson),
5
Vico, Giambattista, 84, 138–39
Victor Emmanuel, King (of
Italy), 125, 131
Vidal, Gore, 34, 121
Vier, Jacques, 47
Virgil, 13, 56, 57

Waiting for Godot (Beckett), 99
"Wanderer, The," 100
War and Peace (Tolstoy), 1, 26
War of the End of the World, The
  (Vargas Llosa), 212
"Was" (Faulkner), 172–75
Washington, George, 70
Waste Land, myth of, 93, 100,
  105, 112, 116–17, 135–36
Waste Land, The (Eliot), 100,
  116, 135
Waterloo, battle of, 20
Wells, H. G., 9–10
Whatley, Janet, 33
White, Hayden, 14, 138
White, T. H., 165
White Aryan Resistance, 110
White Goddess, 15
White Goddess, The (Graves), 123
White Hotel, The (Thomas), 10,
  27, 123, 124, 192; alleged
  plagiarism in, 149–50,
  223n22; and Babi Yar, 144,
  145; critique of modern
  metaphysics in, 142, 143,
  164; doubling in, 150–52,
  153, 154, 163–64; epigraph,
  158–59; Freud and
  psychoanalysis in, 141, 142–
  49, 152, 153–55, 159; myth
  in, 148–49, 155–58;
  narrational features of, 149–
  50; prescience in, 144–46;
  significance of its esthetic,
  153; and spiritual alternatives
  to scientific materialism, 160,
  161–62, 163, 164; symbolism
  of "the camp," 161, 162, 163,
  223n26; symbolism of train

journey, 143–45; symbolism
  of white hotel, 143–45, 146;
  and World War II as culture-
  wide abreaction, 141–42,
  159, 160, 163
White Patriots, 110
Whitman, Walt, 25
Wieland, 101
Wife of Bath, 114–15
Wilder, Thornton, 34
Wille zur Macht, 80
Williams, John, 33, 34
Wilson, Edmund, 7
Winesburg, Ohio (Anderson),
  169
Wittgenstein, Ludwig, 19, 29,
  226n33; quoted, 210
Woolf, Virginia, 36, 153
Word. *See* Logos
World War I: novels of, 2
World War II, 24, 29, 30, 165,
  192; in *Gravity's Rainbow*,
  212–13; in *The Naked and the
  Dead*, 2; in *The White Hotel*,
  142
Wordsworth, William, 162
Wyss, Ulrich, 193

Xenophon, 46

Yeats, William Butler, 207, 208;
  source of epigraph for *The
  White Hotel*, 158–59
Yin and yang, 98
"Young Goodman Brown"
  (Hawthorne), 112
Yourcenar, Marguerite, 9, 27,
  30, 32, 74, 75, 132; See also
  Memoirs of Hadrian

DAVID COWART, professor of English at the University of South Carolina, took his doctorate at Rutgers in 1977. He also holds degrees from the University of Alabama and Indiana University. A specialist in twentieth-century American and British literature, he is a winner of his university's Amoco Outstanding Teaching Award. He is the author of numerous articles, as well as *Thomas Pynchon: The Art of Allusion* (Southern Illinois University Press, 1980) and *Arches and Light: The Fiction of John Gardner* (Southern Illinois University Press, 1983). He considers his best piece of work, however, to be his daughter Rachel.

DATE DUE